Praise for the novels of Brenda Novak

"Novak elevates mystery elements that **will appeal to readers of Colleen Hoover**."

—*Booklist* on *Tourist Season*

"Filled with **mystery and drama**, coupled with themes of family ties and secrets. This page-turner **will not disappoint**."

—*Booklist* on *The Seaside Library*

"*The Bookstore on the Beach* is **a page-turner with a deep heart**. You'll cheer for these admirable, complicated women. **You'll be breathless (and smiling)** when you read the surprising end. (Don't peek!)"

—Nancy Thayer, *New York Times* bestselling author of *Girls of Summer*

"Novak handles difficult topics with sensitivity, making for a heart-tugging romance. **Readers are sure to be sucked in**."

—*Publishers Weekly*, **starred review**, on *The Bookstore on the Beach*

"The prose is **fast-paced and exciting** making this **a breathless page-turner** with the conclusion proving no problems are too difficult to solve."

—*New York Journal of Books* on *The Bookstore on the Beach*

"I adore everything Brenda Novak writes. Her books are **compelling, emotional, tender** stories about people I would love to know in real life."

—RaeAnne Thayne, *New York Times* bestselling author

"**Heartwarming, life-affirming, page-turning** . . . I can always count on Novak to make me weep, laugh and fall in love!"

—Jill Shalvis, *New York Times* bestselling author

Also by Brenda Novak

The Summer That Changed Everything	*Come Home to Me*
The Banned Books Club	*Take Me Home for Christmas*
The Messy Life of Jane Tanner	*Home to Whiskey Creek*
The Talk of Coyote Canyon	*When Summer Comes*
Talulah's Back in Town	*When Snow Falls*
Tourist Season	*When Lightning Strikes*
Summer on the Island	*In Close*
Keep Me Warm at Christmas	*In Seconds*
When I Found You	*Inside*
The Bookstore on the Beach	*Killer Heat*
A California Christmas	*Body Heat*
One Perfect Summer	*White Heat*
Christmas in Silver Springs	*The Perfect Murder*
Unforgettable You	*The Perfect Liar*
Before We Were Strangers	*The Perfect Couple*
Right Where We Belong	*Watch Me*
Until You Loved Me	*Stop Me*
No One But You	*Trust Me*
Finding Our Forever	*Dead Right*
The Secrets She Kept	*Dead Giveaway*
A Winter Wedding	*Dead Silence*
The Secret Sister	*Cold Feet*
This Heart of Mine	*Taking the Heat*
The Heart of Christmas	*Every Waking Moment*

For a full list of Brenda's books, visit www.brendanovak.com.

Look for Brenda Novak's next novel, available soon from MIRA Books.

Meet Me in Italy

BRENDA NOVAK

/‖/MIRA

⁄‖ MIRA

ISBN-13: 978-0-7783-0581-1

Meet Me in Italy

Copyright © 2026 by Brenda Novak, Inc.

Illustrations: © Annykos/stock.adobe.com (sailboat); © Denys/stock.adobe.com (waves).

Recycling programs for this product may not exist in your area.

All rights reserved. No part of this book may be used or reproduced in any manner whatsoever without written permission.

Without limiting the exclusive rights of any author, contributor or the publisher of this publication, any unauthorized use of this publication to train generative artificial intelligence (AI) technologies is expressly prohibited. Harlequin also exercises their rights under Article 4(3) of the Digital Single Market Directive 2019/790 and expressly reserves this publication from the text and data mining exception.

This is a work of fiction. Names, characters, places and incidents are either the product of the author's imagination or are used fictitiously. Any resemblance to actual persons, living or dead, businesses, companies, events or locales is entirely coincidental.

For questions and comments about the quality of this book, please contact us at CustomerService@Harlequin.com.

TM is a trademark of Harlequin Enterprises ULC.

MIRA
22 Adelaide St. West, 41st Floor
Toronto, Ontario M5H 4E3, Canada
MIRABooks.com

HarperCollins Publishers
Macken House, 39/40 Mayor Street Upper,
Dublin 1, D01 C9W8, Ireland
www.HarperCollins.com

Printed in U.S.A.

To Leanne Luttges—
For opening your heart to my daughter, Alexa, and loving her so completely. Knowing she has such a wonderful mother-in-law—that you'll be there for her if ever there comes a time I can't—is one of life's sweetest comforts. And please know, I'll always be there for Vinny, too.

Our children's wedding in Italy will forever be among my most treasured memories—and the one that inspired this story.

You may have the world if I may have Italy.

—Giuseppe Verdi (1813–1901), Italian opera composer

chapter 1

Charlotte Williams-Jackson was about to lose her married name. Her husband of only four years wanted a divorce. The reality of that—the mere weight of the D word coming out of nowhere—hit her, once again, like a gut punch as she walked through the front door of the sprawling LA mansion he'd purchased just after they were married and saw the leather carry-on Cliff had packed in anticipation of his trip to New York. The text she'd received while she was at yoga said he wanted her out by the time he returned.

Out. Gone. But they hadn't even been fighting!

She covered her mouth with one shaking hand as tears welled up. She'd be divorced before she turned thirty. That had to be unusual. These days, people weren't even marrying until then. And not only would the split be painful, but it'd also be humiliating, embarrassing. Their relationship had been almost as public as that of Travis Kelce and Taylor Swift.

At least she wouldn't be left destitute. As an NBA player who'd just negotiated a huge contract, he'd asked her to sign a prenup, but the settlement was more money than most people her age would ever have the chance to earn. Since they hadn't been married long and didn't have any kids, she'd get the minimum amount specified, but eight hundred thousand dollars was still a lot of money.

Maybe he was breaking things off because she'd been pressing him to start a family. He was probably afraid she'd go off her birth control and get pregnant even though he wasn't ready. She wanted to believe he knew her well enough to trust she'd never try to trap him, but there were plenty of professional athletes who'd faced such a scenario or worse, and he'd heard all the horror stories.

Before he'd left their bed to sleep in one of the many guest rooms last night, he'd said he hoped she wouldn't try to break the prenup. She'd told him she wouldn't, and she meant it. Besides the settlement, she still had royalties coming in from her first novel, a "sports romance." She wanted to think her book had sold over a million copies because it was just *that* good, but she knew debut authors typically didn't see such numbers. Her success had to be largely due to her connection with Clifford, who was one of the best shooting guards in the league. Thanks to him, she'd had over a million followers on social media before she'd even been published, giving her an incredible platform.

But she hadn't married him for his fame or his money. She'd married for love, and although her parents and friends had warned her that being the wife of a professional athlete wouldn't be easy, she'd thought she could defy the odds. She'd never dreamed she and Cliff wouldn't even make it to their fourth anniversary.

Numb inside, she lifted the hand that held her phone. She'd replied when he'd said he wanted her out before he got back, but he hadn't answered. Couldn't they talk through whatever had upset him? Go to a counselor?

She'd suggested as much last night when he'd asked for a divorce, but he'd refused, said he just didn't want to be married anymore. When she'd pressed him for an explanation, he'd added that he didn't know how long his NBA career would last and he planned to enjoy these years while he could.

Apparently that meant *unencumbered*. But why couldn't he enjoy playing ball while he was with her? How had she been getting in the way? Didn't he love her enough to *try* to salvage what they had?

The door opened behind her, and she turned to see his driver, whom she'd passed in the driveway when she'd pulled in a minute ago.

"Mrs. Jackson." Jeremy nodded politely, but he wouldn't look her in the eye. She could tell he already knew that she was now persona non grata. Cliff must've told him he was kicking her out, which made everything she planned to say, after a morning spent reassuring herself that her husband would view things differently once he came back to himself, seem pointless.

"Have you seen Cliff?" she asked woodenly.

"No, ma'am. He called to tell me to get the car ready shortly after you left, but I haven't seen him yet," he replied. Then he grabbed the luggage and beat a hasty retreat.

Was there another woman? Charlotte wondered. She had a feeling Cliff had strayed a time or two. Last night, he'd insisted he hadn't, that he simply wanted his freedom. But professional athletes—at least those at his level—were constantly faced with temptation.

A bead of sweat rolled down between her shoulder blades. It was only eleven, but LA could get warm, even in April.

Footsteps sounded above her. She looked up to see her husband striding toward one of two matching staircases that swept down to the first floor. It appeared he was leaving for his trip to New York to play the Knicks in an important play-off game sooner than expected.

When he noticed her, he stopped as if he didn't want to confront her. She got the impression he'd been trying to get out of the house before she returned. But then he squared his shoulders and continued, jogging down the stairs.

"You're back from yoga already?" he said.

She tried to hide the hurt, but the emotional blow he'd struck was still so fresh it was impossible. She blinked rapidly but couldn't hold back the tears. "I'm actually home later than usual," she said. "I wanted to give you plenty of time to sleep in. I know you have to be rested for the game." She'd also been hoping he'd be in a better frame of mind. "So I ran a few errands after my class and stopped by my mother's house. She hasn't been feeling well."

"There's always *something* wrong with her," he said dismissively.

Surprised by this callous response, she stiffened. "Lupus is like that."

"Maybe she's got lupus and maybe she doesn't. Has that really been determined?"

"That's what the doctor told her."

"Either way, she loves the attention being sick brings her. Every time she says she's not feeling well you run over there, which is exactly what she's after."

He'd made similar comments before, but her mother would not say she wasn't well unless it was true. Charlotte opened her mouth to defend Penny, as she always had, but the words froze in her throat. If he wasn't going to be part of her life in the future, what did it matter?

He pulled his phone out of the pocket of his slacks and glanced at it. "Anyway, I have to go."

She fixed her eyes on the thick gold chain hanging around his neck because she couldn't bear to see the hardness in his eyes. "You rarely leave this early."

"I've got lunch with some of the guys."

As if he wouldn't have enough time with his teammates on the long plane ride. "That's it then?" she said. It was all so sudden she had whiplash. But she didn't know how to fix anything. Cliff was completely unemotional, indifferent; she almost didn't recognize him. He'd been an asshole at times, sure. But he'd grown up with a difficult father who'd been in and out of his life—until he'd gotten rich and famous. Then Richard was always hanging around, looking for a handout.

Cliff was also in an unusual and demanding job, despite its perks, and sometimes suffered from anxiety and depression due to the constant pressure to perform and the very public backlash if he didn't.

She'd tried to be understanding, tried to see the best in him. She'd meant what she'd said when she'd sworn to love him for the rest of her life. But if he wanted to end their marriage, there was nothing she could do to stop him. The helplessness she felt was probably the worst aspect of what was happening. He wouldn't even give her the chance to change whatever was bothering him.

"Have a safe trip," she said dully.

The door opened behind her, and Jeremy stepped in. "Car's ready," he announced.

Relief flooded Cliff's face. "Great. Let's go."

Charlotte thought he'd simply circumvent her and leave without so much as a goodbye, but as he brushed past, he muttered, "I'm sorry."

Then he was gone.

Charlotte had packed a suitcase and moved back in with her parents, who lived in Newport Beach, while Cliff was gone. She wasn't going to stay where she wasn't wanted; it'd been his money that'd bought the house in the first place.

But even after living an entire week in her old bedroom, whenever she opened her eyes and took in her surroundings, she felt strange, as if she'd stepped into a time capsule. Her parents hadn't changed a thing since she'd graduated from high school and left home. Her yearbooks were stacked in the closet, the cluttered bulletin board above her desk held, among other things, a picture of her and Doug Green at senior prom, along with the dried-out corsage he'd given her, various notes from the friends she'd been closest to at the time, her SAT results, her acceptance to Stanford and her old book lists, which were extensive because she knew, in order to become a writer, she needed to be well-read. That she'd been able to achieve her dream of getting published by a major publisher and hitting *The New York Times* bestseller list so easily and early in her career certainly wasn't typical. But she hadn't marveled at the anomaly too much. For her, nothing had seemed off-limits. As far back as she could remember, the world had bowed at her feet. She'd always felt loved, valued, capable, happy.

Until now. Now the world had, without warning, become completely hostile. The press was having a field day with her divorce ("Clifford Jackson Kicks out Queen of the 'Sports Romance'"; "NBA Star Leaves 'Queen of Sports Romance'"; "'Sports Romance' Author Unable to Create Her Own Happily-Ever-After"; "Clifford Jackson Giving up on 'Storybook' Romance"), so she wasn't just brokenhearted; she felt like a laughingstock. It didn't help that the friends she'd made since marrying Cliff had become unresponsive to her; apparently, they'd decided they'd rather remain friends with him. She didn't even know if she'd have the emotional wherewithal to finish the second book on her contract, so her career might go the same way as her marriage. The manuscript was due in just three short months, and because she'd been so intimidated by the success of her first book, so scared she wouldn't be able to top it, she'd started five different stories only to abandon them all.

Now the fear was worse than ever—overwhelming, paralyzing, suffocating. The fact that Cliff was responsible for so much of the word of mouth she'd received when *Playing for Keeps* was released made her feel like an imposter, as if she hadn't deserved what she'd received in the first place, and her second book would reveal just how inept a writer she really was.

She pulled the blankets over her head to block out the light. Her mother had come in an hour or so earlier and put up the shades. Penny was making lunch—or dinner; Charlotte couldn't keep track. She just knew that her mother wanted her to come down to eat.

But she had no desire for food. She'd been in bed since she came home and still couldn't summon the strength to get up. Everything she'd built since she'd left this room eleven years ago had been leveled—or soon would be.

She heard someone at the door but didn't pull the blankets down so she could see who it was. Her father, a hedge fund manager, didn't usually get home until six, and it was somewhere in the middle of the afternoon, somewhere in the middle of the week, so she was fairly certain he was still gone. It had to be her mother, who'd been a tennis instructor at the local club before her health had started to deteriorate. The longer Charlotte stayed in bed, the more Penny began to hover. She said encouraging things, offered to take Charlotte shopping or to lunch. She'd even mentioned getting her a good therapist. Her family was wealthy, so they could afford that kind of help. But right now, even those baby steps seemed too daunting.

"You're not coming?" her mother said.

"I'm not hungry," she replied.

The bed dipped as Penny sat beside her and tugged the covers down. "That can't be true," she said as she smoothed the hair out of Charlotte's face. "You've hardly eaten for days."

"I'd rather sleep."

Her mother's eyebrows shot up. "That's all you've been doing!"

"I must be catching up," she muttered.

Penny's cool, gentle hand cupped her face. "What about your book, honey?"

Just the mention of her book caused fear to burn like acid in Charlotte's stomach. "What about it?"

"Isn't it due soon? Don't you need to write?"

"I've got time," she lied.

Her mother studied her with concern. "I'm *so* worried about you."

Charlotte curved her lips into as close an approximation of a smile as she could manage. "I'll be okay."

"I can't believe Clifford would do this to you," she responded. "You . . . you haven't heard from him, have you?"

The first few days after she'd moved back in with her parents, Charlotte had checked her phone religiously. She couldn't help hoping Cliff would change his mind, feel *some* regret. She hadn't done anything wrong; she'd been a loving, devoted wife. Surely, he'd realize he was tossing away someone who was important to him, someone he missed and needed in his life.

But no . . . She winced as she remembered how torturous it'd become as the days passed and she received no calls from him—no messages, either. The Lakers had managed to beat the Knicks, and he'd scored over thirty points. She'd been hoping he'd do well because that usually made him eager to celebrate with her. But he still didn't call.

Then she'd made the mistake of googling his name to see what was going on in his life—or what the press was reporting about it, anyway—and came across a headline that'd nearly made her throw up: "Clifford Jackson Seen in Vegas with Model Marija Vidmar." There'd been a picture to corroborate the brief sighting—of her husband holding hands with the tallest, most beautiful woman she'd ever seen—and she hadn't picked up her phone since. For all she knew, the battery was as dead as her marriage.

"I haven't heard from him," she mumbled.

"Then you need to let him go."

"I know that." Instant annoyance had caused her to speak too sharply, but if it was *that* easy to get over Cliff, she would've done it already.

"Time heals all wounds," her mother said, attempting to soothe her, but it was difficult to believe anything could help. Charlotte could barely open her eyes they were so red and swollen from the crying jags that would hit her out of nowhere.

Her mother stood, then bent over to gather the balls of tissue that'd avalanched onto the carpet from the nightstand. "You have to keep up your strength. Come on down and at least try to eat something."

Charlotte allowed her heavy eyelids to close. "Not tonight."

"But I have a surprise for you." Penny was clearly disappointed. "Something guaranteed to cheer you up."

She forced her eyes open again. Unless her mother could put her marriage back together, *nothing* would cheer her up. "Mac and cheese won't do it this time, Mom," she said. "But I appreciate the effort."

"It's Julian," Penny said.

Charlotte shoved herself into a sitting position. *"Davis?"*

Lines of confusion creased her mother's forehead. "Do you know another Julian?"

She didn't, but she hadn't heard from her best friend's twin brother in years. He'd hung out with them a lot in high school. But when they graduated, they all went off to different colleges. He'd gone to a school on the East Coast to play lacrosse, found a girlfriend and gotten busy. She'd only remained in contact with Sloane. The last she'd heard about Julian, which was a couple of years ago, he'd become a landscape photographer who traveled extensively for work but was now based out of Moab, Utah, where he'd opened his own gallery, and he'd become engaged to some woman who worked for one of the travel magazines that featured his photographs. She probably would've heard more about him, but Cliff hadn't liked Sloane, and Sloane hadn't liked Cliff, so even her relationship with Julian's sister had been mostly nonexistent in recent years, especially once Sloane got married and moved to Seattle just after telling Charlotte about Julian's engagement. "What does *he* want?" she asked her mother.

"Didn't say. He just came to the door to see if you were home, and I invited him to join us for dinner."

She groaned. "You *didn't* . . ."

"Why wouldn't I?" her mother replied. "You've always loved Julian. *I've* always loved Julian. I was happy to see him, especially because I thought . . . Well, I thought he might be able to help me pull you out of this . . . funk."

Her sinuses were plugged, making her voice sound nasal. "I'm going through a divorce. It's not a funk. Anyway, look at me." She grabbed a tissue and held it up before blowing her nose, which she'd wiped so often in the past week she could've played Rudolph in a Christmas show. "I haven't showered for three days. I don't want him or anyone else to see me like this."

"Then take a few minutes to clean up," she said. "You'll find us in the kitchen when you're done."

"I can't face getting ready! Tell him I don't feel well," she said to her mother's retreating form and flopped back down on the pillows.

Penny turned at the door. "Charlotte, please. Staying in bed isn't doing you any good."

It was better than allowing others to witness the depth of her devastation. That was probably what Julian had come to see; it was what everyone on the internet was speculating about. Millions of strangers were talking about her online, probably dying to catch a glimpse of her. If someone happened to take a snapshot and post it on the internet, she could only imagine the number of views it would get . . .

The world was no longer safe. "I'll eat later," she said.

"You've been putting me off for days." Her mother gestured at the rumpled bed. "I can't see you like this anymore. If you won't come down, I'll call him up."

Panic gripped Charlotte, causing her to bolt back into a sitting position. "No!"

Her mother didn't even hesitate. "Come on up, Julian!" she yelled in a fatalistic voice.

The sudden movement had made Charlotte's head swim. She put a hand to her right temple. "Mom!" she said, her voice a harsh whisper.

Penny winced as she glanced back, but she was far more determined than Charlotte had expected. When Julian came, she merely turned to the side to make room for him to get past her in the doorway before she left.

"*You* look good," he said sarcastically.

All too aware of her greasy hair, swollen eyes, red nose and blotchy face, Charlotte sniffed. "That's the first thing you're going to say to me?"

"Pretty hard to ignore the obvious."

Unfortunately, *he* looked incredible. Of course that would be the case. These days, everything seemed to be engineered to make her feel bad. No longer the scrawny late bloomer he'd been in high school, with terrible acne and braces on his teeth, he had a clear, unblemished complexion, broad shoulders and well-defined biceps. And the white cotton of his T-shirt contrasted nicely with his dark tan and cornflower-blue eyes. Those long, golden eyelashes matched the lighter streaks in his hair and had always been attractive, but now they were positively dreamy.

She preferred the tall, lanky physique of her husband—soon-to-be ex-husband—she told herself. She'd always liked basketball players. But she could see how some women would find Julian's stockier frame appealing. He looked incredibly strong.

"You don't feel even the least bit sorry for me?" she said.

"Looks like you've got that covered." A crooked smile coupled with a wink softened his words, but she took exception to them all the same.

"My husband just . . . My husband dropped me without any warning and hasn't looked back since, Jules," she said, easily and automatically falling back on the nickname his closest friends and family had always used. "This was the man I was hoping to have a family with—the man I was hoping to grow old with."

His muscular shoulders lifted in a shrug. "He's also the man who doesn't deserve you. Good riddance to Clifford Jackson—that's what I say."

"Because he's a professional athlete?"

"Because he's a selfish bastard."

She stiffened in surprise. "How would *you* know?"

"It's obvious from the way he plays ball." He opened the doors to her closet and stepped inside.

"What are you doing?" It looked like he was rifling through her suitcase, which was lying open on the floor. She hadn't bothered to unpack. Why would she? She'd been hoping Cliff would invite her back to the gorgeous Malibu mansion she used to call home.

"Finding something for you to wear," he replied.

"I'm *not* coming down to dinner," she reiterated.

"I know." There was a plop as he tossed some of her clothes to the side. "We're going out."

"*What?*"

His voice drifted to her, once again, from inside the closet. "You heard me."

"I'm not going anywhere," she argued.

He took a moment to poke his head out. "It might look weird if I'm carrying you over my shoulder, but I guess that's up to you."

She felt her jaw drop. "You're saying you'll haul me out of here if you have to?"

"That's exactly what I'm saying."

"*Why?*"

"Because we're not going to let Clifford Jackson get the best of you—that's why."

She considered his response, found it somewhat empowering and, therefore, appealing. "How do you propose we stop him?"

"We're going to be seen around LA, make sure we're photographed together and leak those pictures to every online source that might be interested."

That would be a long list. For the news outlets, it'd be almost like receiving shots of Hailey Bieber hanging out with another man if she ever split with Justin. "You want to make him think we're seeing each other? That I've already moved on?"

"He can think whatever he wants as long as he knows you're not sitting in your room—" he poked his head out again "—crying over him."

"What about the evidence?" she grumbled. "You don't think my swollen eyes and red face will give me away?"

"That's what makeup and sunglasses are for."

She nibbled on her bottom lip as the nasty online comments she'd read about herself floated through her mind. It wouldn't help her broken heart, but maybe it *would* feel good to salvage a portion of her pride . . . "You really believe we can sell it?"

"Why not? Any woman would want to be seen with me. After all, I'm a hell of a good-looking guy."

That made her laugh out loud in spite of everything. "You're definitely not bad."

"You probably think Clifford's hotter, but I'm cutting you

some slack for being delusional at the moment." He came up with a shirt and a skirt from two different outfits and held them up before tossing them over to her as if he'd decided they'd do. "Here you are."

"Those don't even go together," she informed him.

"Now you're questioning my fashion sense?"

"I'll pick my own clothes, thank you—if you'll just step out of the room." She wasn't wearing anything other than a tank top and a pair of panties, so she couldn't get out of bed until he left.

"I'm not that stupid," he said. "Once I'm gone, you'll just lock the door."

She laughed again, and the sound of it reminded her of who she normally was. This was what friends were for, she reminded herself. They picked you up when you were flat on your ass and compelled you to journey on. Her problem was that she'd let her friends go because of Cliff, had let him dictate who they saw and what they did. She'd felt she had to do that to keep him happy.

Little good it had done her . . .

"Then turn your back," she said.

He instantly obliged, and she dragged herself out of bed and over to her suitcase. "Where's your wife, by the way?" she asked. "Won't she mind you taking me on this little escapade?"

"I don't have a wife."

She'd just pulled the rest of her clothes out of her suitcase and hadn't found anything that wasn't too wrinkled, so she was going through what he'd already tossed aside. "Sloane told me you were engaged."

"I was."

"What happened?"

He kept his back to her. "My fiancée came to her senses, I guess."

"She broke up with you?"

"Went back to her douchebag ex, who, it turned out, had been calling her. So don't tell *me* I don't know how bad you're feeling."

"That would hurt," she acknowledged. "But as long we're comparing war wounds, *I* was actually married and thought we were ready to start a family—and all of America was paying attention to our relationship and is now witnessing my fall from grace."

"You've got a backbone. You'll get through it."

Would she? That remained to be seen. "How long ago did your fiancée leave you?" she asked as she pulled out a clean pair of panties.

"It's been about fourteen months, but it was only nine weeks before the wedding. We were just about to send out the invitations when she realized she'd rather be with him."

"That sucks. So . . . are they married now?"

"No. Didn't work out between them *again*. I, of course, wasn't surprised—but neither was I interested in taking her back."

"You were over it?"

"I was more than over it. I was *grateful* she'd left me—feel like I dodged a bullet. Distance gave me a certain perspective I'd lacked before."

After nearly drowning in feelings of inadequacy and allowing her own internal critic to beat her up over and over again by suggesting everything she should've done differently so she wouldn't have been tossed out by the one person she loved more than any other, it felt like Julian was throwing her a life preserver. She hated that he was seeing her at her most vulnerable, especially because it was the first time they'd been together in over a decade. But he wouldn't let her send him away, and his tough-love approach—although, admittedly, a little callous—was actually helping. He was essentially saying, "Shit happens to everybody—get over it." And he was right. What other choice did she have?

"You're lucky," she agreed.

"So are you. You just don't know it yet."

She was far from feeling the gratitude he felt, but she certainly hoped he was right.

"What are you doing in town, anyway?" she asked as she finally settled on a casual black spaghetti-strap dress. She'd always loved yoga, had stayed in shape, so at least she wouldn't look too bad if she could fix her face and hair.

"My mother had to have a full hysterectomy, and my father had to get an operation on his hemorrhoids," he replied matter-of-factly.

She covered her mouth. "I'm sure your father wouldn't want you telling people about that!"

"Let it be a lesson to you. Eat more fruits and vegetables or suffer the consequences. Anyway, Sloane's design business is so new I didn't want her to leave it."

"So you stepped up. That was very good of you."

"I have my moments."

She dropped her tank top on the floor before yanking the pool dress over her head. "I'm decent."

He turned around. "Nice. Now you just need to wash your face and comb your hair."

Fresh tears filled her eyes—out of nowhere—but these tears weren't for Cliff. "I've missed you," she admitted, somehow feeling as if she'd suddenly come across an important part of herself she'd lost along the way.

His smile softened. "Yeah, well, you might think of me more as a pain in the ass before this is over."

Impulsively, she walked into his arms—and her bruised ego and broken heart felt just a little better as he hugged her. "You're going to be okay," he murmured in her ear. "Let's go."

chapter 2

"So how is this going to work again?" Charlotte asked, glancing around. She wasn't so famous that everyone she passed would be able to identify her—especially without her husband at her side, towering over her—but there were a lot of Lakers fans in the area who would know who she was. *Someone* was bound to notice her.

Julian clasped her hand more tightly, steadying her. He'd driven her over to Westwood, one of the most popular neighborhoods in Los Angeles. It was a fun place to hang out, with trendy shops and eateries, movie theaters, the Hammer Museum and UCLA—and there was usually a crowd of people milling about the streets, especially on a warm spring evening like this one.

Tonight proved no different.

"I texted my friend, told him where we'll be. He'll snap a few pics and email them to various online sites."

She smoothed her dress with her free hand. "How do I look? Okay?" She'd decided she couldn't go out without washing her hair, so she'd ended up showering, and he'd visited with her mother while she put on makeup.

"Much better," he said. "Relax."

She slid her sunglasses higher on her nose. There hadn't been anything she could do, even with makeup, to hide her swollen eyes, so she had to cover them. "Where are we going?"

He scanned the crowd. Now that he'd dragged her out among the wolves, he seemed determined to make sure she didn't get eaten, and his protectiveness helped. "To a little French bistro."

"Is the food good there? Because I'm suddenly famished."

"I'm not surprised. Your mother said you haven't eaten for a week."

"I've eaten," she argued, but when he challenged that statement with a pointed look, she broke eye contact. "Just . . . not a lot," she admitted.

As they reached the restaurant, a man stepped out of the shadow of the building and started taking pictures of them. Julian feigned outrage at the invasion of their privacy and yelled for him to go away—all while making sure he angled aside so the lens could catch her face well enough to make her recognizable—and the attention made others turn to look. Soon, several people were murmuring about them and lifting their phones for photos.

Charlotte forced a smile as she clung to Julian. "You're sure this is a good idea, right?" For a second, she was afraid this would mean Cliff would never take her back. She knew she probably shouldn't want that, not after what he'd done, but she did.

"You've got this," he responded.

"Charlotte! Charlotte Jackson! Over here! Is that your new man?" someone yelled from not too far down the street.

Charlotte struggled to broaden her smile as she turned. "Just a friend I went to high school with!" she called back.

"Perfect. You're doing great," Julian told her and led her inside.

While they waited for the hostess, the door opened behind

them and a group of teenagers who'd seen the commotion on the street poked their heads in. "Do you think that's her?" . . . "No, dude. She's not that tall." . . . "You're just used to seeing her with Clifford Jackson, who's, like, six-nine!" . . . "I heard someone call her name." One of them tried to get a snapshot of her and might have succeeded had the manager not shooed them out.

"This isn't going to be as bad as I thought," she told Julian after the hostess had seated them. She probably couldn't have braved going out on her own, but she felt safe with him.

"It'll get even easier from here," he said. "You just have to take one small step forward every day."

The waitress came to bring water. "Everything looks delicious," Charlotte said, scanning the menu.

She chose the French onion soup and pistachio-topped salad. He chose the salmon and lentils with capers.

"Look, this place is also a cooking school." She pointed at the back of the menu.

He leaned over to read the information. "I didn't realize that."

"They offer classes—the Art of Making Pasta, Date Night, Springtime in Paris. It'd be fun to sign up for one."

"Maybe you should."

She frowned. "I have to finish my book before I do anything else."

He spread his napkin in his lap. "Your mother mentioned you were on deadline. How's your second book coming along?"

"Great," she lied.

He called her bluff with a skeptical look, but she nodded, trying to convince him.

"Your first book was good," he said.

Her hand froze with her water halfway to her mouth. "You read it?"

"I did. I downloaded it shortly after Sloane told me you'd been published."

"That's *so* nice!" Her own husband hadn't read it. Cliff had acted proud of her, but he wasn't much of a reader.

"I knew how much it would mean to you to see your name on the cover," Julian said.

"Too bad I didn't use my maiden name on the cover," she grumbled.

"You can change it for the next one."

"Not really. Not without hurting sales. An author's name is more than a name. It's a brand. If I go back to Williams, the readers who liked my first book might not even realize I've written another one."

"So you'll stick with Jackson," he said with a shrug. "No big deal. Anyway, I liked the story. You're going to be fine."

She took a drink before putting down her glass. "Do you typically read romance?" she asked with a grin.

He winked at her. "Only yours so far, but I might read more in the future."

When the waitress came to pick up their menus, they agreed to get a bottle of white wine, and he ordered it. "So . . . are you going to continue living with your parents?" he asked.

"For the time being, I guess."

He arched an eyebrow. "Because you're hoping Clifford will take you back?"

"Yes." She gave him a pitiful look before reversing her answer. "No."

"It would be a mistake to go back to him, Char."

"I know. But when you love someone . . ."

"He'd just dump you again, and maybe by then you'd have kids, which would make it that much harder."

She knew he was right. "Did you see that picture of him online with Marija Vidmar?"

"I don't follow him."

"Then how'd you know we split up?"

"My parents said something about it. My dad's a big Lakers fan. I prefer college ball. Who's Marija Vidmar?"

"Only a model," she said. "*And* the most beautiful woman in the world."

"In the whole world, huh?" He grinned. "Wow, that *is* beautiful."

She called up the picture on her phone and turned it to show him. "See?"

"She's not bad," he allowed. "But Sloane told me Clifford picked you out of the crowd at one of his games and sent someone over to ask for your number."

"He did."

"So *something* must've caught his eye, and it couldn't have been your sparkling personality." He waved a hand. "Anyway, who cares? Let her have him. You have a book to write. That's what you need to focus on—the opportunities that lie ahead of you."

If only she had the confidence she needed to make the most of those opportunities. "I don't think I can write it, Jules. I . . . I'm going to blow the only thing I've ever really wanted to do."

"No, you're not," he said, growing resolute again. "You can do it. Your first book proves it."

"My first book only proves that having a big social media following can turbocharge a writer's career—and I got that by dating and then marrying Cliff."

"Your book was *good*," he reiterated.

She wanted to believe him, but the doubt was too crippling. She took another drink of water before asking, "What about you? Do you still have an art gallery in Moab?"

"It's not a full gallery—just my work. It gives me a direct

outlet in a place that sees a lot of tourists, thanks to the national parks in the area."

"Who works the store when you're off taking pictures?"

"I have an employee. She can't be there all the time, of course, so she just tailors her hours to fit her schedule. That's how a lot of places do it down there. And we also sell online."

"I've seen some of your work," she said. "You're incredibly talented."

"I love what I do, mostly because it gives me the opportunity to travel."

"You've been all over the world."

"I've seen a lot of places, but there are still destinations on my list."

"Like . . . ?"

"Lençóis Maranhenses National Park, for one."

"Never heard of it."

"It's in Brazil. There're too many places to name, actually. The world is a big place."

It *was* a big place, with so much to discover—and yet she'd been living her life as a satellite to someone else. Had she truly been happy?

She'd been grateful, felt lucky because so many women would be eager to trade places with her. But Cliff never seemed to care much about *her* goals and dreams. His were much more important. They always came first.

"What are you thinking?" Julian asked.

The waitress appeared with their food. Charlotte leaned back and waited until the woman had set down their plates before responding. "I'm thinking I need to quit wallowing in self-pity and start writing my next book."

He seemed pleased to hear it, but then the smile slipped from his face. "Wait a second . . . Did you say *start* writing your next book? When's it due?"

She gave him a sheepish look. "In three months."

He sat back. "Can *anyone* write a book in that amount of time?"

"It's possible," she said. "But it won't be easy—especially for a newbie like me."

When he got home, Julian found his mother sitting on the couch in a robe watching TV. "Where's Dad?" he asked.

"Went to bed."

"It's barely ten. He feeling okay?"

Although his mother was sitting in the dark, the TV made it possible to see her face as the colored lights flickered across it. "I think so. He got up early. And he typically beats me to bed these days."

"You weren't waiting up for *me* . . ." Julian said. She'd been so interested when he'd said he was going to visit Charlotte, he'd half expected it.

"Maybe I was," she admitted with a laugh. "I've been curious. How'd it go with Charlotte?"

"Better than I expected. She's resilient. She has a tough road ahead of her, but she'll rise to the occasion."

"She must've been surprised to see you. It's been a long time."

"Since the summer we graduated from high school." They'd made the most of those final, sun-filled days by lying out at Charlotte's pool, playing sand volleyball at the beach, going on their friend Trevor's sailboat—his parents were even richer than Charlotte's—and partying with another friend whose parents were always going out of town. So being back in LA conjured up memories that'd made him eager to reconnect.

"Even Sloane hasn't talked to Charlotte for a while," his mother said.

"It's been over a year."

"Why, do you think? Sloane and Charlotte were always so close."

"Sloane says Cliff cut her out. She claims he would only accept his own family and friends. To get along with him, Charlotte had to become part of his world and leave her own behind."

"It would be easy to resent that."

Julian nodded. "But she was trying so hard to make her marriage work, I got the impression she never even considered the cost."

She adjusted the small blanket draped over her lap. "Is that why her parents have been so reticent about their son-in-law?"

"I didn't know they *had* been reticent."

"We ran into them at a charity function—a firefighter's fund raiser—last summer. Everyone was excited to hear about the NBA star who'd joined their family, but they didn't say much, didn't seem all that happy to have such a close connection with him, which took me by surprise."

"They were probably sorry to see their only child marry someone who wouldn't accept them into his life."

"Makes sense. Penny seemed kind of sad, to be honest."

Julian thought of the shots his friend had gotten tonight. He couldn't wait until they were splashed all over the internet to show Cliff that Charlotte would be just fine without him. The friend he'd asked to take those shots would be compensated, since he'd be able to sell them for a good price, so everyone came out a winner—except Cliff, who deserved a dose of his own medicine. "Now that he's moved on, Charlotte *and* her parents are better off."

"It's hard to be tossed aside."

"She'll get over it eventually." He started to cross the room to the hallway, but she spoke again.

"Did you tell her?"

He knew what his mother was talking about; the gravity in her voice made her meaning clear. "No."

She twisted around to face him. "Why not?"

"Because I don't want *anyone* to know—other than you, me and Dad."

"You said you'd talk to Sloane."

"I will, when the time is right."

"When?"

He couldn't say. He sensed something was going on with his sister. Until he had the chance to spend some time with her and figure out what it was, he wasn't going to dump his problems at her feet. It'd be different if there was anything she could do to help—but there wasn't. "When I'm ready."

"Your friends and family should have the opportunity to love and support you through the coming months just like you're trying to support Charlotte."

"My situation's different," he pointed out.

"How? She's facing a challenge. You're facing a challenge."

He frowned. "Not one that I can win," he said and continued on to his room.

Sloane sat behind the wheel of her car at a stoplight, staring off into space, worrying about her marriage and where it was going—which wasn't anywhere good. Ben was a wonderful man and a great spouse, but if she couldn't wrap her mind around having children—and soon—where would that leave them?

The car behind her honked. She hadn't realized the stoplight had turned green.

Glancing in the rearview mirror to see the angry driver behind her, she gave her Subaru some gas. She wished she and Ben could find a compromise, but either they had children or they didn't. And the push/pull over that subject was putting so much strain on their relationship, they were killing what they had. Sure, they still came home from work, made dinner together and acted as if everything was okay. But then she sat, numb, as they had a drink before bed, and he talked about his two nieces and nephew and how he couldn't wait to be a father.

He'd been pressing her to get pregnant—to at least start *trying*—but she hadn't yet visited the doctor to have her IUD removed. She kept telling him the doctor was booked solid and the earliest appointment she could get was months away. But she hadn't even spoken to anyone at the doctor's office. Every time she picked up the phone, she had a panic attack and hung up during the "Press 1 for English" recording that came on as soon as the call connected. She liked her life the way it was, didn't want it to change. Even seeing her husband's nieces and new baby nephew didn't evoke the response she felt it should—a burning desire to become a parent herself. She was excited for Caitlyn, Ben's sister. She thought Caitlyn's children were sweet. She even offered to babysit when Caitlyn needed help. But that was enough "kid time" for her. When she imagined living Caitlyn and John's life—when she saw firsthand the huge commitment raising a family entailed, the *lifelong* commitment and how it changed absolutely everything—she felt positively claustrophobic.

The worst part about it? She'd thought she wanted children when she first met Ben. It wasn't fair that she'd changed her mind. But how could she force herself to go through with something that impactful if it wasn't what she wanted now? She preferred to focus on her career and not take on that added responsibility, couldn't even imagine trying to juggle being a good mom with being a good decorator and business owner.

She pulled in behind the small downtown boutique she co-owned with her college friend, Rory Gaiten. Despite knowing how difficult it would be to start their own interior design firm, she and Rory had moved ahead with their dream and were making it happen. The business was still in its infancy—they were relieved whenever they covered overhead by mid-month—but they were gaining more clients as time went by, so Sloane hoped they'd be on safer ground soon. They'd recently been featured in a local magazine that praised them as being "fresh, innovative and extremely talented," so this month was proving to be an especially good one.

"There you are!" Rory said.

Sloane checked the oversize watch she wore. It'd belonged to her grandfather before he passed. "Am I late?"

Slight and clean-shaven in a fitted white shirt, tailored gray slacks and Italian loafers, Rory cleared his desk, which he never let get very cluttered, by putting a piece of paper in his drawer and centering his coffee mug on its coaster. "Later than usual."

"Traffic was bad." She tossed her keys on her desk, which faced his in the back section of the store. "And the line at Starbucks was out the door." She set down her to-go cup and circled around to take her seat. "Did the paintings come in for the Jones house?"

Rory shook his head. "Not yet."

"Damn it! She's entertaining for her anniversary next weekend and wants us to be finished—understandably."

"I'll email the artist again," he said and started typing.

"Thanks."

Rory looked up from his computer as she put her purse in her drawer. "Do you feel okay?" he asked.

She looked up. "Of course. Why?"

"I don't know. You seem . . . tense."

Her personal life was starting to bleed into her professional life. She needed to find a resolution—the sooner, the better. "It's just . . . been a hectic morning," she said.

"Except you seem to be getting worse by the day," he pointed out.

"It's nothing." She'd have to bury deeper the way she felt about the disintegration of her marriage, improve her acting . . . *something*.

He frowned at her. "You're not going to tell me?"

Tucking her dark hair behind one ear, she put even more effort behind her smile and hoped it would be convincing. It was the best she could do when she felt trapped between two choices—neither of which she liked. "There's nothing to tell," she said as brightly as possible.

chapter 3

When Charlotte came down for breakfast carrying her laptop the next morning, her mother beamed at her. "Well, look at you! I'm *so* glad to see you—and you're even showered."

Charlotte drew a deep breath. "I'm trying to keep putting one foot in front of the other."

"You can do it. How'd it go with Julian last night?"

"We had fun," Charlotte admitted, but one night out with a friend couldn't fix what was broken in her life. The fact that her mind kept circling back to Cliff and the pictures of him with that woman proved it. But after Julian's kindness and support, at least she had the energy to try. She'd needed to hear what he had to say, and she believed him when he said that surviving her heartbreak would be easier if she didn't let the rest of her life fall apart at the same time.

The last thing he'd said to her when he dropped her off was that it would be difficult "digging out from beneath the rubble" and warned her to do whatever she could do to make the comeback easier—which was, basically, not to let herself sink any lower.

So here she was, up and about, even though she still didn't feel like getting out of bed.

"I see you have your computer," Penny said. "Does that mean you're going to write today?"

Charlotte wished she could say yes, but she was empty inside. Too empty to create. She couldn't even contemplate staring at her computer screen, trying to force a story, and having a blank page gazing stubbornly back at her. "Not today. I just brought this down so I can check my email while I'm here in the kitchen with you. I haven't done it in a while."

Her mother nodded encouragingly. "That's a step in the right direction."

Maybe, but if she didn't write today, she'd fall another day behind, ratcheting her tension even higher.

Charlotte tried not to let that freak her out. *Be kind to yourself.* Julian had said that, too. Although her deadline was marching inexorably closer, she could still finish her manuscript in time if she could get on her feet soon. And that was exactly what she was all about today. "I'm thinking of looking for an apartment. Would you like to come with me?"

"You don't want to stay here with us for the time being—in your old bedroom?"

She heard the disappointment in her mother's voice. At least she still had people who cared about her. "I might. But shopping for an apartment will give me a reason to leave the house. I just want to see what's out there, get a feel for the market."

"Sure, I'll go with you. Let me make you some breakfast first." Her mother took out a frying pan. "How many eggs would you like?"

Charlotte was still too upset to crave food. But, again, she decided to push past the pain and behave as normally as possible, regardless of what Cliff had done. "Just one. That's probably all I'll be able to get down."

"I've got bacon, too."

Fortunately, bacon always sounded good. Charlotte imagined that even during an apocalypse people would still be eating bacon. "I'll have a couple of slices."

"And toast?"

"No, that'll be enough."

Her mother chatted about the weather, Sloane's design business, which Julian had apparently told her about while Charlotte was getting ready last night, and how busy Charlotte's father had been lately. "Should I call your dad?" she asked. "See if he can pull away for lunch?"

"That's a good idea," Charlotte replied. Her father had always treated her like a little princess, but he worked long hours. It would be great to have him join them for a change.

"He mentioned he had meetings this morning, but maybe he'll be free in a few hours. I'll check with him."

Although Charlotte nodded, she was paying more attention to her computer. The pictures of her having dinner with Julian had started appearing online before she'd even gone to bed. Ten hours later, they were proliferating like ants pouring out of an anthill. They were everywhere, and after seeing how they'd turned out, she was satisfied that no one would be able to tell how devastated she was on the inside. She looked okay, she thought, and Julian looked better than she'd even realized while she was so worked up about the dumpster fire her life had become. A lot of people in the comments, especially women, stated that she'd traded up and they were happy she'd landed on her feet.

She found that interesting . . . Maybe the world didn't begin and end with Clifford Jackson. Maybe she'd just let *her* world shrink that small.

Her mother slid an egg onto a plate and called her father as she clicked away from the celebrity gossip sites—because there were also harsh comments she couldn't bear to see in her current frame of mind—and checked the sales rankings on her book. *Playing for Keeps* was experiencing another surge in sales—a byproduct of everyone talking about her online again.

At least that was positive.

She could hear her mother speaking to her father while she logged into her email account. Besides plenty of spam from the retailers she liked best, trying to tempt her back to their stores, she found some fan letters asking for the title of her next book. She had a release date, but no title. Sadly, no book, either.

She fumbled through those responses, asking her readers to sign up for her newsletter so she could keep them informed. Then she read an email from her web gal asking for any monthly updates she wanted on her website.

She hadn't even looked at her website, so that would have to wait. She replied that they'd catch any fixes next month and moved on to a message from the publicist at her publisher. Shauna wanted to see if she was okay since she hadn't been returning calls or emails.

Charlotte reassured her. Then she came to the email she'd spotted first thing. It was from her editor. She'd saved that one for last—and wished she could avoid it altogether—but she knew she had to respond before logging off. Megan Schwimmer was a wonderful person, but she had a job to do and that was to get Charlotte's manuscript in and edited on time so they didn't hold up the other departments at her publisher and her book could come out on its scheduled date.

"He said he can make it," her mother announced when she disconnected from her call and carried Charlotte's plate to the table.

Charlotte got up to gather her own silverware while her mother poured her a glass of orange juice.

"Anything interesting?" Penny asked, indicating her computer.

There was nothing from Cliff. Email would be an unlikely way for him to contact her, and she knew that, but hope reigned supreme. "Just something from my editor."

Penny had returned to the sink and was scrubbing the frying pan. "What does she have to say? Do you think she'll give you an extension?"

Charlotte didn't see how that would be possible. Her release date in the fall was a coveted one—typically reserved for the big-name authors who could make or break a publisher's entire quarter. An extension would screw up everyone. "I don't dare even ask. I know they have high hopes for my second book."

"Has she heard about the state of your marriage?"

That was, no doubt, what had prompted the email. Megan had already let her know she was eager to see some sample chapters or, barring that, a synopsis giving the basic premise of her next book. But Charlotte still needed to decide on what that premise would be.

She ate slowly, putting off the inevitable until after she'd pushed her plate away.

"Finished?" her mother said.

She glanced up to see Penny watching her and nodded before opening her editor's message.

Megan told her how sorry she was to hear about her split with Cliff. She didn't act as though losing one of the most famous shooting guards in the NBA would hurt Charlotte's career, but Charlotte knew she had to be afraid it would. Charlotte was afraid of that herself. So now was not the time to admit she hadn't even started her next manuscript, that she was entirely blocked. She knew the panic it would cause at her publisher—and that it would only bring more emails and unsolicited suggestions for what her new story should be. She'd welcome that if she thought it would truly help, but she couldn't write according to someone else's vision. The premise had to stir her imagination—had to call out to *her*.

Taking a deep breath, she wrote a brief reply:

> It's so nice of you to check in. I'm sure, with time, I'll
> be fine. I'm staying with my folks, so I'm in good hands
> despite what you may see online. And don't worry about
> my work in progress. I'll be putting my nose to the
> grindstone over the summer. At least now I won't have
> Cliff's busy schedule to distract me. Ha!

After reading that email several times, just to make sure it struck the right tone, she hit Send. But she was painfully aware of the words she'd chosen. "Work in progress" wasn't really accurate. All she had was a work that had yet to be started.

She sighed, lifting her glass of orange juice.

"Everything okay?" Penny asked.

Nothing was okay, but she offered her mother a feeble smile. "It will be eventually."

"I'll finish cleaning up in here while you get your makeup on," Penny said, taking the empty glass from her. "Are you sure you don't want to buy a house? Should I call my Realtor friend, Jenny?"

"I'm definitely not ready for that kind of commitment. I don't even know where I want to live."

"So how will we find any apartments you'd like to see?"

"I'll look online. Maybe I'll rent a townhouse or condo." She was just getting up when her computer dinged, signaling a text message. She'd left her phone in her room, but since her phone was synced up with her laptop, she could receive messages on either device.

Hoping it was Julian—she could already use a little more of his resilience and strength—she sank back into her seat. But it wasn't Julian; it was Cliff.

> Hey, hope you're doing well. You have a shit
> ton of mail piling up over here. Are you ever
> going to come get it?

Why didn't he just box it up and send it to her? Didn't he have her parents' address?

He'd had it at one time. Maybe he'd deleted it. It had never really meant anything to him.

She almost told him to ship her the mail, but he hadn't mentioned the clothes she'd left behind—or asked when she planned to collect the rest of her belongings. That gave her enough hope that she couldn't deny herself the opportunity to have another conversation with him. Even if they never got back together, maybe they could gain some closure which would make the next few months easier. Part of the hurt she felt came from the fact that he hadn't explained why he was throwing her away, why he'd changed his mind about them. Certainly, he could do that much.

> **I'm happy to come get it. I'll also put in a forwarding address. When would you like me to drop by?**

If he said he'd just set it outside or that she knew the code to the house so she could get in while he was gone, she'd tell him to mail it, she told herself. But he didn't.

What's wrong with today? You busy?

She should be writing, could've used that excuse. But she didn't.

> **Today's fine. I'll be there in an hour.**

He gave her a thumbs-up, and she closed her laptop.
"What is it?" her mother asked.
"Cliff wants me to pick up my mail."

Her eyes widened. "You're going over there?" She didn't sound excited by the idea.

"Just to get my mail," Charlotte reiterated, but what she was really after was answers.

"Would you like me to go with you?"

"No, I'm afraid that'll make it too hard for us to talk."

"What about looking for apartments?"

"We'll do it after we have lunch with Dad."

Her mother finished wiping the counters. "Okay."

Charlotte thought about Julian as she went to put on her makeup. She doubted he'd think it was a good idea for her to go over to Cliff's house. But Cliff's house still felt like *her* house—like *home*. And a small part of her couldn't help wishing that when she got there, everything she'd been through during the past nine days would simply dissolve into the past.

Even if it did, however, even if he wanted her back, could her heart ever truly forget how pitiless he'd been when he told her he wanted out of their marriage? Or that picture of him with Marija Vidmar?

After ringing the doorbell, Charlotte clasped her hands tightly together. She'd used her key card to open the gate so she could drive onto the estate. Fortunately, Cliff hadn't changed that, probably hadn't even thought about it. But she felt so estranged from him that she wasn't comfortable just walking into the house any longer—although ringing the doorbell at the home she'd shared with him for more than three years felt odd, too.

While waiting for him to answer, she imagined him reclining on the couch, a remote in one hand, as he watched the Golf Channel. When she lived here, she'd always been the one to get the door. He hadn't cared enough to bother interrupting whatever he was doing.

She knocked in case he hadn't heard the bell, and he finally opened the door looking like he'd just rolled out of bed. He was wearing a pair of basketball shorts with no shirt or shoes. Clearly, he'd been lounging around, probably watching TV as she'd imagined. They'd had so much fun together on days like this—going out to get coffee and a doughnut or bagel, spending time barbecuing in their backyard, entertaining his family or friends.

Seeing him so relaxed and accessible again made her miss him. But she didn't move in for the hug she craved. "Looks like you have a new tattoo." She pointed at his right shoulder. She knew every inch of his body, would've noticed it no matter what, but the plastic wrap that protected it from getting infected made the new ink obvious. "You went for an alien, after all, huh?" She tried to keep the censure from her voice. He'd been talking for a while about getting a *Predator* tattoo—from the old Arnold Schwarzenegger movie of the same name—but she'd always managed to discourage him with the question "Are you sure you want that on your body for the rest of your life?"

Now that he was unfettered, however, he'd apparently decided to disregard her advice.

"Yeah. And I like it," he said defensively.

She nodded. "That's . . . good."

His eyes narrowed. "Are you trying to make me feel bad?"

She blinked innocently. "No!" She just thought it looked ridiculous—exactly as she'd imagined it would when he first started talking about it—and was having a hard time pretending otherwise. She kept seeing it through Julian's eyes, knew how hard he'd laugh and felt her own mouth begin to twitch. She could hear her friend's voice: *Do you really want to be with a dude who has a* Predator *tattoo?*

"Then why do you look like you're about to crack up?" Cliff demanded.

Because she *was* about to crack up. Covering her mouth to try to stop herself, she said through her fingers, "I don't know what you mean. I'm just . . . smiling," but busted up right in the middle of that statement. It was terrible timing—not the smartest thing she could've done when hoping to have a heart-to-heart with the man she loved. But the harder she tried to stop, the funnier his tattoo seemed.

He looked stunned. Not many people laughed at him—at least not to his face—and that it was her, his *wife*, who'd always done all she could to protect his ego, had to be a shock. "That's it. I'm not even giving you your mail," he said and slammed the door in her face.

The *wham* startled her enough to bring her out of it. Sobering, she wiped her eyes. What was wrong with her? She'd never get him back by making fun of him.

But did she really want him back? Wasn't it already too late, anyway?

She couldn't answer that question; her emotions were all over the place.

She turned to leave, but then she remembered his bewildered expression when she didn't like his tattoo and gathered the nerve to open the door. She could've been kinder . . .

"Cliff?" she said, poking her head into the entry. Fortunately, he hadn't locked it. Although she had her key, it would've been harder to go that far.

He stood about ten feet away, wearing a sullen expression and holding a beer in one hand. She thought he might tell her to get out. But he didn't. He seemed okay with the intrusion, so she let herself in and closed the door behind her. "I'm sorry."

"You don't seem sorry," he said.

She could see why. Just talking about it was tempting her to start laughing again. What was wrong with her?

She lowered her eyes, hoping that would help her maintain control. "Can I . . . can I go ahead and get my mail?"

He walked into the kitchen and returned with a bag full of what appeared to be mainly adverts.

"Isn't most of this for you?" she asked as she reached in and flipped through it.

He shrugged. "You were always the one who dealt with it."

That essentially released it to her, so there couldn't be anything important for him in there—or he was relying on her to get it back to him if there was. "Okay," she said and turned to go.

"Is that all you came for?" he asked petulantly.

Hope flared within her as she faced him again. "Isn't that why you messaged me? Because you wanted me to pick it up?"

"I also wanted to see what the hell's going on with you."

Bewildered, she shook her head. "I don't know what you mean."

"That dude you were with last night. You're already seeing someone else?"

The irony—and the fact that he didn't recognize the irony or care about it even if he did—flabbergasted her. *He* could see someone else, but she couldn't? That was so egocentric; it made her want to applaud Julian for insisting they go out last night. "I was just with a . . . a friend," she stammered. If he'd ever shown *any* interest in the people she cared about, she would've given him Julian's name, but there was no point, since he wouldn't recognize it.

"Yeah, that's what it looked like!" he said sarcastically. "Almost everyone I know has been blowing up my phone, telling me my wife's already fucking another dude."

He'd always used profanity; she'd grown used to it. But today the harshness of his language grated on her. He could've shown her a *little* more respect. "I'm confused," she said. "*You* kicked *me* out. You said you wanted a divorce, remember? And you're seeing someone else yourself—a model."

"There's nothing going on with Marija. We just . . . went out one night."

"Went out," she repeated. "But . . . that's exactly what I did."

"Look, a split is going to be hard enough. Just . . . don't embarrass me, okay?"

"You mean by moving on with my life?"

"I mean . . . can't you lie low for a while? Give it some time, for God's sake, before you're all over the next guy?"

Nothing he was saying made sense. He could be seen with other women, but she couldn't be seen with other men? "Are you listening to yourself?" she asked.

He seemed frustrated—teetering on anger. "Work with me here, Char. Our breakup isn't like other breakups. You should know that."

"Because you're special?"

"Yes, if you want to put it that way! Fame changes everything. You knew that before we were ever married. I'm under a microscope all the time."

"You don't care how our divorce affects *me*."

"Of course I do! It's just that *you* can slink off into anonymity. I don't have that luxury."

Neither would he want it. He was addicted to the upside of fame—the attention, praise and money. But he didn't think he should have to tolerate any of the negatives, and he expected her to mitigate what she could, even though he was cutting her out of his life. In other words, he expected her to continue to protect him as she always had—to have empathy for his situation when he had none for hers.

"I'm just going to live my life the best way I can," she said. "That's it. It won't have anything to do with you, so don't take it personally."

"What does that mean?" he demanded.

"It means I'll continue seeing Julian if I want to."

His shoulders drooped. "You like him?"

She lifted her chin. "I do."

He gave her a skeptical look. "What's so great about him?"

"My feelings matter to him, for one. With you . . . I don't even know what I did that made you want out of our marriage."

He scratched his neck. "I've been trying to figure that out myself. I think it was just that you're . . . I don't know—too nice."

"Too *nice*?" she repeated, dumbfounded. "Are you saying I'm boring?"

"Not boring. Too accommodating, I guess," he said with a wince.

"Oh, I see. How could you possibly put up with someone who was too accommodating? God, that must've been terrible! I mean . . . the pain! The suffering!"

"Okay! I'm sorry!" he snapped.

She hefted the mail to her other arm. "No problem. Since it's easier *not* to be nice and accommodating, I should be able to fix that, right?"

He didn't seem to know how to respond. "I guess." He peered more closely at her. "Are you saying you want to try to save our marriage?"

"No, I'm not saying that," she said. "I'll be looking for someone else—someone who doesn't have a stupid *Predator* tattoo." Whirling around, she took the mail with her as she stalked out.

"What the hell, Charlotte? This is a cool tattoo, just like I thought it would be. Anyway, you're acting like . . . I don't even know you right now." He followed her as far as the front stoop as she hurried to her car. "You're going to be sorry!" he yelled, but for the life of her, she couldn't figure out what she had to be sorry for. She'd given him and their marriage her very best. He was the one who'd torn it to shreds—because she was *too nice*!

"Let him get with someone who *isn't* nice," she muttered. "See if he likes that any better."

chapter 4

Julian stared at his hand, waiting to see if the tremor that'd almost caused him to spill his orange juice would come back. Having a diagnosis for the symptoms he'd been experiencing provided *some* relief. At least he knew what was wrong with him and could seek whatever treatments might help—after he decided between the options his doctor had presented to him. But knowing he had an incurable disease also came with a certain debilitating fatalism. He wasn't sure which was worse—worrying about his symptoms without knowing the underlying cause or facing the truth.

It didn't make things any easier that he felt cheated. He was too young to have Parkinson's. It certainly wasn't a rare disease, but most people didn't develop it until they were in their sixties.

Michael J. Fox was a notable exception. He'd been diagnosed in his twenties. The good news was that he was still around almost forty years later. The bad news was that he appeared to be in decline. And Julian had no way of knowing how difficult the movie star's journey had been. All he'd ever seen were the pictures and articles that appeared in the media.

At least Michael was always smiling. Julian wished he could tell him how much that helped. Maybe *he* could be like Fox. Fight the disease for decades before his symptoms became unbearable. Be grateful for the life he had. Keep his chin up.

Right now, that didn't feel very likely. Whenever he imagined the years ahead, he just felt sad and scared. Mostly scared, which was such a foreign emotion to him. He'd never had reason to be frightened of anything—except the bear that'd charged him when he was in Alaska a year ago. That had caused a bolt of alarm before he played dead and the bear moseyed off into the woods.

He should still be out there, facing bears and moose and whatever other wild things crossed his path. He shouldn't have this disease. Not only was he in the prime of his life, but there was no genetic component. Parkinson's didn't run in his family. The doctor couldn't pinpoint a cause—unless he'd been exposed to some toxin he wasn't aware of that'd caused his body to start misfolding the alpha-synuclein protein that was now destroying part of his brain.

How long would he be capable of hiking to the remote areas he liked to photograph? Of holding a camera steady? Would he be able to make enough money before he could no longer work to carry him through the rest of his life? And how would this diagnosis change the coming years in other ways?

There was no question that his future would be very different from the one he'd envisioned for himself. Now he didn't even know if he'd ever marry, have kids. He couldn't imagine any woman wanting a partner already so compromised. If he'd already been close to someone, he could conceivably see her sticking around—the way Michael J. Fox's wife had remained committed to him over the years. But he hadn't been dating anyone when he realized his body was no longer functioning correctly. And if a woman knew he was damaged goods before she fell in love with him, why wouldn't she simply choose another man for the sake of her own future?

His mother came into the pool house his father had converted into a home office—Jerry was at his company's headquarters downtown—and laid a hand on his shoulder.

"What is it?" he asked, twisting around to look up at her. He'd been using his laptop all morning, was supposed to be editing pictures. He loved the process of perfecting the shots he took. But since his latest muscle spasm, he'd been buried in his own thoughts, didn't even know how long he'd sat there, inert, before she interrupted.

"Charlotte's here. It's *so* good to see her again. She brought me flowers, which is lovely, but she also brought your father a special pillow to sit on." She arched a reproving eyebrow at him. "I wonder how she knows about his surgery . . ."

"Whoops," he said with a laugh. "I shouldn't have told her, but I had no idea she'd bring him a butt pillow."

"You're incorrigible." His mother rolled her eyes. "I'll just hide it for a few days, and if he's still experiencing tenderness in that, um, area, I'll bring it out and pretend I bought it for him myself."

"Steal Charlotte's credit and lie to him to keep him from getting mad at me? That's positively diabolical." He grinned. "I like it."

"I wouldn't have to steal her credit and lie to anyone if you could keep your mouth shut." She gave him a playful swat on the back of the head as she left. "Hurry," she called before the door could swing shut. "Charlotte's waiting."

He smoothed the hair she'd mussed and studied his reflection in the glass door, searching for some telltale sign of his disease—something that marked him as defective. But he still looked perfectly healthy. Most of the time, he felt perfectly healthy, too.

He wondered how long that would last . . .

Charlotte was sitting at the kitchen table with a glass of water when he walked in, and his mother was trying to press every treat they had in the house on her. He heard her politely refuse a lemon square and a soda before Karen offered her a cookie. "I'm fine, really," she murmured. "But thank you."

The moment Charlotte saw him, she smiled in what he thought was relief. "Want to go grab a coffee?" she asked a little too brightly.

"I've got plenty of good coffee here, and it won't cost you a cent," his mother volunteered, but he grabbed Charlotte by the hand and led her straight to the door, saving her from the most persistent food-pusher on earth.

"I think we'll go out," he told his mother. "We'll see you in a bit."

"Goodbye, Mrs. Davis!" Charlotte added.

"Have fun!" she called but looked slightly crestfallen that he'd stolen the object of her attention.

"What's going on?" he asked once they got outside. "Everything okay?"

"I'm not sure." She lifted her own keys to show him since he was digging his out of his pocket. "I'll drive. My car's behind yours."

"I see that now." He got into the passenger side of her expensive Range Rover—a vestige from her marriage to someone who made an obscene amount of money. He assumed the vehicle was paid off and she wouldn't be strapped with monstrous car payments—if she got to keep it—but now was not the time to ask. She was upset. He could see that even if his mother hadn't realized it. "I assume you've heard from Cliff. Is that what's wrong? Has he seen the pictures?"

"Yes."

"Oh, boy! I bet he wasn't happy."

She backed out of the drive. "He wasn't. He asked me to lie low and not embarrass him again."

Julian turned down the music that'd come on with the engine. "How are you embarrassing him?"

"By being seen with another man in public, I suppose." She waited for a break in traffic before pulling into the street.

"Like *he's* lying low and not embarrassing you with that ugly model?"

"Ugly!" She gaped at him until she realized he'd been joking. "Yes, exactly," she said, calming down.

Hoping she'd held her own and hadn't let Cliff get the best of any argument, Julian scowled. "And did you promise to do that?"

"No. I told him I hated his new tattoo and left."

She sounded so proud of herself he couldn't help but smile. "Wow. You did that? Said you hated his tattoo? Brutal! That must've torn him up."

She shot him a dirty look. This time, she knew immediately that he was baiting her. "He's sensitive, Jules. It really *did* bother him."

"Do you honestly hate his tattoo?"

"Of course," she replied with a grimace to show just how much. "He had *Predator* from the Arnold Schwarzenegger movie—which is how many years old now?—tattooed on his shoulder in the weirdest colors." She tapped her right deltoid. "It looks positively ridiculous."

He could tell she thought he'd agree with her, which was why he had to tease her instead. "That movie might be old, but it's still cool."

Her gaze narrowed. "Maybe so, but why would anyone have something so tacky tattooed on their body? Can you imagine seeing that in the mirror when you're seventy-five?"

"You're right. It's tacky. I don't like it, either," he said as if he was just sucking up, and laughed when she swatted him like his mother had earlier.

"Quit messing with me!" she said, but he enjoyed doing it. Spending time with her helped—worrying about her problems distracted him from his own.

"In all seriousness, I love that you're standing up for yourself—in whatever small way."

"It wasn't a small way," she insisted. "He was really mad."

Julian laughed even harder. "Good. I'm happy to hear it."

She glanced at him, a thoughtful expression on her face. "He asked me if I wanted to try again, Jules."

"And you said . . .?"

"No."

"Because you'd never be that naive, right?"

Tears welled up as she pulled into Barista Ted's Coffee and Confections. "Right," she mumbled, but that word was barely audible.

"I'm not sensing a lot of conviction here," he said.

"I'm *trying*," she responded. "I really am."

"I know," he said with a sigh.

Once they got inside, they each ordered an espresso before sitting down among the smattering of people who'd come to work on their laptops.

"Do you need me to go with you to get the rest of your stuff from Cliff's house?" Julian asked. "The day's young. We could rent a moving van right now."

"I won't need a moving van," Charlotte said. "I'm almost positive everything will fit into my SUV."

"Seriously? With the kind of money you've had over the past few years? I assumed you'd need a fleet of moving vans."

The barista called out their order, and she got up to retrieve their drinks.

"I'm only leaving with my clothes and a few personal items," she told him once she'd sat down again. "All the furnishings will be staying with the house."

"I guess that simplifies things. Still, I say we go over there, get whatever's yours and be done with it."

She looked appalled, as if he'd just suggested they blow up the place. "No! I'm not ready to face him again. Besides, I don't want to get you into a fight. Cliff's *very* territorial."

"He's the one who let you go! Besides, I'm not afraid of him. It would suck for you to have to go there and pack up yourself."

"The whole thing sucks . . ."

Julian took a sip of his espresso. "Have you heard from your in-laws?"

"Nope, and I don't think I will. They'll be especially loyal to Cliff since he's the one who pays their bills. His mother raised him as a single mom, had a hard life. I can understand why he wouldn't want her to continue working as a motel maid. But his father and his sisters always have their hands out, too."

"That would drive me nuts."

"It was definitely annoying," she admitted. "But it was mostly his money. And when you marry someone, you marry their family, too."

"Someday he'll regret losing you." Slouching more comfortably in his seat, he crossed his legs at the ankles. "When you do go get your stuff, let me know. I'd like to see the house."

"It's gorgeous."

"Not tacky?" he said with a taunting smile.

"It probably would've been without me—and Sloane. We spent weeks decorating that place."

Julian's phone buzzed with a call. "Speak of the devil."

"What do you mean?" Charlotte sat back. "It's Sloane?"

He nodded as he sent the call to voicemail. He didn't want to take it in the coffee shop. "Have you talked to her recently?"

"No. I've been wanting to reach out. It's just . . . I'm afraid she's mad at me. We got into an argument about Cliff the last time we talked."

"You know Sloane. She's passionate and excitable but quickly forgives and forgets," he said while he texted his sister that he was with Charlotte and he'd call her back in a few minutes.

Charlotte shifted in her seat. "Was that my name? You told her you were with me?"

"I did." Sloane would already know he'd been in contact with Charlotte again, except he'd been avoiding his sister. His mother had been badgering him to tell her about his diagnosis, but the more people who knew, the more real it became, and he wasn't ready to shoulder his twin's sadness along with his own.

"And?" she prompted.

He turned his phone so she could read Sloane's response.

That asshole Cliff better hope I never get hold of him.

"I'd say she's still on your side," he said wryly, but that only made Charlotte choke up.

"I don't deserve her support. Or yours," she said. "I let my own friends and family down trying to appease my husband."

"You're feeling terrible enough already. Let's not worry about that," he said and stood up. There was a middle-aged woman eyeing them from the corner. "Grab your cup and let's get out of here," he said.

But the other patron got up, too, and hurried over, catching them just before they went out the door.

"Aren't you Charlotte Jackson, Clifford Jackson's wife?" she asked. "I'm a *huge* fan—loved your book! Can I get a picture with you?"

Charlotte looked as if she wished she could disappear, but

Julian accommodated the woman by taking a selfie of all three of them.

"Thank you *so* much!" the woman gushed.

"No problem," he said. "Be sure to post that and tag Cliff." He wanted to make it clear that Charlotte wasn't going to put her life on hold just because Cliff didn't want her to be seen with another man.

The woman looked a little startled by the request but quickly acquiesced. "I will!"

"Are you trying to get me in trouble?" Charlotte whispered as they left the shop and started across the parking lot.

He put his arm around her. "I'm trying to get you *out* of trouble," he said.

chapter 5

Sloane typed Clifford Jackson's name into Google and pulled up several more articles. But they all said essentially the same thing as the one that'd caught her attention while she was sitting at her desk eating the lunch she'd grabbed from the Thai place next door. They showed a picture of Charlotte with Julian outside a restaurant in Los Angeles, stated that Clifford Jackson and his wife were separating and speculated that both of them were already seeing other people.

Charlotte and Cliff had split up? How could that be? Charlotte had been so committed to him!

The phone rang and her brother's name popped up on her screen. Julian was calling her back. Rory was still out to lunch, which meant she was running the store alone, but she didn't have any customers.

She hit the green button. "Julian, what's going on? It's all over the internet that Charlotte and Cliff are no longer together. Is that true?"

"I'm afraid it is," he replied. "We're in her car right now. Want me to put the phone on speaker?"

"Of course."

When Charlotte spoke, she sounded subdued. "Hey, Sloane."

"Char, are you okay?" Their last conversation had been over a year ago, and it hadn't gone well. Sloane had called to see if Charlotte would be interested in meeting her in San Francisco for a "girls' weekend," but Cliff had decided he didn't want her to go, even though he'd be out of town himself. The fact that Charlotte wouldn't fight him on it made Sloane mad. Cliff rarely let them see each other. And if Charlotte was going to allow him to stand between them, there was nothing Sloane could do to maintain the friendship.

"I feel like roadkill right now," Charlotte said. "But I'd be a lot worse off if Jules wasn't here."

"What'd Cliff do?" she demanded.

"He told me he wanted a divorce."

"*Why?*"

"That part isn't entirely clear."

Sloane remembered the picture she'd seen of Cliff with another woman while googling his name to learn more. "It's not because of Marija Vidmar, is it?"

"You saw that picture?"

"I've been digging for details ever since the first article popped up."

"It could be. They looked pretty cozy—don't you think? But the only thing he'll say is that he doesn't want to be married anymore."

Sloane winced. "Do you think it's over for good?"

There was a slight hesitation, but then Charlotte said, "I do."

"I'm sorry."

"So am I," she said. "I know I wasn't the friend I should've been while I was married to him. I just . . . I was trying so hard to keep him happy. I really wanted to make our marriage work. And maybe I compromised too often. Actually, I *did* compromise too often."

Little good it'd done her. Sloane wanted to say as much. But she couldn't pile on. Her best friend had been hurt, and that made her too defensive to worry about her own complaints over the last few years. "He's *such* a douchebag. Not because he wanted out, but because he was downright controlling while you were together. So what are you going to do from here? Where will you live?"

"I'll probably stay with my parents for the time being. It doesn't feel great to be home again at this age. It's like being sent back to the starting point of life. But I don't have the mental energy to do anything else. I have to write my next book. It's due in three months."

"And are you pretty far along?" Sloane asked hopefully.

There was a pause, then Charlotte said, "Not really."

"What does that mean? How many more pages do you have to go?"

"Like . . . four hundred."

"*Four hundred?* That's basically the whole novel!"

"Yeah. And I have to come up with an idea before I can start."

"Oh, my God!" Sloane said. "Char, what can I do to help? Do you need me to come to California? I can see if Rory will cover the store."

"No, definitely not. I could never ask you to leave your husband and your business, especially when I'm the only one who can get me out of this jam."

Sloane couldn't help feeling slightly disappointed. The business could take all the time and energy she had to give it, but she needed a chance to get her own head together. "Are you sure?"

"I'm positive. But . . ." Charlotte's voice grew wobbly. "I love you. I'm sorry I neglected you and Jules. You two are the ones who really care about me."

"Don't apologize," Sloane said. "That's the last thing you have to worry about."

"I've told her that," Julian piped up.

"He's right," Sloane told Charlotte. "You're going to get through this, you know. And if Cliff gives you any trouble, you just tell me." She'd love to give that man a piece of her mind and say all the things she wished Charlotte had said but didn't.

"I'll get through it," Charlotte echoed. "Anyway, enough about me. How are *you*?"

Sloane wished she could answer honestly. The truth sat on her chest like a giant anvil, almost crushing her to death. But now was not the time. Maybe the right time would never come.

Drawing a deep breath, she injected more energy into her voice as she said, "I'm doing great. Everything over here is . . . just great."

"Is the business taking off the way you'd hoped?"

Cliff probably didn't know it, but she'd supplied a lot of the furnishings for his house. She'd traded hundreds of photos and ideas with Charlotte right after Cliff bought their mansion, so she'd had a big hand in the interior design. She'd had fun with it. Sloane knew Charlotte liked her style. She also knew Charlotte had been trying to help her get her design business started, and she was grateful for that, even though she'd been disappointed in how things had gone between them since. "I don't know if you could say it's 'taking off.' That remains to be seen. But we're building a good client base, and this has been a great month, thanks to an article that was printed in a local magazine."

"Send me a copy of it," Charlotte said. "I'd like to see it."

"I will." She shoved the empty containers from her lunch into the sack. "Jules, your calls and texts have been pretty scarce lately. How's it going with Mom and Dad?"

"I've just been here working my fingers to the bone, doing your share as well as mine."

Sloane smiled as she got up to toss the bag in the wastebasket. "You're the one who insisted on taking care of them," she reminded him.

He chuckled. "I know. They're doing great. Dad even has a new butt pillow, thanks to Charlotte."

Sloane returned to her seat. "Charlotte, you gave Jerry a butt pillow?"

"I know. It's kind of weird," Charlotte said. "But I was in the drugstore picking up something for a headache when I saw it and couldn't resist. I thought it might make a big difference, since he sits behind a desk most of the day."

"Oh, he's going to love it!" she said with a laugh.

"Just so you know, Char, we're going to pretend our mom bought it," Julian said. "Hope that's okay."

"I actually feel more comfortable going in that direction," she said and laughed with them.

For a moment, it felt like old times. Sloane had missed her best friend. She'd missed her best friend's brother, too. And California! She'd moved to Seattle for Ben's sake; this was where he'd been offered the best job when he got out of pharmacy school.

If only she wanted children—then maybe her marriage wouldn't feel so precarious, and she wouldn't question whether she'd launched the business in the wrong city.

At work, Ben was usually too busy to think about anything but prescriptions. But on this unusually slow day, the feeling that something wasn't right with Sloane crept in again. The longer they were married, the more remote and distracted she seemed to be. Sometimes he'd let the door slam before speaking, and she'd still startle when she heard his voice as if she'd been so deep in the well of her own thoughts she hadn't even realized he was there.

Something was wrong. He was certain of that. But what?

He'd asked her several times, but she always gave him that determined smile of hers and insisted it was nothing. Or that she was just worried about work. It wasn't as if he thought she was having an affair. She was always with Rory, and Rory had a husband. Besides, she'd shown no signs of having another man in her life. She came home after work, wasn't remotely guarded with her phone and was always where she should be.

Was it about money? He brought home a good paycheck, but he was carrying a lot of student debt, plus housing in Seattle was expensive and the money they'd invested in the store didn't leave them with a lot of extra. She could be stressed about their finances, feeling as though the store wasn't going to make it...

It wasn't easy starting a new business, especially in an industry that was so sensitive to the state of the economy and whether people had discretionary income. But Sloane was an exceptional designer. If anyone could make it in that field, he believed she could. Their home was a beautiful example. It looked like something out of a magazine even though she'd had to decorate it on a budget. No one knew how to put things together quite like she did. She could make even garage sale finds look stylish.

But he was losing her. He just couldn't figure out why.

The bell rang, signaling that someone had come to the pharmacy at the back of the store to pick up a prescription. Sandra, the middle-aged woman who worked the same schedule he did and typically handled the register, was out sick today, and there'd been no one who could come in to replace her, so he walked around the tall shelving that usually hid him from view. "Can I help you?" he asked a young woman waiting with an older gentleman who was in a wheelchair.

"We're here to pick up my father's blood pressure medication," the woman replied.

Ben got the man's name and started digging through the bins filled with sacks of medication that'd been alphabetized by customer. "Here we go," he said when he found it. "You already know how to take this, right?" he asked the man.

"Oh, yes." His daughter spoke for him. "He's been on it for years."

Ben rang it up, gave them the medication and told them goodbye. Then he went into the back, downloaded a new batch of prescriptions and started filling them. Still, his mind stayed on his beautiful dark-haired, dark-eyed wife and the disquieting thought that he had to act before it was too late.

But what should he do? What *could* he do?

Penny wasn't feeling well again, so Charlotte insisted on making dinner.

"You seem to be doing better," her father commented as she served him some of her tomato-lentil soup. Penny had gone to lie down and didn't plan on joining them, but she'd indicated she might have a bowl later.

"I *am* doing better," Charlotte said. "Thanks to Julian and Sloane. You find out who your true friends are when you go through a setback like this."

"Isn't that the truth." He pulled a roll from the pan she'd just taken from the oven and slathered it with butter. "You three have been friends for a long time."

The yeasty smell of homemade bread made her eager to eat, too. She was getting her appetite back, she realized. "Ever since junior high," she told him as she sat down with her own bowl and reached for a roll. "Sloane and I go back even further than that, but Jules wasn't interested in hanging out with girls back then. He was still pulling on our ponytails and running away to make us chase him," she said with a laugh.

Her father watched her blow the heat from her first spoonful of soup. "It's good to have you home, honey," he said.

She smiled. "Thanks, Dad. 'Home is the place where, when you have to go there, they have to take you in.' Isn't that what Robert Frost said?"

"I don't know what he said. But you're always welcome here."

He'd been careful not to say too many derogatory things about Cliff. She knew her parents had been disappointed that her husband hadn't been more willing to embrace them, so the fact that they were being so cautious had surprised her at first—until she realized they were merely being diplomatic. They didn't want to create an even bigger gulf, be even more alienated from him, if she put her marriage back together.

"Thanks. I'm hoping the security I feel here will make it so that I can get writing again."

"I do, too. How's the book going so far?"

"It's not," she said ruefully. "I haven't even started—not yet."

He glanced up from his meal. "I was under the impression, and I think your mother was, too, that you only needed to finish. Which would be daunting enough," he added.

"Yeah, it's a lot more daunting than I let on," she admitted. "I couldn't face what was ahead of me, didn't even want to acknowledge it. Besides, giving Mom more reason to worry is never a good thing."

"You can say that again," he said. "So . . . are you going to be able to get it done in time?"

She was feeling only about ten percent better, but just that small improvement was making a huge difference. As soon as she finished cleaning up after dinner, she planned to scour the internet for ideas. She hoped reading about other books and movies, and surfing through articles, would ignite her imagination. And since her parents went to bed before she did, she'd have several uninterrupted hours in which to decide what her next story would be. If she was *really* lucky, maybe she'd even be inspired to write the first few pages.

"We'll see." She was afraid to promise too much; just because she was feeling a slight lift at this moment didn't mean it would last. A wave of grief could crash over her and drag her back out to sea, erasing her progress in an instant.

"Do you need me to find you a ghostwriter, honey?" he asked. "A creativity coach? A therapist? Whatever it is, I'll make it happen."

Like Sloane and Julian, her parents were there for her. So many people who went through a divorce didn't have the friends and family she did. She should consider herself lucky. In many ways, she *was* lucky. With time, her broken heart would heal, and as Sloane and Julian predicted, a life spent without Cliff might prove to be a happier life in the end.

"I'm going to see what I can do first."

"You sure?" he pressed. "Because I bet we could find just the right person."

Finished with her soup, she left her spoon in the bowl and enjoyed the rest of her roll with a generous amount of salty, melted butter. "It's enough just knowing how much you love me," she said.

She really felt that way. But when she finally made it to her room, she decided to go through the mail she'd picked up from the Malibu mansion before opening her laptop. She knew she was procrastinating the hard stuff. But her book was so daunting, such a difficult mountain to climb, she told herself she needed to get organized first.

"Junk, junk, junk," she muttered, tossing one ad after another into the trash. There was a fashion magazine and several home decor magazines she pitched, too, as well as a health insurance bill set to autopay. But then she came to a letter addressed to her from Heidelman & Heidelman, Attorneys at Law.

A sick feeling came over her as she stared at the envelope. Was this about the divorce? From what she'd read online, Cliff had to serve her before doing anything else, and that hadn't happened yet. So what was this?

Taking a deep breath, she opened it and felt her heart leap into her throat—and then plunge. The letter had nothing to do with Cliff or the divorce. As far as she was concerned, it was worse, because it wasn't anything even time could change.

chapter 6

This couldn't be happening, not at the same time as the implosion of her marriage. Her family was the one thing she'd always relied on; she was relying heavily on them now. No way was she willing to believe they'd lied her entire life, especially about something so fundamental, so *foundational*.

Charlotte started to read the letter again, but her hands were trembling and tears were beginning to blur the words. Wiping her eyes, she struggled to navigate the landmines.

She wasn't who she thought she was. That was the main takeaway. But the details were just as shocking. She'd been adopted at birth and yet her parents had never let on. And now her birth mother had died, leaving behind another daughter named Lilly, who was twelve. No one knew who Lilly's father was, so her mother's boyfriend was caring for the girl until more permanent arrangements could be made, but he'd only been with Sabrina—that was the name the attorney provided for the woman who had supposedly given birth to her—for a few months and didn't want permanent responsibility. Something had to be done about the child, so this attorney, who'd been searching for Sabrina's relatives, was reaching out to see if Charlotte might be interested in meeting and possibly taking custody of her only sibling.

Custody of a twelve-year-old. Her sibling. Her *sister*.

"Oh, my God," she said aloud and dropped the letter before picking it up and reading it one more time, just for good measure. There was another astonishing detail in it that she'd stumbled over while trying to process all the rest.

It only took a moment to find it. There it was—in the last paragraph. Although Lilly was born in the United States, it had been Sabrina's dream to live on the Amalfi Coast, so she'd taken Lilly and moved to Italy only a few months ago—to a small town called Praiano.

Charlotte had never heard of it. It was half a world away, in a foreign country. And this sister—

"No," she said aloud. She was not the person Mr. Heidelman was looking for. She needed to write back immediately, say she was terribly sorry about the girl's plight, but she'd been born to Penny McCord, who'd grown up in Orange County, been a D-1 collegiate tennis player, coached for her alma mater for ten years and then, later, gave lessons at the club while married to Don Williams, a hedge fund manager who also came from affluent parents. The attorney needed to look elsewhere for Lilly's half sister, because this terrible situation had nothing to do with Charlotte Rose Williams-Jackson—minus the Jackson soon, she reminded herself.

For a second, she felt an upwelling of relief. The attorneys at Heidelman had made a mistake. That had to be it. But she was off-balance enough to carry the letter out to the living room, where her father was watching television.

He glanced up with a look of expectation on his face when he heard her. "I thought you were going to start writing."

"I was," she said. "But I decided to go through the mail I picked up at the Malibu house first."

He muted the TV. "Don't tell me there are divorce papers in there."

"No."

"A letter from Cliff, reneging on the prenup?" he asked, trying again.

"No." She was having trouble finding the words. How did she ask her father if he was really her father?

But he could tell something was wrong, and she didn't want him to keep guessing, so she blurted out, "Was I adopted?"

The blood rushed from his face, telling her the letter was no mistake. She'd been tricked, or lied to, or . . . or encouraged to assume something to be true that wasn't. She couldn't say if there was anything wrong with what her parents had done. She wasn't sure why they'd done it, or if she would've done the same thing in their shoes. She just knew that she felt robbed. Violated in a very personal, deeply emotional way. Because her adoptive parents had withheld the truth from her, she'd never had the chance to meet her birth mother, and now she never would. Was it fair to make that decision for her?

It didn't *feel* fair. "Dad!" she said, the word a hopeless groan as she sank onto the couch.

He came over and knelt at her feet. "Honey, who told you? Did Cliff do this to hurt you—hurt us all—by tearing our family apart? How'd he find out?"

She was so choked up she couldn't answer. She handed him the letter, but he didn't take it right away. His eyes remained fixed on her. He obviously didn't want her to be crushed, but she could tell he knew she was and felt terrible about it.

Finally, he accepted the letter she held out to him.

After he read it, he closed his eyes and shook his head. "I was afraid something like this would happen. I told your mother we *had* to tell you, but there was never a good time."

"Never a good time?" she echoed. "How could that be

true? I've been around for nearly thirty years. Surely, you could've found a moment. What about when I was in fourth grade and brought home Hannah Jones, and she told me *she'd* been adopted? I remember Mom explaining to me exactly what that meant. You were there at dinner, too."

"I don't remember. I just know you were thriving, like we wanted you to. We couldn't bear the thought of doing anything that might threaten your sense of security, your happiness. We were afraid it would only make you crave something you couldn't have. And we loved you so much we didn't think a . . . technicality like DNA really mattered."

They'd been good parents. *Stellar* parents. She couldn't complain about the job they'd done raising her. But the decision they'd made . . . Was it better for her *not* to know?

Maybe it was. But now she *did* know and knowing brought a tidal wave of pain and *so* many questions. It created a hunger in her soul—a hunger to know more.

"Why did my birth mother give me up?" She was prepared for him to try to evade the question and was relieved when he didn't. Instead, he spread his hands wide as if he'd tell her anything she wanted to know.

"She was barely eighteen when she had you, still had a year left of high school."

"And my father? Was he another kid who was too young to take on the responsibility?"

"No. We were told he was a much older man, a neighbor from down the street who already had a family."

"Ew!" Could this day get any worse?

Her father didn't say anything. Apparently, he didn't know how to respond to that, except with a frown.

"Where is he now?" she asked.

He shook his head helplessly. "We don't know. We've never heard from him, and we've been glad about that."

Because it had allowed them to keep her origins a secret? "And my birth mother? Sabrina? You never heard from her, either?"

"No," he said softly.

They were probably happy about that, too. Otherwise, they might've been forced to tell her the truth. Had they been more afraid of what the news would do to her—or to them?

That was an ungenerous thought. She hated herself for having it. They'd always put her first. But she was so rattled she wasn't thinking clearly. "She must never have changed her mind about me," she said, the knife of that intimate rejection plunging deep. "Never wanted to meet me."

"Situations like this . . . They're not that simple, honey," he said. "I'm sure she would've loved to meet you, but didn't want to intrude for fear it would confuse or upset you. Maybe it was too painful for her to even face the fact that she'd already had a child. If I had to guess, I'd say that's something a woman never really gets over. It's not like she had to worry that you'd go without the love and care you needed. We assured her and her family from the very beginning—through the adoption agency—that we'd give you *everything* we possibly could."

And they'd done that. But this blow . . . She couldn't get over the sense of betrayal—overlying the painful rejection—that was digging into her with talon-like claws. "So what do I do?" she asked.

He blinked. "What do you mean?"

She indicated the letter. "I have a half sister who needs someone to take care of her. I can't continue living my life as if she doesn't exist."

"We'll send for her—bring her here," he said. "Your mother and I would love another child."

They were too old to become parents again. Her father worked long hours, and her mother was no longer healthy.

"Don't you think we should meet her before we make a decision like that?"

"Actually, we probably should," he said. "We have our passports. We'll all go over there."

"I don't think we should go over and just grab her, if that's what you're suggesting. It'll take time to assess what's best for her. She's just lost her mother. Uprooting her right now could be the worst thing in the world for her, especially if she's happy living where she is."

"So what are you getting at?" he asked. "We can't stay more than a week or two. I have work, and it probably wouldn't be wise to take your mother out of the country for too long."

"*I'll* go," she said. "It's not like I have a husband to worry about anymore."

His eyes widened. "What about your book?"

"I can write from anywhere," she said—*if* she could write at all. That remained to be seen, especially now. She'd been in an emotional tailspin *before* receiving the news that she'd been adopted, her birth mother had just died and she had a younger sister who needed her.

He didn't seem convinced she'd be better off on her own. "We should probably go over with you—"

"Dad," she broke in. "I'm nearly thirty years old. I'm an adult, and I'm going alone."

"Shouldn't we include your mother in this conversation?"

She stood. "I'm willing to hear her opinion, but I don't think it'll change my mind."

He got to his feet, too. "But you're already dealing with a painful divorce . . ."

"Dad, there could be worse things than going to Italy." She offered him a feeble smile, and he pulled her into his arms.

"I'm sorry," he said and kissed the top of her head. "This has been such a nasty surprise. But I hope you know we've only ever wanted good things for you. We love you more than life itself."

She *did* know that. It was what was going to pull her through.

Sloane was building a color scheme—holding fabric swatches to paint chips and imagining what furniture would work with them—when she received a text from her brother.

You're not going to believe this.

Curious, she took a break from work to message him back.

> What is it?

Charlotte's heading to Italy.

> For vacation? I wish I could go with her. How long will she be gone?

Indefinitely.

> To get away from Cliff and the fallout caused by the divorce? Staying out of sight for a while might be a good idea. People on the internet can be ruthless.

Her going has nothing to do with Cliff. She's flying over there to meet her younger sister.

Sloane frowned at his response. How could Charlotte be going to Italy to meet a younger sister? She was an only child.
Unless . . .

Shocked by the implication, she called her brother, who answered on the first ring. "Don't tell me Don has a love child!" she said, keeping her voice low since Rory was working at his desk directly across from hers.

"Nope. Her sister is no relation to Don or Penny."

"So . . . how could she have a sister?"

"Turns out Charlotte was adopted at birth. The sister is her biological mother's."

"What?" The outburst caused Rory to glance up, so she lowered her voice again. "Did *she* know she was adopted? Because I've never heard a word about it."

"Just found out. Got a letter from an attorney telling her that her birth mother has died and left a twelve-year-old girl who needs a guardian."

Sloane shot to her feet.

"Everything okay?" Rory asked, sitting up taller.

She lifted a hand to let him know there was nothing to worry about and hurried out the back, into the alley, so she wouldn't continue to interrupt her partner while he was trying to work. She'd known Charlotte and Charlotte's parents almost her entire life. There was no way what Julian had just told her could be true. "There's got to be some mistake," she said as the metal door clanged shut behind her.

"I might've thought that, too, except Charlotte's already confronted her father about it."

Sloane edged away from the reeking dumpster between her store and the Thai food place. "Oh, my gosh! She must be devastated!"

"She was already devastated. Cliff took care of that. But, yeah, she's reeling from this second blow."

"I'm shocked! Absolutely stunned. You could never have guessed the Williamses weren't her biological parents. She even looks like them."

"Not really," he said.

"She doesn't look as though she's from a different family!"

"True."

What'd happened in the past and how would it inform—and transform—the present?

Sloane had so many questions. But she started with "Why's Charlotte's little sister in Italy?"

"She lives there, in Praiano, which is close to Positano on the Amalfi Coast."

Someone came out into the alley from the restaurant and dumped two food crates in the garbage, prompting Sloane to step even farther from the dumpster. "Was she born there?"

"I don't remember if Charlotte told me that. She doesn't know a whole lot, just what came in the letter. This morning, she tried calling the attorney who sent it, but he wasn't available. She should learn more when he calls back."

"How'd her birth mother die?"

"We don't have that information yet, either."

She nudged a rock in the loose gravel with the toe of her high heel. She usually dressed up when she was in the studio. Looking her best helped create credibility in an industry where people were relying on her to have good taste. "Will Charlotte's parents be going to Italy with her?"

"No. She said they wouldn't be able to stay very long even if they did, and she doesn't want to take the girl out of the environment she's accustomed to until she's decided what would be best. Charlotte's not even sure whether she should take custody. Depending on how close the girl is to other relatives, maybe someone in her birth mother's family would be a better option."

"Those people would be Charlotte's family, too," Sloane pointed out. "Wouldn't it blow your mind—to find out you have this whole other family you never knew about?"

"I think it's safe to say her mind *is* blown."

"Meeting them would be so odd," she added, imagining it.

"It would be. It could be a lot of other things, too, depending on how receptive they are, right?"

"Not meeting Charlotte would be a mistake. They'd be the ones missing out."

"We might be a little biased. Anyway, there are so many things to consider, so many unanswered questions. All she told me was that she's going to move there for the next few months and try to write her book while getting to know her sister and determining how she can help."

Sloane kicked the rock she'd been playing with and watched as it skittered toward the tires of her car. "So where will she stay?"

"She's planning to rent a house."

"On the Amalfi Coast."

"Yep."

"And she's going there alone?"

"That's what she's telling me."

"What's the weather like this time of year?"

"The weather?" he echoed. "I've been there before in the spring. It's gorgeous. Why?"

"How many bedrooms will she have?" she asked instead of answering.

There was a slight pause. She could tell he hadn't expected this question. "As far as I know, she hasn't found a place yet. I repeat—*why?* What's with the weird questions?"

The uncertainty Sloane was feeling in her marriage suddenly created the desire to escape. What she needed was time—time to figure out who she was and what she wanted. Maybe, just maybe, if she went to Italy with Charlotte, she could get the separation she needed from Ben to figure out if she wanted to stay with him for the rest of her life—or how to handle her marriage if she didn't. "I want to go with her," she said.

"Without Ben?"

"I need a month—a month to find *me* again."

This comment was met with silence. "Don't tell me there's trouble brewing in your marriage. You two aren't considering breaking up, are you?"

"As far as I know, *he* isn't."

"But you are?"

A lump rose in her throat, making it difficult to speak. "Something's wrong, Jules."

"What?"

"I don't know. If I knew, maybe I could fix it. That's the thing. I need . . . I need some time to myself. To make up my mind. To regain clarity."

"If Charlotte's there, you'd hardly be alone."

"Being with her would be different. It could be good for both of us. I can support her through the coming weeks, and she can help me just by being who she is. She's always grounded me. Maybe together we can fight our way through the dark."

He didn't respond.

"Jules?"

"You're scaring me, Sloane. Ben's a good man. You don't want to lose him."

She lifted a hand to block the sunlight stabbing through the huge canopy of the tree overhead. It was a sunny day in Seattle—after weeks of rain—and the light seemed to warm her soul. The good weather felt like a sign, as if the universe was telling her to take a month and figure out what to do with the rest of her life.

"That's what I keep telling myself," she said.

"But . . ."

"We don't want the same things anymore," she replied.

"What does that mean?"

"He wants kids."

"And you don't?"

"No. Not at all," she admitted, and there it was—the truth.

"That's hard to believe."

"Because *you've* always wanted children?"

"Yes."

"Kids aren't for everyone."

"But they are for Ben."

"He can't wait to start a family."

"Shit."

"Exactly."

"If you go to Italy, what will you do about your business? How will you get away for an entire month?"

"I'll have to check with Rory, see if he can manage without me. Leaving him on his own wouldn't be ideal, of course. But I'm desperate enough that . . . that I'd do it."

"Do you have a passport?"

"Ben and I went to Aruba on our honeymoon, remember?"

"Oh, right. But even if Rory will cover the store, what's Ben going to say?"

She stared down at the tough little weeds fighting their way through the gravel. "I don't know. But this might be the only way to save our marriage." The eagerness and hope she felt at the prospect of breaking away from her current situation was so overwhelming it nearly brought her to tears. "If Charlotte won't mind me coming along, I think . . . I think I *have* to do it."

"I bet she'll welcome the company. What she's facing wouldn't be easy to handle on her own, especially while going through a divorce and being so far from home."

"That's another reason I want to be there. I miss her, Jules. I miss the friendship we had before her arrogant ass of a husband came between us."

"Well, damn," he said. "If you're both going to Italy, so am I."

She lifted her head. "What?"

"You heard me. I can take pictures of whatever I want. There are plenty of gorgeous landscapes to capture in Italy."

"What about Mom and Dad and staying with them after their operations?" If she hadn't been trying to land the biggest remodel of her career a couple of weeks ago, which had subsequently fallen through anyway, she would've volunteered to look after their parents herself. But she'd also known that being around them while trying to conceal how she was feeling about her marriage would be difficult, so she'd been relieved when Julian said he'd do it. She certainly hadn't expected him to step up; he was usually globe-trotting all over the world.

"They're fine," he said. "Mom's pretty much recovered. Dad might need the butt pillow Charlotte bought him for a few more weeks, but he's back at work."

"Okay! If Charlotte will have us as companions and roommates, let's do it!" she said, smiling freely for the first time in ages.

"Are you sure?"

"I'm positive. Let's take a time-out, run away to Italy and use thirty sun-drenched days to refocus and reset—gain clarity about what we want for the future."

"I'd be happy just to have one," he mumbled.

At least, that was what she thought she heard. His voice had been faint, and what he'd said didn't make any sense, so she figured she had to be wrong. "What was that?"

"I said I think that's a great idea," he replied, speaking more stridently. "Here's to a month in Italy!"

"A month in Italy!" she repeated as if it was a toast and, closing her eyes, turned her face up to the sun. Going to Praiano with Charlotte and Julian felt right.

Now she just had to make it happen.

chapter 7

The villa Charlotte had found on Airbnb was spectacular. Muted pink stucco with white trim, it offered an incredible view of the sea, a large red-tiled patio where she could eat outdoors in the temperate climate, a hot tub on the deck and four bedrooms, each with its own bath. A high wall surrounded the property, except where the deck faced the sea, which had a beautiful arched gateway that led into the villa from a street so narrow it was only a footpath. Not only did that high wall guarantee she'd have the privacy she craved, but it was also draped in white bougainvillea.

She clicked on pictures of the inside. Decorated with the blue-and-yellow fabrics, tile and pottery the Amalfi Coast was so famous for, it was filled with antiques and had high ceilings and large, spacious rooms.

"Lovely," she murmured, but bit her lip when she saw the price. The house was expensive. But she didn't like any of the other accommodations she'd seen nearly as much. At least it was right in Praiano, where Lilly was living, as opposed to Positano or Amalfi. Those other towns weren't far away—Positano was just five miles to the west and Amalfi eight miles to the east—but according to what she'd read, there was only a narrow, winding road cut into the cliff to connect them, and that had a lot of traffic, so five miles could take twenty or thirty minutes by car. Walking would take even longer, of course, but that wasn't a viable option, anyway. The road barely fit vehicles.

She continued to search for something else, something cheaper, but kept going back to the same place—and eventually decided to show it to Jules and Sloane, hoping they'd agree it was worth the cost. She needed a house that would make her feel safe and happy and would inspire her writing, and this felt like the one.

It didn't take long to hear back from them. They loved it as much as she did, insisted she book it before someone else could, so she did. Then she sat back with a smile. Crazy things were happening in her life, but at least there was Italy.

Excited to show her father what she'd found, she was just texting him at work from her laptop when her phone rang. Mr. Heidelman was calling her back.

She tensed as she set her computer aside and hit the talk button on her phone. She had no idea what else he might reveal—or what it might do to her. But she needed to speak to him, to learn more, even if she was frightened about what he might say.

He greeted her politely and thanked her for getting back to him. Then he got down to business. "Before my letter, were you aware you had a sister?"

"No," she replied. "Until I got your letter, I didn't even know I was adopted."

He paused for a moment. "I'm sorry if that came as a shock."

"It was definitely a shock," she said with a wry chuckle. "But what happened in the past is certainly not your fault. I'm not blaming you."

"Still, it's a touchy situation. Please forgive me. My only goal is to do what's best for Lilly."

"I understand."

"And I'm afraid I have a bit more to tell you."

"I'm terrified to hear what you're going to say next," she admitted.

"I can see why, but you should know this before you make any decisions. I wish I could say her mother left behind enough cash or other assets to pay for her care, but other than a few personal effects, she's been left with nothing."

Charlotte exhaled in relief. This was what he'd been afraid to tell her? No problem. She'd expected it. And she felt it was probably for the best, at least in one regard. If there'd been money, the boyfriend might have kept Lilly for that alone. And then who could say what would happen once he ran through it?

"That's fine."

"I'm glad. Thank you for taking it so well. I was afraid she might be too big a burden for someone your age, but then . . ."

His words dwindled off as if he'd suddenly thought better of what he was about to say, so she finished for him. "But then you learned who I was and knew if anyone my age could afford to take in a child, it would be me?"

He laughed. "I wouldn't have stated it that way, but . . . yes. I was hopeful that maybe you'd have the resources, as well as the interest, to be involved in her life."

She noted his euphemisms. Be involved in her life? He wasn't talking about having Charlotte join some weekly Big Sister program. He wanted her to become Lilly's full-time guardian and solve the problem. Period.

But it wasn't quite that simple. First, she had to make sure Lilly would want to live with her—see how they got along as sisters. Could they grow any real affinity? Because what a child needed more than anything else was love, and Charlotte wanted to be absolutely sure she could offer as much as Lilly would require.

"I'll do what I can. But the hard decisions will come later. First, I need to meet her."

"I understand completely. It's my job to alert you to the situation and let you make the decisions from there. That's what I've been hired to do."

"By whom?" she asked. "Who's paying your fees?"

"Luca Versetti, the man who's taking care of Lilly."

"He's spending his own money?"

"He didn't specify."

"Does he seem like a decent man?"

"I guess. I've never met him, so I don't have a good read on him."

"Do you have any pictures of my birth mother or Lilly?"

"Unfortunately, no—but I can request them."

"I'd appreciate it if you would. I believe that would help me in some way—to have faces to put with these names. Right now, I feel like I'm flying completely blind."

"I'll email him after we hang up."

She went through the pictures of the villa yet again while she talked. "Can you tell me how Sabrina died?"

"Some sort of accident, I believe. I don't know the details."

That didn't tell her much. "Does Luca speak English?"

"He does, but with a heavy accent that can make it hard to understand him, and his vocabulary isn't very wide."

At least she'd be able to communicate with him. She was relieved he spoke English for Lilly's sake, too—that the girl hadn't been left with a man she'd known only a few months and couldn't really communicate with. "And does Lilly speak Italian?"

"He claims she's picked up a little of the language."

"If I decide it's for the best, is she going to want to come back to the States?"

"I'm afraid she doesn't have many options."

In other words, she'd have to do what she had to do. Charlotte shook her head at that thought. To be so vulnerable, so at risk . . . She'd been lucky to have the parents she'd ended up with, the stability. "What about extended family?"

"I've been in touch with an aunt, but she's in no position to take on a child. Her husband wouldn't allow it even if she was. And Lilly's maternal grandmother is too old and too ill. She also doesn't have the resources."

"Is there anyone else?"

"Who could possibly step in? No."

"That leaves me."

"That leaves you," he echoed. "Would you like to meet her? I could ask Luca, Sabrina's boyfriend, to put her on a plane, but the cost of the ticket would have to be covered by you or someone else. He feels he's done his part. And just so you know, I'm not sure he'd take her back if you . . . if you decided you weren't up to the challenge."

"No need to put her through that. I'm going there—to Italy," she said. "I've already rented a villa in Praiano. I'll arrange my airfare today."

"That's wonderful," he said, obviously surprised. "How long do you plan to stay?"

"I have the villa for a month, but I'll stay as long as necessary—or as long as it's best for Lilly."

"Sounds good. Once you've finalized your plans, I'll let Luca know."

Why couldn't she communicate with Luca herself? She almost told Mr. Heidelman to pass along her email address but stopped short. She didn't know Luca. Maybe, for the time being, it was best to have an intermediary. It provided just enough distance while she struggled to adjust to this new development. "I'll send my itinerary as soon as I have it."

After she hung up, she heard movement in the doorway behind her and turned from her desk to see her mother bracing herself with one hand on the doorjamb. She was in a robe and slippers and had dark circles under her eyes.

"Do you want to talk?" Penny asked, her voice reedy thin.

Charlotte knew her father must have told Penny that she'd learned the truth. But her mother hadn't come out of her room since Charlotte had opened the letter last night.

Obviously, Penny wasn't feeling well. She looked pale, seemed almost too weak to stand. But Charlotte could easily imagine that, besides suffering from lupus, she'd been putting off this moment. As shocking as the truth was for Charlotte, it had to be equally shocking for Penny to learn that the secret she'd hidden for so long was out—just when she'd probably begun to believe it was safe.

The sense of loss that had to engender, and the fear of how Charlotte might react, certainly wouldn't have been conducive to helping her get back on her feet.

Although Charlotte hadn't gone in to see her mother, either—had been trying to come to terms with what she'd learned first—seeing the situation through her adoptive mother's eyes brought some compassion.

Getting up, she beckoned her into the room. "Yeah, I'd like to talk. Why don't you come over so you can sit down?"

She helped her mother across the room before sitting on the bed beside her.

For a moment, neither spoke. They could see each other in the mirror over the dresser, but Penny didn't seem to know what to say until Charlotte smiled and took her hand. Then her mother began to cry. "I'm sorry."

"It's okay," she said.

Penny finally looked her in the eye instead of at her reflection. "Your father and I . . . we didn't know what would be best for you. We just knew you were perfect and happy the way you were."

"I know."

Her mother searched her face. "You're not upset?"

"I'm hurt and confused. But I know you love me, that you've always loved me and that you did your best to give me everything you could." Charlotte couldn't promise she wouldn't feel resentment in the future, but she'd been close to her parents and that made it easier to forgive them. Had she known, maybe she would've insisted on finding and meeting her birth mother, and maybe that would've changed the dynamic of her childhood—made her less content.

"What will you do now?" her mother asked.

"Didn't Dad tell you I have a sister?"

She nodded.

"I'm flying to Italy to meet her."

"We'll travel with you," she said decisively. "I don't want you going to face that alone. We'll do it as a family."

Her mother started to stand, but Charlotte put a hand on her arm. "Mom, look at you. You don't feel well enough to go anywhere. And Italy is a very long trip. You and Dad need to stay here. *I'll* go. I won't be alone. Sloane and Julian are going with me."

Her eyes widened. "They are? But . . . what about their own lives? Sloane's married. Is her husband going, too?"

"No, but Ben doesn't mind her being gone for a few weeks. If it turns into a problem, she can always come back early. And Julian can work from anywhere. He's been to the Amalfi Coast before, knows what to expect and has already mentioned a few places he'd like to photograph. He might even take a weekend here or there to go to Venice or Lake Como."

"That sounds ideal. But where will you all stay?"

"Right in Praiano. I've already booked an Airbnb." She

dragged her laptop closer to show Penny the listing. "Check it out."

"Wow!" Penny said on a breath. "That's going to be lovely."

Italy *would* be lovely—and, she hoped, serene. But Charlotte couldn't say what kind of turmoil would be going on under the surface. That would depend on what she found when she got there.

chapter 8

Sloane was leaving for an entire month. Rory had agreed to take care of the design business while she was gone, and Ben had been surprisingly supportive of her going. He said Charlotte needed her, and he could get by for a few weeks without her—even though he'd miss her.

His attitude made Sloane feel even guiltier for the relief that consumed her at the thought of having thirty days to herself in a place like the Amalfi Coast. Surely, with the sun and the sea, the charm and great food of Italy, the companionship of her brother and best friend and the time to heal and reflect, she'd be able to figure out what to do—whether she should agree to have children, or give Ben up so he could have children with someone else.

"I'll call you often," she promised as they pulled up to the curb of the Seattle-Tacoma International Airport.

He put the car in Park and opened his door to get her luggage. "Don't feel any pressure," he said. "I'll be here whenever you want to talk, but you'll be nine hours in the future, so our days and nights won't be the same. Just get away from it all and enjoy yourself."

She opened her door. "Do you mean that?" she asked as she followed him to the back of the car. "You don't secretly resent me for leaving—even with the cost?"

"You've put in countless eighty-hour weeks trying to get A Personal Touch off the ground. I think a vacation will be good for you. I certainly don't begrudge you this trip."

He was generous that way, which was another reason she felt like a terrible person for even contemplating divorce. He worked hard, too—deserved a vacation as much as she did and yet he wasn't complaining, wasn't saying, *What about me?*

"I appreciate that, Ben. I really do."

Their eyes met and held, and he smiled warmly. "Stop feeling guilty. You'll ruin it."

She smiled back. "Okay. Thank you. I mean that."

"No problem." He got her suitcase and her carry-on from the back of their SUV. "Julian and Charlotte are on the same flight out of LA, right?"

"No. I couldn't work that out. We'll meet up in Naples, but they get in only a few hours after me, so that's almost as good."

"You'll wait for them at the airport?"

"Yes. Then we'll take the train to Sorrento and a bus to Praiano."

"That villa Charlotte found . . ." He shook his head. "That's a pretty incredible place."

"Maybe you can join us at the end of the month for a week or so." She offered that even though she knew inviting him would partially defeat the purpose of her going—because she really *did* care about him and felt bad leaving him out.

"We'll see," he said noncommittally.

She blinked when he didn't jump at the chance. "You're not that interested?"

"We can't afford another plane ticket. Besides, there's a lot going on at work. We've been trying to hire someone and thought we had, but then she found out she was pregnant and quit before she even started, so we're still shorthanded. Besides, I want you to have this trip just for you."

"I appreciate it," she mumbled.

He rested his hands on her shoulders and gazed down at her. "Are you excited?"

She perked up because she *was* excited and nodded.

"Good." He pecked her lips before dragging her luggage closer to the wide automatic doors. "Have a wonderful time."

"I will," she said and watched, stunned, as he got back in the car and drove off.

What was going on? He was acting very . . . distant. Polite and kind, but distant. Did that mean something? Was it for the best? Maybe he was ready to give up on her.

She didn't have a lot of time to think about it. She couldn't miss her flight, or she'd be in a mess. She stood there only until he disappeared from sight. Then she rolled her luggage inside the terminal. She was waiting to check in when she got a text from Julian.

Make your flight?

At the airport now.

Same with me and Charlotte.

Can you believe we're actually doing this?

I can't believe *you're* doing it. What did Ben say when he dropped you off?

> To have a good time.

More proof that he's a great guy.

She felt a little queasy when she thought of her husband. Would this make the difference in their marriage? Or would it spell the end?

> I know.

What in the world was she going to do? She couldn't divorce Ben—she was still in love with him.

They'd just settled into their seats on the plane when Julian noticed that Charlotte kept glancing at her phone and frowning.

"Is that Heidelman?" he asked.

"No. He already sent me Luca's contact information so I can reach him when we get there. Luca hasn't sent the photos I requested, but Heidelman says he and Lilly are expecting to hear from us once we get to the villa."

"We have a twelve-hour flight, and we're going nine hours into the future. We won't even arrive until tomorrow."

"I know. I said it'd be around dinner, so I could have a chance to get settled and clean up."

"So what's wrong?"

She showed him a text from Cliff.

> Don't you think we should see each other before you go? Maybe we're getting ahead of ourselves splitting up. Maybe we need to slow down and talk.

"He's having second thoughts?"

"I guess. He wasn't interested in talking the night he told me he wanted a divorce, so something's changed."

The date indicated this wasn't a new message. "Looks like he sent that a few days ago."

"He did. Right after that other picture of us at the coffee shop went viral, suggesting we were still 'seeing' each other."

Julian had to laugh at how easy it'd been to set that up. "You haven't responded yet?"

She shook her head. "I couldn't decide what to say. I'm still hurt that he'd throw me out without an explanation. And I think he only sent that message because he feels threatened by you and the fact that I'm leaving the country."

"He knows we're going to Italy?"

"He knows *I'm* going. I didn't mention you."

"The pictures we post should be fun, then."

She shot him a skeptical look. "I don't know about doing more of that. I think we've probably gone far enough."

"Can you go too far when you're dealing with a megalomaniac like Cliff?"

"I don't want to ruin the playoffs."

"He would never let anything ruin playoffs," Julian said wryly, but lifted a hand in a stop position so she'd know he wasn't going to continue going after Cliff. He knew the way he was talking about her soon-to-be-ex made her feel disloyal. "If you told him about Italy, did you tell him about Lilly?"

"I did. He was asking me to get my stuff from the house, but I was too busy preparing for the trip, and I needed a reason to put him off. I didn't want to see him—didn't think it would be good for my peace of mind. I have to hold it together for Lilly's sake, you know? I can't let my personal problems get in the way of the next few weeks. So I told him to have his driver drop off whatever I left behind at my folks' house and be done with it."

"Does he know you were adopted, too?"

"He knows everything."

With her at the window, Julian reached around to lower the shade so the sun wouldn't keep blinding him. "What'd he say?"

"Not much."

"Because he's only interested in things that are about him?" he said, unable to stop himself.

"Essentially," she admitted reluctantly. "And he doesn't know how to react to the fact that someone else might come to mean more to me than he does. Or more than he did." She waved a hand. "Or . . . whatever."

"He cares about that even though he's trying to end your marriage?"

"You know the saying about wanting your cake and eating it, too?"

"I'm familiar with it."

"Even though he's the one who's calling it quits, he's been everything to me for the past several years and doesn't want my feelings to change. He hates the prospect of losing that security blanket. And yet he wants to be free to enjoy his pro basketball days, which I've come to realize means seeing other women."

"Wait, he's not moving forward with the divorce?"

"Didn't specify."

"Then I hope *you'll* send papers to *him*!"

She sighed and lowered her voice. Someone was putting a carry-on in the overhead bin in anticipation of taking the seat next to him. "One day I might. But I'm not going to worry about it right now. I just need to get through the month and make the hard decisions I'll have to make regarding my half sister. Then I'll see how I feel when I return."

"How would he react if you got back with him but told him you wanted to take in a twelve-year-old?"

"I don't know," she said.

She could probably guess. Even Julian thought he could predict Cliff's response. Cliff hadn't been interested in her family when he married her. Julian couldn't imagine he'd be open to taking in the orphaned half sister she'd just learned she had. But he said, "Okay." He didn't want to upset her, especially because he couldn't criticize her approach. He was taking a similar one when it came to his own problems. He'd told his doctor he wasn't going to start any type of treatment, not until he returned from Italy.

For the next month, he was just going to enjoy whatever he could—and pretend nothing was wrong.

Julian slept almost the entire flight; Charlotte watched movie after movie. She was trying to distract herself from what was waiting for her on the other side of the world, but nothing seemed to work. Her mind kept drifting, her thoughts ping-ponging from Cliff and his sudden change of heart to the ominous words Heidelman had said when they talked right before she left.

> It might be tempting to meet Lilly, fall instantly in love and take her home. By all indications, she's a beautiful girl. But since you have accommodations in Italy for a month, I'd stay the entire time or even extend it.

She'd found it strange that he'd suggest she put more thought into taking responsibility for Lilly as opposed to less. Wasn't it his job to find the girl a home? And wasn't his job over once he'd done that? She would've thought he'd press her to take quick action rather than advise her to be slow and methodical.

Why do you say that? she'd asked him.

> Because it's the smart thing to do. Get to know Lilly before you decide one way or the other. I don't want to

poison you against the girl, but I also want to be totally
transparent with you, so you know what to expect. She
deserves a lot more consideration than she's ever gotten.
But Luca has indicated she can be difficult.

Charlotte remembered how tense she'd felt in that moment. In what way? she'd asked.

He didn't specify. But if I had to guess, she's hurt and angry,
which can make a child strike out. She's also been raised
by a mother who hasn't given her any consistency, any
stability. And when children have too much freedom, they
tend to get willful and stubborn and resist authority.

The last thing Charlotte needed was an angry, troubled teen. Did her sister already fit that category? Because twelve still sounded so young and innocent. Charlotte was only twenty-nine herself.

She's willful, stubborn and resists authority?

I have a teenager so... I'm here to tell you parenting one
can be very difficult. They all test their boundaries.

Great, she'd thought sarcastically. Her sister was already out of control. What did that mean for her? Would she be able to do anything to help? Would she even be able to tolerate the girl?

Maybe this would be a wasted trip, and she'd be heading home before she knew it, feeling guilty because she couldn't be the solution to a problem that desperately needed solving.

That possibility was one of the things that tempted her to

go back to Cliff. If she returned to the marriage, he'd make the decision for her, and she was almost certain he'd refuse to take Lilly. He didn't even want children of his own—at least not at this point. He was unwilling to be inconvenienced in any way. He was too Important.

All the fretting was giving her a headache. Or maybe it was the altitude. One of her legs was falling asleep, too.

She shifted to get more comfortable and realized that Julian was now awake and watching her.

"You don't look happy," he said.

She didn't bother denying it. "I'm not."

"Is it the old problem or the new one that's bugging you?"

"Both. I'm a multitasker when it comes to worrying."

"Try to relax. We've got an entire month to figure it all out."

She nodded and handed him the foil-covered meal the airline had delivered while he was sleeping. "I saved this for you."

He tried to give the roll that'd come with the meal back to her. "At least have this."

She shook her head. "Jules, what would you do if you were me?"

"I'd tell Cliff he doesn't deserve me," he said with a grin.

She rolled her eyes. "I know how you feel about Cliff. I'm asking about Lilly. What if you found out you had a half sister somewhere, and she needed you to take guardianship—at our age?" He and Sloane were only six months older than she was. "Would you do it?"

"To be honest? I don't know. I'm glad I'm not in your situation." He started eating. "On the other hand, finding out about Lilly and having her in your life could be one of the best things ever to happen to you. We just don't know yet."

One of the best things ever to happen to her? Charlotte certainly hoped that would be true—that they'd be the best thing to ever happen to each other—but depending on how "difficult" Lilly was, reality could present her with the exact opposite.

Sloane was exhausted after her flight and the long wait at Naples airport. Although it was exciting to hear a foreign language spoken all around her, especially one as beautiful as Italian, she'd received so many messages from Rory while she was on the plane she was beginning to wonder if coming had been a mistake. Although she'd gone over everything with him before she left, he couldn't find this swatch or that plan, needed her to send him certain design files and had questions on various jobs. He'd also received a call from one of her clients asking for a remodel of a guesthouse.

Sloane hadn't counted on that deal coming through until fall. She wanted to handle it herself, but he was doing her such a big favor she'd replied that he could take it.

Bottom line: what had sounded perfect at first—a carefree month on the Amalfi Coast—wasn't turning out to be quite so carefree. She was worried about her business; Rory seemed at a loss without her. And she was worried about her marriage, for the opposite reason. Ben seemed almost *too* okay with her leaving.

Her phone buzzed with a text from her husband.

Did you arrive safely?

While she was on the plane, he'd been looking up things she could do in Praiano and found a hike to a convent that was built in 1399 but was no longer in use. Ben said she should see it and take a trail called Path of the Gods that continued up the mountain from there. According to what he'd found, the scenery was spectacular—hence the name—and after seven miles or so she'd arrive in Positano, which was arguably the most popular town on the Amalfi Coast.

It's three a.m. on the West Coast. How are you going to get up for work? she wrote back.

I'll manage.

> You need to sleep.

Tried and couldn't.

Sloane felt bad for him, but was actually glad to have a distraction. With Charlotte and Julian's plane still an hour or more out, she wasn't only tired; she was bored.

> Sorry to hear that.

What are you going to do while you wait?

> I don't know. I admit, leaving you & the business for a month sounded better before I did it. 😂

You're probably just jet-lagged. Don't worry about anything. We'll both be waiting for you when you get back.

She wasn't completely confident either her marriage or her business would survive, but she wasn't about to say that.

> I'm going to be so behind! I feel bad imposing on Rory. And I'm afraid I'll lose all my own clients by the time I get back.

You won't lose anything. You'll cover for him
when he wants a vacation. As long as you're
willing to return the favor, everything should
be fine.

Those words reassured her. He was right, she told herself. Now that she was here, she couldn't ruin the next month by second-guessing her decision to come. What she needed was a hot shower and a nap so she'd feel human again.

How long before Charlotte &
Julian arrive?

She checked her watch.

> An hour and fifteen minutes.

Have you eaten anything?

> Only what they served on the plane. I've
> been holding off because I thought it'd
> be fun to try pizza in Naples after everyone
> gets in. Did you know that Naples is
> the birthplace of pizza?

I didn't, but that means you have to try it. Want
me to find you a place?

> If you're sure you can't sleep.

He was the planner, could find anything on the internet in half the time it took her.

Gino e Toto Sorbillo has a lot of great reviews. It's sixteen minutes by taxi, but I'm sure the airport will have some lockers where you can stash the luggage until you come back to catch the train.

> I'll see if I can talk Charlotte and Jules into it.

They really should try the pizza while they had the chance. She didn't know if they'd be able to get back to Naples before they had to fly home.

> Thanks for looking after me.

Always. Let me know if you need anything else. ;)

She smiled at his response. He took care of her and was always so kind and generous about it. How could she ever let a guy like him go?

She couldn't. But if she wasn't going to have the children he wanted, shouldn't she let him build a family with someone else?

chapter 9

Charlotte hadn't seen Sloane since Christmas of the year before. Julian had been in the Netherlands on an important shoot—an assignment commissioned by a magazine or TV network—when Sloane and Ben had come for the holidays. Charlotte had tried to spend time with her that week, but they'd barely seen each other. It'd been strained and awkward even when they did get together, setting the foundation for their falling-out that March over a potential girls' trip.

That Christmas, Sloane had invited Charlotte and Cliff to the neighborhood party her mother was putting on, but Cliff wouldn't go. In his defense, he'd played two basketball games that week. In the last one he'd been fouled hard and knocked to the deck, which had left him scraped and bruised. Yet he'd managed to attend all his friends' Christmas parties that season. He just hadn't been interested in what he considered a long evening spent tolerating people who were only eager to talk to him because he was a professional athlete. He said they'd pester him for signed jerseys or sneakers or Lakers tickets.

Charlotte had never believed those at the party would ask for anything. But she'd known they'd be eager to get to know him, which meant he'd have to be "on" all night, smiling, talking and laughing with strangers he didn't care to know in the first place. He found that unpleasant and taxing, so she hadn't pushed him too hard. Instead, she'd told him she'd go on her own and make up an excuse for him. He'd said that would be fine, but then he'd called her only an hour after she arrived, complaining of a headache and asking her to go the drugstore and bring him some ibuprofen.

He could've had it delivered. He knew she was trying to spend time with old friends. But he always turned to her to make him feel better, no matter what was wrong. He'd just wanted her to be with him. It was one of those rare nights when he didn't have anyone else to entertain him, and he hated to be alone.

Or it was possible, she supposed, that Sloane's interpretation was the correct one, and he'd wanted to force her to choose between them.

To make up for it, she'd asked Sloane to lunch the next day, but then Cliff said he'd already invited her to play tennis with him and his friends. He loved that she was a good player—she'd spent a lot of time at the club while her mother was coaching—and enjoyed having her help him win. They could beat almost any other couple, and he found that especially fun if they were playing his teammates.

In an effort to try to please everyone, she'd invited Sloane to join them at the club instead, and she'd agreed. But once Sloane arrived, Cliff had completely ignored her. Charlotte had once again felt torn between them as she struggled to make up for how Cliff was behaving.

Sloane had ended up leaving the club early, and later that night they'd had a heated phone call about Cliff, part of which he'd overheard. He'd said her best friend had no right to talk shit about him, and yet Charlotte could see that Sloane had a point. It wasn't what Cliff had said or done. It was what he *hadn't* done. But sins of omission were more difficult to hold him accountable for because he refused to understand why anyone would have a problem with him.

"She's just trying to make trouble," he'd said, over and over again.

At least she wouldn't have to face that anymore, Charlotte told herself as she spotted Sloane waiting for her and Julian beyond customs.

As soon as Sloane spotted them in the crowd, she hurried toward them. "There you are!"

"I'm sorry about the girls' trip, how Cliff behaved at the tennis club at Christmas, what he did when I was at your mother's party and . . . all of it," Charlotte said as they embraced.

"Forget it," Sloane responded. "He demanded far more than he should have from you."

She'd been so dazzled and hopeful when they got married. He'd swept her off her feet, shown her only the best side of him—until after they were married. "You're lucky to have someone like Ben—he's so thoughtful. I can't believe he didn't have a problem with you coming to Italy for a whole month!"

Sloane started to say something, then stopped.

"What is it?" Charlotte asked.

"Nothing. I'm glad he was okay with it, too," she said and gave her brother a hug. "What's up with *you*?" she asked him. "How is it that the highly in demand, internationally acclaimed photographer is actually taking a month off to hang with his lowly sister and her best friend?"

"I guess I finally have my priorities straight," he said with a flash of his perfect white teeth.

"Those braces you had in high school really served you well," Charlotte said, noticing how captivating his smile had become.

He laughed. "I didn't have much to recommend me back then."

"You've always had those eyes," she blurted before she could stop herself—and immediately wished she could snatch the words back. She didn't generally compliment him like that, so when he looked at her in surprise, she felt her face heat.

"I'm flattered," he said with a wry grin.

Sloane didn't seem to pick up on how awkward the moment had become. Fortunately, she brushed right over it. "Maybe he'll find a beautiful Italian woman and fall in love while we're here," she said.

"Maybe," Charlotte mumbled and pretended to be preoccupied with gathering up her belongings. She had a hold on her luggage when Julian insisted she trade her big suitcase for his. Hers had a wonky wheel that made it hard to pull, which shouldn't have been the situation considering how much that case had cost. With all the miles his had logged, it looked like it'd been to hell and back, and yet it worked perfectly.

"Where's the locker you texted us about?" he asked.

Sloane gestured for them to follow her. "This way."

"You're not going to respond to my Italian-woman comment?" his sister teased as they started off.

He shot her a sideways glance. "The only thing I'm looking for is food. Let's get out of here."

"Are you nervous?" Sloane asked.

"To meet my half sister? A little," Charlotte responded while they shared a pizza that was every bit as good as it had been billed. They'd ordered the *diavola*, similar to pepperoni but made with spicy salami, which gave it even more flavor.

"She must be nervous, too," Julian pointed out as he took a sip of the cabernet sauvignon they'd ordered to go with their first Italian meal.

Charlotte hadn't told them about Heidelman's warning—

that Lilly could be difficult. She could see why he'd feel the need to prepare her, and yet she almost wished he hadn't said anything. She needed to approach the situation with an open mind. Otherwise, she was afraid she'd allow herself to use that as an excuse to head home without her sister, when she was really just terrified of the responsibility. "How can she *not* be nervous? I can't imagine being twelve years old and losing my only caregiver."

"I wonder if she knew you existed before Sabrina died, or if having a sibling came as a surprise to her, too," Sloane said.

Charlotte swirled what little wine she had left in her glass as she considered the question. "I don't know. Heidelman didn't share a lot of information. Mostly just the logistics on how to reach Luca Versetti, so we can meet."

"Can Heidelman tell us where her father might be?" Julian asked.

"No one even knows who he is," Charlotte said.

"Maybe we should hire a private investigator," Sloane suggested. "If we can find him, he might want to be part of her life."

Charlotte didn't believe the chances of locating him were very high. "Heidelman used a private investigator to find *me*," she told them. "He must've tried to find Lilly's father, too. Maybe there wasn't enough to go on. Or he's in prison."

"Or dead," Sloane said. "Where was Sabrina living before she came to Italy?"

Julian had asked many of the same questions on the plane. Problem was, Charlotte had no answers. "I'd love to know all this, but I have very little information."

Sloane leaned back as the waitress came to take away the empty plates and ask if they'd like anything else. Sloane immediately said no, but Charlotte had spotted tiramisu on the menu. She ordered some for dessert and so did Julian.

"Whoa, you don't generally like sweets," Sloane said to her brother. "What happened to being a health nut?"

He shrugged as the waitress left. "Might as well eat, drink and be merry . . ."

"For tomorrow we die?" she joked, finishing the biblical reference. "I hope not."

"You never know." He lifted his glass of wine toward her as if in a toast. "Either way, we're on vacation, so it's time to cut loose."

"I can go along with that." Sloane clinked her glass against his before turning back to Charlotte. "There are so many ramifications to what you've learned."

Charlotte wasn't sure what, specifically, she was referring to. "Like . . ."

"You could have several other siblings! Getting into contact with Lilly could open up a lot of . . . issues."

Charlotte waved her off. "Don't start pointing out all the possibilities quite yet. First let me adjust to what I'm facing now."

Sloane frowned. "You haven't submitted to one of those ancestry sites, have you?"

"I did, actually. Just a couple of days ago. I thought it might help me find other relatives—maybe someone it will be important for Lilly to find or know."

"When will you get the results?" Julian asked.

"In four to six weeks."

"So not long after we get back," Sloane mused.

"I wish it was sooner," Charlotte said.

Sloane drained her glass. "I can see why."

A ding signaled that Charlotte had received a text message. She was surprised because she knew her folks would be asleep back in California. Even Cliff would be asleep at four in the morning.

But it wasn't someone from America. This person lived in Italy.

> This is Luca Versetti. You coming to Italy?

First contact. Heidelman had told her to text him when she got in and set up a time to meet Lilly, but she hadn't had the chance. If he'd been told the same thing—that she'd text him when she arrived—why was he reaching out to her before she could even get to Praiano? Was he *that* eager to be rid of Lilly?

Charlotte got the impression he was. The question was why? Surely, she wasn't so difficult he couldn't wait one more day.

> I'm in Naples. I'll be taking the train and arriving in Praiano later today.

> What address, please? I will have Lilly and her things ready.

Stunned, Charlotte looked up at her friends.

"What is it?" they both asked at once.

"It's Lilly's caregiver—Luca Versetti."

"Can he speak English?" Julian asked.

"Heidelman said he could, and he wrote me in English."

Sloane twirled her empty wineglass. "What does he want?"

Julian followed up on that question with "Is he trying to arrange a meeting? You didn't set up something for tonight, did you?"

"No. I knew we'd be arriving after twenty-four hours of almost no sleep. I wanted to wait until I was fresh and rested. I was also afraid our flights would be delayed, or we wouldn't be able to get a train ticket or what have you."

Julian shifted in his seat. "So . . . what's he saying?"

Fighting the jitters that were setting in, Charlotte put her phone aside. She got the feeling this wasn't the situation she'd anticipated, where she could come, meet Lilly and make a careful, informed decision. Luca was obviously finished caring for the girl. Now he was just looking for somewhere to dump her as soon as possible. Which meant . . . *what*? "Sounds like he's planning to drop her off on our doorstep as soon as we arrive."

It felt strange waking up without Sloane beside him. Ben usually got up first, put on a pot of coffee and made breakfast—what little breakfast Sloane was willing to eat. She was always in a hurry. Building her business took so many more hours than if she'd just gone to work for someone else.

Sometimes he wished she had. The sacrifice was costing him a great deal, too. But he was proud of the effort she'd put into A Personal Touch. She had such a talent for making homes and offices—even outdoor spaces—beautiful. And he loved the way her eyes lit up when she was talking about a project that excited her.

Her enthusiasm was contagious. But he feared she'd gotten so caught up in what she wanted to accomplish that they'd lost each other.

He adjusted his pillow as he listened to a lawn mower down the street. Someone was getting an early start, which probably wasn't making the neighbors very happy. He happened to like the steady buzz of the motor. It reminded him of his childhood when his father would get up early on a Saturday morning to mow—before he was old enough to take over that chore. Once his father died, he'd had to become the man of the house and do a lot of things his father had done, including trying to cover some of his mother's bills while putting himself through college.

Gazing at the empty pillow beside him, he sighed. Would

he be happier with another woman? Someone who wasn't so engrossed in her career? Someone who was willing to slow down a bit and enjoy life with him? Maybe even have a family?

That was tough to say. It wasn't until very recently that he'd started having such thoughts. When he'd married Sloane, he'd assumed they'd spend the rest of their lives together like his parents would've done had his father not died white-water rafting with some friends. But she wanted different things—more success and money than he craved. He valued quality of life, which meant he wanted to focus on people, spend time with those he loved and have children. That was all he'd ever wanted—a simple life and to be like his father.

Who knew that would turn out to be a problem? But it had. Sloane was drifting away from him, and he didn't know how to stop what was happening. And if she wasn't happy with him, he didn't want to hold her back. People changed, their needs and desires changed and he was a strong believer in letting those around him evolve and pursue what they wanted most. What good did it do to hang on too tightly? That killed any positive emotions, anyway.

Which didn't mean that splitting up wouldn't be painful for him. There were moments when the thought of losing Sloane hit him like a right hook. Other times, he could be more philosophical about it. On some level, he understood that after the pain eventually receded, he might be better off, happier for having gone through it, especially if he could fall in love with someone who wanted what he did.

His phone rang. Since it was only seven o'clock, he expected it to be Sloane, and it was.

"Hey, how's the trip so far?" he asked.

"Good," she replied. "That pizza place you recommended in Naples was out of this world. Now we're on the train to Praiano."

"The pictures I found on the internet of the Amalfi Coast are gorgeous. You're going to love it."

"I hope so."

There was that uncertainty again. He felt bad for her; he also felt bad for himself. "So Charlotte and Julian made it safely, too?"

"Yeah. They're here with me."

"Poor Charlotte. What she's facing wouldn't be easy."

"It might be even harder than we thought. The Italian guy who's been looking after her half sister seems to think she's taking over from here."

"They haven't even met!"

"Exactly."

He got out of bed and went to the bathroom. "Damn."

"I don't know about this," she said. "I'm afraid we might regret coming here. Maybe Charlotte would've been better off in the States, avoiding this whole thing. A week ago, she didn't even know she had a sister. It shouldn't be *her* responsibility to raise Lilly."

"Someone's got to be there for the poor girl," he pointed out.

"I know. But my first loyalty lies with my best friend. She's going through a divorce, for God's sake. To have this happen now . . ."

"Not the best timing," he agreed. "Except the divorce is probably the only thing giving Charlotte the opportunity to have her sister as part of her life."

"And maybe, in the end, she'll love Lilly more than Cliff. I haven't met Lilly, either, but I already like her more," she joked.

He chuckled. He knew how hurt Sloane had been by Charlotte's defection, but he understood why Charlotte had to choose her husband over her best friend. At least she'd given her marriage everything she had. She wouldn't—or shouldn't—have anything to regret there. "I wasn't a fan, either. But it would be tough not to get egotistical and narcissistic in the mind-bender reality that's become his world. It's something very few people experience, so it's hard to say how he should behave."

"As usual, you're far too kind," she said.

Did it bug her that he could always see the opposite perspective? He'd learned over the years that the world was much more nuanced to him than to most people. "Just trying to be fair."

"I know. Did you get any sleep last night?"

What could he say that would adequately explain how empty the house was without her? How hard it would be to break up? He wanted to let her know how much she meant to him, but he also didn't want to cling to her if she needed to move on. "It's strange being here alone. You've been gone before, but . . . I don't know, this time feels different."

His comment was met with a moment of silence. "I shouldn't have left."

"I don't think that's the case." It was time. They had to find happiness with each other or separate and find it elsewhere.

She asked him a few questions about his work. Then she put her brother on so he could say hello. Ben knew that if their marriage ended, it would be hard to lose her family, too. He had a good mother, but he'd had to step into his dad's shoes when he was only fifteen. That had changed the dynamic at home enough that he craved being part of a regular family, and Sloane and Julian's parents were definitely regular—the kind of regular that was as American as apple pie. So were Charlotte's, for that matter. He didn't want her adoption to change the closeness they'd always shared.

After he spoke with Julian for a few minutes, he said hello to Charlotte and wished her well. If anyone could love a sister they'd never known, it would be her. But he had no idea how that sister would impact her life—whether it would be for better or for worse . . .

Sloane came back on the phone once Charlotte said goodbye. "I'll send you a video of the villa once we get there."

"I hope it's as great as the pictures."

"So do I. I miss you," she added.

"Miss you, too," he responded and meant it. Then he disconnected and turned on the shower. He feared what the next few weeks might bring. It felt like a make-it-or-break-it moment in their marriage—and he had no idea which way it would go.

chapter 10

A tall, thin girl with auburn hair falling to her shoulders and wary brown eyes waited with an annoyed expression and a pillow under one arm when Charlotte dragged her luggage down five flights of stairs and a series of narrow, winding walkways to reach the villa. She knew at once she was looking at Lilly and, at first, assumed the girl was alone—that Luca had simply dropped her off along with her belongings. Several suitcases and boxes were piled against the stucco wall that enclosed the villa, near the gate so they were ready to be carried through. But a second later, a man came around the corner from the opposite direction with yet another box.

"You have arrived," he stated in heavily accented English as he stacked that box on top of the others.

Sloane and Julian, who'd taken a few seconds longer to reach the villa—since Julian had been paying the cab up top and wrestling with the bag that had the wonky wheel while Sloane kept stopping to rest because she wasn't enjoying the effort it took to reach a home built on the side of a cliff—came up beside her and stopped, no doubt as shocked as she was to find Luca and

Lilly there waiting for them. Luca hadn't even given them time to move into the villa!

"Yes, I have arrived," Charlotte said, tempering her voice to hide her irritation. "You must be Luca."

He offered her his hand, and she accepted it for Lilly's sake. About forty-five or forty-six—which had to be younger than her biological mother had been—he wasn't very tall, but he was wiry, tanned and attractive. With strands of silver threaded through his longish black hair, he looked quite distinguished in a white linen shirt, which fell partway open at the chest to show a gold chain, tan linen shorts and leather shoes. "*Ciao*." He gestured at Lilly. "This is your sister, *capisci*? She has been *molto entusiasta* to meet you."

"Yeah, of course I have," Lilly added dryly. "And I'm sure you're just as excited to meet me. Who wouldn't want to find out about a little sister they never knew they had and who just happens to need a home and a guardian?"

He shifted awkwardly at the sarcasm. "She is *intelligente*," he explained, tapping his forehead for emphasis. "You wait and see."

Lilly definitely sounded older than her years. Charlotte hadn't expected a miniadult, not at twelve! But she couldn't think about that right now; she was too distracted and preoccupied with Luca. She wanted to ask him so many things. How did Sabrina and Luca meet? What had their relationship been like? How had Sabrina been paying for Lilly's living—and her own—before she died? Didn't Sabrina have any life insurance? Did he know anything about the girl's father—or her own, for that matter? What about Sabrina's extended family? Surely, there had to be more than the members Heidelman had mentioned.

And yet Lilly's care was falling to her, so . . . maybe not.

She also wanted to learn how Lilly's mother—*her* birth mother—had died.

But it felt heartless to talk so matter-of-factly about a woman who'd just passed away and left a twelve-year-old daughter behind to fend for herself, especially while they were standing in the middle of a walkway with presumably everything the girl had in this world piled in boxes beside them. Charlotte couldn't bring herself to do it. There was something in Lilly's eyes that warned her the girl didn't trust easily—and that she could spot a fool a mile away, despite her young age.

Maybe that was why she hadn't gotten along with Luca. Maybe he was a fool—or just eager to get out of a situation he'd never bargained for in the first place. He and her mother hadn't been together very long. It was possible they hadn't been all that close . . .

"Thank you for looking after her until I could get here," she said instead of asking anything.

He gave her a slight bow. "It was my pleasure. And now, I have to get back to my Vespa store."

That was it? He was just going to drop Lilly off and get on with his life as if Sabrina and Lilly had never been part of it?

Charlotte reached out to stop him before he could get too far. "Is there any chance you and I could meet for a cup of coffee in the morning?"

He didn't look as if he welcomed the opportunity. Her first impression had been correct, she decided. He wanted to be done, to be free to move on with his life and not look back. But after he did look back, literally, and his eyes landed on Lilly, he seemed to soften. *"Perché no?"*

"That's a no?" she asked uncertainly.

"It means . . . um . . . why not?" he explained. "There is a coffee shop in town called Gym Tonic. Have you seen the place?"

"No. We just got here. We haven't seen anything."

"It's on the street where the cab probably dropped you off—next to the gym. It serves food, coffee and delicious crepes. Meet me there at ten?"

"*Grazie*," she said with a nod and turned back to Lilly as he walked away without so much as a hug for the girl he was leaving in her care.

"I wouldn't have come all the way from America if I didn't want to meet you," she said to her half sister, but if she thought that would be enough to reassure Lilly and get her to lower her guard, she was sadly mistaken.

Lilly glared sullenly—testing her to see if that was all it required to get her to head back to the States, Charlotte supposed. The girl resented her own need. That much seemed clear.

Julian introduced himself and Sloane, which elicited only a slight nod from Lilly. Then he cleared his throat and said, "Shall we go inside?"

Charlotte's heart nearly broke when she saw Lilly turn toward all the boxes Luca had stacked up as if she didn't know what to do with them.

"I'll get those," Julian murmured. "You go in and have a look around with your sister."

There was a flash of relief in Lilly's eyes—and it was then that Charlotte realized if anyone could win her over it would be Julian. She was *so* glad he'd come to Italy with her.

Being handed to three total strangers made the girl Julian had just met prickly and defensive. She had to be terrified about her future. If he had his guess, her life hadn't been very stable up to this point and had just gotten a whole lot more unstable, so she was braced for further disappointment. That she didn't shed a tear when Luca left, didn't even say goodbye, made Julian respect her strength and self-possession. It seemed she wasn't about to let Luca know how badly his abandonment hurt, wasn't about to let anyone know.

Except she was overcompensating, which made it easier to figure out than she probably thought.

"This villa is pretty cool, isn't it?" he said, walking over to join her when he found her standing at the edge of the terrace alone, staring out at the sea.

She didn't answer. She just watched him warily, as if she didn't dare lower her guard in case whatever kindness he was offering would prove to be a trap.

He persevered with a smile. "I mean, life could be worse than having our own suite—and there's a hot tub with a view of the Mediterranean."

She corrected quietly, "It's the Tyrrhenian Sea."

The Tyrrhenian was part of the Mediterranean, but he didn't bother explaining that. Technically, she was right. It wasn't an important distinction, anyway, especially at this moment. "Whatever it is, I'm certain I've never seen a more beautiful coastline, and I've been all over the world."

She studied him, presumably to decide if he was credible. "Even Antarctica?"

She thought she had him. "Even Antarctica," he replied.

Her eyes widened. "You're so rich you just travel the world?"

"No, I travel for work. I'm a landscape photographer. I take pictures of beautiful places like this and sell them to magazines, online sites and galleries." He pulled his phone from the pocket of his khaki shorts, found his Antarctica album and handed her his phone.

She studied each picture closely, seemingly mesmerized. "I think it's just as pretty as it is here," she said as she handed it back. "Maybe even prettier."

"It's an entirely different kind of beauty. Everyone should see it at least once. But—" he gestured at the houses built on the cliffs to the right and left of them "—this place is much more comfortable."

"Does anyone live in Antarctica?"

"Just scientists who stay at various stations. There aren't any homes or businesses. Did you know that planes can't even fly over Antarctica?"

He could tell he'd piqued her curiosity despite her desire to remain completely aloof. "Why not?"

"Weather's too unpredictable."

"Where else have you been?"

"Russia, China, India. Lots of places."

She peered over her shoulder toward the villa as if checking to make sure they were alone. And they were. Charlotte and Sloane were still inside getting settled in their rooms. "Are you my sister's boyfriend?" she asked.

He shook his head. "Just a friend."

"Like . . . really?" she said skeptically.

"Like really," he echoed with a chuckle. "We've known each other since grade school. She's been Sloane's best friend since I can remember, and Sloane's my twin sister."

"How can Sloane be your *twin*? You don't even look alike—not very much, anyway."

"Fraternal twins don't share identical DNA."

She wrinkled her nose. "That's weird."

"It is—kind of. But sort of fortunate, too. At least my parents weren't tempted to name us Riley and Kylie or something like that."

This elicited a small grin.

"Or dress us alike," he added emphatically. "Can you imagine what that would've been like for me—going through school always matching my sister?"

Her smile broadened, though grudgingly. "She's still your same age. Did you like that?"

He lowered his voice as if confiding a great secret. "Early on, I would gladly have traded her for a brother. But when I started getting interested in girls, her cute friends were coming to the house all the time, so I felt like the luckiest guy in school."

She laughed out loud, then clapped a hand over her mouth as if the sound had escaped in spite of her attempt to squelch it.

"I had lots of acne and braces back then, so I needed all the help I could get," he said, and that made her feel comfortable enough to drop her hand.

"So . . . she's cool?" she asked uncertainly.

"My sister? *I* think so. We've managed to get along despite being the same age. I think you'll like Charlotte, too."

She reached down to scratch her ankle. "Mr. Heidelman told Luca that Charlotte's married to an NBA star. Is that true?" She gestured around them. "Is that how she has the money for a place like this?"

"The three of us are sharing expenses, which makes our accommodations a bit more affordable. But what Mr. Heidelman said *was* true. Until a couple of weeks ago, she was married to Clifford Jackson."

"From the Lakers?"

He nodded.

"What happened a couple of weeks ago?"

A soft wind ruffled his hair as he turned his face up to the sun. "They split up. He wants to be free. And since he's famous, you can read all about it on the internet, which, as you can imagine, isn't very much fun for her."

"That would suck," she admitted.

"It does. Bottom line, you're both going through a pretty shitty time. But it'll all work out in the end."

His swearing startled her, but she also relaxed immediately after. "What makes you think so?"

"I don't know if I've ever met a nicer person than Charlotte. She'll get on her feet eventually—and, if I know her, she'll be there for you."

She fell silent for a few seconds. Then she said, "What about your sister?"

"What about her?"

"She married?"

"She is—to a guy named Ben."

"Where's he?"

"Back in Seattle, where they live."

"He couldn't come?"

"Had to work." He leaned forward, trying to catch her eye after she turned away. "Aren't you overwhelmed enough with three of us?"

She bit her lip. "I don't know yet," she said, looking worried again.

"You're going to be okay," he reiterated.

The door opened before she could respond, and Charlotte stepped out. "There you are, Lilly. Jules, I thought you'd be taking a nap."

"Is that what Sloane's doing?"

"She was so jet-lagged, she fell right into bed. But she told me to wake her when we go to dinner."

"You know people eat a lot later here in Italy, don't you?" he said.

"I didn't know, but that works well for us. She'll be able to rest a little longer that way."

Wanting to give Charlotte some time alone with her newly found sister, he backed away, leaving Lilly at the railing. "I think I'll lie down for a bit, too," he said and gave Charlotte a nod of encouragement as he went inside.

chapter 11

Once Julian was gone, Charlotte felt a moment of panic. She didn't know this girl she was suddenly responsible for—without ever having made the decision to become her guardian. She supposed she could refuse to take Lilly home, but what would happen to her then? How could she abandon this child the way Luca had when he'd dropped her off with all her belongings—as if he couldn't get rid of her fast enough?

"How are you feeling?" she asked.

"I don't know," Lilly murmured with a shrug.

"Why don't we put on our swimsuits and get into the hot tub?"

Lilly looked startled, as if she'd been expecting a heavy—and potentially heartbreaking—conversation. They needed to have a serious talk at some point, but Charlotte didn't want to hit her with painful and difficult questions before establishing some kind of rapport, especially since she couldn't offer any promises that might make the girl feel better—not without the risk of letting her down again later.

Lilly blinked, clearly thrown off balance. "You want to get into the hot tub?"

Charlotte gestured around them. "It's breezy and cool this afternoon. I think it'd be fun, don't you?"

She nodded.

"You have a swimsuit?"

"In my suitcase."

"Perfect. I'll meet you back here after we change."

Charlotte smiled to reassure her before leading the way into the house. Lilly had to feel as if she was lost at sea, but Charlotte felt just as lost—completely unsure of her future, especially with her impending divorce. Nothing was turning out as she'd expected, which had to be what Lilly was feeling, too.

She'd just fastened her bikini top when she got a text message from Cliff.

We beat the Cavs. Did you see it?

She'd missed the game. She wouldn't have watched it even if she hadn't been on a plane when it was taking place. She doubted she'd ever watch basketball again. That was one of the few positives of her divorce. She would no longer have to stress over a sporting event, whether or not her husband would perform to the best of his ability—and what would happen if he didn't.

As precarious as her situation with her younger sister was at the moment, at least now she had something in her life that was powerful enough to distract her from the misery of her impending divorce.

Uncertain as to whether she even wanted to reply—she felt sick whenever she thought of Cliff—she tossed her phone on the bed and went into the bathroom to twist her hair up. But just as she was about to leave the room, she went over and grabbed it again.

> I'm afraid I missed it, but that's fabulous news.
> Way to go.

She was about to ask him if he'd found an attorney and when she should expect divorce papers. She hadn't consulted an attorney herself, didn't know the rules of such a process—how much time she'd have to respond, what would happen if she missed that deadline because she was out of the country, how many months it would take before she was officially single again.

But in the end, she couldn't bring herself to address that issue. It was too upsetting. So she left what she'd said as it was—after all, it was the rah-rah he was looking for—and dropped her phone on the bed again. She didn't even want it with her, didn't need any reminders of the life she'd lived before.

Dressed in her orange one-piece, which was getting well-worn but was still her favorite, Lilly waited at the railing, overlooking the ocean exactly where she'd stood before. She wished the man who'd come to Italy with Charlotte would be getting into the hot tub with them. Julian had kind, patient eyes. The way he spoke to her made her feel safe, as if the ground weren't about to open up and swallow her whole. That was what it'd felt like since her mother died, as if she was in the middle of an earthquake and had no idea what would be left standing when the shake-up was over. But Julian had gone inside to take a nap, and his sister was already sleeping, so it would be just her and Charlotte.

If she said or did something wrong, would she be packed up and dropped off somewhere else? Because she couldn't get it right all the time. Why even try?

She'd probably wind up in foster care no matter what she did. And she'd seen what foster care was like in the movies and on TV. If she was put into some mean stranger's home, she'd run away again and again if she had to. She didn't want to be a charity case, nothing but a bother. She wouldn't feel comfortable enough in that situation to so much as eat, let alone figure out the rest of her life.

She was tempted to run away now. Why not take off while she could?

Because she was in Italy. Where would she go? And how would she communicate? She had no friends here. Her mother had been homeschooling her, which meant she'd been schooling herself. Sabrina had never really gotten involved other than to tell her to go do her homework. She had to get back to America before running away would even be an option.

Maybe her sister would make that trip happen, but Lilly couldn't imagine someone Charlotte's age being willing to take care of a twelve-year-old who needed food, clothes, a place to live—everything a mother would normally provide, especially if that sister no longer had a husband. Charlotte would probably prefer to be out finding another man, not stuck taking care of a preteen she'd just met.

Biting her bottom lip, she gazed worriedly out at the sea. Most people saw a beautiful ocean with cliffs to the right and left bearing colorful houses. This was a vacation spot. The place to be. There were shops and restaurants and beaches. But she saw only the hopelessness of her current situation.

Life was going to be so different now that her mother was gone. Sabrina hadn't been the best mother. She'd dragged Lilly around wherever she wanted to go. And the men in her life, even though they filtered in and out and never stayed for long, had always come first.

But at least Lilly had known Sabrina loved her. Maybe not as much as some mothers loved their children—the kind who actually made meals, helped with homework and chaperoned field trips. But Sabrina could be generous when she was happy. She'd taken Lilly to so many fun places over the years, and they used to laugh and talk a lot, especially when her mother was between boyfriends.

At least, Lilly had known what to expect—and what not to expect—with Sabrina. There was a level of predictability even in her mother's unpredictability.

The door opened and her sister stepped out wearing stylish white-framed sunglasses and a matching bikini that had only a single shoulder strap. She looked like one of the models Lilly had seen when *Sports Illustrated* came to town to shoot their swimsuit issue, which frightened her. Why would anyone so young, glamorous and rich want a twelve-year-old she hadn't even known existed a week ago?

Although . . . Angelina Jolie was like that. Angelina had adopted several kids, just to help out.

Too bad Lilly didn't know how to reach Angelina . . .

That was a stupid dream, anyway, she decided. Angelina wasn't going to take her in even if Lilly could figure out how to contact her. No one was going to take her in—if her sister wouldn't.

"All set?" Charlotte said.

The false cheer Lilly heard made her feel like throwing up. She'd been nauseous all day, even though she'd barely eaten, and she wasn't sure getting into hot water would help. But she felt shivery at the same time, as if the wind was blowing right through her, so maybe it would be okay.

She stepped into the water, found it wasn't as hot as she'd anticipated and breathed a sigh of relief as she moved around to the opposite side to get out of the way. Then she watched beneath her eyelashes as her beautiful older sister climbed in.

Maybe if she'd had the same dad, she'd look like that, she thought. Instead, she was too tall for her age, all skinny arms and legs. She remembered Luca teasing her when he first met her, telling her she looked like a fawn that was barely learning to walk. He'd also said, with his heavy Italian accent, "Eyes too big, teeth too big, feet too big."

He and her mother had laughed as she'd stormed out of the room, but her mother had called after her saying she'd grow into everything eventually.

She tucked her feet underneath her so that Charlotte wouldn't notice how big they were.

"What do you think of Italy?" her sister asked.

After being gone for three months, Lilly missed America. It was home. But she didn't dare admit it, didn't dare let anyone know how badly she wanted to go back. Everyone thought Praiano was paradise. "It's hard to live somewhere when you can't understand what people are saying."

"Don't most people here speak *some* English?"

"If they work in a shop or a restaurant. But if you go outside of town, where there aren't many tourists, a lot of people, especially the older ones, don't speak any English."

"I see. What made your mother—" she cleared her throat "—*our* mother choose Praiano?"

That question surprised Lilly. Maybe most women wouldn't leave their home country for a man, but Sabrina would do anything. "Luca lives here."

"How'd they meet?" Charlotte asked.

"On a dating app." Sabrina would have Lilly take photograph after photograph to send to the men she was talking to. It seemed Lilly could never get the right shot the first time. Her mother wanted her to take the picture in such a way that she looked prettier or younger or skinnier—a lot of times when she was in a swimming suit.

"Do you like Luca?"

Lilly shrugged. What she felt for her mother's latest boyfriend was hard to explain. He hadn't been *terrible* to her, but he'd only been putting up with her for the sake of her mother, which was why he'd been so eager to get rid of her as soon as Sabrina was gone.

Charlotte leaned forward. "Was he kind to you?"

"He wasn't *un*kind," she replied.

"Did he seem to be in love with your mother?"

Charlotte didn't change "*your* mother" to "*our* mother" this time. But Lilly didn't say anything. She was too busy remembering the six or more men she'd called "father." At first, they all seemed to be in love with Sabrina. But their love never lasted. Lilly couldn't say exactly why. She thought part of it was how much her mother changed once they moved in together, how much she started to demand and expect and how little she was willing to give in return. Sabrina would start to complain—always wanting more time, more attention, more money. And they grew tired of it, some sooner than others.

Lilly could always tell when Sabrina's latest boyfriend was getting ready to move on. Even if her mother hadn't died, Lilly believed her relationship with Luca had been nearing an end. They'd begun to fight, and Luca had often slept on the couch or stayed with family or friends during the last few weeks.

It was a cycle she'd seen before . . .

Lilly had wanted to tell Sabrina that she shouldn't be so hard to live with. But how could a daughter say that to a mother? "I guess he loved her as much as any of the others," she said.

"The *others*?" Charlotte lifted her sunglasses.

"Her other boyfriends."

Charlotte slid around the bench, closing the gap Lilly had purposely put between them, which made Lilly shrink away. She needed space, couldn't let anyone get too close. She couldn't love someone who'd only walk out of her life again. She felt as if she'd crumble, disintegrate altogether and blow away like dust if it happened one more time.

"Were there a lot of them?" Charlotte asked.

When adults drilled her with a question like that, it was usually to find fault with her mother. But Lilly couldn't detect any judgment in Charlotte's voice. It sounded more like concern, and that helped. She was tired of having to defend Sabrina from those who labeled her as "bad." Sabrina had just been trying to be happy. When Sabrina had pulled her out of school to move to Italy to be with Luca, one of Lilly's teachers had muttered that she'd never met a more selfish woman. That was probably true. Sabrina could also lose her temper quickly and lash out. But she forgave just as quickly and provided the love Lilly hadn't been able to find anywhere else.

"Enough that I've started to forget some of them." It felt great to finally admit it, to state the truth instead of trying to think of clever ways to deny it.

"How would she meet the men she dated?"

"Wherever she was bartending. At a club after work. Through a friend or someone she worked with. Online."

"Did you typically get along with them?"

"Some of them." *All of them except one*, Lilly corrected in her mind. Walter had shown a little *too* much interest in her, which was why her mother had left him. Lilly had always wondered if Sabrina was mad at her for ruining that relationship—if it was the one that might've worked if not for her.

After they moved out of Walter's house, Sabrina had never mentioned the day they'd found the camera hidden in the bathroom only Lilly used, but she'd worried ever since that her mother blamed her for being the reason she couldn't find someone who'd love her enough to stay. Walter's house had certainly been the nicest one they'd known.

"And the others?"

"I don't want to talk about this." The words came out before she could stop them. But Lilly couldn't address *that* topic. She was too raw inside, too *damaged*. That was the only word she could think of to describe how she felt.

Fearing her refusal was all it would take to make her sister mad enough to drop her off somewhere else—Italy's version of foster care—she steeled herself for Charlotte's reaction.

But to her surprise, Charlotte smiled kindly. "Okay. No problem. You don't have to talk about it."

Silence fell. Lilly wished she could think of something to fill it. She always felt awkward around strangers, and she was even more uncomfortable now that she was with a sister who was also a stranger. People typically didn't have to deal with that kind of thing.

She pretended to be absorbed in finding a jet that would massage her back, but eventually she had to look up, and when she did, she found Charlotte watching her with her sunglasses still on top of her head.

"What *would* you like to talk about?" she asked. "Is there anything you'd like to ask *me*?"

Lilly shook her head to indicate she didn't have any questions, but that wasn't true. There was so much she was dying to learn. She just didn't dare speak up for fear she'd say the wrong thing.

"There's got to be something," Charlotte coaxed. "Come on, nothing's off-limits. It's your turn to put *me* on the hot seat."

Lilly weighed the question that was uppermost in her mind and, when the silence began to get uncomfortable again, she finally caved into the expectation that hung in the air. "Okay. Is it weird for you, knowing you had a different mother than you thought?"

"Very," Charlotte admitted. "My parents never told me I'd been adopted, so getting Mr. Heidelman's letter came as a shock."

"You thought you were theirs all along?"

"I did."

"Do you look like them?"

"Maybe not, but I don't look too different from them, either."

"Finding out you're adopted—that would suck."

"It did, but everyone has challenges in life, right? I'm trying to work through mine just like you're trying to work through yours. And I think we can both do it."

Her open and honest response gave Lilly the courage to ask another question. "Do you like your parents—the ones who raised you?"

"I love them dearly. They're wonderful people, have been very good to me."

"You're not mad at them?"

Charlotte took a moment to think. "I won't lie to you. At times I feel some resentment, mostly because Sabrina is gone and I can't meet her now even if I want to, you know? But they did what they thought was best for me—and maybe they were right. Maybe it *was* best for me."

"Don't you think they should've told you?"

"That's hard to say. Would I have been any happier if I'd known? It would've introduced questions and issues that I probably would've had a hard time dealing with at a younger age. I had a great childhood. Maybe I should just be grateful."

Charlotte was very different from Sabrina, Lilly decided. She couldn't imagine her mother ever saying anything like that. She was pretty sure her mother would've been mad, felt ripped off somehow. She always seemed to feel ripped off.

"Did your mother ever mention me?" Charlotte asked.

"Mention you?" Lilly echoed, stalling for time.

"Tell you she'd had another daughter?"

Did Charlotte want to hear that Sabrina thought of her often? Missed her? Regretted giving her up? Wouldn't any daughter want to believe that? But Sabrina wasn't the type to ever look back. There was always too much to forget.

"Not to me," she admitted. Afraid her sister would be disappointed, Lilly followed that up with another question, hoping to keep Charlotte from dwelling on what her answer might mean. "What're your parents' names?"

"Don and Penny. They live in Orange County."

"Where's Orange County?"

"You've never been there? It's part of the Los Angeles area. Southern California. Where did you and your mother live before you came to Italy?"

"We've lived everywhere. Denver, Seattle, Portland, Salem, Fort Bragg, a little place called Cherokee. That's in Iowa," she clarified. "That was when my mom was with Steve. He was a farmer. I liked him best." She smiled as she remembered the blind dog who'd hung out in the barn. He'd become *her* dog—until Steve had asked them to move out because he and Sabrina were fighting too much.

"Sounds like you relocated a lot."

"We did."

"Your mother was a bartender?"

"Yeah. If she got fired or hated where she was working, we'd just move on. She liked trying different places." Sabrina had once made a joke that she was trying to outrun the past. Lilly hadn't understood what her mother meant at the time, but she thought she did now. If they didn't keep moving, it felt like everything bad in their lives would catch up with them.

Charlotte wiped away the moisture collecting on her upper lip. "Did *you* like moving?"

"Not really." Over the years, she'd pretended otherwise—to protect her mom. Now that Sabrina was gone, she didn't have to do that anymore. But she still felt slightly guilty, as if she was letting her mother down.

"Were you upset when she decided to come to Italy—take you clear across the ocean?"

Guilt caused her to back away from the honesty that'd just felt so freeing. "I didn't have any choice."

"Having no choice is different from having no opinion."

The longing she felt for Sabrina created a physical ache in Lilly's chest. Almost everything to do with her mother had been hard and confusing, even when she was alive. Now that she was gone, that hadn't changed. "She made Italy sound like a pretty cool place," she said. "And I like pizza."

Charlotte laughed. "There's the silver lining!"

"The . . . what?"

"It means something good coming from something that's also difficult—a part you can be happy about."

She no longer had to start over and over again as Sabrina met one man after the other—no longer had to worry about another "father" spying on her like Walter had done. That had to be a silver lining. But with her mother's death, her life had gotten worse, not better. Maybe Sabrina hadn't been totally reliable, but now Lilly had *no one* to look out for her.

"Luca said you write books," Lilly stated.

"I've written only one—and I need to write another."

"But you're famous?"

"Not really. It's my soon-to-be ex-husband who's famous."

"Clifford Jackson with the Lakers."

"Luca told you about him, too?"

Lilly was glad Charlotte had brought Clifford into the conversation because she hadn't dared to, didn't want to make Charlotte feel bad since it sounded like it was Clifford who wanted the divorce. "Yeah. Luca said you were rich." Luca had actually said that Charlotte could take care of her because she had more money than she knew what to do with. But Lilly didn't add that part.

"*Cliff* is rich," Charlotte clarified. "But we're no longer together, and we weren't married very long, so he's keeping most of his money. I moved in with my parents before I left the States. Being single again is still very new, and it feels . . . odd."

Lilly didn't know what to say. If Cliff was keeping most of his money, that couldn't be good for her. And she could hear the sadness in Charlotte's voice, didn't want to make it worse. Once her mother had split up with whoever she was seeing she'd never wanted to speak of him again. Was it the same with Charlotte? "Sorry. You said I could ask anything," she mumbled.

"I did, and I meant it. You can always talk to me, even about Cliff. The divorce won't be easy, but grief has a cycle. Did you know that? You go through stages, and you hang on through those stages hoping that, in the end, things will get better."

"*Will* they get better?" Lilly desperately wanted someone to promise her the grief and fear she felt would go away, because everything in her life just seemed to get worse.

"I believe it will," Charlotte replied. "But I'm not going to promise you anything. I can't say something just to make you feel better. I want you to know that if I say something you can count on it, okay?"

Those words weren't the promise she'd been hoping for, but they seemed honest, and that made it easier to trust Charlotte. "Okay."

Water dripped from Charlotte's hand as she lifted it to gesture around them. "Why don't you tell me about this little town?"

"I can see why my mother liked it," she replied. "She loved being by the ocean."

"What do you like here?"

"The pizza."

"Of course," Charlotte said with a grin. "Sounds like that hasn't let you down."

"No. The pasta is good, too," Lilly added. "So is the lemon *sorbetto*. They serve it in a giant lemon."

"I've never seen that in the US."

"I think you can only find it here—but it's all over the Amalfi Coast."

"I'll definitely have to try it. Pizza, pasta and gelato, huh? I'm afraid I'm going to gain quite a bit of weight this month!"

This lighthearted talk made Lilly feel like she could breathe again. She hadn't even realized she'd been holding her breath, but the tightness of her chest eased just enough that she no longer felt sick.

Charlotte scooped a dead bug out of the water and tossed it over the side. "What's your favorite restaurant?"

"I don't remember the name, but I know where it is," Lilly told her. "It's in Positano."

"From what I've heard, Positano isn't far."

"It's not. But it's a different town. You have to take a taxi, which costs money," she pointed out. That had always been her mother's reason for saying no whenever Lilly wanted to go there, but her mother had never had any money. She'd had to depend on the men in her life to provide a lot of what they needed, and after a while those men got tired of it. Some resented Lilly even more than Sabrina because she had nothing to offer.

"Sounds like it's worth the trip. Should we go there tonight? Do you know if we need a reservation?"

She shook her head, but for the first time since her mother died, she was tempted to smile. Dinner at a fancy restaurant would feel like a celebration, and it'd been a long time since she'd had anything to celebrate.

"I'll google it after we get out." Her sister sat up on the edge of the Jacuzzi. "I understand that you're in a frightening and difficult situation, Lilly, and I hope to make that easier on you—in whatever way I can."

Lilly felt her smile falter. Those words sounded good, but she didn't know what they meant—not exactly. Maybe Charlotte didn't know what they meant yet, either. "Thank you."

chapter 12

Julian stood at the window of his sister's room, looking down at the deck below where he could see Charlotte and Lilly sitting in the hot tub.

"Did you just say Char's out there with Lilly?" Sloane stirred on the bed. As soon as he'd gotten up from his own nap, he'd knocked and awakened her because he wanted to go out and get something to eat. But when he'd raised the blind to let in the sun, thinking that would finally rouse her, he'd realized Lilly and Charlotte were still in the midst of getting to know each other, and he felt he and Sloane probably shouldn't interrupt.

"Yeah. I guess you can go back to sleep." He sent her a sheepish look for barging in too soon. "Sorry."

She sat up. "It's okay. I need to get going. If I nap too long, I won't be able to sleep tonight." She covered a yawn before continuing, "Does it look like they're doing okay?"

"It does. If I'm not mistaken, Lilly's smiling."

"No kidding? She was so jittery when we first met her, I was afraid she'd bolt and we'd never see her again."

"Do you think Charlotte should take guardianship?" he asked as he continued to watch the scene below him.

"Hard to say," she replied. "It's such a gamble."

"You're afraid raising Lilly might be too difficult?"

"It has nothing to do with Lilly specifically. At this point, taking on any child would change Charlotte's whole life. She should be healing from her divorce and trying to meet someone new. She wants a family of her own. But if she takes Lilly, she'll have to worry about what's happening with her whenever she's out, spend a lot of money to care for her and make sure she's in a good place emotionally, which could require a therapist. Who knows how taking on a twelve-year-old girl will alter her future, or what opportunities might come her way if Charlotte remains on her own? Lilly's old enough that it'll be weird for any guy Char gets serious with—I know that."

"Weird?"

"Most thirty-year-old men wouldn't want the responsibility of a twelve-year-old sister."

"I think you're wrong. I'm thirty, and I wouldn't mind."

"Not all guys are like you, Jules. What if she meets the love of her life, but he resents having a minor—someone who costs so much time and money—living with them? What if he doesn't want to compete with Lilly for priority?"

"A lot of people have unconventional, blended families and make it work just fine."

"And that's a wonderful thing. What I'm saying is we have no way of knowing whether that's best for Charlotte. I'd hate to see her give up so much of her time and resources to make someone else happy when it could mean she'll miss what she should be enjoying at this age."

"What about Lilly's happiness?" he asked. "Doesn't she deserve to be happy, too?"

"Yes, of course. I feel sorry for her. But my loyalty lies with Charlotte. We don't know how Lilly was raised, what issues

Charlotte might encounter with her. There's a lot to consider, especially for someone who hasn't had a child of her own yet. Charlotte doesn't know how to be a parent."

"Someone's got to step up," he said, the thought stirring something deep in him. "Maybe I could help."

"From Alaska or wherever you go next?"

She had him there. He had to work while he could. He didn't know how long he'd be able to earn the money he needed to support himself.

On the other hand, maybe he'd never become a parent any other way...

"We can't just...ignore her need," he said.

"You're making me feel like a coldhearted bitch for arguing that Charlotte should even consider making other arrangements. It's not that I don't want things to end happily for Lilly. It's just that Charlotte might not be the best answer as her caregiver. She can still be a good sister and support her in many ways. Let's see what her extended family's like—what they might be able to do before we go too far. I also think we should find her father and talk to him—if possible."

That made sense. Taking responsibility for a child wasn't a decision to be made lightly. "We have a month. We might as well wait and see what develops as Charlotte gets to know her."

"Exactly. There's no rush."

He moved away from the window. "So what are you hearing from Ben?"

She climbed out of bed, went into the bathroom and started brushing her hair. "Everything's fine back home."

He crossed over to the bathroom and leaned against the doorway. "Not according to what you told me on the phone before you left Seattle."

She turned away from the mirror, her hairbrush still in one

hand. "It's a possibility that I'm not as quick as you are to tell Charlotte she should take guardianship of Lilly because I'm not excited about becoming a parent myself, Jules."

He scowled at her. "I've been thinking about that. Maybe that's a short-term thing while you build your business. It's difficult to be a parent *and* build a business."

"That's not all of it. It's the whole picture."

"What whole picture?"

"Parents are shamed at every turn. Everyone thinks they have the right to criticize how you're treating your children, especially on social media, and they feel so self-righteous doing it. They feel they're speaking for an innocent—never mind that they might be wrong about the whole situation."

"People shouldn't be so quick to judge," he conceded, "but it's tough to know where to draw the line—when a child needs your voice—and that's where the problem comes in." He stepped away from the window. "You'd be the first to try to defend an innocent if you thought it was necessary. That's starting to sound a lot like justification to me."

"What are you talking about?" she grumbled as she put the tie in her hair.

"I think you're feeling guilty about not wanting kids, and you're looking for a way to justify it."

"I don't need to justify it," she said, tossing her brush onto the vanity with a clatter.

He raised his eyebrows. "Not even to Ben? Because the last I heard, a family was important to him."

She froze for a moment, then sighed as she faced him again. "Fine. Maybe a little. I don't want to disappoint him. I also don't want him to feel I pulled a 'bait and switch' since he thought I wanted kids when I married him."

"Having your spouse change his or her mind about that

would be tough," Julian pointed out. "How does he react when you tell him you no longer want children?"

She slid past him. "I haven't said it flat out. Not yet. I just keep putting him off."

He watched as she rummaged through her suitcase and came up with fresh clothes. "Then he's ready to start trying."

"He's been ready for a while," she admitted.

Julian moved toward the hallway so he could step out and give her the privacy she needed to change. "Businesses come and go, Sloane," he said, pausing at the lintel. "Family is forever."

"See? Even *you're* on Team Baby!"

"I can't imagine you won't be glad you did in the end."

"Not everyone wants the same things out of life."

What he wouldn't give to be in her position—to have a steady partner to love and support him through the coming years, one who also wanted to start a family. All the trips he'd taken, the incredible sights he'd seen, even the photos he'd captured—none of it seemed to matter as much after his diagnosis.

"Even if that costs you Ben?" he asked in disbelief.

"You think I should have kids for his sake? That I *owe* him that?"

"I don't know," he admitted. "I'd just hate to see anything tear you two apart—and something like that could have the teeth to do it."

At his response the fight drained out of her, and her shoulders slumped. "Exactly."

The conversation she'd just had with Julian kept scrolling through Sloane's mind like a newsfeed she couldn't close the entire time she was sitting on the deck waiting for Charlotte and Lilly to get ready so they could catch a taxi to Positano. She didn't know where her brother had gone, but he wasn't around, and she was glad of the reprieve. He'd seemed horrified by her responses to his questions about her marriage and having children. What she'd said sounded selfish, even to her. Ben deserved to have kids if he wanted them. But she also deserved to live her life as she saw fit. So where was the compromise? Wouldn't it be better to break up and go their separate ways? Find partners who were more suited to them in their current evolution?

The thought of divorce made her sick to her stomach. After being with Ben for the past few years, she couldn't imagine moving on without him. And yet the very idea of escaping the heavy weight of his expectations and the guilt she'd been carrying for letting him down seemed to provide so much relief. She didn't want to feel such a strong sense of obligation to do something she didn't want to do. But she was also afraid that if he agreed they wouldn't have a family, he'd begin to resent her, feel he was missing out and eventually regret his decision.

There was a lot to consider. It didn't seem fair, even to her, that she'd changed her mind. But how could she make herself want something she didn't? If she agreed to have children just to mollify him, she was afraid *she'd* be the one who'd begin to resent it, that she'd long for what her life could've been if she was free to focus on her career.

"We're all set," Charlotte said as she came outside with Lilly close behind her.

She wore a long white sundress layered with a sheer shirt and a straw hat. Lilly trailed behind in cutoffs and a shabby Ferrari T-shirt she'd hacked into a midriff top. Sloane couldn't help thinking if that was the best the girl had to wear out to dinner, the first thing they needed to do was get her some new clothes. "Great," she responded. Where's Jules?"

"I have no idea." Charlotte gazed around the deck. "He's not in the house, and this is the only yard."

Sloane sent her brother a text message and immediately heard back:

I walked down to the sea to snap a few pics.
Coming now.

"He's on his way."

"Any word from Ben?" Charlotte asked as they waited. "How's he getting along without you?"

"He's at work now. I'm sure he's fine. He actually sent me a list of good restaurants to try."

"We'll get around to them. Tonight we're letting Lilly choose."

Lilly's eyes widened. "It doesn't have to be *my* pick," she protested.

Sloane had heard only that they were going to Positano for dinner. She hadn't realized this was meant specifically to please Lilly. "You can choose tonight. We'll be here an entire month, so we'll have plenty of time to try everything." She lifted her phone, which held the list she'd been referring to. "Some of these—the ones in Praiano—we'll probably visit more than once."

"Kasai is really good," Lilly told them.

"What do you like there?"

"They have a supergood truffle pasta."

"You like mushrooms?"

She made a face to show she didn't. "I don't think there are any mushrooms in it."

Truffles *were* mushrooms, but Sloane didn't want to spoil her favorite dish by telling her. "I definitely want to try that while we're here," she said and smiled at Charlotte, who grinned back at her as they walked out to meet Julian in the narrow walkway that snaked through the houses crowded onto the cliff.

The restaurant Lilly couldn't remember the name of—but loved—was a place called Il Tridente Positano. She had more trouble finding it than Charlotte had expected. She'd sounded so confident before. But finally, as the taxi drove slowly through the narrow streets, constantly stopping to wait for the tourists crowded all around them to drift slowly to the sides, she recognized it. When they asked her to explain how she'd discovered the restaurant in the first place, since it didn't seem like the type of place a young girl would choose, she said it'd been her mother's favorite, and her mother and Luca had taken her there for both her mother's birthday and her own.

Once they'd been seated and served, Charlotte thought the food was every bit as good as she'd been promised. They shared the buffalo carpaccio. Then Lilly ordered the potatoes and saffron gnocchi, Julian got the pasta with baby octopus, Sloane raved over a tubelike pasta with shrimp and other seafood and Charlotte chose something called *spaghettoni* pasta with black garlic that also had shrimp.

"Ben said we should try the fried artichokes while we're in Italy," Sloane said. "Apparently, they're very popular here."

There hadn't been any artichokes on the menu at Il Tridente, but there'd been a risotto with cheese that, according to Sloane, Ben had also recommended they try while they were in Italy. Sloane had ordered that in addition to her meal so she'd be able to tell him they'd followed his advice and give him some feedback.

Charlotte liked the risotto almost as much as her main meal but wouldn't have wanted it as her only entrée. "He was certainly right about the rice, so I'm willing to try the artichokes next time." She turned to Lilly. "What do you think? Have you ever tasted them?"

"My mom made me try them once," she replied. "I didn't like them."

"She liked them, though?" Charlotte couldn't help being curious about Sabrina.

"She said they were good, but she likes—" her voice faltered as she realized her mistake and changed tenses "—she *liked* the ones that aren't fried." Her voice grew even softer as she finished with "I don't think I've ever had those."

Sloane shot Charlotte an apologetic glance for bringing up the artichokes. "How about we get some tiramisu?" she asked, probably as an attempt to prop up Lilly's spirits.

Julian set down his now-empty glass. "Another Ben recommendation?"

"We're in Italy," Sloane said. "He didn't have to recommend that to me."

"I say we walk around a bit and see a little of Positano before it gets too dark," Charlotte said. "We can get some tiramisu later."

"The tiramisu at Kasai is the best," Lilly said, her voice barely audible.

"Back in Praiano?" Charlotte clarified, obviously attempting to draw her out.

She nodded. "The owner's mother makes it."

Lilly hadn't spoken much at dinner, so Charlotte was surprised she'd volunteer this. "Do you think they'll be open late?"

"If they're busy."

"They don't have set hours?" Julian asked.

"Not in Italy," she said. "But most restaurants stay open late now that it's spring. You'll see people eating at ten, eleven, even midnight."

"Have you been anywhere else—other than the Amalfi Coast—since you arrived here?" Julian asked.

"Rome and Florence."

"What about Lake Como?" Sloane asked.

She shook her head. "I don't know where that is."

"Venice?" Julian ventured.

Another shake of her head.

"Maybe we should do some traveling while we're here," Charlotte suggested. "I think we can take public transit almost anywhere."

Lilly said nothing, but Julian and Sloane agreed.

"Did you get some good pictures while Lilly and Charlotte were getting ready?" Sloane asked her brother.

"I didn't bring my big camera with me today, didn't want to mess with it. But I got a few nice shots with my iPhone." He navigated to his albums to let them look, and Charlotte paused on a photograph he'd taken from a second-story window at the villa before leaving the house. She could see Lilly and her in the hot tub with the large red tiles of the deck and then the deep blue of the Mediterranean Sea spreading out beyond them. The white bougainvillea climbing on the house showed in the foreground, giving the picture depth and perspective.

"You *do* have an eye," Charlotte told him. The picture he'd captured made everything look so perfect and serene. No one would be able to guess the roiling angst she'd been feeling at the time.

He smiled as he reclaimed his phone. "I'm glad we came."

She could tell he was trying to encourage Lilly, to suggest she should be glad, too. But Lilly was so hard to reach. Charlotte thought she'd made some progress with her in the hot tub. But since then, her half sister had retreated behind the walls she'd built to keep the rest of the world at bay, making Charlotte wonder if she'd ever be able to bridge the gap between them.

chapter 13

"So how do you think it went with Lilly today?" Julian asked.

The villa had gone quiet except for the rhythmic pulse of the waves against the cliffs. It was late in Italy—almost one a.m.—but only midafternoon in California, so he, Charlotte and Sloane were still wide-awake. They sat around the dining table on the deck, where a lantern flickered, drawing moths that tapped faintly at the glass.

"Tough to say," Charlotte said, her voice low.

They were keeping their voices down. Lilly had gone up to her room an hour ago, but it was possible she hadn't fallen asleep and could hear the conversation.

A gust of wind nearly yanked away the umbrella that had provided shade earlier, so Julian got up and secured it. "Seems like a sweet girl."

Charlotte sighed. "*Sweet* wasn't the word the attorney used."

"What did *he* say?" Julian asked.

"That she could be difficult—apparently that was something Luca shared. And in truth, she comes off as a bit sullen. But it could all be a defense mechanism, an attempt to push people away before they could reject her."

"She's going through a lot," Julian said.

"So are you," Sloane pointed out. "Have you heard from Cliff?"

They'd purchased a bottle of limoncello while walking around Positano. Almost every shop—except for those selling handmade leather shoes, Amalfi-made ceramics or linen clothing—sold it, along with lemon candies, cookies, even lemon-coated almonds. His sister had told them Ben had sent her the recipe for a limoncello spritz, saying it would be fitting to enjoy a popular Amalfi digestif on their first night. So they'd purchased the vodka, club soda and Prosecco the recipe called for at a small family-owned grocery store in Praiano before starting down the path that would take them through the labyrinth of cliffside houses to their villa. Then they'd waited for Lilly to go to bed before actually making the spritzes and going outside to talk.

"He texted to ask if I'd watched his game."

Sloane gaped at her; Julian felt the same surprise. "Are you kidding me? You were on your way to Italy to meet a sister you didn't even know you had, and he wants to know if you watched *his basketball game*?"

Julian was tempted to throw a little shade at Cliff, too, but he bit his tongue. Cliff's indifference had to hurt; Julian didn't want to deepen the wound.

"They beat the Cavs," she said without much inflection.

Sloane rolled her eyes. "Who gives a damn?"

Charlotte shrugged as if to say it wasn't all that important to *her* anymore, either. "He can be . . . self-absorbed. But in his defense, he's used to people making a big deal about his ability to play ball. In his world, that's all that matters."

Julian could tell she was used to relying on that excuse. It was handy, ready, on the tip of her tongue. She'd probably been telling herself the same thing since the day she met him, because there had to be *some* justification or it would be too difficult to look beyond the narcissism.

"*You* should've mattered to him," Sloane grumbled. "What you're going through—what *he's* putting you through—should matter to him."

"I just need to get over him," Charlotte said.

Julian swatted away a mosquito whining in his ear. "The split's still new. Don't worry, it'll happen."

Sloane tilted up her glass while holding back the slice of lemon and mint leaf. "I wonder if he's still seeing that model."

Julian scowled at his sister. "Let's not talk about her. We have enough going on."

Sloane put down her drink. "You're right. Sorry, Char. I'm just so mad at *Clifford*," she said, mocking his full name.

Charlotte added more limoncello to her glass. "The shock and hurt I felt at first is turning into anger for me, too. It's almost like he flipped a switch one day and became someone else, someone I don't know—or an exaggerated version of his worst self. When I think about it, I'm stunned, so shocked I feel frozen solid, unable to move. But I have to keep functioning, have to keep moving forward, or my whole life will collapse."

Julian propped his legs up on the empty chair beside him. The moon seemed huge tonight. The way it hung low over the water made him wish he could capture it through his lens. But night photography required hours of effort. He'd been out many times, from dusk until dawn, chasing enough light to photograph the red rocks of Moab with the stars filling the sky beyond them.

Fortunately, he'd managed to get one shot he was particularly proud of—something different from all his competitors, who were also out in that area, trying to do the same thing. Prints of it sold quite well at the gallery. But he didn't plan to do any night shooting in Italy.

"So let's imagine a life without Cliff," he said. "Where would you ideally want to live?"

"Once I finish my book and have some breathing room, you mean? Until then I'm playing it safe and staying with my parents."

Sloane lowered her voice. "If you bring Lilly home, will they let her stay there, too?"

"They will. My mom isn't feeling well a lot of the time, but I'll be there to take care of both of them."

"While you write?" Julian said.

Charlotte shrugged. "Other people have to deal with life while they work."

Other people weren't on such a short deadline. Other people didn't have their whole career hanging in the balance. But Julian didn't say anything. Why add even more pressure when pressure was the biggest problem she faced? "What happens after you finish your book?"

"I think I'll buy a house with the money I'm getting from the divorce."

"In LA?" he said. Even small, middle-class homes in Orange County, where her parents lived, cost well over a million dollars. She'd still have a mortgage to pay.

"Or maybe San Diego," she said.

That area was no cheaper.

"Something close to LA," she continued. "I'm an only child. After all my parents have done for me, I feel I should stay close as they age."

"Do you have much money left over from your first book?" Sloane asked. "It was on the bestseller lists forever, right?"

Charlotte shifted uneasily at this question. Julian could tell by the way she hesitated that he wasn't going to like her answer.

"Everything Cliff wanted to do or buy cost so damn much,"

she explained. "I couldn't contribute equally, so I just gave him everything I had."

Julian dropped his head back with a groan.

When he looked up again, he found Charlotte giving him a disgruntled look. "I thought we'd be married forever, Jules, like my parents. Why wouldn't I share everything I have? Anyway, I just got a royalty check that was decent. It came into my account, and I haven't switched it over, so he doesn't have that. I'll be getting another one the first of August. And I'll get a progress payment when I turn in some sample chapters of the new book—if my editor likes them enough to sign off on the proposal."

"She'll like them," Sloane said, but Julian wasn't convinced and Charlotte couldn't blame him. She didn't seem capable of writing anything. She'd lost all confidence. And that scared him. The money she was getting from the divorce sounded like a lot, but it wouldn't even buy her a house—not if she paid cash—so if she couldn't maintain her career, she'd be broke before she knew it. And what if she was supporting Lilly?

Her parents would probably come to her rescue, he told himself. They were incredibly supportive. But she wouldn't want to be bailed out, especially after being on her own for so long. That would cost her some self-respect, make her more depressed.

He didn't like the setup, could see it all going badly very easily.

"Are you nervous about meeting with Luca?" Sloane asked, changing the subject.

"Sort of," Charlotte admitted.

Sloane pushed her glass aside. "What are you going to ask him?"

"I want to know what my birth mother was like. What kind of childhood Lilly had so I'll know what issues she could be facing. I also want to find out what he knows about any extended relatives."

"And Lilly's father," Sloane reminded her. "Don't forget to ask if Sabrina ever said anything about him."

"I won't forget. I also want to know if he can tell me anything about my own father."

Dropping his legs to the deck, Jules sat up straight again. "We'll take Lilly to the beach in Positano tomorrow, so don't feel you have to hurry."

Charlotte's expression showed relief as she met his gaze. "Thank you."

"You bet." He wanted to ask when she was going to start her new manuscript. He knew it should be right away. But she'd just met Lilly and had so much to figure out, especially if she was going to try to contact other family members or reach Lilly's father. That meant the book would have to wait. But . . . until when?

As they sat on the deck, Sloane finally began to relax. They were in Italy, looking out at the coastal lights, a blanket of stars across the sky and a vast inky ocean after one of the best meals she'd ever had. Julian had queued up "Bella Ciao," "Volare," "Con Te Partiro" and other classics—along with a bit of Italian opera. The music drifted out to them through the open doors of the villa while they discussed Lilly and Charlotte's situation.

Sloane was glad the conversation never turned to her and what she was facing with Ben. She didn't even want to think about the choice she had to make. She'd come to Italy to catch her breath and draw strength from two of the people she loved and trusted the most, and that was exactly what she planned to do.

"What are you thinking about?" Julian asked, cutting into her thoughts.

Surprised that she'd drawn his attention—he'd just been

speaking to Charlotte—she blinked and sat up straighter. "Nothing, why?"

"You went quiet on us, and you had a dreamy smile on your face," he replied, smiling himself.

"I just can't believe we're here—that we have this time to be together in this truly amazing place," she replied. "It makes me feel stronger, as if we can handle anything."

"I hope we can," he replied.

She leaned forward until the moonlight revealed his face. "Doesn't it do the same for you?"

He reached over to pour himself more limoncello spritz from the pitcher Sloane had made, then turned his chair slightly to look out at the scene she'd been taking in. "I guess it does."

"Italy's magical," Charlotte agreed. "I feel it, too."

"If we can't sort out our lives in a place like this, we're hopeless," Sloane said jokingly.

"The next few weeks probably won't be easy—but they will certainly be better because we're here. And because we're together," Charlotte added.

Sloane held up her glass. "To a month in Italy!"

"To a month in Italy!" they both said in unison and leaned forward to clink their glasses against her own.

Charlotte couldn't sleep even after Julian and Sloane called it a night. She went to her room at the same time they did, but after about thirty minutes of tossing and turning, she sat up, grabbed her phone from the nightstand and opened her Instagram app. She'd been avoiding social media since Cliff kicked her out, but she'd been so active since her first book was published that she knew her prolonged silence had to seem strange to her followers. She needed to tell them *something*. She was flooded with direct messages from fans who were worried about her.

OMG! Are you and Clifford breaking up? Tell me it isn't so.

I cried all day. You and Cliff are perfect for each other. Don't let anything happen to your marriage!

This can't happen to today's Barbie and Ken! But whatever's going on, please know that he was lucky to have you.

You're just as pretty as that model he's with now. Prick!

There were also a lot of mean messages, people who were eager to celebrate her fall from grace. She didn't understand trolls. Maybe seeing her suffer made them feel better about their own lives. Getting dumped made her human—knocked her off the pedestal some people had put her on—and there were as many gloating about her downfall as mourning it.

She winced as she read some of the comments that said she should "eat shit and die," that she was never good enough for Cliff to begin with, that she was a gold digger or that now she must finally realize she was no better than anyone else. Hurtful comments always seemed to carry the most weight. But she felt a responsibility to the many people who were being kind—or trying to be.

What could she say to them? She didn't want to reveal that she'd just learned she'd been adopted and discovered that she had a half sister. She wouldn't have wanted to reveal the news about her divorce, either, but it was already out there. It was time to make a public statement. But she had to be careful how she went about it. She couldn't risk coming off as disingenuous, flippant or angry. She cared about her readers, but she needed them, too—now more than ever. If they didn't continue to follow her and buy her next book, she'd soon be out of a job even if she managed to get a new manuscript completed. She'd always known the second contract was the one that could finally pay well. Signing a new author was so speculative, a publisher couldn't offer as much as they could to someone who had a good track record. But to get that next contract, she had to stay relevant and connected on social media, and that meant keeping the content going on Insta, which was her main platform, so readers wouldn't forget her—wouldn't drift away and start spending their time and money on someone else.

> Sorry I went AWOL. First, my mother was ill. Then I had to rush to get ready for a trip to Italy to meet some of my family. But I wanted to let you all know that I'm fine. You've probably heard Cliff and I have split up. Sadly, we grew apart and had different goals in the end. But it was a mutual decision, one made very amicably. We plan to remain friends and continue to support each other in the coming years, so please be kind to us both as we navigate these tricky waters. Transitioning back to single life won't be easy, but I can't think of a better place to do it than on the Amalfi Coast, where I'm hard at work on my next book. I can't wait to see what you think of it!

She knew from the many celebrities who'd gone through high-profile divorces that pretending all was friendly and fine would at least put out *some* of the speculation fires burning on the internet. And while she didn't have an expensive publicity firm like most of those people, she could copy their approach. She couldn't see how remaining generous and positive could get her into trouble.

She called up the pictures Julian had taken earlier—he'd sent her and Sloane a few when they'd asked about them at dinner—and picked a shot of the Amalfi Coast that showed a small fortress-like ruin that had once been a watchtower. He'd told them there were about thirty of these round stone buildings—most falling apart to some extent because they were so ancient—strung along the coast from Vietri sul Mare to Positano. They'd once been used as lookouts to warn the local villagers of the approach of Saracen pirates, he'd said, who, according to the internet, first arrived in Southern Italy in AD 711.

That small, resolute, unyielding tower seemed symbolic—perfect for her post—which was why she chose it over a beautiful shot of Positano, visible down the coast, and the Mediterranean Sea. She should've run away the first time Clifford showed interest in her, should've protected her heart. Her parents had tried to warn her of the difficulties she'd face by getting involved with someone who was so famous. And they'd been right. All he'd done was pillage her heart and then burn it to the ground simply because he could.

After posting what she'd written, along with Julian's photograph—he'd made it clear he had no intention of using it commercially, which made it fair game—she put her phone back on the nightstand, scooted down in bed and punched her pillow, hoping she could finally get some sleep. Her meeting with Luca in the morning would come all too soon.

But fifteen minutes later, she found herself getting up again, this time to retrieve her computer. She'd thought she was done with basketball, had found it ridiculous that Cliff would even ask if she'd seen his last game. But it was the playoffs, and she'd spent the past several years making him the center of her universe, had grown accustomed to caring about what he cared about, which was basketball. So she suddenly felt left out, as if the party was still going strong without her and no one even cared that she was no longer there.

As she put on the game, her heart ached when she saw Cliff. There'd been so many challenges to being married to him, not the least of which were his extreme highs and lows and the way he constantly swung between them. Their experience wasn't like that of most young couples, that was for sure. But she'd seen and done so many wonderful things she would not have done without him. And no one was more fun to be with—when he was happy, anyway.

She'd meant only to catch a few minutes, just enough to get another glimpse of her soon-to-be ex-husband in his element, where he did such incredible things—but two hours later, she'd watched the entire game, including the interview afterward, during which tears dripped off her chin as Cliff talked about his performance and smiled proudly for the cameras, seemingly as happy as ever.

Sloane woke up to a message from Ben.

How'd you like the limoncello spritz? (I'd make that plural, but I'm not sure how.) 😂

She sent him a reply for when he got up in the morning saying she'd enjoyed it, that they needed to come to the Amalfi Coast together sometime and wishing him a good day at work. Then she set her phone aside and got up. Julian had suggested they go sightseeing this afternoon. She wanted to have coffee with him, get online and research their options.

When she came downstairs, the house was quiet. Charlotte and Lilly didn't seem to be up yet, but she found her brother sitting on the deck, the umbrella on the dining table once again expanded to block the sun while he read a book called *A Walk in the Park* by Kevin Fedarko.

"Morning," she murmured.

He lowered his book as she came toward him. "Morning."

She laid a hand on the back of the chair facing him, but didn't sit down. "You sleep okay?"

"I did. You?"

He didn't look as well rested as he normally did, but she passed that off as jet lag. "Pretty good." She gestured at the house. "You didn't make any coffee? Should I put some on?"

"I thought it'd be fun to find a shop. We could grab a pastry, too, and look around while we're at it."

She liked the prospect of strolling through the tiny cliffside town in the mellow weather, enjoying a doughnut with an iced coffee. "Now, there's an idea," she said. "What about Charlotte and Lilly?"

"We could wait a little longer for them to get up, or we could text Charlotte to let her know where to find us. She could bring Lilly and come later."

"Except if she sleeps much longer, she might not have time to meet us before her appointment with Luca. Actually, we should be back here by then so she won't have to leave Lilly alone when she goes." Lilly was old enough to be left on her own for a couple of hours, but given the girl's unique situation, Sloane knew today wouldn't be the best time for something like that. "You promised we'd take her to the beach in Positano, remember?"

"Good point." He stood and stretched. "We'd better get going."

"Let me grab my purse." Sloane hurried back to her room to get her phone and sunglasses, too, and found a text from Ben:

> They sell limoncello here in the States. I'll
> get some and make a spritz in your honor.

Feeling terrible for being in Italy without him, especially because he didn't seem to be sleeping well and still had to work, she shoved her phone in her purse before hurrying out to meet Julian, who was waiting for her at the arched iron gate leading off the property. But it was only fifteen minutes later when she was tempted to text Ben about the lemon-cream-filled croissants she'd found. They had to be the best pastries she'd ever tried. It was so hard not to be able to share everything with him.

"How's Ben since we've been gone?" Julian asked when she took out her phone.

"Good," she muttered and quickly put her phone back in her purse and changed the subject. She didn't want to talk to him about her marriage again. It just made her feel guilty, and she already felt guilty enough.

chapter 14

Luca wore linen again—shirt and shorts—with leather sandals and a gold chain. Today he'd added a straw fedora and smelled like he'd put on a whole bottle of cologne. Beneath the hat, his dark hair curled, still wet—presumably from a shower—and he had the dark shadow of beard growth on his cheeks and chin, all of which he'd neatly trimmed.

Charlotte couldn't call him unattractive—he wasn't. He was probably fifteen years older than she was, but he'd aged well and looked younger than that. She could see why her birth mother had been attracted to him. When he held the door for her and flashed her that dashing smile, she realized he was also quite charming.

"Let's sit in the corner," he suggested, immediately taking charge. "Mario will be over to get our order when he has *un momento*." He called out in Italian to Mario, who was working behind a display case that had a pile of menus on top, two of which Luca grabbed before following her over to the table he'd indicated.

The restaurant's wide glass doors were flung open to the street, letting in the scent of salt and citrus. Inside, the air buzzed with English—mostly American voices trading travel tips over cappuccinos. Lemons gleamed everywhere: painted on plates and pitchers, curling across tilework, clustered in bright ceramic bowls. She was growing familiar with the blue and yellow that was so prevalent here, saw the same motif in shop after shop.

"I like all the ceramics you have here," she commented as Luca hurried to pull out her chair. "It's cheerful, clean looking and creates such a unique sense of place."

He took his own seat across from her. "*Fatto a mano, signorina*—It's made here. Some Italian families have been in this business for generations."

"We love the *limoni*. They grow *enormi* in Southern Italy—huge, you know what this means? Some are as big as your head."

"No!" she said disbelievingly.

"*Si!*" he insisted. "The *limone sfusato Amalfitano* is three times the size of your piddly US lemon." He grinned. "But it is the *cedro*—the citron—that is really big. We have *limoni* everywhere, which is why we put them in whatever we cook and on whatever we paint. Have you tried the *pasta al limone*?"

"I haven't been here long enough yet."

"I will recommend a place. But this morning, you must order the *crespelle*. You say crepes, like the French, *si*? Sweet or savory. Both are *deliziose*." When he kissed his fingertips like she'd seen actors do in the movies when depicting Italian characters, she had to laugh.

"What?" he asked, taken off guard.

"That was just a very stereotypical thing for an Italian to do, I guess," she replied.

He winked at her. *"Eh, ma io sono italiano, no?"*

She couldn't help grinning. "And that means?"

He laughed. "I *am italiano*, no?"

She accepted the menu he handed her and decided to get the Nutella-and-strawberry *crespelle* with an oat-milk latte. He insisted the burgers his friend Mario served were also the best in town, but her stomach was churning too much to eat anything as heavy as a burger, especially for breakfast. Although she was starting to like Luca, he was still handing her a very difficult problem. She needed to figure out what she was going to do about it.

When Mario didn't come over right away, Luca called out to him despite all the other patrons in the restaurant. He joked that the owner should get his priorities straight and serve his friends first, and they both laughed as Mario ignored two other customers who'd been vying for his attention to walk over to them.

The two men exchanged a few moments of what sounded like cheerful banter. Then Charlotte heard the word *bellissima* as Mario looked her over with an appreciative eye. "I knew your mother," he said to her in English. "She was also beautiful."

Charlotte felt a pang in her chest. He was talking about a woman she'd never met, would never have the chance to meet, and the finality of that bothered her, even though, logically, she told herself it shouldn't. She'd been far luckier than Lilly; she'd always had everything she needed.

The men sobered when she glanced away. Sabrina was gone, and she'd died quite suddenly. The fact that she was young and healthy at the time, and should've been around to finish raising Lilly, made it even more of a tragedy.

"I am sorry about her passing," Mario said, acknowledging his gaffe with a belated apology.

"So am I," Charlotte said.

After clearing his throat, he asked, far more stridently, "What can I get for you today? Since you are a friend of Luca's, breakfast is on me."

"I don't expect that," she argued. "I'm happy to pay for my meal."

Mario lifted his hand. "I won't hear of it."

Deciding she'd just leave a big tip, Charlotte asked for the crepe and coffee she'd planned to get, and Luca copied her with his order. After Mario walked away, Charlotte indicated Luca's phone. "I asked Mr. Heidelman for a picture of Sabrina, but I didn't get one. Do you have any you can show me? I still don't know what she looked like."

He navigated to his photos before turning the screen to face her.

Charlotte's stomach knotted as she used her fingers to zoom in on the woman who'd given birth to her. They had the same high cheekbones and thick blond hair, the same shade of green eyes and the same squarish chin. Her mother was wearing a black bikini and standing on the beach with Positano behind her. She didn't have a perfect figure, but she had a golden tan and looked healthy and robust. She also seemed comfortable with who she was—there was no self-consciousness in front of the camera, which Charlotte found appealing. Sabrina's smile revealed teeth she'd probably whitened a great deal—they were whiter than most women her age—but what ultimately drew Charlotte's attention was the way her mother's smile brought her whole face alive. She looked as if she would've been the life of any party—and she'd obviously been quite adventurous or she wouldn't have moved to Italy.

"She was beautiful, no?" Luca said softly.

Charlotte thought Lilly looked even more like Sabrina than she did. If Sabrina served as any indication, Lilly would turn a lot of heads in a few years. "Even prettier than I'd imagined."

Luca straightened. "After seeing your own face in the mirror, how can you be surprised?"

"I don't know." She supposed the impression she'd received of her mother, knowing she went from one man to another every year or two, had created an image in her mind that didn't meet with reality. She handed his phone back to him. "Can you send that to me? As well as any others you have?"

"*Si.*" He acted on her request while Charlotte watched. She was looking forward to a quiet moment when she could pore over those photographs in private. Seeing so much of herself in Sabrina was mind-blowing, since she'd always believed she belonged to Penny.

When he finished, he set his phone aside as she asked, "Were you in love with her?"

He seemed surprised by the directness of this question, but Charlotte knew this would very likely be her only chance to learn all he could tell her about her mother, so she wasn't holding back. "I . . . cared for her."

The equivocation of his answer was obvious. "But you didn't love her."

"I *could* have loved her," he said. "I wanted to love her. I was excited when she came here, thought she was the most beautiful woman I'd ever seen. I am attracted to Americans," he confessed with a chuckle. "They are so exuberant, ready to take on the world as if nothing bad could happen. I am drawn to that confidence—the whole American Dream. It's real, you know? But she was *molto difficile*—very difficult. You understand?"

Lilly had already alerted her, but still she asked, "In what way?"

"Like a spoiled child mixed with a bird that cannot be caged. Never fully satisfied. Never at peace. Restless. Always looking for something better and demanding more of those around her."

"Selfish?" Charlotte suggested, summing up what he'd just said.

His expression indicated he hated to speak ill of the dead, but she could tell she'd reached the truth. "I suppose I, too, am selfish," he said, an acknowledgment Charlotte found quite generous. "I never wished her any harm. But when it happened, I was ready for her to go back to America and leave me to my life. Being with her was not as I had imagined. I told her so right before . . . right before she got into the accident."

"What kind of accident was it?" Heidelman hadn't even been able to tell Charlotte how her mother had died. He'd said he'd been told only that she'd passed away and he needed to find her next of kin.

"She got angry when I asked her to move out, stormed from the house and took my Vespa. I tried to stop her, but she almost ran me over as she drove off." He flung his arm out as he spoke to show his shock, but then his arm returned to his side and his voice went soft again. "She was only a kilometer away when she swerved to avoid something in the road and . . ."

His words faded away, but Charlotte could easily guess the rest of that sentence. She'd been killed in an accident. "And what?"

"Collided with a bus."

Charlotte's fingernails curled into her palms. "Please tell me Lilly didn't see what happened."

"No. She was in the other room while we were arguing, doing her schoolwork. She would always disappear when we started to fight. She hated it, of course. What child wouldn't? She didn't even know her mother had left. She had AirPods in when I went to tell her there'd been an accident and we had to go to the hospital right away."

"You're painting a picture of constant emotional upheaval," Charlotte said. "Is that what it was like for Lilly?"

"I'm a passionate person. Sabrina was a passionate person."

"So . . . yes."

"*Sì*," he finally acknowledged in a fatalistic tone.

"Do you know what life was like for Lilly when they were with the man before you? Did Sabrina or Lilly ever talk about that situation?"

"Lilly did. *Un po'*—a little bit. The man with a blind dog."

"Steve. The farmer."

He shifted in his seat. "She's already told you about him? That dog meant everything to her."

"I got the impression she was happiest there."

"I probably could have focused on her more," he acknowledged. "But if it wasn't going to work out with her mother . . ."

"You weren't interested in being a father," Charlotte finished. Clearly, the poor girl had been treated like extra baggage Sabrina had schlepped around. Maybe that blind dog had given Lilly something to love, an animal that had loved her unconditionally, too. Charlotte hated that Lilly hadn't been able to stay in that situation.

Luca frowned as Mario finally brought their coffee and crepes. "So what will you do?" he asked when his friend told them "*buon appetito*" and hurried off to fill his other orders. "Will you take Lilly back to America to live with you and your rich and famous husband?"

To his credit, Luca thought she had a good place for Lilly. Apparently, he'd missed the news of her divorce, which wasn't all that surprising, since he lived in Italy. "I'm not sure what I'll do," she admitted. "Not yet. Do you happen to have Steve's number? Or his address or anything that will enable me to contact him?"

He scowled. "Why do you want to talk to *Steve*?"

"To find out what he's like—and hear what he has to say about Sabrina and Lilly." The only way she had of getting to know her birth mother—and what her sister's life had been like before Sabrina passed—was through others and whatever Sabrina had left behind. She thought if she could establish a friendship with Steve, she could possibly take Lilly to see the dog. That could offer her some comfort at this difficult time.

"I don't know how to reach him," he said. "I remember he

called Sabrina a few times while she was here, but I never spoke to him."

"Maybe his contact information is still in Sabrina's phone."

"If she didn't delete it."

Charlotte hoped that wasn't the case, but Lilly had indicated that her mother had a tendency to cut all ties when she moved on. "Does Lilly have her mother's phone?"

"No. I was afraid to let her see some of the pictures and other things that are on it. I was surprised by what I saw myself."

Charlotte hesitated with her cup halfway to her mouth. "What did you find?"

"She'd been communicating with other men since she came here, sending pictures, texting . . . sexual things." He grimaced as he shook his head.

Charlotte sighed. "So you have her password?"

"It was easy enough to guess, since it was Lilly's birth month and day."

She supposed being able to access Sabrina's phone was a good thing. At least it would enable her to see what her birth mother was like in a different way. "So where is it now?"

"With Sabrina's other things at the house. There was too much to carry yesterday. I boxed it all up, though, and was going to ship it to you when you went back to America."

"I can't wait that long. I'd like to have the phone while I'm here, if you don't mind."

"*Tutto bene*—I don't mind," he said.

They discussed the logistics of getting those boxes to the villa. Apparently, there was a road closer to sea level. He could park on the lower road so there'd be only one set of stairs, instead of carrying everything down several flights from the street above.

"Can you tell me anything about Lilly's father?" Charlotte asked as they finished eating.

"Not really."

She couldn't help being disappointed, even though she'd expected as much. After all, he'd hired an attorney for a reason—and that attorney had come to *her*. "Not even his name?"

He shook his head. "But it could be that you'll find it in some of her journals or other papers."

"You haven't read them?"

"No. I only went through her phone to look for someone to contact about Lilly—and I didn't want to see any more after that."

Perfectly understandable. Charlotte put down her empty cup. "Then I'm guessing you know nothing about *my* father."

"I didn't even know you existed," he said with a wince.

Charlotte set down twenty euros as a tip and stood. "Thank you for taking the time to meet with me this morning—and for helping me get Sabrina's things tomorrow."

"*Prego, signorina.* I am happy to help," he said and seemed sincere.

They thanked Mario, who wished them well while continuing to manage his small restaurant almost single-handedly, and moved out to the street, where Charlotte thanked Luca again.

"I am going to miss Lilly," he told her just before she walked away. "But I cannot become her father. I hope you understand this. Having a teenager is difficult even without all the anger, insecurity and resentment Lilly feels. I am not prepared to deal with that."

Somebody had to care enough to deal with it.

More and more, Charlotte realized that somebody would most likely be her. "I understand," she said and meant it. Luca really wasn't the right person to be raising Lilly. She knew that much.

chapter 15

"How'd it go?" The late-morning sun shimmered off the water and the scent of salt and sunscreen hung in the air as Sloane bent the brim of her beach hat to shield her face in case Lilly happened to look up from where she and Julian were wading in the surf about fifty yards away. She didn't want Charlotte's half sister to know she was talking about her or her situation.

Charlotte had just arrived by taxi at Spiaggia Grande, the world-famous beach in Positano. She was also wearing a wide-brimmed hat, as well as a black knitted cover-up over her white swimsuit. After dropping her bag on the large towels Sloane, Julian and Lilly had spread out when they claimed their spot two hours earlier, she'd suggested they go get a drink. So Sloane had gotten up to join her, and they were now walking to the closest bar, which was among a cluster of shops and cafés at the edge of the beach.

"My meeting with Luca was fine," Charlotte replied. "I like him a lot. He's actually a pretty decent guy, but he couldn't tell me much."

Disappointed for her friend, Sloane frowned. "Why not?"

"Because Sabrina wasn't with him very long. She didn't talk

a great deal about the past, either. And even though he speaks good English, there's still a bit of a language barrier, not to mention a culture barrier. He's never been to the States and has a romantic view of Americans, something he must've picked up from the movies."

"Not only from the movies." Sloane gestured at the crowded beach, shops and restaurants. "Lord knows he sees enough Americans around here."

"You think most of these people are from the US?"

"Judging by the English I've heard, I do. And since he owns a rental shop for Vespas, he'd interact with a lot of tourists. What does he know about Lilly's father?"

"Nothing. Not even his name. But Luca's willing to stay in touch, so I can speak to him again once I've been able to wrap my head around everything I've learned so far. Maybe he knows more than he realizes and I just didn't ask the right questions."

"I think it's good that we'll be here for a while."

"So do I."

They'd reached the bar, so Sloane ordered three limoncello spritzes and a *limonata* for Lilly.

"He's bringing Sabrina's belongings to the villa tomorrow—including her phone—so that might tell me more," Charlotte said as they waited.

Sloane thought of everything her own phone could reveal about her and had to agree. "That should tell you *a lot*—if you can get into it. Isn't it password protected like everybody else's these days?"

"He knows the password. He's already been through it, trying to find someone to take Lilly."

"If he resorted to hiring an attorney, he must not have come up with anyone."

"True. Still, I want to go through it myself. Read words that actually came from her, see her pictures and check her contacts."

"Of course you do," Sloane said. "That could reveal so much about who she was, what she thought of and dreamed about, maybe even why her life took the path it did."

"I hope so."

The bartender brought their drinks. "*Grazie*," they both murmured and paid before taking one in each hand.

"Have you heard from your parents since you got here?" Sloane asked as they passed through a handful of artists who were busy painting colorful scenes of the beautiful town around them.

Charlotte stopped to gaze at a partially finished canvas depicting the villas stacked up on the hillside above them—the scene that was always in the most famous photographs of Positano. "They both texted me to make sure I arrived safely."

Since they weren't moving, Sloane took a sip of her drink. "I bet they're wondering where this will lead."

Charlotte gave the artist a smile to compliment his work, and he nodded in return as they moved on. "It's definitely been a shock—for all of us."

"They must be curious about Lilly."

"They are. I should call them later today—when it's a decent time in LA—and let them meet her via FaceTime. Or at least send a picture. But I don't want to overwhelm Lilly. I believe we should take everything very slowly. And to be honest, I'm not overly excited about speaking to my parents right now."

Sloane quit walking again. "Why?" she asked in alarm. "You're not going to let this come between you, are you?"

Charlotte turned back, since Sloane had stopped. "I just need some time. I know they're worried and want blow-by-blow information, but including them feels strange. This is so hard for me that I just want to deal with it myself—at least until I can come to terms with it."

"I can't even imagine what you're going through," Sloane said. "I'm sorry."

"It helps to have you here," she responded. "I'm *so* glad Ben didn't mind you coming. I wish I'd married someone more like him," she added with a chuckle.

Sloane felt the heavy weight of the guilt she now hauled everywhere. What was she going to do about her husband? How would she know whether to stay with him or build a life without him? She had no idea which path would make her—and him—the happiest.

Fortunately, Julian and Lilly had spotted them and were coming to get their drinks, because it saved Sloane from having to form a reply.

"Everything go okay with Luca?" Julian asked Charlotte. His voice was light—for Lilly's sake, no doubt—but Sloane knew her brother better than anyone and could tell he would probe deeper later on.

"Great," Charlotte said. "He's going to bring Sabrina's belongings to the villa tomorrow."

"He's bringing them to *us*?" Julian said.

Charlotte nodded as if it was the most natural place in the world for them to go. Then she dipped her head to get Lilly's attention. "You can go through the boxes and have whatever you want. And the rest . . . Well, we'll decide what to do with the rest later. We'll just keep it safe for the time being."

"Okay." Lilly sounded relieved, at least to Sloane's ear, but at the reminder of her mother, her gaze fell to her toes again, which were buried in the unusual black pebbles of Spiaggia Grande.

"I hope the *limonata* soda was a good choice for you," Charlotte said. "I was going by what you ordered last night."

Lilly nodded. "I like it."

"We should get lunch in a bit," Julian suggested. "What's good?"

"Are you asking me?" Lilly touched her chest since he was looking at her.

"Of course I'm asking you," he replied. "You're the expert around here."

This elicited a small grin. Julian could win over almost anyone and had certainly been working his magic on Charlotte's half sister.

"There's a deli up there." Lilly pointed toward the busy shopping district, which had a labyrinth of lanes, stairs and stores, most with apartments or flats on top that had bougainvillea spilling from the verandas and climbing the banisters. "My mom took me once when we came here. It has a spaghetti pie that's pretty good."

"What's spaghetti pie?" Sloane asked.

"It's like—" Lilly made a face as she tried to think of a way to explain it "—gobs of noodles packed into a pie dish that has bits of ham and cheese mixed in. You can pick it up and eat it with your hand like a piece of pizza."

Sloane couldn't picture it. "The spaghetti doesn't fall apart?"

"Nope," Lilly replied. "It's thick and dry, so it sticks together."

"Sounds interesting," Charlotte said. "I'd like to try it. But let's take a few minutes to enjoy our drinks first."

As Lilly and Charlotte walked over to sit down with Julian, Sloane hung back to snap a selfie over by the artists with Positano in the background, which she sent to Ben.

> **Positano is magnificent—every bit as beautiful as people say.**

It was six thirty in the morning in California, so she didn't expect an immediate response, and she didn't receive one. She hoped he was finally getting some sleep. But she took a quick video for him, too.

> Pretty crowded today. That's probably to be expected during tourist season, especially because the beach is only about a quarter of a mile long. But it's easy to see why everyone wants to come here. The striped umbrellas, the intense blue of the water and the pink, white, yellow and blue houses nestled into the cliffs are all so special. Hope you have a great day!

Putting her phone back in the pocket of her cover-up, she started to follow Charlotte and Lilly over to the towels.

Julian looked up at her approach. "Why the smile?"

"I just made a video for Ben," she replied.

"I bet you miss him," Charlotte said, overhearing.

"I do," she said and realized how very much she meant it.

Ben woke up to the picture and video Sloane had sent him.

God, she was beautiful, he thought as he studied her face. He still loved her, wished life didn't have to be so hard—that there weren't differences of opinion and conflicting desires that could tear two people apart who were otherwise perfect for each other. Should he give up on his dream of becoming a father?

He was tempted to try. For her. But he didn't think he could do it. He was stuck between losing the woman he loved and fulfilling a role he'd looked forward to since he was a kid himself.

They'd been so happy in the beginning. What he wouldn't do to get some of that magic back . . .

> Thanks for what you sent. You're stunning. As always.

He heard from her as soon as he got out of the shower.

You're such a good man. I would never want
to hurt you. I hope you know that.

Her response made him love her even more. He'd needed to hear something like that. But her words were bittersweet, because she *was* hurting him, and he was probably hurting her, even though neither one of them meant to do it.

Julian relaxed in a deck chair while Charlotte, Sloane and Lilly sat in the hot tub nearby. He wasn't in the mood to get in with them. He preferred to embrace the cool night air coming from the sea and stare up at the stars blinking in the sky while listening to the three of them talk. He paid special attention whenever Charlotte had something to say. He'd always believed her to be a wonderful person and being around her again reminded him of the wholesomeness he'd found so appealing back then.

Had things gone differently, he believed they might have started dating. While they were growing up, Sloane hadn't wanted him to get romantically involved with any of her friends, and he could understand why. She was afraid something would go wrong, and she'd be forced to choose between them. He'd felt the same about her dating *his* friends. During their sophomore and junior years, Charlotte had already had a boyfriend, anyway, so it was a moot point. And by the time she broke up with him, they were in their senior year, and he'd had a girlfriend.

The timing was never right, but he'd often thought that maybe one day . . . Then they'd graduated and life had pulled them in different directions, only to bring them back together again at this juncture—when he felt he couldn't even show any interest. She was still in love with Cliff. He didn't want to get involved with anyone who was on the rebound, couldn't risk the damage that could cause in his own life, not when he was already dealing with so much. Even if her heart was open and free, Julian didn't feel he had enough to offer her, not with his recent diagnosis. He didn't want to put her in a position where she felt she couldn't say no—or saddle her with someone who could easily become a burden. He hated the thought of her getting into a relationship with him only because she pitied him or felt a sense of obligation arising out of their long friendship.

The girls were talking about the linen clothes they'd purchased at one of the little boutiques they'd passed on the narrow, crooked streets of Positano. While Charlotte and Sloane were shopping, Lilly had hung back with him near the entrance. She didn't have any money. But Charlotte had eventually prevailed upon her to try on a white linen sundress, and it'd looked so good she'd insisted on buying it for her.

Julian would never forget the look on Lilly's face when she took hold of that sack and left the store. She'd been trying not to smile, and yet he could tell she really liked the dress and felt accepted and included, since Charlotte and Sloane had each gotten something, too.

Lilly seemed to be warming up to her half sister. At least, there were moments when it felt that way. At various points during the day, she'd let down her guard enough to give them a glimpse of the person she was when she wasn't being so defensive—a very likeable, bright and pretty young woman, but also one who'd been abandoned and was now alone in the world and terrified to trust.

In an odd way, Julian could identify with her. He was protecting himself, too, couldn't let anyone, even his sister, know about his Parkinson's, because once the word got out there'd be no taking it back. She wouldn't even see why he'd felt the need to hide it. But he didn't want others to value him any less than they did now, while he was seemingly as healthy as could be.

"The dress you got looks *so* good on you," Sloane was telling Lilly.

"Thanks," Lilly said. "I've never had anything so nice. I'm not sure where I'll wear it."

"The design is such a simple one," Sloane told her. "You could wear it anywhere."

"Sloane would know," Charlotte agreed. "As an interior designer, she has excellent taste."

"You decorate houses for a living?" Lilly said.

"I do," Sloane told her. "I opened my own business with a partner in Seattle not too long ago. It's called A Personal Touch."

Lilly seemed emboldened by the conversation. She certainly hadn't asked anything about Sloane before. "So you don't live close to Charlotte?"

"No. We both lived in the LA area while we were growing up, but when I married my husband, I moved with him to Seattle because he had a good job offer there, and we had a lot of student debt to pay off," she added with a laugh.

Charlotte's phone went off. She twisted around and, being careful not to drip water on the device, checked to see who was calling her. Then she silenced her ringer and put the phone down again.

"Was that your folks?" Sloane guessed as Charlotte settled back in the water.

Charlotte nodded.

"You're not going to take it?"

Julian could hear the worry in his sister's voice.

Charlotte's response was subdued. "I'll call them back later—or maybe tomorrow."

Julian noted Sloane's expression when she glanced over at

him. She was concerned. Charlotte had always had such a good relationship with her parents; neither one of them wanted to see that put in jeopardy.

But Charlotte didn't allow any more conversation on the subject. Reaching back, she grabbed her phone again. "Here, let's take a picture of the four of us," she said. "Julian, will you get in?"

"I'll be the one to take it," he offered.

"Are you sure?" she said. "I'd rather have you in it."

He was wearing his swim trunks, so it wasn't any bother. He pulled off his T-shirt, tossed it aside and climbed in to pose with them.

Initially, he sat next to his sister. In his mind, it was better to avoid getting too close to Charlotte. But Charlotte had him come over next to her. His arm was the longest, so he'd get the best angle—and she wanted the moon over the water in the frame.

As they moved closer together so they could all fit inside the frame, he felt the side of her breast against his arm. It was only incidental contact—she probably didn't even notice—and yet the sexual awareness that suddenly flowed through him made him wonder if coming to Italy was going to be the best thing for him, after all. Maybe it would just make him yearn for something he couldn't have.

Lilly fingered the crisp fabric of her new dress, which was draped across the bed next to her. She loved it. When she was wearing it, she felt pretty—more like her older sister, who'd been so nice to her today. Would that last, she wondered—the niceness? Was it real and permanent or just a passing polite phase while Charlotte was in a good mood and having fun on vacation?

Because the hope rising up inside her scared her. She didn't want to start expecting something good, couldn't take the disappointment she'd face when Charlotte put her wherever she was going to put her once she was done sightseeing in Italy.

With a sigh, Lilly got up and hung her dress carefully in the wardrobe that served as a closet at the villa. Luca would be bringing Sabrina's clothes, jewelry, papers and other things tomorrow. She'd been worrying about that all day. She was afraid there were items in those boxes she didn't want Charlotte to see—items that might make her mother look bad. She didn't want her mother to embarrass her yet again.

There could even be stuff of hers Sabrina had kept, stuff she'd rather Charlotte not see. She'd been so upset about her mother's death—so shocked by it—that she hadn't paid any attention to what was left. At the time, it didn't seem to matter. Sabrina had never owned anything valuable, so there was nothing to help Lilly moneywise. And no keepsake was going to bring her mother back. Lilly hadn't wanted some picture or perfume bottle sitting on her dresser to remind her of Sabrina. Why would she want anything to remind her of her mother storming out of the house without so much as a goodbye—and then veering in front of a bus? The very thought of Sabrina doing what she always did—throwing a fit and yelling and screaming and acting like a child so that she couldn't drive right—made Lilly so angry it brought tears to her eyes.

But now she wished she'd packed those boxes herself like Luca had asked her to, because she didn't know exactly what was there. Had her mother kept her report cards?

Probably not. Sabrina had never been one to hang on to much. They'd moved around; having a lot they had to carry with them only made life harder. But Lilly was still a little apprehensive. She didn't want Charlotte to know she hadn't been a good student. She'd let school go, had been too busy trying to keep her mother happy so their lives wouldn't turn to crap again.

Not that it had ever worked. No matter how hard Lilly had tried to solve their problems—no matter what she gave up or missed in her own life so she could be there for her mother—the same cycle continued.

Still, she'd kept trying, hoping the next time would be different, and now her past could make her unacceptable to the only person who might be willing to help with her future. What if Charlotte thought she was one of those kids who wouldn't pay attention or do homework? No one wanted a kid like that, especially an adult with a choice, and Charlotte definitely had a choice.

There was always foster care. Lilly shuddered at the idea of living with strangers who had absolutely no reason to care about her beyond the money they'd receive. She wished she had a cell phone. Her mother had refused to buy her one, said she wasn't old enough, they were too expensive and she didn't want Lilly to start "running around" or spending hours and hours on social media. But now she had no way to contact Luca—not without asking Charlotte—to see if he'd make sure there wasn't anything of hers in the boxes he was about to bring over.

She doubted he'd go to the trouble of searching them even if she asked, though. He'd think she was worried about nothing, wouldn't believe it mattered. He seemed to take everything with a shrug and a smile. At first, Lilly had loved that about him. Her mother had called him "easygoing." But easygoing also meant he wouldn't stick around when times got tough, and he'd proved that. As soon as her mother grew difficult, he'd wanted them to move out—go back to America—just like that. At least Steve, the farmer, had tried to convince her mother to go to counseling. He'd said she owed it to Lilly—even offered to go with her.

Thinking of Steve reminded her of Old Blue. She missed that dog even more than her mother. He'd made her feel she mattered in the world. They'd needed each other—but no one seemed to care.

She wished she could call Steve. It would be good just to hear his voice. He never really said much, but he was steady and kind. She liked just being in the same room with him and still couldn't believe her mother had managed to mess up that situation. Steve was the best man her mother had ever dated. Even Sabrina had eventually admitted that.

A soft knock sounded on her door. Surprised since it was so late, she froze. Was she going to get in trouble? She was supposed to be in bed, but she'd been too wound up to sleep.

The knock came again, so Lilly walked over to the door. "Yes?" she said softly without opening it.

"It's Charlotte. I saw the light under the door and was worried about you. Are you okay?"

Lilly straightened. She hadn't been okay for a long time, even before her mother died. But she didn't know how to express what was going on inside her—didn't feel she'd ever been heard or understood—so she went with the answer she felt was expected. "Yes. I was just about to turn off the light," she said even though the rest of her wanted to scream and rant and cry for no particular reason.

"Okay. If you need to talk or just be with someone, I'll be sitting out on the deck for a few minutes. Feel free to come out and join me."

Was Charlotte having trouble sleeping, too? If so, why? Was she trying to decide what to do with Lilly?

Her half sister seemed nice. But Luca had been nice, too,

especially at first. That didn't mean there was anything to it. It wasn't as if he wanted to raise her. And Lilly knew that if her mother had ever been put in Charlotte's shoes, she wouldn't feel she should have to take on someone else's child—not for more than a weekend. She'd made a big deal about "getting fixed" so she wouldn't have any more kids and had always talked about how difficult it was to raise one, as if Lilly had been *such* a burden. If her own mother hadn't really wanted to take care of her, what were the chances someone else would?

"Thanks, but I'm okay." She assumed she'd have a better chance of staying on Charlotte's good side if she pretended not to need anything. That was what had always worked best with her mother. She couldn't be a bother or she'd be left behind like all the men her mother had been with in the past. "Good night."

"Good night," Charlotte echoed, and her footsteps moved away from the door.

chapter 16

At ten the following morning, Luca texted Charlotte to let her know he had a taxi—he didn't own a car; he drove one of his Vespas—waiting on the street below them. She'd been hoping Sloane and Julian would be awake and willing to help, but she hadn't specifically asked them, hadn't wanted to make them get up early if they preferred to stay in bed. They were all having difficulty adjusting to the time change. She hadn't fallen asleep until it was nearly dawn.

But she was the only one up at the appropriate hour. She didn't even have Lilly's help. She'd knocked on her half sister's door and been surprised when Lilly said she didn't want to come.

Just before she was about to step outside to go to the meeting place on her own, however, she heard footsteps. She assumed it would be Lilly, relenting, but a second later, Julian came into the kitchen. He was unshaven and yawning—clearly, he'd just rolled out of bed, hadn't even brushed his hair—but he was dressed.

"Is Luca at the meeting point?" he asked.

Charlotte felt her eyebrows slide up. "You remembered he was coming? You got up to help me?"

"Yeah. You mentioned it last night," he said. "But where's Lilly? Doesn't she want to be part of this?"

"Apparently she doesn't."

"Why not?"

"It would be hard for a girl who's just lost her mother to deal with the boxes we'll be carrying back. And Luca was pretty eager to get rid of her. That had to hurt." Charlotte didn't get the impression that Luca and Lilly had been all that close, but it would be difficult, anyway. They were so different. Luca was flexible and carefree; Lilly was serious and cautious and probably a lot less flexible because she couldn't seem to exert any control over her own situation. Because of those differences, Charlotte could see why Luca would think Lilly was difficult. She was completely closed off, wouldn't let anyone in, and once she decided something, changing her mind was almost impossible.

But there were reasons for the way Lilly was behaving, and Luca didn't seem to care enough to even try to understand. He just wanted to move on with his life.

"She's been through a lot, so I didn't push her," she added and, stepping back into the main room, craned her neck to see as far as she could up the stairs. She'd been hoping Lilly would change her mind—that they could find some common ground in taking responsibility for all that was left of Sabrina—but her half sister's door remained closed. "I guess she's really not coming."

"We can manage," he said. "Let's go."

"Okay. Once we get the boxes here, she can go through them at her leisure. Or not at all. It's up to her."

They had to zigzag through several walkways with colorful ceramic sea creatures embedded in the cement walls on both sides and descend a flight of stairs before they came out onto the street where Luca was waiting. It was down near the sea and a hotel. As the road bent to follow the coastline, Charlotte could make out an even bigger hotel on the opposite side of the street, right on the water. This wasn't the town center—with the cathedral and the square—that sat higher on the mountain. But it was the highway leading west to Positano and east to Amalfi, so it was busy.

Luca was leaning against the taxi, which had pulled into a little drive to get out of traffic. When he heard them coming, he glanced up, put his phone away and started handing boxes out of the back seat while the driver opened the trunk so they could get the rest.

They piled everything at the walkway entrance. Then Luca told the driver he'd call when they were done and helped carry load after load to the villa.

It took almost an hour and four separate trips. Charlotte could only imagine how much more difficult it would've been if Sabrina had owned as much stuff as most people her age. "We're lucky this is all of it," Charlotte muttered to Julian as they stacked the boxes in a storage room off to one side of the deck.

"You wouldn't typically bring furniture or other big items across the ocean," Julian pointed out. "She must've sold whatever she had before leaving the States."

Except Sabrina seemed to have been a rolling stone. Charlotte had the impression she'd never accumulated much. "Whatever the reason, I'm glad."

Luca came up behind them and heaved the final box on top of the rest. "There you go."

"*Grazie*," Charlotte said. "I appreciate your help."

"*Nessun problema.*" He glanced up at the house. "How's Lilly?"

Charlotte followed his gaze, but couldn't see anything except a mirror image of the stunning view they had. "She's going to be okay," she said and hoped she was right.

"*Bene*," he responded and dusted off his hands as if he was releasing himself from all future responsibility.

Considering the situation, Charlotte couldn't really hold that against him. They all said, "*Ciao*." Then he was gone, and Charlotte wondered if they'd see him again while they were in Praiano. It wasn't as if he'd expressed any interest in staying in touch.

"Not a bad guy," Julian commented.

"Because he helped carry a few boxes belonging to the woman he'd been with before she died?" Charlotte said. "He's just relieved to have Sabrina, her daughter and everything that belonged to them out of his house."

Julian dropped into a seat at the outdoor dining table. "Yeah, I get the same impression. He hinted he shouldn't have gotten involved."

She sat across from him. "I didn't hear him say that."

"It was on one of our trips to the house."

"Thank you for getting up to help me. It would've taken *so* much more time without you."

"It was nothing. It's always fun to one-up my sister, *who chose to sleep in*," he added for emphasis.

Charlotte chuckled. "Sloane probably had a hard time falling asleep last night just like I did."

"Excuses, excuses," he teased.

"Not everyone comes through the way you do," she told him. "You're like Ben—a really good guy."

"I'm a hell of a lot better than Ben," he said with a mock scowl.

Her mind immediately went to her own situation. "Well, if you're better than Ben, Cliff must not be any competition whatsoever."

"I thought that was a given."

She rolled her eyes. "I guess I should've married *you*."

He didn't laugh like she'd expected. Her last comment hung awkwardly in the air, making her wish she could snatch it back. There'd been moments when she *had* been attracted to Julian; maybe that was why. The joke had landed closer to the truth than she'd intended.

She felt her face heat up as he stood.

"You definitely don't want to marry me," he said, suddenly serious, and went inside.

Lilly stayed in her bed all morning, waiting to make sure that Charlotte and Luca had done whatever they were going to do with her mother's stuff before she so much as ventured from her room.

When she finally did come down, she was relieved not to see a single box.

"Did Luca show up this morning?" she asked Charlotte, who was sitting at the indoor dining table working on her laptop.

"He did," she said rather absent-mindedly.

"He didn't want to talk to me?"

Charlotte had been scowling at her screen, but at this, she looked up. "He asked about you, wanted to be sure you're okay."

"What'd you tell him?"

"I said you're going to be fine, because I believe you *will* be fine." She gestured toward the kitchen. "I made a caprese salad for breakfast if you'd like some. There's also fruit and granola with yogurt."

"I'm not hungry."

Charlotte checked her watch. "It's nearly two," she said in that way adults had of letting her know she'd given the wrong answer. "Are you sure?"

"I'm sure."

Lilly thought Charlotte would press her to eat, but she didn't. "Okay," she said. "It'll be there waiting for you when you're ready."

Lilly looked around, expecting to see Sloane and Julian, but Charlotte seemed to be alone. "Where is everyone?"

"Julian grabbed his camera and went out to take some pictures. Sloane's not up yet. She's still on California time. Sadly, so am I, but I have to work so I can't stay in bed. Would you like to start going through your mother's belongings while I take care of a few things here?"

Luca's delivery had been on Lilly's mind all night. She didn't want there to be anything that made her look like someone who shouldn't be taken in, but even still, she couldn't bring herself to touch her mother's possessions.

"I don't want to see any of it," she said.

Charlotte scooted her chair back. "Because going through those boxes would make you too sad about your mom?"

"I guess," she said. "I just don't want to deal with it. Where are they, anyway?"

"The boxes? In the storage room outside."

Lilly thought of her report cards. "Did you already look through everything?"

"No. It felt a little intrusive to just . . . dive right in. I wanted to wait for you."

Lilly had never had an adult treat her as if her thoughts, feelings and opinions really mattered. "You care about that?"

"Of course I do."

"What if I don't want to see any of her stuff ever again?"

"That would be okay. Just let me know."

"Why do *you* want to see it?" she asked.

"Because other than talking to you, it's my only way of getting to know Sabrina. But there's no rush. We can wait a few days, see how you feel. Maybe you'll change your mind. I have a lot to do, anyway."

Lilly threaded her fingers through the strings hanging from her cutoffs. "What do you have to do?"

"Start my next book."

"Is that what you're doing now?"

She sighed. "I wish. I'm answering emails. My editor is asking which narrator I'd prefer for the audio version, so I've been checking out the options. She's also looking for some input on the cover, but it's hard to say what the cover should be like when I don't even know what the story's going to be about."

Lilly typically tried to keep her distance from Charlotte and Charlotte's friends. She had to depend on them for everything, but the last thing she wanted was to let herself get sucker punched by hoping for and expecting a good outcome only to be handed off to some authority or other. Still, at Charlotte's remark, she stepped forward.

"You don't know what your next book is about?"

Worry lines creased Charlotte's forehead as she shook her head. "I've been surfing the internet, trying to find a good idea."

"How long does it take you to write a book?"

"Well, I've only written one, and the first isn't anything to judge by. With *Playing for Keeps*, I was sort of feeling my way through the dark, teaching myself the craft as I went along, so it was an extended process."

"You'll be able to do it faster this time?"

"Theoretically."

Lilly knew what that word meant and hated the concern that welled up. She didn't want to feel what she'd felt so often for her mother. It was too hard to take care of the adults around her. She'd done her best with Sabrina, but nothing seemed to help. Someone always said something he or she shouldn't, or her boss insisted she do something a different way and she didn't like it, or a customer tried to stiff her and that gave her an excuse to lose her temper, which meant she'd get fired if she didn't quit.

Usually, Sabrina quit. Then she acted as if she'd had no choice, that the working conditions were just too terrible to stay. And the same thing went for the men she got with. It was all great at the start, but only went downhill from there.

"How long do you have?"

"Just a few months," Charlotte admitted. "But don't worry. I'll figure it out."

What if she couldn't? What would happen then? She no longer had Cliff and his money to rely on. She'd made that clear. Would she have no way of paying the bills?

"Do you have writer's block?" Lilly asked, trying harder to understand the murky boundaries of her new situation—and the pitfalls and obstacles she might encounter.

"Maybe that's it."

"You don't know? Have you ever had it before?"

"I hit some difficult patches with my first book."

"How are you going to get over it?"

"That's a good question," Charlotte replied. "I guess I'm going to give myself permission to write something terrible."

Lilly felt her eyes go wide. "Why would you do that?"

"I need to turn off my internal editor somehow. That bitch has a stranglehold on me."

When she laughed, Lilly felt better. Because Charlotte wasn't taking it too seriously, and she hadn't felt the need to use different language than she would with Sloane—language more appropriate for children—Lilly felt more hopeful that Charlotte would be able to fight through her problems, even though Sabrina never could. "You'll come up with something?"

Charlotte must've heard the fear in her voice because she got up to come around the table. At first, Lilly was afraid she'd try to take her hands or hug her or something, which made her go cold inside, but she didn't. She just leaned against the table a foot or so away. "Even if I can't write this book and my publisher won't give me an extension, I'll make sure you have what you need and we both get through this, okay?"

Lilly wasn't convinced. Sabrina had always said she'd make things work, too—and never could. "How?"

"Because I'm capable and resourceful and I'll find a way."

Maybe that was true. Maybe Charlotte *would* find a way. But if times got even harder, it would decrease any chance Lilly had of finding a home with her half sister.

Charlotte's phone went off, and she went back near her laptop to check who it was.

Lilly's stomach sank when her half sister began rubbing her forehead as if she didn't like what she saw on the screen. "Bad news?" she guessed, feeling the panic she'd battled so often start eating at her again.

"It's my parents," Charlotte replied. "I'd better take it."

Lilly was curious about Charlotte's parents. How she interacted with them. What her life had been like. If it'd been better than living with Sabrina. If it was Charlotte who'd been the luckier of the two of them, even though she'd been the one who was put up for adoption. But she didn't want Charlotte to think she was in the way or being too nosy, so she said, "I'll get some breakfast," and went into the kitchen.

Lilly had left the room, but Charlotte carried her phone into her bedroom and closed the door anyway. She was doing her best to be kind and reassuring with her half sister, but this situation wasn't easy for her, either. The way she'd been blindsided made it difficult to forgive her parents. She also didn't want to be quizzed by them when everything was still so up in the air.

But she felt she owed them more than to grow sullen, angry and uncommunicative. They'd been good to her and weren't totally responsible for this situation.

Still, suddenly feeling so indebted to them for the rights and privileges she'd taken for granted when she thought she was a natural-born child was part of the myriad emotions she was struggling with.

"Hello?"

"There you are," Penny said. "How are things going?"

Charlotte could tell she was trying hard to compensate for the recent drama. "Fairly good, I guess."

"What does that mean? What's Lilly like?"

"She's guarded, defensive, frightened—as you can imagine."

"I was hoping you'd send us a picture, at least. I'd love to see her. Maybe we could even have a Zoom call where you introduce us."

Her mother was obviously insecure about what was happening and eager to be part of it. But this was something Charlotte had to work through before everything could go back to normal. "I'm not ready yet."

There was a prolonged silence. Penny wasn't used to meeting with any resistance, not when they were getting along, and they were almost always getting along.

The sudden guilt she felt for being the one to change that added to the other negative emotions Charlotte was experiencing.

"Okay," her mother said at length. "Well, I'm here when you're ready."

Squeezing her eyes closed, Charlotte began to knead her temples. "Lilly's a pretty girl and will be beautiful one day," she volunteered, just to have something to say that wasn't emotionally charged. "She looks like her mother. Did you ever meet Sabrina?"

"No. Our caseworker had us come get you from the hospital. We were open to meeting her in person, but she didn't feel up to it and, of course, we didn't want to make the situation any harder on her. The agency agreed to deliver a letter we wrote, thanking her for letting us have you and promising to do all we could to give you a good life. We hoped it would reassure her. Of course, she already knew a great deal about us from the application. She picked us from among many families. We submitted pictures and everything."

This revelation only made her feel worse. Penny was clearly proud to have won the parent lottery, but Charlotte could only focus on the fact that her birth mother had never even tried to see her. "So it was an open adoption, but she never reached out?"

Charlotte had looked up the difference on the internet. A closed adoption meant no identifying information was shared with the adoptive parents, and there was no ongoing contact. An open adoption meant that information, updates and sometimes even visits were allowed.

"It was a semiopen adoption, I guess you could say," Penny explained. "Her parents didn't hide her identity. They allowed us to have a few pictures, her medical records and background information. We wanted to be sure she hadn't been taking drugs, you know, and tests revealed she hadn't. But we didn't have any other contact."

Why not? Charlotte wondered. Sabrina hadn't been curious about her? Hadn't wanted to meet her first child, even after she became an adult and had Lilly? Why had Sabrina simply given Charlotte up and walked away without ever looking back? And what about Sabrina's parents? Why weren't they ever interested enough to contact her?

Charlotte couldn't wait for the results of her DNA test with Ancestry.com, but she was scared about what they might reveal at the same time.

"What does she have to say about her father?" Penny asked. "And her grandparents?"

"I haven't asked about them yet."

"Why not?"

"Because she's twelve, Mom, and her mother died only a short time ago. Not only that, but I'm still almost a total stranger to her. I don't want to make it sound like I only came to Italy to pawn her off on someone else. I want to build a relationship with her before going after certain information. If I can get her to trust me, she might open up and say more than she otherwise would."

"I understand that. I just thought . . . She hasn't volunteered anything about her relatives? I assumed she would've said *something*."

"She hasn't. Not a word. So far, she's been reluctant to talk about her mother at all—doesn't even want to go through Sabrina's belongings."

"Did they not have a good relationship?"

"That's hard to determine."

"The Italian man they were living with can't tell you that much?"

"They lived with Luca for three short months, and he and I have only had two conversations, both of which revolved around logistics—like getting Lilly and her things and Sabrina's personal effects."

"He gave you Sabrina's stuff, too?"

"He had to do something with it."

"What about shipping it to her parents or a sibling or something? What will you do with it?"

"It should probably stay with Lilly. Anyway, I have to see what's all there before I make any decisions."

"When will you go through it?"

"When Lilly has a chance to decide if she wants to do it with me. At the moment, she doesn't seem eager to do so."

"Maybe it's too painful for her to think about her mother."

"Probably. I'm giving her time to adjust to everything before I bug her about it. I have to get a few things done for my editor today, anyway."

There was another pause. "Speaking of your editor, have you started your new book?"

The panic Charlotte felt clamped down harder. What was she going to do about her book? "Not yet. But I'm looking for an idea right now, and once I find one, I'm going to stick with it and push through. No more changing my mind. No more uncertainty."

"Okay. If you need me to fly over there and help with Lilly so you can sequester yourself away and concentrate, let me know."

She knew it was not an empty promise—her parents would do whatever they could—and that made her feel she was being too hard on Penny. "Thanks, Mom," she said.

"I have always loved you so much," her mother said.

Charlotte dropped back onto the bed. "I love you, too."

"Let us know how it goes."

"I will," she promised and disconnected. She was about to return to her computer—she had to power through or the tension and stress would only ratchet higher—but at the last second, instead of getting up, she called Julian.

"Where are you?" she asked as soon as he said hello.

"There's an old convent above Praiano. I hiked up to it. Why?"

She didn't know why *exactly*. She'd just needed to hear his voice. "I was . . . curious."

"Do you need me for anything?"

She tried to think of something but couldn't. "No."

There was a long silence. Then he said, "So this is work avoidance?"

She covered her eyes with one arm. "Maybe."

"Okay, that's it. I'm going to call Sloane and have her bring Lilly here. The climb will be good exercise for them—whether they will like it or not—and everyone will be out of the house for the next several hours so you can concentrate."

As nice as that was, *she* wanted to be the one to go find him. She didn't care how high she had to climb. She didn't want to think about Cliff or her divorce or her deadline or what she was going to do about Lilly. She definitely didn't want to write in her current frame of mind. She just wanted to enjoy Italy at Julian's side. There was something cathartic about his presence, his humor, his smile.

"You're trying to take photographs," she said. "They'll be fine here."

"Charlotte."

"What?"

"Block everything out and write five pages. That's it. That's all you have to do. Then the four of us will get some cheese, salami, dates, nuts, apples and other charcuterie fixings, along with a nice bottle of wine, and enjoy a relaxing evening so you can recharge and get up tomorrow and write five more pages. One day at a time. That's how you're going to approach this—a little progress every day so nothing's too overwhelming."

He made it sound easy. But the constant emotional upheaval was killing her creativity. "What should I do with Sabrina's stuff in the storage room?"

"You don't have to decide now. It's not going anywhere.

And there's no rush to make any decisions regarding Lilly. We'll all just live in the moment—enjoy our stay here in Italy while you write your book and see where life leads us."

"And my divorce?"

"Leave that in America for now."

"But I don't want to write, Jules. I want to be with you," she admitted.

He hesitated before saying, "That's your fight or flight kicking in. You're trying to flee to safety, but I can't let you. You need to stay in the fight and battle it out. I'm here to help, though. We'll get through the next month together, taking it one day at a time, like I said."

She drew a deep breath. "Okay. But I'm going to call you as soon as I get to five pages—even if they're terrible."

"That's fine. Just write them. You can always fix them later."

She was so grateful for him and his friendship at this critical moment, tears sprang to her eyes.

"You okay?" he asked when she didn't say goodbye.

She sniffed. "Yeah."

When he spoke again, his voice was filled with conviction. "You can do it," he said.

"Okay, coach," she responded, and she kept repeating what he'd told her as she went back to her computer and started a story about a woman who had a near-death experience that changed everything about the way she wanted to live the rest of her life.

chapter 17

Sloane was beginning to get the feeling that something was bothering her brother, something much bigger than jet lag. Julian wasn't quite present, not in the way he normally was. But Sloane couldn't even begin to guess why. He smiled and joked like his usual self, and yet, when he didn't think she was watching, the smile slid from his face and he seemed to get lost in his own thoughts.

She and Lilly sat on a stone bench at a right angle to the seat he'd taken a few feet from them while listening to two men, one on a flute and the other on a tuba, play classical music in the courtyard of the Convent of San Domenico—a concert they hadn't known about but chanced upon when she and Lilly arrived to meet Julian. She watched him stare at the grass as the wind stirred it at his feet and got the impression he wasn't even hearing the music.

Lilly leaned toward her. "Is something wrong?" she murmured, keeping her voice low so she wouldn't bother a smattering of other tourists and locals who'd made the trek up the mountain to hear the concert—or just to see the area, like they'd done.

Sloane quickly masked her concern. "Nothing. I'm just tired. Aren't you? We climbed so many stairs."

"One thousand," she said proudly.

Sloane shifted to get more comfortable on the hard surface. "Exactly a thousand?"

"I think so. I don't know for sure. I've just heard that the convent is a thousand steps above Praiano. The locals say it all the time. But the climb's worth it, don't you think?" Lilly stretched tall to look out over the sea. The convent had a spectacular view of the deep blue water below them, Positano and even the Island of Capri, much farther away.

"For this view? Absolutely. Although…if we climb anymore, I might need a sherpa," she said with a laugh. "How often did your mother bring you up here?"

As they were walking, Lilly had mentioned that she and Sabrina had done the same hike. "Only once. We brought a picnic."

Sloane set the program a woman had given her listing the various pieces to be performed to one side. "Did Luca come with you?"

She shook her head. "He had to work."

"Must've been a fun mother-daughter outing," Sloane said, watching for her reaction. Lilly was obviously bottling up a lot of emotions, and if Sloane had her guess, most of them were negative. Sloane wished she could let them out, believed she'd be better off if she could, but she was far too wary—and, Sloan suspected, too loyal to her mother.

"We always had fun when it was just the two of us," she said wistfully.

"How often did you get away alone together?"

Closing her eyes, she tilted her face up toward the sun. "Not very often once we came to Italy. She was with Luca most of the time. But we had a few months together after we left Steve and the farm in Iowa and moved to California."

Was that what Lilly clung to? The memories of what her mother was like during the rare times Sabrina wasn't with a man who took all of her time and attention?

Sloane wanted to put an arm around the girl's shoulders, but she knew Lilly would only pull away. Lilly wasn't comfortable with physical contact, dodged it whenever she could.

"Sometimes mothers are so busy trying to fulfill their own needs they can't see beyond them," Sloane said softly, hoping that by understanding, Lilly could also find forgiveness and healing.

"My mom didn't do anything wrong," she said. "I wasn't saying that. She was a good mom."

Lilly came to her mother's defense so often. Sloane wanted to say, "The lady doth protest too much, methinks," but she was fairly certain Lilly had never read *Hamlet* and wouldn't understand such an allusion. "Of course she was," she said instead. "But being a mother is a hard job, and no one's perfect, right?"

Lilly seemed to relax. Then she leaned over to whisper again. "What's Penny like?"

"The woman who raised Charlotte? She's a very nice person—but also not perfect," Sloane added with a grin.

Several people who'd paused to listen for a few minutes slipped away from the small gathering and continued the trek up Monte Sant'Angelo a Tre Pizzi, which was the name of the mountain. Before the concert started, Sloane had seen knots of people moving above them on the famous hike called Path of the Gods (Sentiero degli Dei). Julian wanted to try it, but Sloane wasn't ready for that—not today. They'd gotten too late a start, for one. And they'd already climbed nearly four hundred feet.

"Is she upset that Charlotte had to come to Italy?" Lilly asked.

"Charlotte didn't *have* to come to Italy," Sloane replied with a smile. "She came because she wanted to—to meet you."

Julian left his camera on the bench near them as he got up and walked over to the two-foot stone wall enclosing the grounds, closer to the cliff. He'd bought coffee from the man who sat at the entrance with a sign listing prices, in euros, for a few limited refreshments, and carried his cup, sipping from it as he stood facing the sea.

"Excuse me for a moment," Sloane said to Lilly and walked over to stand next to him.

When he noticed her presence, he turned slightly but didn't react.

"Are you going to tell me what's going on?" Sloane whispered.

He lowered his coffee cup. "Not sure what you mean."

"I'm your twin sister, Jules. And, yes, I've been absorbed with my new business and my own problems for the past year or more, but you've been absorbed, too—and happy, as far as what you've told me. But something's wrong. I can always tell. At first, I chalked it up to jet lag, but now . . ."

"It's nothing," he insisted.

She glanced over her shoulder to make sure they weren't bothering anyone by talking, but they were far enough away from the group and the performers that no one seemed to be paying any attention to them.

"Bullshit," she said, turning back. "You volunteered to help Mom and Dad through two minor surgeries."

"So? I'm a nice guy," he said with a grin.

She couldn't argue with that. But that grin didn't reach his eyes. It'd been manufactured for her benefit. "True, but normally it would be me."

He put his cup in his other hand. "Consider yourself lucky, then."

"The problem is that you don't seem to be in any rush to get back to your job. Have you grown bored with it?"

"No, I love my job."

That was what she'd thought. "So . . . is it the gallery? Was it a mistake to take that on? Tell me, Jules. If you need money, I'll come up with it somehow—help you get a loan, sell anything I own. Don't box me out."

"I love you, too," he said, "but I'm not ready to talk about it."

Her stomach plummeted. There *was* something wrong. "But . . . it's nothing serious, right?" she said imploringly. "There's some stupid woman who's broken your heart or something like that. You'll get over it in time, right?"

"It's nothing serious," he echoed, but something about his words didn't ring true. Maybe it was that he was staring out at the sea instead of meeting her gaze and really trying to convince her.

The panic inside her notched a bit higher. "Then why won't you tell me?"

"Because I need time to deal with it on my own."

She looped her arm through his. They'd both been busy leading their separate lives over the past several years, but he was her rock, her foundation. Nothing could happen to him or her whole world would fall apart. It'd been the two of them—always on the same side—since the womb.

"Whatever it is, we'll take it on together," she whispered fiercely.

A sad smile curved his lips. "I appreciate that, but this is one battle I'm going to have to fight alone."

She leaned her head on his shoulder. "You're scaring me. It's not cancer, is it?"

"No, it's not cancer."

"Something just as bad?" She searched his face for some indication of just how worried she should be.

His jaw tightened. "Stop," he snapped, and that was probably the most terrifying thing of all because there was nothing playful about it, and he was almost always playful. "I need more time."

She gripped his arm tighter. "Okay, I'll back off. But—"

"No, you won't back off. I shouldn't have said anything," he broke in and pulled away from her to stride over to where he'd been sitting before, close to Lilly, who'd been watching them as if they'd disappear if she so much as blinked. No doubt she could read the tension in their bodies and was so used to the adults around her not being completely reliable that what she saw alarmed her.

"Everything's okay," Sloane murmured as she returned to her seat and patted the girl's knee, and Lilly was so busy watching them for any telltale sign that everything *wasn't* okay that she didn't even bother to slide out of reach.

Ben was just leaving work when his phone went off. Surprised to see that it was from his wife—it was one in the morning on the Amalfi Coast—he answered on Bluetooth as he backed out of his space. "Hey, you're still up?" he said.

"I don't think I'll be able to sleep," she replied.

"The time change is brutal."

"It's not the time change."

He stepped on the brake. "Then what is it?"

"It's Julian, Ben. Something's wrong with him."

He pulled back into his space and shifted into Park so he could concentrate on the call instead of rush hour traffic. "Can you be more specific?"

"He won't tell me what it is. But he's not himself. He's quiet, takes off on his own as if he needs time to himself, seems a bit listless and won't really engage because he doesn't want me to badger him."

"Then *don't* badger him," he said. "Give him time."

"That's easier said than done when I'm *this* worried."

He'd known when he married a twin that he'd have to share more of his wife than he would have otherwise. Fortunately, he loved Julian—had never resented his presence or his close relationship with Sloane because Julian had been an incredible brother-in-law. "What do you think it could be?"

"I asked him if it was cancer."

Ben gripped the steering wheel tighter. "Cancer! Oh, God. Tell me it's not that. Does he *look* like he has cancer?"

"No, he looks healthy to me—mostly. Maybe a *little* less robust than usual. It's more that he's preoccupied and upset about something."

"Would your parents know what it could be?"

"I doubt it. I'm not even going to ask them. I know he wouldn't appreciate that. If he won't tell me, he's not telling anyone."

"Good idea. I can just see your mother calling him immediately. Karen means well, but she won't let him rest if she thinks he should tell her what's going on."

"Exactly."

"Maybe it has to do with his work."

"He claims all is going well there. Still, I'm hoping that's it. Problems at work would be better than so many other things. We could help him with money, if he needs it."

They didn't have a lot of extra money themselves, but Ben would help Julian, no question. "He's there in Italy with you. He'll talk to you when he's ready."

"So I need to calm down and wait?"

"That's what I'd do."

"Because *you* are a calm person. I am not. I'm high-strung and totally freaked out right now."

He chuckled. "I love you just the way you are."

"I wish you were here, Ben. I always feel better when you're around."

"I wish the same thing."

"Come over for the last week," she suggested once again. "What the hell. It's Italy."

"I can't, and you know it. We already used my vacation days when we went to Niagara Falls for our anniversary six months ago."

"I hate that you're so tied down."

"The curse of working for someone else."

"Actually, I put in as many hours—or more—than you do," she pointed out.

And he could let his work go once he left it each night. So there was that. "Pros and cons."

"Do you miss me?" she asked.

"Of course I do."

There was a slight pause. Then she said, "Do you think we're meant to spend the rest of our lives together?"

He felt his chest tighten. That was the big question, wasn't it? "I think it's time we figured it out."

She went silent.

"Sloane?"

"I was hoping you'd reassure me."

"I'd like to do that. But we'd better start talking about the issues that stand between us. And somehow it's easier while you're gone."

"Is that why you were so supportive of me leaving?" she asked.

He pulled out of the parking stall and rolled to the light. "I wanted you to be able to support Charlotte. But, yes, that was part of it."

"Are you not happy being with me?"

"I'm happy being with you. But will I be happy staying with you if our lives don't include children? You don't want them, right? That's what's standing between us. I know you'd rather not admit it, but it's becoming obvious."

"What if I have them anyway?" she asked.

"I don't want you to 'have them anyway.' I don't want to feel like you're doing me a favor. I want you to *want* children, and I can't make that happen and neither can you. So where do we go from here?"

"I wish I knew," she said. "Why does it have to be this hard?"

"If marriage was easy, the divorce rate wouldn't be so high."

"I love you," she said. "I hope you know that. I don't think I could find anyone who's half as good a person as you are."

"I hope you're not out there looking," he said jokingly.

"Of course not."

"Then relax and get some sleep. Things will be better in the morning."

"Okay," she said, and the call disconnected.

Ben remained in his car for several minutes even after he reached home. It was hard having Sloane gone, but he felt it was important they finally address the uncertainty that'd been eating away at their peace of mind. He was also worried about Julian. Was Sloane right? Was something wrong with him? And, if so, how would that impact her?

The next morning, while everyone else was still sleeping, Lilly stood outside the storage room that held her mother's belongings. For the most part, she knew what she'd find in the boxes Luca had brought—Sabrina's cheap costume jewelry, the clothes she bought even when they didn't have the money, a few knickknacks she'd kept on her dresser and case upon case of makeup and perfume.

Sabrina had always gotten what she wanted when it came to beauty products, even when they should've been paying for other stuff instead. They couldn't pay their rent, and yet she'd come home with a new outfit or spend over a hundred dollars at Sephora. It'd cost two thousand dollars for her to get hair extensions before they moved to the Amalfi Coast; then they'd left their one-bedroom place in Fort Bragg without paying the last month's rent or the electric bill.

The landlady had called several times, but Sabrina had already spent the money. She finally just blocked her. Lilly had seen her do it. The knowledge that they hadn't paid the nice woman who'd let them move into the small house in her backyard—when they had nowhere else to go and couldn't afford a place that required first and last month's rent and a security deposit—made Lilly's stomach churn with embarrassment and humiliation. But it didn't seem to faze Sabrina. She wouldn't even talk about it.

Lilly opened the door. She should get her mother's phone, if it was there, but just the sight of those boxes made her eyes burn with unshed tears. Seeing and touching her mother's things—especially her phone—would make the fact that Sabrina was never coming back too real. That phone had meant more to Sabrina than anything else. Sometimes, Lilly couldn't even get her mother to respond to her, she was so caught up in doing something on her phone. She had it in her hand all the time, was constantly on one of her dating apps or Instagram—or texting some guy, even if she already had a boyfriend. She'd once joked that it never hurt to have a Plan B. She'd said that when they were with Steve. It was what had alerted Lilly that even though they'd finally found a wonderful home and a really good person to share their lives with, neither would be theirs for very long.

"Hey, what are you up to today?"

Lilly turned to see Julian, who'd come out of the house carrying his camera. He was always the first to get up, seemed more accustomed to jet lag than his sister or Charlotte.

"Nothing," she replied, even though she'd been thinking that if she could find her mother's phone, she could call Steve.

He'd always been kind to her, had tried to make them a real family, so maybe he wouldn't mind hearing from her. Lilly knew he'd called to check on her now and then, even after they left the States. She'd heard her mother tell him not to bother them again, that what she did with her own daughter was none of his business.

Julian gestured toward the storage room. "Are you ready to go through your mother's things? It's a nice quiet morning, might be a good time."

She closed the door. "Not really. Not all of it, anyway. I was just wondering about her phone. Unless someone pays the bill, it won't work very long, so I was thinking that maybe . . . maybe I should write down some numbers before they're gone."

"That's a really good idea," he said. "Hopefully, it hasn't been turned off already."

The fact that it might be added a jolt of alarm to her other emotions. She had to dig into those boxes—and the sooner the better. Her mother was always behind on the bills. They'd shut off her phone service before, and she'd had to pay a penalty and reconnection fee. Lilly remembered her cursing about it. It'd also caused a fight with Luca because she'd wanted him to pay it for her, and he wouldn't. He'd said she hadn't even tried to pick up any extra shifts at her bartending job, and she'd said that was because she'd wanted to spend time with him and thought he'd wanted to spend time with her. It had been their first fight.

"Do you know if Luca even brought it?" Lilly asked hesitantly.

"I'm assuming he did. Why wouldn't he?"

Because Sabrina owed Luca a lot of money and that phone was the only thing he could sell to get some of that money back. He'd said as much when Lilly had asked if she could have it—a request he'd shot down right away, saying she was too young and wouldn't be able to pay the monthly bill.

"No reason," she mumbled. "I just . . . I thought maybe he gave it to Charlotte and didn't put it in with her other things."

"Charlotte hasn't said anything. But you could ask her."

"Yeah, I'll check with her when she wakes up."

"That could be a while. I got a text from her in the middle of the night telling me she'd finished the first five pages of her new book."

"That's good, isn't it?"

"It's fantastic, but it also means she needs to get some sleep. Sloane's already rumbling around. She's about to take a shower and begin her day. Is there any chance you'd like to go for a walk with me?"

"Where are you going?"

"Don't know yet. Sometimes I just go out to see what I can see—and if I'm feeling it, I take some pictures. Are you hungry? We could grab some breakfast while we're roaming around."

She wanted to find her mother's phone before it got shut off so she could save Steve's number and check on Old Blue. But she wasn't even sure the phone was in the boxes, which she didn't want to touch in the first place.

Besides, there was something about Julian that reminded her of Steve—he wasn't only nice; he was steady and reliable. Just the sound of his voice made her feel better. She craved more of that steadiness, and now that she knew Charlotte had started her book, she'd probably have to continue working on it, and Lilly would be left alone with Sloane, whom she didn't trust as much, so she decided to go with him. She didn't know him that well, but he typically didn't ask her a lot of dumb questions, didn't try to get her to talk about things she didn't want to and seemed fine just taking things as they came.

"I don't have any money," she said. "So I don't want to eat. Going out costs more." Luca always complained about that when Sabrina wanted to eat out. "But I'll walk with you."

"Lilly, you're only twelve," he said. "Quit trying to carry the world on your shoulders. I don't expect you to have money. If I offer something, you're welcome to take it. If I don't want to pay, I won't suggest it in the first place, okay?"

She felt her body sag as some of the worst of her emotions eased. She hated being so needy, hated that she was too young to take care of herself. So many of the men her mother had been with resented the money she cost them. But at least Julian wasn't making her feel terrible about it. "Thank you."

He grinned at her. "Let's get out of here and see what we can find."

"Shouldn't I leave a note for Charlotte?" she asked hesitantly.

"I'll text her."

chapter 18

Charlotte woke up relieved because of the progress she'd made on her new book. Not only had she written five pages last night—she liked them. That was huge. She could already tell that Josie, her heroine, would be forced to rethink her marriage. The conflict wasn't villain vs. angel; it was a partner who wouldn't change when thriving—for Josie—meant moving in a different direction.

When was it ever right to walk away? That was the big question. And there was no perfect answer—no answer that would fit everyone. Josie might decide that living her best life required a different partner, which would be painful.

Exploring that idea was giving Charlotte a fresh take on marriage—making her more willing to remain vulnerable, more honest about growth and change, and more open to splitting when commitment became a cage. It might draw pushback from some readers, but since it was helping her through her own divorce, she believed there would be others like her who needed to hear the same message.

So . . . if she could just maintain her level of enthusiasm for the story, really get her heart and imagination into it instead of fearing and dreading it, she might enjoy the process the way she had with her first book.

She had a long way to go before "The End," and the pain in her personal life would intrude when she least expected it. But having started the manuscript and having a sense of direction with it took some of the pressure off. At least she could give her editor a paragraph or two about the story so the art department could get going on the cover. Then she'd do exactly as Julian had said and focus on the five pages she needed to write each day. The rest would take care of itself.

Last night, she'd counted the days until her deadline. Five pages wasn't a quick enough pace to finish in time, but it was doable, even in her current situation, and would put her within reach of the finish line before she was *catastrophically* late. She hoped her publisher would be able to live with that since it was the best she could do at the moment—unless she miraculously got so swept up she somehow managed to produce more.

She yawned, stretched and pulled her phone into bed with her. She'd heard from Cliff, she realized. His name was bolded to signal the fact that he'd sent a message she hadn't yet seen, making her grimace. He'd hurt her so badly she didn't even want to read it. If he was asking for her address in Italy so he could mail her the divorce papers, it would just prove how tone-deaf and insensitive he really was. What was the rush? Why force her to deal with the logistics of their split on top of everything else she was going through right now?

And if he'd changed his mind and wanted her back? She wasn't convinced that would be any better. If he softened any more than he already had, it could create a desire to give up the battle she was waging to save her career and do the right thing by her half sister. For the most part, she'd been happy when she was married to him. Could he have been a better person and husband? Of course. There'd been bumps along the road.

But she'd always focused on the good times and making the relationship work, so she certainly would never have left him.

Knowing whatever he'd sent would evoke strong emotions either way, she decided not to look. She couldn't risk letting him upset her when she'd just started her book. She had to protect her muse. And she couldn't risk what could happen to Lilly if he wanted to repair their marriage.

Ignoring it, she clicked on a new message from Julian instead.

> Hey, sleepyhead. Took little sis out for breakfast and a walkabout to give you the chance to go through Sabrina's phone without her being around.

If Luca hadn't already mentioned the sexual nature of some of the text messages he'd discovered on Sabrina's phone, Charlotte probably wouldn't even have considered going through it on her own. Since Sabrina had always been a stranger to her, doing so felt invasive and weird.

But Lilly was too young to see some of the things Luca had indicated were there. Charlotte had taken a break from writing to discuss the situation with Julian last night before he went to bed. After that odd moment on the deck when he'd helped her move Sabrina's boxes into the storage room and she'd made things awkward by saying she should've married him instead of Cliff, she hadn't seen much of him. But she'd approached him last night while Sloane and Lilly were playing checkers in the house to make sure everything was as it had always been between them. What he said and did helped and comforted her. He'd sort of taken over Sloane's position in that regard, which was a little surprising, but she had enough to think about, wasn't going to worry about that, too. She was enjoying

Sloane, as well, and was glad the way she'd behaved when she was married to Cliff—giving in to the pressure he put on her instead of doing more to insist he accept her friends and family the way she'd accepted his—hadn't permanently damaged their relationship.

How long will you be gone? she wrote, responding to the message he'd sent this morning.

As long as you need us to be.

I'll find her phone and text you when I'm done. Thank you!

Again, she recalled the comment she'd made about marrying him and cringed. He must have found that *way* out of line. He'd been around so much while they were growing up, and they were so familiar with each other and each other's families. He probably looked at her like a second sister and was put off by the idea of anything romantic between them. That had to be why he'd reacted the way he did, even though she'd only been joking.

Well, she'd *mostly* been joking. A woman could do a lot worse than marry Julian. Not only was he handsome, he was clever, fun, warm, protective, kind and demonstrative.

There you go again! Quit thinking about him in that way, she chastised herself and jumped out of bed.

After pulling on a lightweight sweatshirt and a pair of shorts, she shoved her feet into some flip-flops and was almost out of the room—wasn't even going to brush her hair or teeth since she didn't know how long it would take to find Sabrina's phone and wanted to get to it right away so she didn't strand Julian for hours—when she remembered Cliff's text and stopped dead in the doorway.

What was he saying? Was he finalizing the divorce or wanting to get back together?

Closing her eyes so she wouldn't actually see what he'd written, she clicked on his message to remove the bolding that set it apart from the messages she'd already seen. She didn't want that notification glaring at her every time she glanced at her phone, didn't want to be reminded that he'd sent *anything*. She had to deal with her book and her sister. That meant forgetting about Cliff, at least while she was in Italy, whether he still wanted her or not.

Shoving her phone in the pocket of her cutoffs, she rushed into the living room and kitchen area and was heading straight for the doors that led onto the deck when Sloane startled her by calling out from not very far away.

"Hey, you just getting up?"

Charlotte whipped around to see her friend lounging on the sofa reading the latest Kristin Hannah novel. "Oh, I'm glad you're awake," she said. "Come help me find Sabrina's phone. I need to go through it."

"Why the rush?" Sloane asked, but set her book aside as she got up.

"I want to do it before Lilly gets back."

"Because . . ."

"Because Luca told me Sabrina was sexting other guys. I don't want Lilly to see anything like that. It could traumatize her for life."

"Are you sure *we* want to see it?" she asked, wrinkling her nose in distaste.

Charlotte would've laughed at Sloane's response, but she was in too much of a hurry. "Better us than a twelve-year-old."

"I can't say I've been all that impressed with what I've learned about Sabrina so far," she admitted ruefully. "This might come off as insensitive, but I think you should be glad she gave you up."

Charlotte paused to respond more thoughtfully. "I'm well aware that I was much better off with Penny and Don. But I'm trying not to be too hard on my birth mother. Who knows what drove her? To me, it seems as if she was more than a little lost—always chasing something she couldn't find."

"That's very generous of you. But I still say she should've been a better mother to Lilly."

Charlotte couldn't argue with that. Sabrina was almost assuredly the person responsible for the fear, uncertainty and insecurity she saw in her younger sister's eyes.

They stepped out into a gusty day with sunlight dripping over the sea like paint rolling down an artist's canvas. "What are you going to do with Sabrina's phone when you're done with it?" Sloane asked.

"I don't know," she replied. "Why?"

"You should give it to Lilly."

"She's too young for a phone," Charlotte said, closing the door behind them.

"I don't think so," Sloane argued. "I googled it just this morning. Most guidance says thirteen or fourteen is the appropriate age for a smartphone."

"Lilly's only twelve."

"She's twelve and a half. What's a few months? Besides, thanks to the kind of life she's lived, she's probably older than her years. She doesn't talk much, but there's a lot going on behind those big eyes of hers."

Charlotte had so many decisions ahead of her she wasn't particularly interested in making this one right now. "We'll see," she said and lifted the top box out of the storage closet.

"That phone is all her mother left her," Sloane continued as she took a different box and carried it to the table. "It might give her a feeling of independence and power at a time when she really needs both. Who's she going to call, anyway?"

"It's not about who she'd call, Sloane. It's about what she might find on the internet."

"She already has a tablet for her schoolwork. She can go on the internet whenever she wants. And there are restrictions you can put on phones that block children from certain sites."

"Even if that's true, a smartphone will give her greater access to social media, and social media is so unhealthy for young girls. I don't want her to compare herself to other kids her age who seem to have everything—or constantly feel left out because it appears as if everyone's having fun except her."

Sloane opened her box. "She has to be feeling pretty left out *now*. I think a smartphone would reconnect her. Make her feel less vulnerable. Besides, we can teach her the proper perspective."

Charlotte looked up in surprise. "*We can teach her the proper perspective?* In a month?"

"Probably not in a month, but . . ."

Charlotte set the curling iron and other hair care products she'd found in her box to the side. "I thought you were against me keeping her."

"I'm just being more cautious than Julian. I want to be sure it's what's best for *both* you and Lilly. But since you lead with your heart, just like my brother, you'll probably do it, regardless."

Charlotte started to laugh.

"What?" Sloane grumbled with a scowl.

"Lilly's growing on you already, isn't she?"

Sloane responded with a sheepish shrug. "She's not a bad kid."

Charlotte was about to say Lilly was a *good* kid. She was truly beginning to believe that, despite Luca's take. But the words caught in her throat. She'd thought it might take an hour or more to dig through all the boxes and was frustrated that Luca would mix something as important as Sabrina's cellphone in with all her other belongings. But Sabrina's purse was right beneath the hair tools—and the phone was inside it.

"So would it be okay if we talked about your mother a little bit?" Julian asked as he watched Lilly pick at the chocolate-filled croissant he'd just bought her. They were sitting at a table on the narrow street that went through the heart of Praiano, taking in the sights and sounds of the quaint little town. A few cars and several Vespas zipped by, but most people were on foot. Tourists were scarce this early; it was mostly locals buying groceries, sweeping sidewalks and opening shops.

"What do you want to know about her?" she asked, keeping her gaze on her plate.

Julian took a drink of his oat-milk latte. "Nothing too personal, just general stuff."

Her expression still wary, she glanced up. "Like . . ."

He shrugged, keeping it casual. "Was she a happy person?"

Lilly seemed to be okay with that question. "Most of the time, I guess."

"What kinds of things did she like to do?"

"Shop. Go to the beach. Shop," she said again with a fond smile.

Lilly had a sense of humor, Julian realized and smiled back. "What kinds of things did she buy?"

"Clothes, shoes, makeup."

Julian assumed those things weren't for Lilly or Lilly would've made that clear. "She liked to dress up and go out?"

She nodded. "I think that's why she didn't want to stay in Iowa."

"Because there was nowhere to go?"

"It was a really small town. She used to tell Steve, 'It doesn't even have a movie theater.' And we lived out on a farm with nothing but corn around us."

"Did you hate it there, too?"

She took a bite of the croissant. "No," she replied as she chewed. "I *loved* it."

"What did you love about it?"

She thought for a moment. Then she said, "A lot of things. The tire swing Steve put up. The big porch on the old house where he'd sit in the rocking chair that used to belong to his parents and have a drink at night. The apple tree—apples have never tasted so good. But mostly Old Blue."

"Who's Old Blue?"

"My dog. Well, Steve's dog. In a way. He didn't buy him or anything. He said Old Blue just showed up one day and moved in, and Steve allowed him to stay. Blue was blind and lived in the barn. I tried to get him to move inside the house with me, but he liked to be by the horses."

"You two became friends?"

"*Best* friends," she confirmed.

"Is that the only pet you've ever had?"

"I had a cat once. But my mom made me give him away when we moved because he shed a lot and scratched up the furniture. And she said it was too expensive to take care of him, that it was hard enough just to take care of me."

"How long ago was that?"

"I was in the fourth grade."

She seemed to feel safe and unthreatened by the conversation, so he continued, "Have you had any contact with your grandparents over the years?"

"No."

"Why not?"

She frowned. "They didn't get along with my mom, didn't like what she did."

"All that shopping?" he asked with a grin.

A brief smile curved her lips, but then she looked down.

"And all the men. Moving around. Leaving me home to go out. That sort of thing."

"They made that clear?"

"I could hear them fighting. They fought a lot," she added ruefully.

"Did they like the farmer?"

"Steve? They never met him. They were out of our lives by then."

They hadn't tried to stay in contact with their granddaughter? That was unfortunate. She'd obviously needed them, but maybe Sabrina had made it impossible.

"Where do they live? Are they still in California?"

She shrugged.

He wanted to ask more about Sabrina's parents but didn't want to make her feel bad, especially when she was just coming out of her shell a little bit. "What about aunts and uncles? Do you have any of those?"

"My mother's sister was the good daughter. My mom used to say she was the black sheep of the family."

He crossed one leg over the other and leaned back. "Meaning your mother was the bad daughter?"

"I guess. Aunt Justine had a skiing accident and is in a wheelchair these days, I think." She pushed her plate away, leaving her croissant only half-eaten. "Are you looking for someone to take me? Are you going to ask about my dad next? Because he says my mother got pregnant on purpose, to trap him, and he doesn't care what happens to us."

"How do you know that? You heard him say it?"

"My mom told me." She sighed. "Steve's the only one who ever wanted me. I would've stayed there, but my mom said he must be a perv like Walter to want to keep a young girl in the house."

Apprehension bit deeply as he asked, "Perv as in pervert?"

She nodded.

"Who's Walter?"

Her face went dark. "The guy we lived with in Colorado."

"What was he like?"

"Never mind. I don't want to talk about him," she said and the way she clamped her lips into a thin, straight line told Julian she was done talking.

He didn't press her. He wanted her to feel safe, to trust him. But he made a mental note of the name of Sabrina's Colorado boyfriend, and when Lilly went to the bathroom, he texted Charlotte. Is there a Walter in Sabrina's phone?

He didn't get an answer, so he figured he'd have to talk to her about it later. Lilly's whole demeanor had changed when she mentioned that name. Something had happened with "Walter," and it wasn't hard to guess that it'd made a significant impact.

chapter 19

Once they plugged it into the charger, Sabrina's phone revealed more than Charlotte had ever wanted to learn about her birth mother. She'd been hoping to gain some sense of who Sabrina was, where the woman had come from emotionally and geographically—and whether she'd missed out in some sense by being given away. But what she and Sloane read in Sabrina's texts and dating-app messages revealed a part of her birth mother that should've remained private.

"Ugh," Charlotte said with a grimace. "She said whatever she could to keep these guys on the hook."

"Why do you think that's the case?" Sloane asked with a grimace. "It was like she had to have someone in reserve at all times. Why was she never satisfied with who she was with?"

"Hard to say. Insecurity, maybe? She must've fed off the compliments and the chase, which is why she pivoted to sexting so fast. She was always trying to get them stirred up and wanting her."

"Could be vanity."

"Human beings are complicated. It's probably a mixture of things. But wouldn't a stable, loving relationship be more fulfilling than the fleeting attention of so many men?" Charlotte asked, still trying to figure out how this side of her birth mother made her feel.

"Someone who's more mature might realize that," Sloane said, her voice flat with irony. "Sadly, Sabrina seemed pretty shallow."

"I hate that I agree," Charlotte said. Everything she'd seen and heard pointed to the same thing. "Steve's number's in here," she added. "Should I call him?"

"What for?"

"He might be able to put all of this into some context, and context is the only way we can ever truly understand what she was like."

Sloane nibbled at her lip. "If you want to," she said at last. "At least then we can learn more about Lilly, too. That could help a lot."

Charlotte was also curious about Steve himself. What had drawn him to Sabrina? He seemed to be a much more admirable person . . .

With the time change, it'd be six o'clock in the morning in Iowa, far too early to call most people. But Steve was a farmer. She couldn't imagine he wouldn't be up.

Taking a cleansing breath, she hit the number on his contact record.

She was rewarded when he answered almost immediately, and after a heartbeat of silence—during which she thought she could detect surprise—he sounded fully alert. "Sabrina?"

She froze. Did she really have any business bothering a total stranger with her family drama? He was probably relieved to have Sabrina out of his life.

But he'd picked up. And he'd been good to Lilly. "I'm afraid it isn't Sabrina, Steve. My name's Charlotte Williams."

He didn't seem to know how to respond. "Who are you,

and why do you have Sabrina's phone?" he asked after a heartbeat or two.

"I'm afraid that . . . Well, I'm sorry to tell you that Sabrina's no longer with us."

"What does that mean?"

"She passed away."

The resulting silence was filled with shock. "You mean she's *dead*? How? When?"

"She swerved on a Vespa and...collided with a bus."

"A bus?" he repeated. "When she was on a Vespa—*in Italy*?"

"Yes." Charlotte swallowed against a dry throat. "It happened a few weeks ago."

"I'm sorry to hear that. Where's Lilly?" he asked immediately. "Is she okay? Or—"

"Lilly's fine," she broke in. "Or as fine as a twelve-year-old could be in her situation. She wasn't with Sabrina at the time."

"Thank God. But . . . don't tell me she's been left with that guy in Italy."

"She's not with him anymore. I have her now."

"And you are . . .?"

"Her half sister."

Again, she could feel his surprise. "I wasn't aware she had a half sister," he said slowly.

"Sabrina put me up for adoption when she was eighteen. I . . . I never even knew I was adopted. The people who raised me acted as if I was their own. I would've kept believing that, but after Sabrina died, I was contacted about my half sister because she now has no one to take care of her."

"Sabrina never mentioned she had . . ."

When he let his words trail off, Charlotte assumed it was because he'd realized how that might make her feel.

"Another child?" Charlotte finished for him. She'd had a good life; it shouldn't hurt as much as it did that Sabrina had never acknowledged her existence. But she couldn't override the pain.

"Where'd you grow up?" he asked.

"In LA."

Silence fell. Then he said, "I guess, on some level, that doesn't completely surprise me. What's going to happen to Lilly?"

"That's what I'm trying to decide. I'm twenty-nine and about to be single. I'm not sure I'm her best long-term option. But there doesn't seem to be anyone else. You don't know anything about her father, do you?"

"Not a lot. Sabrina told me he lives in Mexico. Owns a fishing charter down there."

"Do you know if Sabrina had any contact with him?"

He didn't hesitate. "I don't think so. He hated her. Accused her of getting pregnant on purpose—as an attempt to trap him—and he wasn't having it."

Charlotte gripped her phone tighter. Just how terrible a person was her mother? Although it didn't seem as if Lilly's father was much better. Hers probably wasn't, either. "After knowing Sabrina, would you say you believe that or . . .?"

"Are you looking for the truth?" he asked.

She winced and braced herself. "Of course."

"I could believe she'd do something like that, yes—if it suited her."

Feeling even more deflated, Charlotte dropped her head in her hand and immediately felt Sloane touch her arm in a show of empathy. "He should still have to pay child support," she pointed out.

"If he ever comes back to the States, maybe you could go after him," Steve said. "But it costs money to track someone down—probably more than you'd ever get out of him. Since he's in business for himself, it's pretty easy to hide money. It's not right, but it happens."

So . . . the cost of trying to collect would outweigh the recovery. "That's not hopeful."

"There's what's right, and then there's what's practical. Believe me, if Sabrina thought she could get him to pay, she would've tried."

Another comment that made her believe her birth mother leaned on others—mostly the men in her life—whenever she could. "I see." She cleared her throat. "What about Lilly's grandparents?"

"Sabrina was an unexpected pregnancy herself. Her mother was on drugs and wasn't reliable, so she was raised by her grandparents, and they're far too old to take on another child."

"But they're still around?"

"To a point, I guess. While Sabrina was with me, her grandmother had a stroke. Her grandfather spends what time, energy and money he has left taking care of her."

"Even if . . . if they can't help, it might be good for Lilly to reconnect with them—providing they're willing. Do you know their names or how I could contact them? I don't see them in Sabrina's phone—but I also don't know what name to look under. There's nothing obvious like 'Mom' and 'Dad' or 'Grandma' and 'Grandpa.'"

"Last I heard, there was a big blowup between them, and they were no longer speaking to her. Maybe she deleted them. I'm not sure. Sabrina didn't like to dwell on anything she felt she might be responsible for. For the most part, what I've learned came from overhearing her on the phone or observing her behavior."

"I see." But there had to be someone . . . "What about other extended family? Did Sabrina keep in contact with anyone else?"

"I got the impression the entire family had written her off."

"*Why?*"

A sigh came through the phone. "She burned a lot of bridges, wasn't easy to love in the first place."

"Did *you* love her?" She'd asked Luca the same bold, intrusive question, but Charlotte was willing to risk it—again—because the answer mattered to her. Did Sabrina burn every single bridge? Did she not learn from her mistakes and do better?

"I tried," he said softly.

"What drew you to her in the first place?"

"I live in a small town, was hoping to meet someone. She brought fun and excitement. She was always up to something, always laughing. For someone who's been entirely about work since I can remember—I was raised on this farm—that was appealing. *Too* appealing," he added.

"So what went wrong?"

"There wasn't enough there beneath the shine," he replied.

"What about Lilly? You cared for her, didn't you?"

"I did. I feel bad for her. She's a good kid. Deserves better."

"She says you tried to give her 'better.'"

"I hated to see her taken away from the farm. She was happy here. Loved Old Blue like nothing and no one else."

Imagining what *could've* been nearly brought a lump to Charlotte's throat. "Old Blue's your dog. Luca told me about him. He's blind, right?"

"Yeah, he's blind, but not as old as you might think—only about five. I just call him 'old' because he reminds me of a horse I used to have when I was a child. The horse was old," he said with a chuckle.

"And Lilly and Old Blue were close?"

"Inseparable."

"Can you send me a picture of him I can show her? She's going through such a tough time. Maybe it'll help."

"You bet. They hit it off immediately," he told her. "Whoever owned Old Blue before he found a home here with me abused him pretty badly—that's what happened to his eyesight. The poor boy doesn't trust easily, but he trusted Lilly."

Horrified to think anyone would mistreat a dog, especially to the point of blinding him, she straightened. "He lost his eyesight because of . . . because of abuse?"

"At best, it was negligence. Anyway, I think Old Blue and Lilly were kindred spirits, just trying to heal together."

Steve seemed like such a kind, decent person. "Would there be any chance that . . . I mean . . . would you mind terribly much if I were to bring Lilly to town one day to see you and Old Blue? I think she'd *love* that."

"Of course. Lilly's always welcome here. I'd even . . ." He cleared his throat. "I'd even let her live with me if you don't want to become her guardian, so don't feel as if you're painted into a corner."

Charlotte's jaw dropped. *"You'd take her in?"*

"Why not? I seem to gravitate to broken things," he said with a laugh. "I want to make them whole. You asked me about Sabrina. That was probably the case with her, too. But she wouldn't let me help her, wouldn't let *anyone* help her. I offered to keep Lilly when she left. I truly believed the girl would be better off here. But Sabrina wouldn't hear of it."

"She'd given up one child. She probably couldn't think of giving up another."

He hesitated before saying, "I'd like to think that was the reason. I suppose Sabrina loved Lilly in her own way. But she couldn't seem to put Lilly's needs above her own. That's what made me mad. And when I tried to step in, she accused me of wanting to keep Lilly for . . . for the wrong reasons, which is just plain sad because she should've known me better than that. We weren't together very long, but I've never done a thing to hurt an animal or a child and I never would. I just wanted to give Lilly a stable, loving home. That was what she needed. But because of what Walter did . . . That certainly played a role."

"What *Walter* did?"

"You don't know about that?"

"I don't know about *anything*," she said. "I'm coming into this entirely cold."

He hesitated as if he wasn't eager to explain.

"Steve? If it'll help me understand Lilly better, what she's been through and what she might need, please tell me."

"I'm sure it's something she'd rather you not know. It's probably something she'd rather no one knows. According to Sabrina, she was pretty upset. So I'm thinking I should let her share what happened. When she's ready."

His loyalty only made Charlotte trust him more. She wanted to press him; he'd raised her curiosity. But she could tell from the finality in his voice that he wasn't going to change his mind. "Okay. Then just tell me this. Who was Walter?"

"The guy Sabrina was with before me, in Colorado."

"I see. And he hurt Lilly in some way?"

"I'll let her tell you," he reiterated.

Charlotte believed Sabrina had made a grave mistake leaving Steve. Just the way Lilly talked about him indicated he was a good man. But Sabrina hadn't been able to stop sabotaging her own happiness, which, unfortunately, directly affected Lilly's.

"I'll keep everything you've said in mind. And when we get back to the States, we'll plan a trip to Iowa."

"Sounds good."

"Don't forget to send me a picture of Old Blue."

"I won't," he said.

Sloane was waiting to comment on the conversation as soon as Charlotte hung up. "What'd he say?"

"He said he'd take Lilly himself."

"That's what I thought he said. Was he serious?"
"Sounded like it."
"But . . . does that mean her grandparents, father and extended family aren't viable options?"
"Sabrina was raised by her grandparents, who are too old these days. He didn't say where her mother is, but she was a drug addict, and maybe she never got clean."
"What about Lilly's father?"
"Lives in Mexico. It wouldn't be worth the time, effort or money to track him down. Even if I could find him, I'd have to force him to pay child support. I don't want to deal with all that negativity." Apparently, Mr. Heidelman had done his job well and found the only viable relation—*her*.
"Do you think Lilly would want to move back to the farm?"
"Possibly. You know how she feels about Old Blue."
"Then that might be the perfect solution."
"Steve seems like a really good guy," she agreed.
"You're taking Lilly to visit him once we get back?"
"I think I should, don't you?"
"Absolutely."
Charlotte was about to set Sabrina's phone aside when it pinged with a text message. Steve had sent the picture she'd requested—a selfie that included him, along with a message.

> Old Blue and I miss you, Lill. Can't wait for you to come see us.

"That's him?" Sloane said, peering over her shoulder.
Charlotte lifted the phone so she could get a better look. "Apparently."
"He has nice eyes, and a seems to have a steadiness that reads as trustworthy."

She adjusted the phone to study the picture herself. Sloane was right. Tall and lanky, Steve was bald and a bit weathered with a full beard that was almost all gray but neatly trimmed, and he had a shy, sweet smile for a man of his size and age. Just looking at him made Charlotte feel he was the kind of person who would keep his word.

She reminded herself that looks could be deceiving, but Lilly's comments and feelings about Steve backed up her opinion. "Would Lilly be better off with him?" She was mostly speaking to herself, but she thought Sloane would jump at the chance to offer an emphatic yes. Sloane was the one who'd been trying to convince Charlotte not to take on a twelve-year-old. But she was surprisingly reticent.

"I don't know. We'll have to see how things go from here."

Charlotte hid a smile. Sloane's tough talk hid a very soft heart. Maybe she didn't know it yet, but this served as further proof that she was falling for Lilly.

As she walked along the shore in Positano next to Julian, who'd suggested they stay out of the house a little longer to give Charlotte more time to work, Lilly saw a man lift his little girl up so he could carry her on his shoulders and was mesmerized by the sight. She'd always wanted to experience that. It was why she'd called so many men "Dad." Sabrina had encouraged it, of course. She'd pushed that sort of connection far too soon. But Lilly had done it, hoping it would make them a real family, which now made her feel like a desperate fool. Somewhere along the line, that sort of thing had become a joke. Other than maybe Steve, each new "dad" was far more interested in Sabrina than he was in her. Lilly was merely an annoyance they had to put up with if they wanted a relationship with Sabrina.

As she stooped to pick up a broken shell veined like lace,

she remembered the fight she'd overheard the night before they left the farm. Steve had caught Sabrina cheating on him with some guy she'd connected with on a dating app and said he was done with her. At first, Sabrina had tried to convince him she wasn't really interested in that other man. Then she'd promised she'd never contact him again. But Steve no longer seemed to care what changes she made. He'd insisted she move out right away, but Lilly remembered hearing him say that *she* could stay.

Her mother hadn't even discussed the possibility with her. Lilly was the one person Sabrina had relied on to always be there, the one person who *couldn't* get upset and leave, no matter what. But what would've happened if her mother *had* left her at the farm? Would they *both* have been happier?

Considering what'd happened since, Lilly certainly believed *she* would've been better off. Had Sabrina died while Lilly lived at the farm, Lilly would probably have gone on living there. With Old Blue. No change.

The thought of Steve's beloved dog always hit her hard. But even if her mother had allowed it, she couldn't have lived with a man who was no relation to her while Sabrina moved on without her, especially after what had happened with Walter. Walter was always there in the back of her mind, making her distrust all the "dads" who came after.

So what was going to happen now? As nice as her sister seemed to be, Lilly didn't know if she could truly rely on Charlotte. With Charlotte's marriage falling apart, there wasn't currently a guy in her life. That was when her promises were most likely to be broken—if there was a chance her pro basketball, rich-as-fuck (something else Lilly had heard her mother say) husband ever came back around. How could anyone say no to a pro basketball player? Someone who wasn't just rich but famous, handsome and athletic? If Sabrina were in Charlotte's shoes, *she'd* go back to him, and Lilly knew it. Sabrina had never been able to pass the guy test, and she'd never been tempted by anyone as desirable as a pro athlete.

"Why do you think Charlotte's husband is breaking up with her?" Lilly asked Jules.

He was too busy eyeing a seagull that was strutting confidently toward them to answer—and caught her arm so she'd stop walking.

"Is something wrong?" she asked, blinking up at him.

"I don't like birds," he said.

She laughed at the expression on his face. "You're *scared* of them?"

"I didn't say that. I said I didn't *like* them."

He *was* scared of them. Lilly could tell. Flapping her arms, she chased the bird away before returning to him. "Don't worry. I'll protect you," she said with a teasing grin.

He arched an unappreciative eyebrow. "I could've done that. I was just . . . waiting to see if it would be necessary."

He wasn't even attempting to sell the lie. He was laughing, too, and that made her like him even more. He wasn't all that different from Steve, she realized—so real he could laugh at himself for being afraid of something as harmless as a bird.

"You're funny, you know that?" she said.

He flexed for her. "Just so you know I'm also strong and masculine and perfectly capable of protecting you from . . . everything except birds."

This time when she laughed, it felt perfectly natural to slide her arm through his as they continued to walk, which was such a rare thing for her—she couldn't believe she was that comfortable with him. Jules felt like an older brother.

"So are you going to answer my question about Cliff and Charlotte?"

He glanced down at her arm. "Look at you—growing all confident and brave."

She felt her face heat as she withdrew, but he reached over and put her arm back inside his. "I don't know why he left her," he said.

"You must have *some* idea," she insisted.

"Other than that Cliff's an asshole? I actually don't."

She let go to bend over and pick up another broken shell, which she transferred to the hand holding all the others. "What are the chances he'll want to get back together with her?"

"Once he realizes what he's lost, I'd say the chances are good. He'll never find anyone better. But maybe he's not even as smart as I think he is, in which case he'll never realize it."

"You really like Charlotte," she commented.

He shifted his gaze to look out at the sea. "I know what kind of person she is."

"Do you have a girlfriend?"

"Not right now."

"Why not?"

His grin slanted to one side. "What woman would want a man who's afraid of birds?"

"Yeah, that's intolerable," she said, joking back with him, and picked up another shell.

"Why are you only going for the broken ones?" he asked when he saw her stow it with the others.

"Just because something's broken doesn't make it worthless," she pointed out.

Lines appeared on his forehead as if he might argue with her, but then they disappeared, and his smile grew easy again. "You're wiser than your years, you know that?"

"I only had my mother. *One* of us had to be an adult," she muttered and felt a little lighter when he chuckled as if he understood and found another broken seashell he handed to her.

chapter 20

The image of Sabrina that had emerged in Charlotte's mind made Penny look like the best mother on the planet—so much so that Charlotte called her before going to bed. She'd also sent her and Don a few pictures of the villa, Praiano and Lilly, as she would have done already if she hadn't been so torn about the latest developments in her life and her parents' role in them.

Charlotte could tell how relieved they both were to be forgiven and she felt guilty for ever being angry with them. They'd faced a difficult decision and felt they'd made the right choice. Considering what she was learning about Sabrina, it probably *was* the right choice. Not many people had the kind of parents she'd had, biologically linked or otherwise, and she was determined to show a great deal more gratitude.

At least she seemed to be working her way through *that* aspect of the mess her life had become. Anything was an improvement.

She'd just set her phone on the nightstand and curled up to go to sleep when her phone started to ring. Assuming her mother was calling back to say something she'd forgotten to get in before, she checked. But it wasn't Penny; it was Cliff.

She'd been ignoring his texts. She didn't know how to respond to him. Why wasn't he out having the fun he'd been craving when he blew up their marriage?

She let it transfer to voicemail. Then she sat up and scooted back, using the headboard for support while searching his name on the internet. She hadn't let herself look for what had been posted about him lately, not since she'd found that picture of him with Marija Vidmar. She knew she shouldn't be doing it now, but the temptation was simply too great.

She found pictures and video clips of him from his last game and the spate of interviews that had followed, but when she discovered nothing else about Marija or any other woman, a wave of relief crashed over her so powerfully it was impossible to ignore him again when he called right back. Part of her still insisted that this whole thing was merely a terrible mistake—a nightmare that would eventually go away and all would be well again. They'd had so much fun together in the beginning.

Bracing for the sound of his voice and the memories it would evoke, she answered.

"There you are," he exclaimed. "What the hell do I have to do to get a response from you?"

She didn't owe him anything. Not anymore. But she didn't want to start a fight. Tonight, after her call with her parents, she was all about mending fences and finding her old equilibrium. Could that happen with Cliff, too? Could they reconcile and forget he'd ever asked for a divorce?

It didn't seem too farfetched at the moment—if she refused to acknowledge the past couple of months and focused only on the commitment she'd felt when they were together. "I've been . . ." *decimated, hurt, drowning in confusion* ". . . busy," she finished.

"With what?"

Had he been paying *any* attention to what was happening

in her life? "Starting my new book. Learning about my birth mother. Getting to know Lilly."

"What's she like?"

The thought of her half sister caused a warm feeling to bubble up from somewhere deep inside. "Like a fawn that suddenly finds itself alone and doesn't know where to turn. She's always watching what's going on around her, hanging out on the periphery, in case she needs to bolt."

"You and your analogies," he said, the eye-roll audible.

Charlotte had been trying to convey something that was meaningful to her—the insecurity Lilly felt and what a beautiful, innocent creature she was. But he was obviously irritated by the way she'd chosen to express it. Or just didn't care enough to understand.

"What's that supposed to mean?" she asked.

"It's just the way you talk. You're the only one I know who does it."

"I'm sorry," she said, stung.

He offered no apology, which was ironic since, in her opinion, he was the one who should've been apologizing. "We made the finals. Did you see?"

Not until she'd googled his name a few seconds earlier. "Yeah. Congratulations. You must be thrilled."

"I am. I scored twenty-eight points, turned the final game around. We couldn't have pulled it off otherwise."

"And the other guys?" She said that to emphasize that he was part of a team, but he didn't seem to catch on to the fact that she was pointing out what *he* always did—and that was make everything about him.

"They helped."

It was a throwaway statement, as if to say they'd contributed only a small amount. "That's . . . wonderful."

"I wish you'd been here to see it."

"I'm glad you're being successful and enjoying your career. That's why you said you wanted a divorce, right? So you can have some fun during your basketball days?"

"Stop it," he said. "I didn't mean that the way you're taking it."

How else could she take it, especially after he showed up in Vegas with a beautiful model? "Are you still seeing Marija?"

"No. She has no sense of humor, no personality at all."

"I didn't know it was her personality you were after."

"Come on, Char. I know you're upset. But everyone has second thoughts once in a while. The important thing is . . . I miss you and I'm sorry for what I did."

"Are you saying you want to get back together?"

"I do. Life isn't the same without you. I want to see if we can make our marriage work."

This was exactly what she'd longed to hear, and yet . . . it didn't make anything better. She got the impression he was simply lost, didn't know what he wanted and was flailing around. Trusting him again would be like walking across a bridge that had already given way and let her fall through once. Did she really want to take the risk a second time?

"Char?" he prompted when she didn't respond.

"Would you be willing to let Lilly come live with us?" she asked, just to see how far he'd go to get her back.

"You want to bring your sister *here*?"

He didn't sound excited by the idea. But she'd known he wouldn't be. He wanted kids of his own eventually, but he'd indicated he wasn't ready. So why would he agree to become the guardian of one? "She doesn't have anywhere else to go," she said, which, of course, he should already have known.

He hesitated. Then, obviously sensing the trap she'd just laid for him, said, "Sure, why not? This place is big enough for an army."

Under the circumstances, it was the only way to avoid looking like a bad guy. Problem was, she didn't believe he'd stick by those words, not once she went back to him. As soon as they ran into any inconvenience caused by Lilly's presence—something she had to attend at the school when he wanted her to be at his game or whatever—he'd start pressuring her to make other arrangements. And that was if he didn't change his mind about *her* and their marriage again and throw her out.

"Thank you." She'd said it without any real feeling, but he didn't seem to notice.

"No problem. So . . . does that mean you'll be coming home sooner rather than later? I mean, as long as she can come here, there's no reason to stay in Italy, is there?"

"I've already paid for the villa."

"So? You're missing the playoffs!"

"I have a book to write, Cliff."

"And how much will you make off that book?"

Nothing compared to what he made. That was his point. But it was money she'd need if they couldn't make their marriage work. "It's my *career*."

"I get that. But it's the playoffs, for God's sake! Tell your publisher you'll get to it when you can. They'll understand."

Just because he could throw his weight around didn't mean she could. She covered her eyes with one hand. "I'll think about it. I'd better go. It's late here, and I have to get up early and write."

"Okay, but tune in for tomorrow's game. It's going to be a good one. Maybe you can get home before the next one."

"I'll think about it," she repeated and told him good night before disconnecting.

A lump grew in her throat as she stared at her phone for several seconds. She'd lost more than her marriage, she realized. She'd lost faith in the man she loved. He'd proved himself to be far different than she'd once believed him to be. But she knew in her heart that she'd been turning a blind eye to his less favorable traits for a long time.

Too upset to sleep, she texted Jules.

> You awake?

To her surprise, she got an almost immediate response.

> Just sitting out on the deck, editing a few pictures. Something wrong?

> Where's Sloane?

> Sleeping.

So was Lilly, which meant they could get away for a little while on their own.

> Will you go for a walk with me?

> Where to?

> That restaurant—Kasai—if it's still open. I'd like to have a glass of wine and some tiramisu.

> You had me at Kasai.

She smiled. What would she have done these past few weeks without Jules? Thank you, she wrote back and meant it.

"Lilly's starting to get more comfortable with us, have you noticed?" Jules asked as he watched Charlotte dip her spoon into the tiramisu they served at Kasai's. Here the tiramisu leaned sweet and creamy, the coffee and booze barely a whisper.

"Are you referring to something specific?" she asked.

They were sitting out on the street, with people strolling between them and the restaurant, at one of five tables that were all filled despite the late hour. "Today, she took my arm while we were walking on the beach," he told her. "Can you believe that?"

She scooped up another bite of her tiramisu. "That's a bold move. But you've been her favorite from the beginning."

"I'm not sure about that. Even if it's true, we're talking about *Lilly*. The girl who could barely meet our eyes when we were introduced to her not very long ago."

Charlotte chuckled. "You really like her, don't you?"

"I do," he admitted. "She's a sweet kid."

"Yeah, well, you're a pushover," she said teasingly.

"It's not just me. Sloane likes her a lot, too."

"I've noticed," Charlotte said. "She's losing the fight to stay objective—"

"Despite her best efforts to decide what's best for each party."

"I know. Some of that might be pity. Sloane certainly has no love for my birth mother."

He'd skipped the tiramisu, was happy drinking a glass of merlot. "She told me about a few of the things that were on that phone," he responded with a frown.

"That stuff was nothing I ever wanted to read, I can promise you." She grimaced. "Telling one guy she wanted to blow him and another that she'd do a threesome?"

"I see what you mean." He held his glass loosely in one hand. "So why are we out here, enjoying this beautiful evening, when you're supposed to be getting some sleep so you can continue writing your next blockbuster?"

Her smile disappeared; he'd known something was wrong despite her casual behavior. "Cliff called tonight."

"Let me guess—he wants you back."

She gave a small shrug. "That's what he said."

Julian felt an immediate reaction—the desire to punch Clifford Jackson in the face—but tried to remain impassive. "Already."

"It doesn't feel quick to me."

Nothing seemed fast when you were going through hell, which was part of the reason he wanted to punch Cliff in the face. He was the one who'd put her in a bad place. "Depends on who you ask, I guess."

"You're not surprised?"

"No. So what are you going to do?" He held his breath while he waited for her answer.

"I don't know. It's so hard to walk away from all the time and effort I've already invested in the relationship."

"If you go back, you can avoid the hard months ahead, you mean."

"There's that. Maybe he's learned his lesson, Jules."

"And maybe he hasn't. Sometimes you have to cut your losses no matter how much you've invested."

"You don't think I should go back to him."

"I don't think he'll ever treat you the way you deserve to be treated."

"He agreed to let Lilly come live with us," she volunteered, as if that should make all the difference.

He clinked his glass against hers. "What a guy."

"Jules, I know Cliff has his shortcomings. But no one's perfect."

"That's true. You could get with a guy who has a debilitating disease, for instance," he mumbled.

"Where did *that* come from?" she asked with a laugh.

"Just showing you it could always be worse, I guess. Don't listen to me. I've had too much to drink." He'd had a shot at the house after receiving an email from his doctor urging him to begin treatment. Since everyone else was in bed, it hadn't seemed to matter if he numbed his feelings with alcohol. He certainly didn't have to worry about his health any longer. He was already fucked there. But then Charlotte had asked him to go to Kasai's with her, and he'd had two glasses of wine in addition to the whiskey he'd been drinking at the villa, and it was all going to his head. "I need to stop."

He pushed his glass away, but she filled it again before topping up her own. "Why quit now?" she said. "If ever I needed to forget my problems and have a little bit of fun, it'd be tonight."

Charlotte was drunk. But she didn't care. The heartache was gone. The worry was gone. The fear that she might make the wrong decision where Lilly was concerned was gone, too. She felt free and fully alive for the first time in what seemed like forever.

"Fuck Cliff!" Jules nearly shouted as they finished the bottle they'd been drinking, and she was actually able to laugh. The more Jules drank, the funnier he got; the more she drank, the more she could appreciate his humor. She was laughing and hanging on to him so she wouldn't trip on the cobblestone street as they walked away from the restaurant.

He steered her toward home, but she wasn't ready to go back to the villa. Her problems resided there. The reality of her situation, including the impending loss of her career if she couldn't overcome the fears and anxiety that were holding her hostage, were waiting for her there. She wanted to avoid that place for as long as possible and simply continue to feel good.

"Let's not go back quite yet," she said.

A cat slunk past them as Jules looked down at her. "Where else do you want to go?"

"By the water."

"What do you want to do there?"

The world spun as she shrugged, so she tightened her grip on him. "Look at the coastline, I guess. Howl at the moon. It's so bright this evening. Maybe we can get a picture of it."

"I'm a good photographer, but I'm not *that* good," he said. "Not without the right equipment."

She rolled her eyes. "Well, it might not be up to your high standards, but it'll still make a nice memory."

"Okay," he relented.

"Do you know how to get there?" she asked.

"To the beach? Yeah." He winked at her. "I can get you anywhere."

"I believe it," she said. "But I wasn't even sure Praiano had a beach. To me, the coast looks mostly like big rocks jutting out of the sea with no sand around them."

"There are a couple of tiny beaches," he said. "And I think I know how to get to both of them. But just in case I'm wrong, I'm going to take you to the one I've already visited. It'll mean several hundred stairs, though. To get to any beach we have to go down." He swayed before catching himself. "Are you sure you're up to it?"

She heard the bang of a shutter and the whine of a Vespa or two in the distance as she gave him a cocky grin. "I am if you are."

"It's climbing back up to the villa that'll be hard," he warned. "At least in our current condition."

She didn't care about that. They'd make it somehow, even if they had to stay out long enough to sober up. She felt safe and warm and happy with Julian. "Then maybe we'll sleep down there."

His gaze seemed to take on a sexual undercurrent. But she told herself she had to be mistaken. She'd made that one comment to him the day he'd helped her carry Sabrina's things, and he'd distanced himself immediately.

"That'd be okay with me," he said, but then he paused, seemingly confused, as he looked around them. "Wait. First, I have to figure out how to get to the town square. If I can do that, I'll be able to find my way from there."

A couple passed by, talking earnestly. "*Scusi*," Julian called out. "Can you tell me how to get to Piazza San Gennaro?"

The man tried to tell them in heavily accented English how to get where they wanted to go, but they were too inebriated to remember his instructions thirty seconds after he'd finished speaking.

"*Grazie*," Jules said and as soon as they were gone, he laughed and shrugged. "We'll find it. I have faith."

She had faith in *him*, but she had to wonder if her faith had been misplaced when they got lost in a rabbit warren of stairs and walkways. They had to double back twice before they eventually found the piazza and took a street called Via Masa.

"Now I've got it," Jules announced when they spotted signs for the beach.

"We might be sober by the time we get there," she said.

"I doubt it," he responded. "We're pretty drunk."

Her phone buzzed as they were struggling to navigate one of many flights of stairs. She used it as an excuse to take a rest.

"It's a text from Cliff," she said.

Jules leaned against the rock wall to one side. "What does *he* want?"

"He's telling me to forget about my book and come home."

"Oh, yeah, that'd be really smart—for *him*. Without your career, you'd be even more dependent on him."

Jules's sarcasm spoke volumes. "Yeah. Not a good idea," she agreed. "He doesn't care that writing is my dream. He cares only about his own dreams."

"Fuck Cliff!" Julian said, revisiting his earlier sentiment.

"Yeah, fuck Cliff!" she said and, ignoring her estranged husband's text, put her phone in her pocket before once again taking Julian's hand.

When he looked down at their clasped hands, the sweetest smile appeared on his face. "There you are," he said.

She didn't know what he meant by that, but she could tell he was talking to himself so she didn't question it.

They laughed and talked until they reached the water, where they found themselves alone. Apparently, descending close to five hundred stairs wasn't all that appealing to anyone else, not at this time of night.

A tiny beach tapered down to the water, the moon hung low in the sky and white-crested waves slammed against the magnificent cliffs on either side. Way off in the distance, they could see some twinkling lights she assumed were on the Isle of Capri simply because she knew it was in that general direction.

"God, it's beautiful in Italy," she said.

He let go of her hand to grip the railing. They were standing on a small platform, hadn't yet descended all the way to the sand. "The world is a beautiful place, Char, and I've been lucky enough to see most of it. For a guy my age, that's a lot of traveling."

"What's your worst fear?" she asked as she gazed at the moon.

She thought he'd need a few minutes to think about it. That wasn't a question someone asked every day. But he answered immediately. "Being incapable of doing what I love," he said, and for a moment he seemed so sad she put her hand over his.

"That will never happen."

He turned to face her. "Yes, it will."

"Years and years into the future," she insisted.

When he remained silent, she looked up to find him studying her. "It's too bad," he said.

"What's too bad?" she asked.

"That we never got together in high school."

She knew that if she was in her right mind, she'd be shocked that he'd make such a statement. He'd always been careful not to so much as allude to anything romantic between them. "There's always been too much standing in the way—people we were already involved with, the fear of ruining our friendship, the cost to my relationship with Sloane if we did ruin our friendship. But I feel like it was a missed opportunity, too. Maybe we'd still be together," she murmured. "Maybe we'd even have children by now."

"I certainly wouldn't have been stupid enough to let you go," he said.

That statement struck a serious tone despite the alcohol, but instead of moving away from him, she caught his face in her hands. "I wouldn't have been stupid enough to let you go, either," she said and, rising up on her toes, pressed her lips to his.

It'd been an impulsive action, one fueled by alcohol and probably desperation to escape what she was going through. On some level, Julian understood that. But there was also something much deeper there. They'd known each other for years; Lord knew *he'd* certainly flirted with the thought of "what if?" on numerous occasions. So once Charlotte's lips touched his, he couldn't bring himself to set her away from him. He told himself he could allow this much—no more, but this much.

When he hauled her tightly against him, as he'd wanted to do for the past week or more, he was surprised she didn't immediately come to her senses and pull away. Ever since they were kids, they'd been so watchful, so careful not to cross this line. Straying from the friendship they'd always had was risky, even now. And yet she not only parted her lips, but she also moaned when her tongue met his.

Such an enthusiastic response nearly caused his knees to buckle. He'd expected to enjoy kissing Charlotte if he ever got the chance, but he'd never dreamed the pleasure would be quite so overwhelming. He'd been filled with such despair since his diagnosis that the hormones ripping through him in that moment created a slingshot effect, taking him higher than he'd ever been.

"God, I love the way you kiss," she muttered, her lips still against his as she spoke. "I should've known you'd be good at this. You're good at everything."

Except self-control, apparently. Somewhere in the dim recesses of his mind, he knew he was doing her a disservice. She didn't know there was something terribly wrong with him, didn't know that she'd only wind up feeling disappointed and betrayed in the end. He didn't want to blindside her with the terrible news he'd been hiding—wasn't ready to face it himself. He'd promised himself he wouldn't have to deal with it here. Italy was his last chance at normalcy before he had to face everyone finding out and deal with the pity that would inspire.

So after several even more feverish kisses, when he felt her hands go up his shirt and was tempted to put his hands up hers, he gathered the strength to step away.

She was breathing heavily and so was he. "What is it?" she asked, blinking up at him. "What's wrong?"

"We can't do this, Char. It's only going to get us into trouble."

Her eyebrows drew together. "In what way?"

When he didn't answer immediately, she said, "If you're worried about Cliff, I don't care what he thinks. I'm more heartbroken over my own failure—after giving my marriage my absolute best—than I am over losing him."

"But the devil you know is better than the devil you don't? Is that why you're tempted to take him back?"

"Loss is complicated, Jules. Sometimes it makes you second-guess yourself. But I know I could never really trust his love again, so I'd be miserable, which means it would never work even if I tried to force it."

"Still. It's brand-new. It wouldn't be wise to get involved with someone else so soon."

"I can see why you'd say that," she allowed. "And maybe you're right. Regardless, I don't want to screw up again—definitely don't want to do anything that could possibly ruin our friendship. You mean too much to me."

"I feel the same." He leaned his forehead against hers, wishing he could act on the spark they felt, fan it into something hot and fierce and all-consuming, and then take care of her like a partner should. Especially if it meant keeping her away from Cliff, who he was convinced would just hurt her again.

He would've gone for it—if he could. But he couldn't allow himself to be that selfish. If he really cared about her, he'd protect her from being shackled to someone she'd just have to take care of when his health began to deteriorate. "If only things were different."

"Why are you talking as if it's too late?" she asked. "Why are you acting as if it could never happen?"

"You're not in the right situation." That was an excuse, and he knew it. *He* was the one who wasn't in the right situation. But he had to say something, and he wasn't ready to tell her the truth. She and Sloane were dealing with enough already. Why would he ruin their trip to Italy?

She looked torn, uncertain. "So maybe later . . ."

"Maybe. Let's give it some time," he said and felt his chest tighten painfully because he knew it was time that was working against him.

chapter 21

When Charlotte woke up the next morning, her mouth tasted of stale sugar and wine and her skull throbbed behind her eyes. "Damn it. What'd I do?" she said aloud. Then the memory of kissing Julian rose in her mind, and she realized drinking too much wasn't the worst of it. Thank God *he'd* put a stop to what they'd been doing. There was no telling how far she would've gone. She'd suddenly been willing and eager to make love with him, which was beyond shocking. He was her best friend's brother! Her longtime *friend*! And she wasn't even out of her marriage yet.

"Hey, you!" Coffee drifted up from the kitchen as Sloane cracked open the door and leaned through.

Charlotte managed to rise up on her elbows, but the sight of her best friend nearly made her curse silently. What would *she* think about that kiss?

Charlotte didn't want to find out, so she wasn't going to tell her. She could only hope Julian made the same decision. "Hey," she responded, and gingerly slid back down to lay her head on the pillow.

Concern entered Sloane's expression as she came into the

room. "What's wrong with you? Are you sick? I thought you'd be up writing by now."

Charlotte wished she'd lower her voice, but didn't really care to explain why, so she didn't ask. "I'm okay," she said, trying to speak as loudly as she usually did. "Just . . . slept in a bit. Is Jules up?" She couldn't help wondering what *he* was thinking about what happened last night.

"Not yet. He's been keeping some really late hours."

"He doesn't seem to be sleeping much," she agreed.

"And sometimes, if you look at him when he doesn't know you're doing it, he'll have this far-off expression on his face, as if he's . . . lost."

"What do you mean?"

"He's acting weird, Char. I'm worried." She sat on the corner of the bed. "Have you noticed anything . . . strange going on with him?"

Charlotte sifted through possibilities and tried not to land on last night. Had Sloane picked up on the subtle changes that'd been going on between them since this trip began?

If so, he wasn't the only one acting different. She'd enjoyed kissing Julian, had wanted to go much further.

Where had that come from? Since she got married, she hadn't allowed herself to even think about anyone other than Cliff. And then . . . only a short time after they split up, she was ready to take off her clothes for someone else? Not just anyone but . . . *Julian*?

She was on the rebound, she decided. A person going through a breakup didn't always make the best decisions. "Not sure what you mean," she mumbled.

"He hasn't told you what's bothering him?"

"I didn't know there *was* something bothering him." She'd been so caught up in her own troubles, had she missed signs she should've noticed?

"He probably wouldn't say anything to you. He knows you're already going through too much. Just thought I'd ask."

A fresh wave of guilt gave Charlotte the impetus to drag herself into a sitting position. "What could it be?"

"I have no idea."

"You're his sister," she said. "Ask him."

"I've tried! He won't tell me."

Attempting to ease the pain in her head, Charlotte began to rub her temples. Julian *had* seemed rather pensive at times—when he wasn't trying to lift *her* spirits. "He seems to be over his broken engagement, and he's his own boss, so it's not like he could lose his job."

"He claims the gallery's doing fine, too. So what is it?"

"He's pretty driven. Could it mean something that he'd take off so much time to come to Italy?"

"No. That's not a warning sign as far as I'm concerned. Why would he turn down an opportunity to spend an entire month on the Amalfi Coast? Especially when any pictures he takes here would be commercially viable. It's not like we dragged him to some godforsaken place where there wouldn't be anything appealing to photograph." She grinned. "And he gets to hang with us. What could be better?"

Charlotte could no longer hold her best friend's gaze. "I get that, but it must be work. What else could it be?"

"It's not work," Sloane argued. "If it was, he'd tell me."

"Maybe it's just that he's lost direction in his life. Maybe this trip is meant to be a reset for him. Everyone has those moments . . ."

"So I shouldn't worry?"

"Not until you know there's a good reason to."

She blew out a breath. "Okay. I'll sit on my hands and trust that he'll tell me when he's ready."

"What about you?" Charlotte asked. "How are you and Ben doing?"

She pulled her gaze away. "We're hanging in there."

It'd taken some time, but Sloane had finally started confiding in Charlotte about the decision she was facing. Although she didn't really want to talk about it, a bit more seemed to come out every day. "I'm worried about you."

"I know. But . . . don't. I'll figure it out."

They heard voices downstairs. Lilly was up, speaking to Julian.

Sloane got off the bed. "I'm going down to breakfast. Forget I said anything about Jules. I'm sure it's nothing."

The memory of Julian's lips, soft and pliable on hers, and the taste of Merlot when he laughed against her mouth rose in Charlotte's mind. "Jules is fine," she said aloud, trying to convince herself at the same time. She couldn't bear the thought that anything could be wrong with him.

But if he needed her, she'd be there for him just like he'd been there for her.

Over the next week, Charlotte fell into a productive routine in which she got up early every morning and went to her computer. She told herself she only had to write five pages, but some days she was able to produce more.

Soon she had forty pages finished. She printed the first few chapters, spread the pages on the table, and circled a sentence that finally felt like her voice again. Seeing her words, feeling the forward momentum of the story, felt *so* good. Once she reached chapter five or six, and she'd edited those pages so they were as good as she could make them, she'd be able to send them in to get her editor's opinion—something that both excited and scared her. She liked the story so far, but it was only her second book, and it was dealing with a much more divisive conflict. It was also striking a more somber tone—obviously a reflection of where she was at emotionally. She felt it was engrossing, but she was afraid it wouldn't be similar enough to her first book.

What if her publisher didn't like it? She was under such a tight deadline there was no margin for error, and if they went with it even though they weren't entirely happy and it flopped, there'd be no forgiveness. The people she worked with had their hopes set far too high to be able to take failure lightly. But Charlotte didn't really see how this book could succeed. Once it was released, she wouldn't have Cliff's celebrity to help propel it to the top of the bestseller lists.

The story had to be *so* good, had to stand entirely on its own merit. But better writers had failed to realize the kind of sales necessary to remain in the industry. To achieve that on her own seemed daunting. Still, she kept reminding herself to push forward. She had to try. The last time she'd spoken to her father, he'd said, "Stop sabotaging yourself with all these doubts, babe. Let your publisher be the one to tell you if it's not good enough. Don't destroy your own confidence. Otherwise, you'll go nowhere."

He was right, of course. But imposter syndrome was real and something she had to fight every time she sat down to write.

After she finished work each day, she and whoever hadn't already set off to do something—most often Sloane and Lilly—would go hiking, shopping, sightseeing or exploring the coast. Sometimes Julian joined them. She also spent some of her off-hours scrubbing Sabrina's phone of dating apps, sexts and any explicit photos while keeping the number, the clean pictures and anything Lilly might treasure.

She wanted to pass the phone on to half sister as Sloane had suggested, but she'd been holding back in case some man Sabrina had connected with hadn't gotten the message that she was no longer alive and sent something suggestive or made a comment that wouldn't show Sabrina in the best light.

"You have Sabrina's phone with you today?" Sloane asked.

Charlotte glanced up. Sloane had been inside a nearby bakery, purchasing lemon croissants while Lilly went with Julian to get sorbet, so she'd had a moment alone and pulled out Sabrina's phone to make sure she hadn't received any new messages. "Yeah. I thought I might run into a good opportunity to surprise Lilly with it."

Sloane clapped her hands. "She's going to be so excited."

"I just don't want to do it too soon. I'm still hearing from some of Sabrina's contacts."

A moped coughed past. "Even after you texted everyone?"

"Yeah."

"What are people saying?"

She lowered her voice despite the fact that Lilly wasn't even close. She didn't want anyone else to hear her, either; there were tourists clustered all around. "One guy said he'd never had a better lay."

Sloane curled her lip to show her distaste. "Now I see why you're waiting."

"Another said the world's a better place."

"Ouch!"

She shaded the screen from the bright Amalfi sun. "Maybe I should go ahead and change her number—"

"No," Sloane broke in. "There's something special about keeping it. Lilly told me her mom's phone number is the only one she knows by heart. It'll preserve a part of Sabrina for her."

"And she'll be able to text Steve whenever she wants." Charlotte lifted the phone to show Sloane the screen. "I've left his contact info in here."

"She loved the picture he sent."

It'd been a week since Sloane had helped Lilly find a place in

Praiano where they could get it printed so she could tape it to her mirror. She'd done that to keep Lilly occupied while Charlotte worked. "What are you hearing from Ben?" she asked.

"He's keeping busy while I'm gone," she said, once again veering away from a more serious conversation. She'd shared what she'd shared, but she didn't like to dwell on it. "In his off-hours, he looks things up on the internet and sends me links to fun things we should do."

Charlotte knew about a lot of his earlier suggestions. "What's he sent lately?"

"Says we need to hire a boat to take us to the Emerald Grotto."

"Sounds like something from a Disney movie."

"It's a cave near Amalfi," Sloane told her. "Sunlight comes through an underwater fissure and turns the water a pretty emerald color."

"I definitely want to see that." They hadn't spent much time in the town of Amalfi yet, but she knew there was supposed to be some good hiking there. Lots of cute shops, too, not to mention restaurants and bakeries. She hoped to see it, as well as Sorrento and the Isle of Capri, before they had to go back to the States.

"When should I schedule it?" Sloane asked. "I've been holding off because I wanted to be sure you were at a good place in your book so you could join us."

"Let's go once I submit my sample chapters. That's how we'll celebrate."

"You deserve to celebrate. It's got to be hard to concentrate when we're all enjoying ourselves. Are you still feeling good about your story?"

"I like it," she said.

Sloane peered at her more closely. "Just . . . not a lot?"

"This book is a little more . . . meaningful than the last one."

"And the last one would be considered . . ."

"Playful." She gave her friend a worried look. "I'm afraid readers won't gravitate quite as well to 'meaningful.'"

Sloane looped her arm through Charlotte's while Julian and Lilly walked back holding gigantic lemons filled with sorbet. "Sometimes those are the books that sell the best."

"I hope you're right—because chances are I'll have only one shot at this. If my sales numbers are bad—"

"They won't be bad," Sloane broke in. "Your first book killed it."

That logic didn't help. The performance of her first book is what had created such high expectations. "I'm not nearly as convinced."

"Stop it. I believe in you."

Bolstered by her friend's support, Charlotte did what she could to cast off the nagging worry. But then she met Julian's gaze and noticed how quickly he adjusted the camera strap that didn't need adjusting. He'd barely spoken to her since their kiss and had made himself scarce whenever she was available. His sudden withdrawal made her regret her drunken actions last week even though, especially late at night, she relived the moment he pulled her into his arms.

Club music thumped faintly and sunscreen and salt cut through the heat as Sloane watched Lilly swim in the sea from under the shade of a wide-brimmed beach hat while sitting on an orange lounger provided by One Fire Beach Club. She'd been surprised by how much she was enjoying Charlotte's half sister. Because both Charlotte and Julian had to work in the mornings, she was the only one available to entertain Lilly—something she'd thought would be onerous.

But she'd been pleasantly surprised. They'd been having a lot of fun.

Yesterday, she'd purchased some makeup for Lilly and was

teaching her how to apply it. To Sabrina's credit, Lilly had been told she had to wait until she was thirteen to wear cosmetics, but Sloane figured the girl was close enough now. She'd decided to buy her a few things she could experiment with while they were waiting for Charlotte to join them each day.

Lilly came out of the waves and flung her hair back, completely unaware of the boy, maybe a year or two older, who'd taken an interest in her. Sloane smiled to herself as she watched his eyes follow Lilly.

"How's the water?"

Lilly stretched out beside her and used one arm to cover her eyes to avoid the glare of the sun. "Perfect. Aren't you going to get in?"

"I might—in a bit. I just ordered us a couple of sodas."

After plopping her own beach hat on her head, Lilly sat up and retrieved the digital reader from the basket that held what they'd brought with them. She'd asked to read *Playing for Keeps*, but Charlotte had insisted she wasn't old enough, so Sloane had steered her toward YA, and now *Throne of Glass* had her glued to the screen.

"What's happening in your book?" she asked.

"Oh, my gosh!" Lilly exclaimed. "It's getting *so* good. I don't know how you say the girl's name, but she's in big trouble. The assassins and warriors are dying, and she doesn't even know why!"

"Do you?"

"No. Maybe we will both find out today." She lowered the brim of her hat to provide more shade as she started to read, but when their drinks arrived, Sloane had the chance to interrupt.

"If you had your choice, would you like to go back and live with Steve at the farm?" she asked. "And Old Blue?"

Lilly pulled her bottom lip between her teeth for a moment before answering. "Has Steve invited me?"

"I don't know," she lied, just in case Charlotte might take

exception to her providing this information. "Would you want to go if he did?"

A hint of suspicion entered her eyes. "Is that what Charlotte would like me to do—so she can go back to Cliff or whatever?"

Sloane didn't want her to feel they were trying to get rid of her. That wasn't why she'd asked. She simply wanted to know how Lilly felt. "She hasn't said. You were just so excited about that picture Steve sent—and to hear from him again. It made me wonder if you'd like to go back and be with him and Old Blue, because if that's the case, I could push for it. That's all."

Lilly stared down into the drink the waitress had just handed her. "I don't know," she finally mumbled.

"You don't have to decide today. I just thought you might like to have that as an option."

She nodded as the waitress left. Then she did a double take when she saw the same boy Sloane had noticed earlier. "Why's that kid staring at me?" she whispered warily, her eyebrows drawn together.

"Because you're beautiful," Sloane said with a laugh.

"No, I'm not."

Sloane couldn't believe it. "Haven't you looked in a mirror lately? You absolutely are."

"I'm too tall and too skinny. And my feet are too big."

"I don't think he cares about your feet, and no one else will, either," she said and reached over to give her arm a squeeze to emphasize what she'd said.

Lilly's attention shifted to Sloane's hand, but she didn't pull away. A shy smile dawned on her face, one that told Sloane Lilly was finally beginning to trust her the way she'd begun to trust Julian, and it was then that Sloane knew she never wanted to lose touch with this sweet girl.

She was almost afraid to tell Ben what she was feeling.

At the same time, she couldn't wait.

chapter 22

Lilly spent the next several days thinking about what Sloane had said at the beach club about going to live with Steve. She imagined waking up in her old room, with the frilly curtains Steve's mom had put up that were much too young for her—not that she would ever be ungrateful enough to point that out—and having Old Blue waiting on the porch for her. She imagined the smell of bacon wafting through the house and having Steve call out that it was time for breakfast—and once she'd eaten, having him tell her that she needed to hurry and get ready so she wouldn't be late for school. When she'd lived with him before, he'd packed her lunches and sent her off to the bus stop each day; in some ways, it would feel normal. The farm would also be a quiet, steady-as-morning-chores life. Just what she'd always craved.

But then she imagined not having her mother there with her. While that would be a good thing in some ways—there'd be no more fights or the feeling that she couldn't get too comfortable because it wouldn't last—would she truly fit in? Did she *belong* at the farm the way Old Blue did? If not, *could* she belong there? Or would it be too weird to be raised by someone who was no relation to her? A single guy.

Could Steve ever really love her like a daughter?

She had no ongoing relationship with any of her mom's other boyfriends. He was the only one who'd actually tried to be a stepfather. But she hadn't had a great deal of time with him. Her mother had started acting out after only a few months. And Lilly didn't want to be a burden on him just because he was nice enough to take her in.

She wanted someone to love her.

No, that wasn't enough, she decided. She wanted to be *wanted*. That was what she'd always craved. Her mother had loved her, but she'd also used her to pick up the pieces each time her life fell apart.

"You're quiet today," Sloane commented.

Lilly breathed deeply, smelling sun-warmed asphalt as they walked to the small family-owned grocery store they visited when they needed to get a few ingredients for dinner. Sloane had started teaching Lilly how to cook, which was something she really enjoyed. She'd made a lot of meals when her mom was alive—she'd had to if she wanted to eat—but it wasn't the same. That was mostly packaged stuff, a sandwich or a can of soup. Sloane said that wasn't *cooking*. She was showing Lilly how to make her own spaghetti and pasta sauces, bake her own bread and make polenta, tiramisu, even a chocolate cake with strawberry-and-cream layers. Mostly, they cooked Italian. Sloane said she wanted to remain "fully immersed" in the Italian experience while they were here.

Besides, it was easy to get just the right ingredients, and Lilly loved helping her choose the menu.

Tonight they were going to make an artichoke dip, then some grilled garlic shrimp and follow that up with lemon pasta.

Lilly could already taste the hit of zest and the buttery slide of noodles. Fortunately, she liked lemon stuff because it was *everywhere* on the Amalfi Coast, and Sloane was really excited about it, too, so she always suggested it for meals.

"I'm just thinking about dinner," Lilly commented, even though that wasn't really true.

"Dinner takes that much concentration?" Sloane glanced back with a smile that said she was only teasing.

"I guess not," she admitted, but she wasn't about to volunteer that she was thinking about Steve or the farm, so she said, "I've been wondering whether Charlotte will be able to finish her book on time."

"Maybe not on time, but she should be close. Seems like it's going well so far."

"What happens if her editor doesn't like it?"

They made their way up a set of stairs and shifted left to start another flight. "That wouldn't be good."

"Her career would be over?"

"Maybe they'd pull the book from the production schedule to give her time to change it. I'm not sure."

"I know she's been worried."

Sloane waited for Lilly to catch up with her. The walkways weren't wide enough for them to remain side by side for the whole journey, not if someone was coming from the opposite direction, so Lilly generally trailed behind to allow room for others. "Listen to me, Lilly. You don't have to worry about adult problems anymore, okay? Like I've told you before, Charlotte is smart and reliable. She'll be fine."

She was saying that Charlotte wasn't Sabrina. Only she was doing it nicely. And Lilly was grateful. It was so easy to get caught up in the kind of sick-to-her-stomach worrying she'd done most of her life. In some ways, she'd had less of that since

Sloane, Julian and Charlotte had entered her life. Now she had three capable adults looking out for her, the world seemed a lot safer.

But their time in Italy was almost over. What would happen then? Would she no longer be safe? She had no real assurances, and that made each day feel like she was taking one more step toward some terrible end.

Lilly slung the cute hobo-style bag Charlotte had bought her last night across her body to shift the weight of it. "Do you think she'll go back to Cliff?"

"God, I hope not."

Lilly knew Charlotte hadn't been responding to him. She'd heard her say as much. But she also knew he'd been trying harder and harder to get her back. He'd reached out to Sloane, even though Sloane said they'd never gotten along. She said Cliff was too possessive of Charlotte, that he'd tried to separate her from all the other people in her life who loved her, and that made Lilly wonder what would happen if Charlotte went back to him. She didn't want to lose contact with her sister. She was really starting to like Charlotte. And Charlotte was her only family. Cliff had enough people, possessions and attention. He didn't need Charlotte, too. Did he?

"But . . . what are the chances?" She wanted something to be certain for a change.

Sloane's answer proved, once again, that *nothing* was certain in life. "To be honest, I couldn't even put a number on it," she said. "Let's just be glad she's focused on being here with us and getting her book done. It's giving her some time away from him—time to see that she's better off without him," she added emphatically.

"You're saying the real test will come once we get home."

Sloane cast her a rueful glance, but continued walking. "That's the bottom line, I guess."

Lilly had searched the internet to learn everything she possibly could about Cliff. He was famous enough that there was a lot to sort through. Tons of pictures showed how handsome he was. And from his interviews, he seemed like a fun guy. He was certainly good at basketball. But Sloane didn't like him. Neither did Charlotte's parents, from what Lilly had been able to tell. She'd spoken to them a few times on the phone. They were starting to call regularly—and ask to talk to her after they'd spoken with Charlotte.

Charlotte's mother sounded like the kind of grandma who'd bake cookies and go all out for Christmas—nothing like the tired and frustrated person who'd been her real grandma. Charlotte's dad sounded patient and kind and sort of indulgent toward the women in his life. Lilly liked how he'd just chuckle whenever Charlotte and Penny got carried away with an idea.

"What would Charlotte's parents do if she went back to him?" Lilly asked. "Would they put a stop to it?"

"They probably wouldn't say anything. It's Charlotte's decision, right?"

"I guess." Disheartened, she walked a bit slower—and stopped briefly to run a finger over the blue ceramic octopus tile embedded in the wall. No one had ever been able to tell Sabrina what to do, either. That was part of the reason she'd never gotten along with *her* parents. "What about Julian?" She and Sloane were together so much these days that they talked all the time, but this conversation went a little deeper than others, making Lilly feel as though she was stepping onto thin ice.

"What about him?" Sloane asked, pausing to wait for her.

"He'd be the most upset if she went back to Cliff."

At this, Sloane retraced a few of her steps. "Why? You mean because Cliff doesn't treat Charlotte like he should?"

"I mean because . . . because Julian likes her himself, doesn't he?"

"Not in that way," Sloane said. "We all grew up together. It's not romantic."

Lilly didn't say anything when they started walking again, but that wasn't the impression she'd gotten. The way Julian looked at Charlotte, especially when she wasn't paying attention, was more like . . . like he cared about her in a *completely* romantic way. And Sloane didn't like Cliff, but Julian took that to a whole other level. He wasn't only protective of Charlotte; he was jealous of Cliff.

Or was she wrong about that? She'd spent her whole life trying to read the various men her mother had been with. She'd had to—to get some idea of what was coming. She could always tell when her mother's latest boyfriend was angry, frustrated, happy or even when he lost interest.

But maybe Julian was different . . .

"Have you heard if Ben will be able to get enough days off to come over?" she asked, changing the subject. She'd also spoken to Ben and really liked him. He was similar to Julian, only not quite as funny.

"The pharmacy's too busy this time of year, and he doesn't have the vacation days. We have only ten days left, so there's not really time to arrange it anyway."

"That's a bummer."

"Yeah. He'd really like to meet you."

"I'd like to meet him, too."

"Maybe we can have you over when we get back," she said as they reached the street where the store was located.

"You mean if I'm not in Cherokee?"

"A minute ago, you didn't sound totally convinced you wanted to live with Steve. Have you changed your mind?"

She hadn't, because going to the farm would mean leaving Charlotte, and that wouldn't be an easy choice—if it *was* her choice. Maybe Charlotte wouldn't want to keep her even if she didn't go back to Cliff. "I don't know what I want to do yet."

The sound of the door alerted Sloane that Charlotte had just come out of the house. She knew it wasn't Lilly, not this late. Lilly had taken her e-reader and gone to bed over an hour ago. She was so engrossed in the second book of Sarah J. Maas's series that nothing short of an earthquake or a fire would make her leave her room now that dinner was over and she had the chance to read. And Julian hadn't returned after being gone all day. Sloane had been waiting for him to come through the gate. After what she'd just seen, she needed to talk to him.

"There you are," Charlotte said.

Fortunately, that comment didn't require a response, so Sloane took a moment to compose herself. She'd been hoping for some privacy until her brother got home, had thought she'd be able to safely find it on the deck. She'd heard Charlotte talking to Cliff on the phone earlier and assumed she wouldn't venture out again, if only to avoid what Sloane had to say about the part of the conversation she'd overheard—where it had sounded as though Charlotte was weakening and might eventually cave in to his entreaties.

Pulling the lap blanket she'd carried outside higher around her shoulders, Sloane used it to partially shield her face.

"I thought you went to bed when Lilly did," Charlotte commented.

Sloane kept her gaze on the lights pricking the dark over Amalfi so that Charlotte couldn't see the tears in her eyes. That picture Ben's coworker had sent had leveled her. She felt like she couldn't breathe, let alone explain what was happening, even to her best friend, especially because she sensed that everyone would think she deserved exactly what she was getting. After all, she was the one who'd been unsure whether she wanted to stay in her marriage. "No."

"Where's Jules?"

The sea thudded softly below; the air smelled faintly of citrus and stone as a cool breeze ruffled her hair. "He . . . um . . . I don't know," she managed to say.

Charlotte pulled out a chair and sat to Sloane's right. "Are you waiting up for him?"

Sloane's composure was crumbling. She wouldn't be able to keep up the pretense much longer.

When she didn't answer right away, Charlotte leaned forward, trying to catch her eye. "Seems like he's gone all the time these days."

Sloane drew in a deep breath. "He's been—" she swallowed hard "—spending a lot of time in Sorrento."

"Sorrento? Without *us*?"

"He told me there's a lot to photograph, so . . ."

"I get that," Charlotte said. "But it's dark now. Well past dark. Seems like he should be home."

Sloane didn't say anything. It was too hard to speak.

"Sloane? Did you hear me? I said it seems like he should be home by now."

"What do you want from me?" she snapped, too upset to be able to hold back. "He's not!"

"What's wrong?" Charlotte asked, grabbing her arm to get her to turn and make eye contact.

The concern in her friend's voice broke what was left of the dam holding Sloane's emotions back. She could no longer speak as the tears began to stream down her face.

"What's happened?" Charlotte asked again, clearly alarmed.

Sloane figured she might as well show her now. Shoving her phone at Charlotte, she squeezed her eyes shut before covering them with her hands.

"What's this?" Charlotte asked.

"Can't you see it?" she choked out, dropping her hands. "That's Ben!"

"I know it's Ben, but it doesn't look like he's doing anything wrong. He's got a kid on his shoulders, but he's not with a woman. He's just . . . outside in a parking lot."

"That's not just any kid, Char. That's Colt, the son of the woman his pharmacy hired right after I left. Her name's Adele something. You can't see her in the picture because she's bent over putting groceries in her car."

"You're not saying . . . You don't think Ben's having an *affair*. Chances are he only met this woman when she started."

"I don't think he's having an affair. Not yet."

"But . . ."

"But I could easily see it moving in that direction. She's divorced and her husband isn't a good father. I'm sure Ben would love to step in. He wouldn't even have to wait through a pregnancy."

"How do you know she's divorced and the boy doesn't have an involved father?"

"Ben told me."

Charlotte gestured at the phone. "So wait . . . Where is this?"

"Right by the pharmacy. There's a big grocery store next to it."

"So he probably came out of work, saw her loading her groceries and is entertaining her son while she does it. Isn't that his car parked right next to hers?"

"Yes, but—"

"Sloane, according to what you just told me, he's been open with you about the new hire, who happens to have a young boy he's trying to help with. How does that change anything?"

"Don't you see it? How happy he is? He wants children,

Char. Sandra, his coworker who sent me this picture, said he and Adele are getting close. That's why she contacted me! She's concerned. She must have reason to be."

"She could be wrong—"

"I'm holding him back. If I don't agree to have kids, he'll leave me. If not now, eventually." She gestured at the photograph Sandra had snapped of Ben helping to entertain Adele's five-year-old. "Maybe even for her."

Charlotte sighed audibly. "Sloane, no! Ben loves you. He's always been true to you. Why would you doubt him now?"

"Because I can feel us drifting apart! We're changing, have different interests. I don't think I'm the right person for the person he's turning into."

"Have you two talked about this?"

"Not enough. We don't want to acknowledge it. But we need to. We want different things."

"Are you ready to let go of your marriage?"

Slumping lower in her seat, she finished the last sip of wine in the glass she'd brought outside. "I don't know. I'd be giving up such a good man."

"Yes, you would."

"You think I'd be making a mistake . . ."

Charlotte seemed to choose her words carefully. "I can't say that. Sometimes two people aren't right for each other even though they're both good people. That's actually what I've been writing about, and that could be the case here. But you've always been so much in love. It's hard to choose divorce when you're not splitting up for . . . for something that makes the decision necessary."

"We just want different lives!" she reiterated.

"Are you sure you don't want children?"

"No," she admitted. "But I also don't want to feel forced into having them."

"I can understand that. I wanted children, but Cliff wasn't ready—"

"Ew!" she broke in, using the back of her hand to wipe her nose. "Don't compare me to Cliff."

"I know you don't like him, but—"

"Are you going back to him? Because his opinion on children isn't the problem. He doesn't want you to have any of your friends or family in your life. That selfish bastard wants you all to himself, so you can focus your time, effort and energy exclusively on him. Then in a few years, he'll probably cast you aside for a much younger woman."

"Ouch!" Charlotte said.

Sloane knew she was going too far, but she couldn't help it. She was hurt and upset, and feeling she had only herself to blame just made it worse. Why oh why couldn't she crave babies like so many other women did?

"If I don't say it, who will?" she said, doubling down instead of shutting up like she knew she should. "Do you think I should bite my tongue and let you go back to him when he doesn't deserve you? When the life you'd live wouldn't be the kind of life you could have with a better partner? Money's great and all that, but what about feeling safe, secure, loved and supported? What about your needs being as important as his for a change?"

"You mean how will I live without all the truly important things—like the ones Ben's given *you*?" Charlotte snapped, finally getting upset. "Well, look how far that's gotten him!"

Sloane felt like she'd been punched in the gut. Maybe she deserved it. She'd raised her voice first. But she was in a hollowed-out kind of despair, afraid it was already too late to save her marriage.

"Obviously, you've got Ben's back. I'll be sure to let him know you're in his corner," she said and stalked into the house, where she went straight to her room and threw herself on the bed.

Charlotte's heart thudded as she stared at the blanket Sloane had dropped, now pooled at the chair's feet. The air on the deck still felt charged, sharp with what she hadn't meant to say.

"Damn it," she cursed. She loved Sloane, wanted to be there for her no matter what. But they were both on edge, worried about their marriages—or their divorces, as the case might be. Sloane was also concerned about leaving her business languishing in the hands of her partner for so long. She'd been starting to talk a lot about that and spending more time on the phone and computer. And after being gone for almost three weeks, she had to be a little homesick. Then to receive a picture of Ben laughing while holding his new coworker's darling son when the issue tearing them apart revolved around having kids . . .

Charlotte could totally understand why that would hurt.

Still, she had no right to judge her or be critical.

She should've handled the situation better, been more supportive, she decided. But Sloane had struck a nerve with what she'd said about Cliff. She hadn't needed to say it; Charlotte already knew the truth. She understood, just as Sloane did, that he was unlikely to change. In her view, it was more a matter of timing. If she went back to him, she could get her feet under her again. She'd have somewhere she and Lilly could stay until she finished her book, and the reconciliation would make her second book sell as well as the first. That seemed *so* vital to her right now. If her marriage fell apart after one last, concerted effort, at least trying again would've bought her some time. Time to keep her money separate from his so she'd have some reserves. Time to get some counseling and prepare herself emotionally. Time to focus on her future deadlines so she'd never fall this far behind again.

She'd been blindsided when he asked for the divorce. She just wanted to regain her equilibrium and have some way to plan what she'd do if her marriage *did* fall apart.

While she hated herself for even gaming it out, that would be the easiest path in so many ways, which was why, when she was at her weakest, it was tempting.

But she also knew, in her heart of hearts, that she could never really do it. Cliff had broken something when he kicked her out—had made her look at him from a critical point of view, which she would never allow herself to do when she was busy being the dutiful, long-suffering wife. She couldn't put what they'd had together again. He called her refusal a lack of forgiveness. Made her feel guilty for being unable to let it go as a mistake. But she wasn't a hard-hearted person. She believed it was her intuition, warning her to stay away from danger.

It was also what she'd begun to feel for Jules . . .

With a sigh, she got up and went inside to apologize, but Sloane wouldn't open her bedroom door. Charlotte called out—softly, so she wouldn't disturb Lilly—and Sloane replied just as softly that they'd discuss it in the morning, when she wasn't feeling quite so raw.

Charlotte accepted that because she knew it was probably a good idea. She wasn't in the best frame of mind herself. Not only was she stressed out about her marriage and her career, but also she was concerned about Julian. She missed him. She needed him. She wanted to know, if it was their kiss that'd made him retreat from her, if they could get beyond it somehow. If that required an apology for crossing the line they'd always respected in the past, she was willing to give it to him.

So instead of going to bed, she went back to the deck and waited until he finally came through the gate.

chapter 23

Julian waited to come home until he was sure Charlotte would be in bed. She typically didn't stay up late. That made it too hard for her to write the following morning. So he was shocked when he got back to see that the rest of the house was quiet and dark, but she was sitting at the table on the deck with her computer.

"Are you writing?" he asked.

The sea kept an even hush below as she closed the laptop and shook her head.

"Then . . . what's wrong? Why are you out here all alone?"

"I've been waiting for you."

He felt his stomach sink. He'd planned to muddle through this trip until he could get back to his normal life, whatever that was going to be like now that he was dealing with a debilitating disease. He didn't want to get in her way or make anything worse for her. But he could tell she wasn't going to let him skirt past her too easily. "What for?"

"Sloane and I had an argument tonight."

That happened occasionally. Sloane was a passionate, animated person. Charlotte was usually a bit more levelheaded, but she stood her ground, especially when Sloane went too far. "About what?"

"I told her I think she's crazy for even considering leaving Ben. And she told me that Cliff is a total asshole, and I'd be a stupid idiot to go back to him."

Julian wanted to say that both of those things were true. But he bit his tongue.

"I didn't hear you," Charlotte said.

He spread out his hands. "I didn't say anything."

"Exactly. If you were being the you *I* know, you would have. You had plenty to say the night you dragged me out of bed for dinner right after Cliff dumped me."

That was before he'd realized his feelings had shifted. "Yeah, well, I haven't changed my mind about Cliff. I think you already know that. And you seem to be back on your feet now."

She jumped up. "I do? Because I feel like I'm drowning, Jules. And you just . . . disappeared on me. Is it about that kiss? *One* kiss? Are you kidding me? God, was it *that* terrible?"

It hadn't been terrible at all. It'd been revealing—*too* revealing. It'd felt as if their childhood had set them up for a lifetime of love and happiness—except for the part where she wouldn't want him because he was about to fall apart. Even if she did want him, he'd hate for her to accept anything less than what she deserved.

"That kiss had nothing to do with it." Other than show him what he'd be missing. As if he'd needed *that*.

"I don't believe you. You haven't even been willing to look at me since. I wouldn't have done it if I'd known how you were going to react. I'm sorry."

"You don't have to apologize," he said gruffly. "It wasn't just you. We both know that."

She stepped closer, wearing a confused and hurt expression. "Then why are you avoiding me? What have I done? One kiss makes me poisonous?"

The disappointment he'd been feeling since his diagnosis cut even deeper than usual. "I'm trying to stay away from you, okay?"

Her eyes widened, and she blinked. "*Why?* That's what I'm trying to find out!"

"Because I want you too badly, damn it!" He gripped the chair back until his knuckles turned white. He'd said too much. But he'd been drinking again and had lost his usual restraint. After he'd finished photographing the harbor and daily life in Sorrento, he'd taken the bus back to Praiano, but there'd been nothing better to do while he waited for everyone to go to bed at the villa—so that he wouldn't run into Charlotte again—than to relax with a beer and then another and another.

Her mouth fell open. "That can't be the problem. You . . . you view me as a sister or something. When I kissed you, it gave you the *ick* factor, and now you won't even look at me."

"I *wish* that were the case," he muttered, too low for her to hear.

"What'd you say?" She stepped up to him, challenging him.

He moved back. He couldn't see this going anywhere it should. "Nothing."

"I enjoyed that kiss. *I* wanted more, but you . . . you weren't interested."

"You're thinking about going back to your husband, remember?" It was an excuse, something he wasn't nearly as afraid of as the truth. But at least she'd find his response believable.

"So you *don't* think of me like a sister . . ."

Apparently, he'd done a better job of hiding his attraction to her than he'd thought. "Look, I've had too much to drink. *Again.*" The bite of beer lingered on his tongue. "And I'm tired. I'm heading to bed before— I'm heading to bed," he said, cutting off his prior sentence so he wouldn't get himself into even more trouble.

"Julian . . ."

He told himself to ignore the plea in her voice and go inside. But he cared too much about her. He turned back.

"You don't think . . . You don't think you and I could ever . . . that we'd ever . . . you know, have a chance at something more than . . . what we've had in the past?"

He could tell it'd been a hard question for her to ask. They'd labeled their relationship as "friends" for so long it was difficult to take that next step and feel sure about it. But the fact that she seemed interested in him romantically was as crushing as it was remarkable. He'd never dreamed she'd be able to imagine them together, especially while she was still trying to break away from Cliff.

But plenty of people struggled to know who and what they really wanted when they were on the rebound, he reminded himself.

"Maybe if circumstances were different," he said. "But they're not."

Sloane had tried calling Ben last night—several times—but she'd been unable to reach him, which she found a little odd. He was usually good about responding. Because she didn't hear from him, she'd tossed and turned, imagining that he was hanging out with his new coworker, mowing her yard, fixing a leaky faucet or teaching her boy how to play ball. It would be just like him to offer his help. He'd see no point in remaining home alone. Since she'd been gone, he'd attended trivia night with his friends, played in his weekly softball league game and visited a sports bar a couple of times to watch playoff basketball, and she didn't mind. He, too, had the right to have fun. She just didn't want that fun to include Adele—not when she felt her marriage was so fragile.

She must've worried herself ragged because when she finally dropped off, she slept like the dead. It was several hours later when the sun came through the cracks in the shutters and woke her the next morning.

"Shit," she said as all her worries—and the memory of her argument with Charlotte—came crashing down on her.

She felt around for her phone. She hadn't let it go—even to charge it—so it had vanished into the blankets.

She found it under one of the pillows. There were several messages from Ben. But no missed calls. That seemed significant and gave her the impression he hadn't been all that anxious to talk to her.

What's going on?

Is everything okay?

Sorry I wasn't able to respond. I was playing poker at Tony's.

Tony was a coworker. He managed the store in which the pharmacy leased space. Ben hung out with him occasionally. They both liked to mountain bike. But the fact that Tony was also associated with the pharmacy made Sloane wonder if other coworkers were invited—like Adele.

Was the new girl there?

She held the words on the screen a full three seconds, then deleted them. She didn't want to come off as a jealous shrew, even though she currently *was* a jealous shrew.

A knock sounded at the door.

"I'm up," she called out.

Charlotte came in wearing a sheepish expression. "Morning."

Sloane slid up and combed her fingers through her tangled

hair. "Morning," she said, feeling contrite about how she'd behaved last night.

"I just wanted to say . . . I'm sorry."

"So am I," Sloane mumbled and set her phone on the nightstand. "I was . . . worked up. You're going through a lot, and I should've taken that into account."

"We overreacted. We're both struggling, and we both have difficult decisions to make."

"Who could've guessed our lives would come to such a turning point? Maybe we'll both wind up single," she added with a humorless laugh.

Sloane assumed Charlotte would make some wise crack about becoming roommates and growing old together. Something with a sentiment akin to "at least we have each other." But she didn't. She became even more serious and reflective. "Here's the thing, Sloane. I don't think *you* have to wind up single."

Because Ben was such a good husband. But he'd been a good husband all along. That didn't solve the problem of whether she wanted to have children. "You're saying you do plan to end your marriage?" She was interested in Charlotte's answer, but she also wanted to keep the focus off herself.

Charlotte crossed the floor, threw open the shutters and stood in a pool of sunlight as she stared out the window. "Yeah."

"You really mean it this time?" Sloane had heard a note of commitment in Charlotte's voice that hadn't been there before.

"Do you mean that?" she pressed when Charlotte didn't immediately respond.

"I do. Letting go all at once was a big step. A lot has happened in a short time, so it took me a minute to get my bearings. But I'm there now."

Sloane got up and walked over. "You don't need him, Char. You've got us."

"I appreciate that." She smiled. "So . . . what are *you* going to do?"

Sloane wished she could say she'd also come to a decision, but she hadn't. "I don't know."

"Fortunately, you don't have to make up your mind this minute. Why don't we take the day to go see the Emerald Grotto?"

"But . . . you haven't sent in your pages yet."

"I'm close. I need the support of my friends today. And Lilly. I'll send them late tonight."

"Okay. I'll buy the tickets and you and Jules can Venmo me."

Lilly had been enjoying herself as much as she could, considering she had no idea what would happen when their stay in Italy came to an end. But today felt special, like a holiday, so she wasn't going to let anything sad or worrisome intrude.

First, she, Julian, Sloane and Charlotte took a bus to Amalfi. The driver tapped his horn around the blind curves as they traveled along the narrow, winding highway that connected Positano, Praiano and Amalfi—and other towns on the coast—like the thread going through a strand of pearls. Then they enjoyed Nutella croissants, which shattered into sweet flakes, and coffee—she got hot chocolate—at a sidewalk café not far from the huge, ornate cathedral that sat in the middle of the town square.

After that, they walked around the cobblestone streets to visit the surrounding shops before catching a small boat, one that could only seat six people, at Pennello Pier.

Charlotte and the others had decided to pay for a charter despite there being cheaper ways to get to the grotto. Lilly had heard Julian say they could even reach it by land. But Charlotte wanted to spend a couple of hours on the water—not just be ferried back and forth—and Lilly was glad Sloane and Julian had agreed. To her, being on the boat was one of the coolest things in the world. The coast was gorgeous from the sea! All the buildings—even the huge cathedrals with their domed tops—looked like miniatures. And the colorful houses cascading down the cliffs resembled jewels the mountains were pouring into the sea.

Lilly especially enjoyed looking at the ancient towers that'd been built to protect the old villages from pirates. There were more than she'd ever imagined. The Saracens must've been a big problem. The round stone towers—some crumbled, some almost intact—reminded her of tiny castles. Charlotte said they were built fifteen hundred years ago, which made them almost a thousand years older than America!

That something could last so long filled Lilly with a sense of wonder. Of all the sights they saw while they were on the boat, she loved the towers most because they captured her imagination.

But some of the cathedrals in Italy were almost as old, she reminded herself.

The wind flung her hair around as she sat in the bow, the sun causing the water to sparkle and shimmer all around her. She felt so grown-up in her swimsuit. It was a blue one-piece, not a bikini like her mother had always preferred. But she thought it was pretty. She was also wearing a cover-up very similar to Charlotte's—Charlotte had bought them both at the same place—and the same beach hat as Sloane. From a distance, she probably didn't look much younger than her sister and her sister's friend because she was as tall as they were.

Maybe one day she really would grow into her feet, she thought, examining the bright orange polish on her toes. Just before they'd left the villa, Charlotte had offered to paint her nails, and they'd turned out so pretty it no longer seemed to matter that her feet were too big.

"Look at you—grinning like you've never been on a boat

before," Sloane said as the outboard hummed steady as a bee. "You're obviously not seasick."

She *had* never been on a boat before. But Sloane already knew that. "Nope." Standing, she held out her arms like Rose in the movie *Titanic* and let the wind ripple through her cover-up. "I *love* the movement. Don't you?"

"*I* do. It's my stomach that's not all that excited about it," she said with a pained expression.

Lilly felt guilty for wishing their trip would continue forever. "Will you be okay? Should we go back?"

"No. The skipper gave me some Dramamine. I should be fine in fifteen or twenty minutes."

Lilly asked to stop for a swim, and the skipper found a small cove near Positano, where they all jumped into the water.

"Good idea, Lilly," Sloane said as they cooled off. "This should give the Dramamine time to work."

Julian had hung out with her a lot at first, but recently she'd been spending most of her time with Sloane. Maybe that was another reason she was enjoying herself so much. He was with them today. Charlotte was, too, and she wasn't so preoccupied. She seemed to have forgotten about her divorce and her book, at least for the day.

After they swam for a while, when Sloane was finally feeling better, they climbed back into the boat and motored to the Emerald Grotto, which was closer to Amalfi than to Positano. The cave wasn't as big as Lilly had expected, but she loved the light hue of the water and smiled happily for a picture with Charlotte, then one with Charlotte and Sloane and a selfie of all four of them that Julian took because he had the longest arms.

Her sister and her sister's friends didn't treat her like a nuisance, she realized. They didn't act as if they didn't want her around, the way so many of her mother's boyfriends had. They treated her like she was a valued member of the group.

"I'd never even heard of a grotto until I moved here," Lilly told them as their skipper maneuvered carefully around all the other boats jostling for a turn inside the cave. "Do we have any in America?"

"Good question," Charlotte responded and checked the internet on her phone. "Apparently, we do," she said after a quick search. "Religious grottoes, man-made grottoes *and* natural ones."

Lilly wrinkled her nose. "Isn't the point that they're natural?"

"You'd think," Sloane said.

Charlotte tipped the brim of her hat to remove the glare from her screen. "I guess man-made ones are a thing. Says here that the Midwest has a whole bunch of Catholic grottoes—the largest collection in the world."

Disappointed that the ride was almost over, Lilly watched the opening of the cave and all the boats waiting around it disappear from view. "What are *Catholic* grottoes?"

Charlotte, who'd gone back to reading, looked up. "Grottoes made by German Catholic immigrants, evidently. This article says they're considered folk art."

Lilly tightened the string under her chin so that her hat wouldn't blow away now that the skipper was going so fast. "I can't even imagine what a fake grotto would look like."

"Maybe you should pull it up on your phone," Charlotte said.

Lilly blinked. "What phone?"

A smile spread across her sister's face right before she dug inside her bag and pulled out Sabrina's phone. "On *this* phone, which belongs to you now," she said and handed it over.

Lilly had wanted a phone since forever. "Are you kidding?" She searched her sister's face to be sure she wasn't going to add "while we're in Italy" or something else that suggested she'd take it back.

"I'm not kidding," Charlotte said. "It's all yours."

"*Forever?*"

Charlotte laughed. "For the next year, at least. Then you'll probably want an upgrade."

A bolt of excitement charged through Lilly. The thin, sleek metal object in her hand signified freedom and the ability to do so much more for herself. "Thank you," she said. "Thank you, thank you, thank you!"

The smile on Charlotte's face looked . . . affectionate. "You're welcome. I've been very excited to give it to you. I was just waiting for the right moment."

Lilly knew it was stupid to allow herself to feel so happy. Something terrible always seemed to come right after. But it was starting to feel as if she still had family in the world, and that maybe her sister *wouldn't* abandon her in the end. "You're the best thing to ever happen to me," she said and threw her arms around Charlotte.

Charlotte seemed bowled over at first but quickly rallied and returned the hug. "I'm glad," she said, laughing, "because I'm not going anywhere."

Breaking away so she could see Charlotte's face, Lilly stepped back. "Do you mean it?"

Charlotte lifted Lilly's hand, the one holding her new phone. "Look at this. Here's my number," she said, navigating to Contacts. "No matter what happens, I'll only be one call away, from this day until forever."

Owning a phone, having a way to reach Charlotte at any time, day or night, seemed to offer a safety net, which was something she'd never had. It also made Lilly feel connected and important to someone—besides a dog. But it was what she saw when she exited out of her contacts that brought tears to her eyes.

The wallpaper on her new phone was a picture of her with her mother on her last birthday—what *had* been her favorite day.

Until this one.

chapter 24

Ben was eating lunch when he received a text from Sloane.

> Is there something going on I should know about?

Surprised and a bit confused, he was about to ask her to clarify what she was talking about when Adele, who was now replacing Sandra on Mondays, Tuesdays and Thursdays until two o'clock, peeked into the back room. "Hey, you. I made something for you last night."

Her bright, expectant smile—and how often she'd begun seeking him out—made him wish he'd been more guarded. He hoped he hadn't given her the wrong impression. He liked her, but he'd only been trying to make her feel welcome. His father had died when he was just starting high school, so his mother had been forced to soldier on alone, and he knew how hard that could be.

He set down his sandwich as she came in, carrying a plate. "What is it?" he asked.

Warm vanilla and chocolate drifted up as she peeled back

the foil. "The best cookies you'll ever eat—oatmeal chocolate chip. I heard you tell Sandra they're your favorite and that you can hardly ever get them without raisins. So I set out on a mission to find the very best recipe."

"You shouldn't have gone to so much trouble," he said. "That . . . that was very nice of you."

"I wanted to do it. You're the reason I'm excited to come to work each day."

Yikes! Had he said or done something that could've made her think his interest went beyond that of a friend or coworker? He was pretty sure he'd mentioned that he was married. Even if he hadn't, he wore a ring!

"We're all happy to have you here," he said, keeping his voice neutral. "We really needed another person."

"That's what Sandra told me." She stepped close enough for her perfume to drift over as she pulled a folded sheet from her back pocket. "By the way, Colt drew this for you."

It was a picture of a horse. Or a turtle. Ben couldn't decide which. Maybe it was neither. "Very nice."

"He wants to know when he'll get to see you again. I told him I'd ask if you'd like to join us for a picnic this Saturday. I thought I'd make my mother's potato salad, some sandwiches, that sort of thing."

Ben cleared his throat. Would it be just the three of them? Because he didn't mind helping her with chores around the house. He'd spent last Saturday fixing a broken sprinkler for her and getting rid of a bunch of cardboard in her garage because she was new in town and didn't have much support from family or friends. But a picnic would feel more like a date than a service project.

When he hesitated, she added uncertainly, "To thank you for all you did last weekend."

"No thanks needed." He lifted the plate of cookies she'd given him. "These are more than enough."

She seemed crestfallen that he hadn't jumped at her invitation, which made Ben grapple for a way out that wouldn't hurt her feelings. "I . . .uh . . .promised my wife I'd get some 'honey-dos' done around our house before she gets back," he added. "Sorry I can't make the picnic."

Her smile held, but the light went out of her eyes. He'd reminded her of his wife, subtly let her know he wouldn't stray. "Of course. No worries. I can't wait to meet her. Name's Sloane, right?"

"Yeah, Sloane," he confirmed. "You'll really like her. She's great at decorating. If you ever want help with that sort of thing, she's the girl to call."

"Right. Okay," she said and went back into the front.

He exhaled. *Awkward*, he thought, and responded to his wife.

> **What are you talking about?**
>
> Sandra says you've been spending a lot of time with the new hire, who's gorgeous, by the way.

Damn Sandra. No wonder his coworker had been acting so waspish. She thought he was starting to creep around.

> **I was only trying to help. There's nothing going on, Sloane. Nothing.**

He'd mentioned Adele to her before, told her he was going to do a few chores around the house for her and didn't get much of a response. He took that to mean she wouldn't mind. But he hadn't added that Adele was their age and incredibly attractive. He hadn't seen any point in making Sloane jealous when they were already going through a difficult period. If she stayed with him, he wanted it to be because she still wanted to spend the rest of her life with him, not because she felt there was someone waiting in the wings to take her place.

> You believe me, don't you?

The answer, when it came, left Ben weak with relief.

I do. I was just... scared for a minute.

He caught his breath as he wrote her back.

> Are you sure you wouldn't be relieved?

So much hung on that question. Did she want to move on without him or not?

I'm positive. I'd feel completely lost
without you.

He'd be lost without her, too, he realized, or he would've moved on already.
Maybe he was just going to have to live without children.

The day had been torture. Julian had wanted to go to the Emerald Grotto at first. He'd known how excited Lilly was at the prospect of the four of them visiting Amalfi, getting on a boat and touring a cool cave. He'd told himself it wouldn't be that big a deal to spend several hours with Charlotte, not if the others were around. But it'd been much harder than he'd expected, especially after she'd announced that she wouldn't be going back to Cliff. That knocked out one of the excuses he'd been leaning on to convince himself he wouldn't have a chance with her even if he wasn't facing Parkinson's.

"Have you told *him* that yet?" he'd asked.

He knew she'd heard the skepticism in his voice because she'd lifted her chin and flashed him that stubborn look—the one that said heaven and hell couldn't move her now. "No. I didn't want to deal with his reaction—didn't want him to be calling and texting nonstop and ruining our plans. I'll tell him tonight."

He'd tilted his head toward her, goading her a bit further. "You're sure . . ."

At that point, she'd looked at Lilly, who'd been dangling her hand in the water while the boat was stopped so Sloane could snap a picture of Positano. "I'm positive."

It'd been easy to tell she meant it. And that Lilly was part of the reason. Considering how much Charlotte was coming to care about her sister, he believed she wouldn't allow Cliff to get in the way.

"You're going to remain available for her sake," he'd said, catching on.

"You bet I am," she'd told him. Then she'd turned away and mostly ignored him for the rest of the day. She was mad at him. Or more likely, she was confused and hurt by his emotional withdrawal at a time when she felt she needed him most. He knew she believed it had to be that kiss or an off comment here or there that'd strained their friendship, didn't understand it was much bigger than that. And he couldn't tell her. He'd rather have her angry at him than feeling sorry for him.

He couldn't allow her to depend on him, anyway, he told himself as he nursed a shot of whiskey long after the others went to bed. She had Sloane. Sloane was dealing with her own shit, but she'd give Charlotte the support she needed. *He* had to decide on his treatment, work hard, save while he could and find something to fulfill him when work was no longer a possibility. It wasn't fair to expect a woman to become the center of his life when he might not even be capable of helping her raise any children they might have.

Tempted to pour himself another drink, he stared at the bottle on the table. But he'd already had too much. He'd been drowning his feelings in liquor since coming to Italy. He'd told himself he wasn't going to worry about it, that the drinking was only a temporary thing while he was on vacation—before he had to go back and deal with reality. But he knew it couldn't be doing him any good, and he proved himself right when he got up and accidentally slammed into the corner of the table while trying to get past it.

Cursing his clumsiness, and the pain throbbing down his leg, the anger inside him suddenly boiled over. Almost before he knew what he was going to do, he picked up the bottle and threw it.

The crack rang too loud in the night, making him flinch. He stood and stared, stunned by his own actions, at the liquid running down the stucco wall and the shards of glass winking in the moonlight hitting the deck.

"Fuck." Now he had a mess to clean up on top of everything else, but he couldn't leave it until morning. He didn't want Lilly, Sloane or Charlotte to see it.

Charlotte heard the crash. She'd been only half-asleep because she'd been getting out of bed every few minutes and going over to the window, where she could see Julian sitting at the outdoor table. She'd wanted to know what was troubling him, why he was out there drinking alone. It bothered her that he seemed so remote and upset and wouldn't tell her—or Sloane—what was wrong. How bad could it be?

She'd wanted to ask. But she'd refused to go down and try to talk to him again, not after he'd rebuffed her last time. She'd had a rough evening herself. Cliff hadn't taken it well when she told him that she wasn't interested in reconciling. At first, he'd been so disbelieving that he'd laughed. But when she'd let him hang up and hadn't called back, he'd eventually begun to realize she'd been serious. Then he'd started calling her incessantly, and because she wouldn't answer, resorted to a series of text messages.

> I never loved you anyway… What a stupid bitch! Do you realize what you're giving up? What could you be mad at me for? So I got confused! That happens sometimes… Look, I'm sorry, babe. Ignore my previous texts. I was angry, that's all. Let's talk. Can we? Please? Will you just answer your fucking phone?

And when she still wouldn't capitulate:

> What the hell is wrong with you? Do I have to fly over there and drag your ass back?

She'd cringed at the idea that he might come to Italy. That was the last thing she needed. But for now, she felt safe. The Lakers were still in the playoffs. He couldn't go gallivanting around the globe.

> Asking for a divorce was a momentary lapse of judgment. If you can't love me through something small like that, you never really loved me to begin with.

After that last message, she'd finally written back.

> Cliff, please stop. Take a deep breath.
> No matter what happens, I will
> always be your biggest fan.

I have enough fucking fans!

> Calm down. You started this.

How?

> You kicked me out!

So you're looking for revenge? You're trying to
make me pay? I just told you it was a lapse of
judgment. I wasn't thinking straight!

> I'm not out for revenge! It's just that I have Lilly
> to think of now.

Lilly isn't your responsibility. Stop acting like
she's the kid you've always wanted.

> She needs me. That's the point.

So support her like a sister should—in
whatever home she goes to. You don't have to
be her mother, for God's sake.

He'd said before that Lilly could come live with them. This revealed he'd never really meant it. And the way he was acting . . . It reminded her of how possessive he'd always been of her time, how little he'd allowed her to include her parents and friends in her life. He'd made her live for him, and she was simply not willing to do that any longer. What he'd done over the past two months had been like throwing a cup of cold water in her face. It hadn't been pleasant, but that—and her trip to Italy, where she remembered what healthier relationships were like—had certainly woken her up.

> I love her.

What about me?

She hadn't known what to say to that. She still loved him—not the way she once had but because he'd been such a part of her life. Her actions now were more about recognizing the truth. She owed it to herself to demand fair treatment, could see that having him break up with her was a gift of sorts—a chance to take a different path—and if she handled it right instead of giving in to what was easiest, she'd be much happier.

Even if she wasn't, at least she'd be able to do right by the other people in her life.

> You won't give me what I need.

I've never been stingy with you!

That was true. But he was talking about money, and that wasn't what she was referring to.

> I know, and I appreciate it. I tried not to take advantage of that.

The way his family did.

> But I think we should at least take a break and
> see how we feel later.

Why? I'm ready to get back together now.

> I need some time to focus on myself—on my
> career and raising my sister.

So you're going to keep her?

> If that's what she wants.

You don't even know her!

> Do we ever really know anyone?

That last text had been a jab at him for turning on her so suddenly, for breaking her heart and upending her life. Truth was, she couldn't trust his love anymore. She simply didn't believe in it. Her marriage felt like it had gone up in smoke so quickly and easily—far too quickly and easily to have been real in the first place.

She checked her phone. Cliff had sent her a lot of other stuff after that. But she'd decided if she didn't stop responding to him he'd go on forever. He wasn't used to hearing the word *no*. She didn't take the time to read the rest of what he'd sent. Julian was outside, trying to clean up something—she couldn't see what but guessed it had to do with the noise that'd jarred her awake again—and she felt he needed her, even though he kept pushing her away.

Leaving her phone on the bed, she hurried downstairs to find Julian kneeling in the silver wash of moonlight, a thin line of blood sliding from a cut on his hand.

"What's going on?" she asked, startled by the wound.

When he looked up at her, he seemed so lost and filled with despair she couldn't help gripping his shoulder.

"Whatever it is, I'm here for you."

Julian wasn't sure how Charlotte managed to get him into the house. The first few minutes after she came out were a blur. He knew she cleaned and bandaged the cut he'd gotten attempting to pick up the glass; he had a Band-Aid on his hand and he wasn't bleeding anymore. He also knew she'd taken care of the mess he'd made on the deck; he could remember hearing her go in and out while she insisted he rest on the couch. Other than those two things, he couldn't say what had happened or how long it took. He'd drifted off while she was gone, hadn't been aware of anything until she came back in and helped him from the sofa to his room.

"Julian, I need you to tell me what's going on," she said, having him sit on the bed while she took off his shoes and socks. "Something's wrong. I can tell. So can Sloane."

"I'm fine," he mumbled.

Standing, she made him raise his arms so she could pull off his shirt. "No, you're not."

"Just had a little too much tonight. That's all."

"You've been having 'too much' almost every night since we got here. Why? Drinking like this . . . It isn't you."

"Vacation."

"It's not that! You're not partying. You're staying away for long periods of time, drinking alone. But whatever's going on with you, we'll help. I hope you know that."

"I know you'd try," he said.

"What does that mean?" she asked. *"What is it?"*

He couldn't help touching her face. She'd always been so goddamn beautiful. "If things were different, I'd marry you," he announced. "Cliff wouldn't stand a chance of getting you back because I'd treat you so fucking good you'd never want to leave me."

Her mouth dropped open in apparent shock, which made him laugh, and that made *her* scowl.

"You don't even know what you're saying," she said.

"I do," he insisted.

"You just said you'd *marry* me."

"I would."

She gave his bare shoulder a slight shove. "You've never shown any interest. You've pushed me away every time I've . . . I've crossed that line!"

"Because I can't have you. But I've always known you were special. The guy who gets you is going to be damn lucky." He thought of her current husband and grimaced. "I just hope it's not Cliff."

"I already told Cliff that I won't go back to him, and I meant it."

"Good! He doesn't deserve you."

"Julian . . ."

He'd just closed his eyes, but the gravity in her voice caused him to summon the energy to open them again.

"You're scaring the hell out of me, you know that?" she said. "What's wrong? Are you *dying*?"

He chuckled. "No." *Not yet, anyway.* He thought he'd rather die than live what he believed his life might become, but maybe he was just feeling sorry for himself.

"Then *what is it*?" she pressed.

"I don't want to be alone tonight," he replied. "Stay with me—at least until I fall asleep."

She looked undecided for a moment. Then, while he scooted down under the covers, she closed his bedroom door, came back and climbed in beside him.

"I wish you'd trust me," she murmured as he found her in the bed, wrapped his arms around her and pulled her up against him.

This was better than nothing, he thought. "I *do* trust you," he said. "I trust you too much. That's the problem."

"How can that be a problem?" she asked.

His eyelids were so heavy, he could no longer keep them open, and neither could he bring the words swirling in his head to his lips.

Charlotte woke up slightly disoriented. She wasn't in her own room. It took a moment, but as soon as Julian shifted beside her, she remembered putting him to bed and how closely he'd held her, seemingly comforted to have her in his arms.

She told herself to get up and quietly let herself out. But his words—*I'd marry you*—echoed in her ears while the memory of that kiss they'd shared on the beach played in her brain. What was going on? Her life was taking some unexpected turns, but she wasn't eager to leave him. Quite the opposite. She wanted to touch him . . .

Her heart banged like cymbals in her ears as she imagined running her hand over his bare chest. She knew what that chest looked like. She'd been trying not to focus on it every time they went to the beach or got in the hot tub. She'd become fixated on him and his body. She'd just explained to Cliff that she wasn't going back to him. Why wasn't she in her room crying? How could she be feeling so much desire for another man?

But this wasn't just any man. Jules had been part of her life long before she'd ever met Cliff. And there'd certainly been periods when she'd flirted with the idea of having a romantic relationship with him. They'd just never really had an opportunity.

Until now. Why shouldn't she take advantage of it? Her marriage was over. And Jules *couldn't* think of her as a sister, not if he said he'd marry her if he could. As much as she'd tried to talk herself out of it, she'd recognized the desire in his kiss . . .

He was shoving her away for some reason. But maybe he needed her . . . Maybe the only way to reach him on a deeper level was to pry away the layers.

She knew it was a risk. If tonight turned out badly, she could lose his friendship. But she also knew that whatever small flame had started to burn inside her felt like a beacon in the storm.

Gathering her nerve, she reached over and smoothed the hair off his forehead.

When he opened his eyes, she slid closer to him, cupped his face in her hands and gently pressed her lips to his.

He stiffened at first, enough to make her fear he was about to break away like last time. But then he groaned and rolled her beneath him while deepening the kiss—and only stopped kissing her long enough to get rid of her shirt.

She wasn't wearing a bra.

Julian had sobered up enough to know he was making a mistake. But he'd been making a lot of them lately, so it didn't seem all that alarming. Charlotte in his bed was just too tempting to resist, especially since she was already wriggling out of her sweatpants.

"Are you sure about this?" he asked as her panties came off right after.

"Stop it," she said breathlessly. "Don't you dare ruin it like you did when we kissed at the beach."

He didn't want to ruin it. He wanted to forget about having Parkinson's disease and make love to her with all the confidence he'd once had. But it wasn't fair not to tell her there was something seriously wrong with him...

Problem was that would *definitely* ruin what they were doing, and she'd just told him not to.

He started to touch and taste her, to give in to what he wanted, but then his conscience got the best of him once again. "Wait. I feel like I need to say something."

Suspicious, she glared up at him with those gorgeous eyes of hers. "Not now," she warned. "If you screw this up, I'll seriously never forgive you."

Her bare body was pressed against his, and he held her breast in the palm of his hand as he nibbled at the curve of her shoulder. Finally making out with her was a heady experience. That and her nakedness were clouding his judgment, but he decided to take her at her word.

"Yeah—fuck it," he said. "There's always tomorrow."

"There's always tomorrow," she agreed and dragged his mouth to hers.

After that, there was no going back. She tightened her arms around his neck as he shifted in the bed and lowered his hand to the moist spot between her legs.

As she gasped and arched toward him, he knew he'd have to answer for this eventually. His sister would probably hate him as much as Charlotte, once they learned the truth.

But the life he'd had, the one he really wanted, was essentially over, anyway. So he let go of the last shred of his restraint—possibly his decency, too—and simply handed himself over to the desire that was driving him.

Almost before he knew it, it was too late to make a different decision. He'd pressed inside her, and she'd locked her legs around his hips as he began to move.

chapter 25

"If I'd known what I was missing, I would've made more of the weeks we've already been here," Charlotte teased Julian as he lay exhausted in her arms. "That doesn't happen to a girl every day."

"Yeah, well, I think we've already established that you've been married to a selfish bastard."

Charlotte had been so used to tolerating Cliff and his behavior—and trying to be the one to make up the difference—that she hadn't even realized how bad it'd gotten or how heavy that role had become.

"I don't want to talk about Cliff." She didn't want to think about him, either. She couldn't believe he'd defected and broken her heart—or that, because of Julian, she was actually feeling better than she had before Cliff had asked for the divorce.

She could only hope whatever this was would last . . .

"No problem," he responded. "As far as I'm concerned, we don't have to talk at all."

"You're not going to get out of it that easily," she said wryly. "What's going on with you?" He'd wanted to tell her something while they were making love, but she'd been too afraid that whatever it was would make him stop touching her, like when he'd ended their kiss.

"Nothing," he replied. "I'm tired. I just want to sleep."

"Okay. I'll go to my room." She started to get up, but he caught her by the wrist.

"I meant with you."

"That's better," she said with a laugh and checked the clock on the nightstand. They had a few hours before Sloane and Lilly got up, so she climbed back into bed.

Once he was settled in her arms with his head on her shoulder, she combed her fingers through his hair. There was no way she'd be able to sleep. She was too shocked by her own emotions. Shouldn't she feel odd being with her best friend's brother like this?

She probably should. Until just a couple of months ago, she'd been with Cliff. And yet she *didn't* feel odd. She felt as if she'd finally found her way home.

"Are you okay about . . . about what we did?" she asked. "I mean . . . we crossed a line I know you've been careful to stay away from. You've been a lot better about it than me. But . . . I hope you don't have any regrets."

"I enjoyed every second of it," he said.

Her breath settled. His weight felt right. "It won't be easy to explain to Sloane."

"No, it won't."

"Is that what you were going to say before when I . . . I told you not to screw it up?"

This time, he didn't speak for several seconds. Then he said, "We'll talk about it in the morning. Just . . . give me this night."

"No problem. But I don't want you to worry. I know you think I'm on the rebound and don't know what I'm doing, but that's not the case. Tonight meant something to me. *You* mean something to me."

When he didn't respond, she continued combing her fingers through his hair. She assumed he was falling asleep—until tears warmed her skin.

"Jules?" she said.

"Tomorrow," he reminded her.

She didn't know what to do. He'd asked for this night, and she'd agreed to give it to him, but . . . "I can't stand it that you're feeling so bad."

"Tomorrow," he said again, more forcefully this time.

"Fine, I'll wait," she agreed. "But whatever it is, I promise it's going to be okay."

An hour later, when he *was* finally asleep, she slipped out of his room to find her own bed. But she was still so terrified about what he was going to say when he finally explained himself that she couldn't sleep.

She'd never seen Jules cry before. What could affect him that deeply?

Charlotte was anxious when she got dressed in the morning. She needed to get some writing done, but Jules had seemed so troubled after they made love . . .

A knock sounded on her door while she was brushing her teeth. "Come in," she managed to say around her toothbrush.

Lilly let herself in and came to stand beside her, where they could see each other in the bathroom mirror. "I want to call Steve today. Would that be okay?"

After rinsing her mouth, Charlotte put her hair into a messy bun. "Of course. His contact is in your phone."

"So I can call the States? It doesn't cost money?"

"Nope. I put your phone on my contract and upgraded to a global plan while we're here."

"That's awesome!" Her little jump of excitement made the extra five bucks a day well worth it.

"I'm sure he'll be happy to hear from you. You should send him one of the pictures from our trip to the grotto. Just remember it's seven hours earlier in Cherokee, so wait until noon, at least. He gets up early, but not in the middle of the night."

"I will," she said and was just about to leave when she peered at Charlotte a little more closely. "Are you okay?"

"Of course. Why do you ask?"

"You look tired."

She *was* tired. She hadn't gotten more than a couple hours sleep even after she'd returned to her bed. She'd had too much on her mind, including memories of making love with Julian. That had been the best sex of her life; she was still excited about it. But she had no way of knowing exactly how it would change their relationship. "I might have to take a nap later."

"Are you going to write now?"

She was going to seek out Julian and finally put the questions inside her to rest. "After I eat," she said, but when she got downstairs, he was gone. Only Sloane was there, making breakfast.

Charlotte pulled her phone out of her pocket and texted him.

> Coward.

> Don't be in such a hurry. How about we just screw around while we're here? Have some fun and face reality when we go home?

Sloane must've heard her footsteps, because she looked back. "Who are you texting?"

"No one." She didn't want to admit she was texting Julian. Normally, that wouldn't be a problem. But after last night? She felt like she had to be careful. "Just reading all the messages Cliff sent me."

"Are there a lot of them?"

"A ton! He's freaking out."

"That's a little worrisome."

"Why?"

"Because I'm afraid you'll go back to him."

"I'm not going back to him. There's no way." Not after last night. He'd never forgive her—even though she'd made it clear she wasn't interested in reconciling. "I'm not even tempted."

Sloane seemed stunned by her confidence. "Whoa! You've come a long way."

"Did you see Jules this morning?" Charlotte asked, trying not to act overly interested.

"Yeah. He was here until just a few minutes ago."

The villa smelled like gardenias—someone had put some in a vase—and butter as she walked over to pour herself a cup of coffee. "Where'd he go?"

"You know him—wherever his art takes him. Are you going to write?"

Charlotte cast a resentful glance at her laptop. She had to forget about everything else until she could get those sample chapters turned in. "Yeah."

"When you're done for the day, let's go to Atrani to see the Torre dello Ziro."

"Atrani?"

"It's another coastal town about twenty minutes from here."

"Okay. What's the Torre dello Ziro?"

"A watchtower. I know we've seen quite a few. But this one is behind the crumbling walls of the Duchy of Amalfi—which was a major trading power in the Mediterranean during the Middle Ages. Should be picturesque."

"Will Jules be going?"

"Said he would. He's the one who suggested it."

She thought about his last message: *How about we just screw around while we're here? Have some fun and face reality when we go home?*

Maybe that was what he needed. Maybe she should back off—relax and give him more room to cope with whatever he was going through.

Patience had never been her strong suit, but she didn't want to push him. They *both* needed time—time to allow for change. She had no idea how difficult Cliff would make their divorce. She was still struggling to save her career. And now that she had Lilly in her life, she needed to be more cautious than she'd ever been before.

There was nothing wrong with slowing everything down. Yes, she was excited about Jules. But she had no idea if last night would lead to anything. If happy for now meant happy forever. They were only at the very start of it.

She had to be careful not to let her expectations run away with her.

"Great, I'll get my pages done," she told Sloane. Then she carried her coffee to her laptop and replied to Julian's last message.

> **Take all the time you need. I'm here when you're ready to talk.**
>
> **P.S. Last night was incredible—did that really happen???**

Lilly curled her fingernails into her palms while waiting for the phone to ring. She'd just sent Steve a picture of the grotto with a message saying she'd gone there with Charlotte, Sloane and Julian, so he had to know it was her. But maybe he wouldn't pick up. Maybe he didn't want to be bothered by the daughter of a former girlfriend.

She nearly hung up. But then he answered.

"Hey, Lilly. How are you?"

The kindness in his voice was nearly enough to make her cry. "I'm . . . okay."

"Are you having fun with your sister and her friends? It sure looks like it in that picture you just sent."

Lilly was lying on her bed, where she'd been reading her book. Grabbing her extra pillow, she put it over her face in an attempt to stem the emotion that was welling up inside her. "Yeah."

"What'd you say?"

She removed the pillow so her voice wouldn't be muffled. "I said yeah."

"That picture was at a cave of some sort?"

"The Emerald Grotto. We went out on a boat."

"What else have you been doing?"

"Shopping. Swimming. Sightseeing. Sloane's been teaching me to cook. And Charlotte's bought me a lot of new clothes."

"That's cool. Are you still doing your schoolwork?"

"Not right now. Charlotte said I didn't have to worry about it, that I can start up again once we get home. She said all we both have to focus on right now is healing."

"And is that happening?" he asked.

She wasn't sure why she was so shaky. She'd been feeling pretty good the past couple of weeks. "I think so. Sometimes . . . sometimes I feel happier than before."

"What about other times?"

"I just feel scared," she admitted.

"About what?"

"About what's going to happen after Italy, I guess."

"There's no reason to be scared. Charlotte will be there for you, and so will I. A little more structure in your life would help, which is why I'd really like to see you back in school."

Lilly wasn't sure she'd fit in with her classmates anymore.

She felt years older than everyone else her age. "I'll go back in the fall."

"You know you can go to school here, right? You can come live with me, and if you're behind, I'll help you get caught up."

She thought of the kids she'd known, briefly, while she was living in Cherokee. She hadn't been there long enough to make any real friends. She'd lived out of town, not in a neighborhood with other kids close by. Her social life had consisted of hanging out on the farm with Old Blue or being in the house with her mother. Her mother had been so bored while they were there; she was always looking for something to do. So they'd played a lot of card games—not that Sabrina paid much attention while they were doing it. She kept checking her phone whenever it wasn't her turn.

"Do you mean it?" Lilly asked.

"Of course I mean it. Charlotte didn't tell you?"

Lilly thought of the terrible things her mother had yelled at him when they stormed out the last time, how she'd accused him of being like Walter. Lilly didn't have to worry about Steve being like Walter, did she? He'd never done anything that made her skin crawl.

But would she be able to count on that if there was no one else around? "We haven't talked about it yet. We agreed not to make any big decisions until we got home. This is . . . this is just a time to get to know each other."

"I see. Well, there's no pressure on my part. I just wanted you to know I'm here if you need me."

"Thanks. I . . . I miss Old Blue."

"He misses you, too. He wandered around this place looking for you for weeks after you left," he said with a chuckle.

She hated that the dog probably assumed she'd deserted him. "Charlotte promised she'd bring me for a visit soon. I can't wait."

He must've heard her sniff because he said, "Are you crying?"

"No," she lied, embarrassed.

"What's wrong?"

"Nothing." She couldn't say it, but she missed him, too. She just didn't know if she could fully trust him, not after Walter.

"Okay, well . . . you can call me anytime."

"Thanks," she said and disconnected.

She'd just set the phone aside, wiped her face and blown her nose before reaching for her e-reader when she got a call.

Although she'd received a few texts from Charlotte, Sloane and Julian—saying things like, Time to eat, or Want to help me decide what to make for dinner tonight? or Want to go get some gelato?—this was the first time she'd ever received a call.

Assuming Steve had forgotten to tell her something, she picked up the phone and saw a picture of Penny on the screen. She hadn't even realized Charlotte's adoptive mother had her number; Charlotte must've given it to her.

"Hello?" she said tentatively.

"Hi, Lilly. It's Penny."

"I know. I . . . I saw your picture."

"I didn't want to bother Charlotte while she's writing, but I thought I'd check in on you and see how you're doing."

"Good," she said automatically.

"I was also wondering what your favorite color is."

Why would she want to know that? Lilly wondered but didn't ask. "Yellow, I guess."

"Then I'm glad I didn't assume it was pink or purple."

It *was* pink. But when she'd told Steve's mom her favorite color was pink, she'd wound up with curtains that were for a little girl. Pink could easily be misunderstood, she'd decided. She didn't see how that could happen with yellow.

"I'm going to buy you a tennis outfit," Penny explained. "I'm not sure I can find a yellow one, but I'll do my best."

"Tennis outfit?" she echoed.

"I'm a tennis player. Well, I *used* to be a tennis player. And then I was a coach. Nowadays I can't play much. But I thought I'd take you to the club and have someone I used to coach teach you the game. That might be fun for you while Charlotte finishes her book. And if you like playing, I'll make sure you get lessons."

Lilly had taken band in the fourth grade. But then they'd moved, and she'd never had the chance to take any kind of lessons again. That was when she'd also had to leave her cat. "Does that mean . . . does that mean I'll be living near you?" she asked.

"I'm hoping you'll be living *with* us," Penny replied. "At least for a while—until Charlotte moves out and takes you to whatever house or condo she decides to buy."

Penny was assuming Charlotte would keep her. But even if Charlotte didn't go back to Cliff, wouldn't she rather be on her own, free to do whatever she wanted? What would she do when she got with another man? Would she want Lilly then?

"I appreciate that," she said because she didn't know what else to say.

"Charlotte doesn't want me to push you. I don't want to do that, either. I just . . . I wanted to let you know not to worry. That you have a home. We'll make sure of it."

"Thank you."

They hung up, but before she even had the chance to think about their call, a knock sounded on the door.

"Come in."

Sloane poked her head into the room. "Hey, you! Ready to go to Torre dello Ziro?"

Lilly scrambled off the bed. "Not yet. Has Charlotte finished writing?"

"She's almost done—so chop, chop," she said jokingly.

Lilly moved toward the dresser to put on a different shirt and a pair of shorts while Sloane continued down the hall, but a second later, Lilly called her back.

"What is it?" Sloane asked, once again poking her head through the doorway.

"Do you still think I should go live at the farm? Because I just talked to Steve. He said I can."

She took a moment to respond, as if she was thinking it over. "That's up to you. What do *you* want to do?"

"I don't know," she said. "It's hard."

Sloane came farther into the room. "It's not like you'll have to let go of anyone either way, Lilly. If you go to Steve's, Charlotte—and me and Julian—will still be part of your life. We'll make sure we talk to you and see you often. And if you stay with Charlotte and her folks, Steve will do the same."

"Steve can't leave the farm. He has animals to take care of," she pointed out.

"That doesn't mean you can't go there and visit for a week every now and then."

The idea that she might be able to have both eased the cramping in her stomach. "Okay," she said and, thankfully, managed to stave off the fresh tears that were burning the backs of her eyes.

Everything was going to be okay. She hoped. But when she'd been afraid her half sister wouldn't want her, Luca had promised he'd stay in touch—check in on her, make sure everything was going okay, at least while they were in Italy—and she hadn't heard from him even once.

Julian sat on a crumbling watchtower below Praiano, letting his legs dangle while the sea breathed in and out below. Charlotte's text glowed on his screen.

Last night was incredible—did that really happen???

Unfortunately, it had. And now he'd have to answer for it.

"Damn." He'd known better than to let things go that far. The last thing he wanted to do was hurt someone else, especially Charlotte.

He watched several seagulls strutting along the coastline and raised his camera to capture them. The setting—with Positano, Capri and the white surf in the background—was pretty spectacular. But then he lowered it again. He'd taken thousands of pictures. He had more than enough. He'd left the villa early this morning because he needed to escape, not because he needed to work. He didn't like birds, anyway.

At the moment, he didn't much like himself, either.

He had to make a decision. Did he tell Charlotte the truth right away? Or did he simply allow himself to enjoy the short time they had left?

Sloane had a case of the jitters as they set off for Atrani. All night she'd been considering something she believed could make a world of difference—to her and to Ben. A solution to their stalemate. A way to save their marriage. She hadn't said a word about it to anyone, but the more she considered the possibilities, the more hopeful and excited she became. She just hoped Ben would be open-minded enough to accept what she planned to offer.

The drive wound between lemon terraces and sea cliffs. Sunlight flashed on the tiled domes; laundry snapped over narrow lanes. It was beautiful scenery, but even after they arrived at Torre dello Ziro, she was only half there. She wandered around, feigning more interest than she actually felt and trying not to miss what the others were saying so they wouldn't realize just how far away her mind really was. She didn't think Charlotte or Julian noticed her preoccupation, but at one point, sweet, serious Lilly edged closer to her and asked if something was wrong.

Sloane was touched that Lilly would be concerned about her. The girl was so in tune with those around her and what they were feeling. Sloane was coming to love Charlotte's little sister like her own.

"I'm fine." She reached out to squeeze Lilly's hand, something she wouldn't have done even a week earlier, and was gratified when Lilly squeezed back before running over to join Jules, who was trying to teach her how to take better photos.

Waiting until they got back to the villa and the others went to bed was agonizing. Sloane wanted to talk to her husband as soon as possible, but the fact that it was midday on a Friday in Seattle, and Ben had to be at the pharmacy, was working against her. She didn't want to confront him at work. She preferred him to be at home, relaxed and ready for a heart-to-heart.

It was after midnight in Italy when he finally responded to the text she'd sent earlier asking if he could set aside a half hour to talk to her tonight.

> Got off work a little early. It was slow this afternoon. Is this a good time?

She climbed out of bed, opened her door and peered down the hallway to make sure the house was quiet and she wouldn't be interrupted. The light was off under Lilly's door. She didn't know where Julian and Charlotte were. She'd left them sitting on the deck an hour ago, hoping that if she broke up the party they'd go to bed. She could no longer see them from her window, but she hadn't heard them come in.

After closing her door again, she went into the bathroom so her voice wouldn't carry beyond her room and sat on the closed lid of the toilet as she dialed Ben's number.

"Hey, what's up?" he said as soon as he answered.

"I'd like to talk to you about something," she replied.

"I gathered that from your text. I don't think you've ever sent me such an ominous message. Now I'm nervous. Have you made a decision about what you want for your future?"

She drew a deep breath. "Yes."

He remained silent for a moment. Then he said, "Does the future you see include me? Because your last text suggested it did."

No longer able to sit still, she jumped up and began to pace in the small room, the tile cool under her bare feet. "It definitely includes you. It also includes children—or a child."

"*What?*"

She hurried to curtail his expectations. "Before you get too excited, let me explain."

"I'm listening," he said cautiously.

Was he hopeful? Skeptical? She couldn't tell . . . "What if *we* take Lilly?"

His earlier emotions had been hard to read—cautious, hopeful, also a little worried?—but now she could feel his shock through the phone. "Charlotte's sister? You want to finish raising her?"

"Hear me out," she said, rubbing her free hand on her thigh. "She's a truly wonderful girl—very sensitive and kind. She's been hurt and is afraid to trust, to truly grab on and connect for fear of being let down again, but she's incredibly smart. I can already see her growing and changing and coming out of her shell. It's all happening right before my eyes. With consistent love and care, I think she'll be able to overcome the trauma she's experienced in her young life."

"I'm glad she's doing so well. Truly. But . . . Lilly's *twelve*."

"So? What does that mean?"

"You really want to start with a child who's on the cusp of becoming a teenager? You've heard how hard they can be, right? For someone who doesn't want kids, that's like . . . like jumping right into the fire."

"Something can be hard and still be worth it."

"True . . ."

"She needs us, Ben. And it would be the perfect solution for Charlotte."

"Have you talked to Charlotte about it?"

"Of course not. I felt it was only right to approach you first. We have to be in this together."

"But you didn't even want *Charlotte* to finish raising Lilly. You thought it might ruin her life. And now *you* want to do it?"

"I want *us* to do it. To give her a home."

"That's a huge commitment. Is this the path you really want to take?"

Squeezing her eyes closed, she dropped her head back. Maybe she should've thought this over a little longer. It did seem impulsive; she hadn't known Lilly very long. But someone had to take her, and this solution seemed ideal for everyone—especially if it would make Ben happy.

"It is." She knew it was fast, but surprisingly, the certainty felt solid in her bones.

After another moment of shocked silence, he said, "Wow. A twelve-year-old."

"If you knew her, you wouldn't even hesitate." When he started to laugh, she gripped the phone tighter. Was this where he was going to tell her she was too late? That he preferred Adele and her five-year-old son, after all?

She knew that was unlikely, but her jealousy suggested it all the same. "What is it?"

"If *you* already love her that much, I'm sure I will, too."

Relief, excitement and terror filled Sloane in equal parts. "Is that a yes?"

"That's a yes—provided Charlotte agrees and Lilly, too, of course. Do you think they will?"

"I have no idea." She knew Lilly had spent more time with her than with anyone else. She knew they got along well and enjoyed each other. She knew she'd do her best to make sure Lilly had everything she could possibly need.

But Steve was offering her a good home, too—one that

included Old Blue. And Sloane had seen the way she looked at Charlotte, as if she admired Charlotte more than anyone else on earth. What if Charlotte made her the same offer?

"If they agree, would you be happy?" she asked. "Happy enough to stay with me?"

His voice softened. "Babe, I could never leave you."

"Not even for Adele and her adorable little boy?"

"Stop it," he said. "I've already told you that. I couldn't leave you for *anyone*."

Tears stung her eyes. "I don't want to feel as though you're settling for less than you really want."

"*You're* what I want," he reiterated. "That's what I've decided since you left. And if I get to be a father to Lilly, too, that's just . . . all the better."

Sloane sank back onto the closed lid of the toilet. Would he regret making this commitment? Wish for more later? She had no way of knowing, but they loved each other enough to continue to try to make their marriage work. "You're going to adore her. And she's going to adore you."

"Wow," he said. "It's hard to wrap my mind around this. I never expected it. Would you just . . . bring her home with you or what?"

"I think so. Why not?"

"That would be okay with me. Let me know if I need to get the spare room ready."

Sloane imagined decorating Lilly's room, getting her back into school and helping her do homework. The responsibility of raising a child—the risk of screwing that up—was a little frightening. It had always frightened her.

But the love she already felt for Ben and for Lilly made her willing to try.

chapter 26

Julian was going to tell Charlotte about his diagnosis. That was why, after his sister went to bed, he'd asked if she wanted to take a walk with him. He'd been psyching himself up all evening, preparing for her reaction and the domino effect it would have as the news rolled out from her to Sloane, Lilly, his friends and, finally, his business associates. Then the metamorphosis in his life would be complete and permanent. He'd be "Julian with Parkinson's" for the rest of his life.

So much for having a month in Italy to prepare for all that . . .

But he hadn't expected what happened last night. That forced his hand.

Once they left the villa, they started navigating the labyrinth of walkways and stairways to the Church of St. Gennaro.

Lanterns glowed in niches along the stone walls, and the timeless scent of the sea drifted on the breeze. He figured they'd stroll through the town square with its timeless mosaic, and there, in the middle of centuries of history and tradition—which was one of the things he loved most about Italy—he would explain why his behavior last night hadn't been fair to her and apologize for not letting her know the truth before they made love.

"How old do you think this church is?" she asked once they finally reached it.

He'd been careful not to have anything to drink this evening. It was alcohol that'd gotten him into trouble last night. But she'd had a glass of wine with Sloane and seemed to be in a happy yet mellow mood.

"It was owned by a noble family from Amalfi and dates back to the late fifteen hundreds," he told her. "Not as old as the convent farther up the mountain, but it's built on top of an older structure from several centuries earlier."

"How do you know all that?" she asked in surprise.

The air tasted faintly of metal and brine; the surf below boomed against the cliffs like a slow heartbeat. "I spoke to a woman who came out of the church when I was here once before, trying to photograph it."

She studied the bell tower with its cupola covered in the same kind of majolica tiles that adorned the floor of the square. "It's beautiful."

"You should see the sunset from here." Although other towns on the Amalfi Coast were also built on cliffs overlooking the sea and had somewhat of a similar view, people claimed Praiano's sunsets were the best, and he agreed.

"I'll have to make sure I see one before we head home."

He wanted to show it to her. He wanted to show her other things, too—wished they were in a different situation so he could take her around and share all he'd learned about Italy, both on his previous trips and while she'd been inside writing. But he had no idea how she was going to feel about him once she heard what he had to say. And he couldn't put off telling her any longer.

They were still standing in front of the church when he took her hand and turned her to face him. "Charlotte, you've been wondering what's wrong."

She grinned up at him. "You're finally going to tell me?"

He couldn't maintain eye contact. Wincing, he glanced to where the mountain fell away and the dark, roiling water stretched out beyond it. "I'm *not* ready," he clarified. "But I feel as though I owe it to you to—"

"Stop right there," she interrupted, a stubborn set to her jaw as she stepped away from him. "You don't owe me anything. You didn't make any commitments last night. If you're dealing with something you don't want to share, then don't. You have that right."

He couldn't keep from tugging her back into his arms and kissing her, something he'd been wanting to do all evening. The way her naked body felt against his had been on his mind ever since she'd left his bed. "But if I don't, I'm afraid I won't be able to stop myself from making love to you again and again and again."

"Would it be so terrible to just let go and have some fun? We came to Italy for Lilly, but also for a much-needed time-out, a chance to get our heads together and figure out where to go from this point. At least, I know Sloane and I came here to do that, and I think part of the reason you joined us was because you needed the same thing. I say we stick with the original plan and give ourselves what little time we have left here."

"But last night—"

"Doesn't change anything. It was my choice, too. Let's just . . . let it be whatever it will be."

"I can't," he argued. "I don't want you to feel as though I've misled you."

Her arms tightened around his neck. "You're forgetting something."

The longing he felt was undermining his good intentions and wreaking havoc with his state of mind. "What's that?"

"I *know* you," she said simply. "I know you're a stand-up guy. And I understand that you're in the middle of something you're struggling to navigate. So if you're not ready to open up about whatever's troubling you, don't. I won't hold it against you. I promise." Rising up on tiptoe, she pressed her lips to his in a sweet peck that quickly grew into something more when he put his hand to the back of her head and deepened their kiss.

"What you do to me," he murmured.

"Allow this to be the escape it was intended to be—for both of us. We'll figure everything out once we get home."

He rested his forehead against hers. "Don't ruin it," he said, echoing what she'd told him last night.

A smile played at the corners of her lips. "Exactly. Don't ruin it."

"But by then I'm afraid you'll be in love with me."

Although he hadn't been joking, she started to laugh, so he did, too. "I admire your confidence," she said. "But right now, I can't promise you anything, either. My life is a mess. So *you'd* better be careful not to fall in love with *me*."

That was the problem. He was pretty sure it was too late. But he didn't say so. She'd just given him nine more days he could spend with her in Italy as if nothing in the world was wrong—and he knew they'd probably become the nine best days of his life. How could he refuse that?

"No matter what, we'll always remain friends," he said solemnly, trying to make it a pact so he could feel a little less selfish about accepting her offer. Then he allowed his hands to travel down her back, pressing her lower body to his.

"Now you're getting the idea." She sounded slightly breathless, which let him know she was as affected by his close proximity as he was by hers. "Let's go back to the villa before you tell me you're too tired."

"There's no chance of that," he said.

"You never know," she teased. "Brooding can drain you."

"*Brooding?* I can't even remember the last time I heard that word," he said and swept her off her feet, laughing as freely as he used to while letting her slide down the front of him—until she found her footing and he found her lips.

There's no place on earth quite so romantic as Italy, Charlotte thought as she lay, exhausted but content, in Julian's arms. They'd gone to his room again. Because of the layout of the house, they had less chance of being discovered if they used his room. But he was now snoring lightly, fast asleep, and she felt he'd likely remain that way for the rest of the night.

She had to get up and find her own bed—she just couldn't move yet.

Closing her eyes, she reveled in the warmth and comfort of his body for just a little longer. The shutters were cracked, letting in a slice of moonlight that silvered his bare shoulder and the sheet tangled around their legs—a welcome sight. Giving him license to simply enjoy what they were feeling had changed him, removed whatever had been holding him back, and that made being with him even more intoxicating.

But what was it he had to reveal? And how would Sloane react to them being together?

She heard a toilet flush somewhere else in the house. Sloane or Lilly was up, she realized, and dragged herself out from under Jules's arm, causing him to stir.

"You're leaving?" he mumbled.

"Yeah, before I fall asleep, too."

"Damn." He sounded disappointed.

"There's always tomorrow."

"The rest of our time in Italy will go too fast," he predicted.

"Don't start worrying yet—I'm not ready to face it," she said and kissed him before climbing out of his bed.

The next day, when Sloane asked to speak to her as soon as Julian took Lilly to the market to pick up a few things for dinner, Charlotte couldn't help growing apprehensive. Her friend looked so serious. Nervous, too. Sloane had been acting strange all day, not that Charlotte had had much occasion to notice. It was Julian who'd texted her about it while she was writing. He'd been hanging around the villa for a change, showing Lilly some editing software for pictures while waiting for Charlotte to get off work. Sloane and Lilly were planning on making a fancy dinner—Charlotte had heard them talking about it at breakfast—and she and Julian had been hoping to escape to the beach for an hour or so while they cooked.

"Of course you can talk to me," Charlotte said. "You can always talk to me. What's going on?" Against all odds, she'd managed to finish her sample chapters and get them off to her editor. She'd been absolutely exuberant after she hit Send, and given her pact not to fall in love with Julian, more excited than she probably should be to spend more time with him.

Now she was worried that she'd been wrong about Ben's involvement with his new coworker, however, and that was the reason Sloane was acting so fidgety and on edge. "Don't tell me it's about Ben."

"Not really, no. I mean . . . he's involved, but . . ."

"He's not having an affair," she clarified.

The smell of fresh bread and espresso still lingered from breakfast and sunlight pooled across the tiled floor. "No."

"Thank God." Relieved, Charlotte pressed a hand to her heart. But an instant later, another thought struck her. Did Sloane know what was going on between her and Julian? Could that be what this was all about? She caught her breath and held it for several heartbeats while waiting to hear what it was, but Sloane still managed to surprise her.

"It's Lilly."

Had she missed something she should've noticed about her sister because she was too preoccupied with her work and Julian? Lately, Charlotte had left a lot of Lilly's care to Sloane. It'd seemed natural to do so, since she had to work and Sloane was available. "What's wrong with her?"

"Nothing. I think she seems happier—more content—with each passing day, don't you?"

"I do," Charlotte agreed. Now she was really lost as to where this conversation was going . . . "So . . . what's up?"

Sloane got off the couch. "I've talked to Ben, Charlotte. We'd like to take Lilly."

Charlotte blinked in surprise. "*Take* Lilly? Take her where?"

"Have her come live with us, finish raising her."

"Are you kidding?" Charlotte sprang to her feet. "Where's this coming from? You . . . you don't want children. You've been adamant about that."

"I didn't. I don't," she clarified. "Not of my own. At least, I don't think so. Maybe that'll change over the next couple of years. I never saw myself doing *this*. But being around Lilly, getting to know her, has made me see things differently."

Charlotte didn't know what to say. "I'm shocked. Where is this coming from?"

Sloane shook her head while holding up her hands. "Honestly, I don't know. I just . . . I *really* care about her."

"I know you do. You're incredibly good to her. But you can't mean what you're saying about . . . about taking legal responsibility for her."

"I do mean it. Ben and I . . . we'd do everything we could to be great parents."

"You don't have to convince me of that," Charlotte said. "I know you'd be great parents. It's just . . ."

Sloane peered at her more closely. "What?"

"I think I want to raise her myself."

Silence followed. Then she said, "Since when?"

Now that Charlotte knew Lilly, she couldn't imagine life

without her. They'd shopped together, painted their nails together, enjoyed the beach, sightseeing and the good food of Italy. They'd spoken to Don and Penny regularly and laughed with each other in the Jacuzzi. Day by day it felt more natural, more real, that she had a sister, and a sister was forever. Although Sloane had probably spent more time with Lilly because of Charlotte's book, there was something about their relation that made them natural companions. "Since coming here and getting to know her, just like you. I'm the only family she has."

"You don't have to be related to be family."

"I agree. I didn't mean that—"

"And I feel Ben and I are in a better position to take on a child right now. We already have a home for her. She'd have a mother *and* a father—you know how wonderful Ben would be to her. We're settled and ready for the next chapter in our lives."

While Charlotte was going through a divorce, had a book to finish and was living with her parents. She saw the practicality of it, but still. "Are you thinking this might save your marriage, Sloane?"

Sloane seemed reluctant to go *that* far, but she said, "I think it would be good for us."

Then how could Charlotte say no? "But Seattle is so far away," she said, mostly to herself.

"We'd come visit you often, and you'd be welcome to visit us whenever you like. I'd love to see more of you, anyway." She dropped her hands. "Besides, Seattle's no farther than Cherokee, Iowa, yet you told her she could live with Steve if that's what she wanted."

"I said that before, when . . . when . . . That was before," she reiterated.

"I'm just saying that we'd be happy to have her."

Charlotte plopped down again. At first, there'd been no one

to take Lilly. Now everyone wanted her. Which option would be best? And if she gave her up, would she be able to live with that decision? "I need time to grow accustomed to the idea," she said.

"I understand. That's why I brought it up now."

"And Lilly's old enough that I . . . I think we should let her decide."

Sloane said nothing, just came over and sat beside her.

"I know you'd be a good mother to her," Charlotte said softly.

"And I know it would be hard for you to give her up," Sloane responded, just as softly. She reached for Charlotte's hand. "But having all of us to love her can only be a good thing."

Provided they could always keep what was best for her in mind.

That was what she needed to do now, Charlotte realized. But this decision wasn't going to be any easier than the other decisions she'd had to make lately.

It was her anniversary. Or it would've been. Considering everything that'd happened recently, it felt weird to think that this day would've marked the fourth year of her marriage.

Charlotte rolled over in bed and reached for her phone, wondering if Cliff had remembered the significance of this day. It was extremely late where he was, but he was a night owl, so she wasn't surprised to find a fresh spate of calls and texts from him. He *had* remembered and was saying how much he still loved her and that he couldn't wait until they could celebrate together.

Why he wouldn't give up, she didn't know. They didn't have any chance of resurrecting their marriage; she'd decided that before she'd started sleeping with Julian.

She wasn't going to respond, she decided. Not now, anyway. She needed to work on her manuscript—like every other day.

But she was so nervous about how her editor might react to what she'd already turned in that she couldn't keep writing, not without some word from Megan to signal she was on the right track. She knew her editor would read what she'd submitted right away; she'd been too desperate to get hold of it to put it off. But that would still take a day or two.

Until she heard, she was going to turn her attention to other things—like going through her birth mother's belongings and finally clearing *that* hurdle.

She was just climbing out of bed to see if Lilly wanted to join her after all when a text came in from Julian.

How long until you're available?

She'd spent most of the night with him again. They weren't getting much sleep, but they were having one hell of a good time.

She smiled at the memories they'd made as she wrote him back.

No clue. Why?

I'd like to take you to Salerno.

With or without the others?

We can all go, I guess. It would be too hard to get away on our own. But I'm already struggling to hide my interest in you, so it's risky.

They'd gone back to the Church of St. Gennaro and watched the sunset last night. They hadn't had time for the beach. But the more they did together, the more they wanted to do.

> Maybe we should tell Sloane, get it out in the
> open. I hate feeling as if I'm doing something
> behind her back.

Julian wasn't the only one who was nervous that Sloane would pick up on the change in their relationship—and not be happy about it.

> We're not making any hard decisions like that in Italy, remember?

She didn't remember agreeing to take the "no hard decisions" edict that far. But she was fine with waiting. She *had* made it clear that this was a safe zone where he could take all the time he needed to work through whatever he was dealing with.

> Then don't look at me the way you
> look at me. 😊

> That's impossible.

She chuckled and was about to put down her phone when she received another text—only this one was from Cliff.

> That dude you were with right after we split
> up is in Italy with you?

He must've seen some of the pictures Sloane had shared on Instagram. Charlotte had been worried about that. But she didn't have the right to ask Sloane not to post. She was using their stay—the architecture, style and furnishings of the Amalfi Coast—to promote her design business.

Charlotte certainly hadn't posted anything that showed she

was with Jules. She'd been trying to lie low so the furor surrounding the implosion of her marriage would die down. If that happened, she thought maybe Cliff would decide he was better off without her. She didn't want him trying to win her back just for the sake of beating out the competition.

> **Jules is just a friend.**

That was no longer true. She didn't know what Jules was exactly. It was too early to define it. But he was certainly her lover, and that was definitely more than "just a friend."

Still, she sent the text. She needed to put out this fire before it could grow into a conflagration. Her relationship with Jules didn't really matter. She couldn't go back to Cliff, regardless.

If that was true, you'd call me back.

> **Lilly is the reason I haven't called you back.**

What does Lilly have to do with our marriage?

> **Everything!**

You're saying you're not fucking this guy?

Dropping back onto the bed, she groaned as she stared up at the ceiling. The fan ticked lazily overhead, its rhythm somehow amplifying the tension coiled in her chest. She was such a terrible liar. If she said no, would he even believe her?

> **We're getting a divorce. You no longer have any say over what I do, so I'm not even going to answer that question.**

You're sleeping with him, aren't you!

Stop! Just stop or I'll have to block you.

He tried to call, but she refused to pick up.
I don't want to talk right now, she wrote.

I'm finally making good progress on my book and feeling better. I can't risk letting you level me again. You have what you wanted. I'm gone. Now leave me alone, okay? At least while I'm in Italy. I'll let you know when I'm back in the States. We can talk then.

They still had to go through the paperwork, but their divorce should be relatively easy, she told herself. She wasn't going to try to break the prenup. She wasn't even going to ask for any of the furniture or other personal property they'd accumulated when they were together. He should be thrilled to get out of the marriage without a long, drawn-out court battle like so many other celebrities faced.

She waited several minutes, but he didn't respond.

Relieved, she got up again and set her phone firmly aside. She could hear movement downstairs, was eager to immerse herself in the life she had since coming to Italy. The transition she was going through was fraught with risk and uncertainty, but change was like that. She was building a vastly different future, one in which her parents, Sloane, Julian and Lilly played a much bigger role, and she believed it would make her happier in the end.

chapter 27

Lilly told Charlotte she didn't want to help search through the boxes in the storage room. She felt bad saying no—it seemed ungrateful after all her sister had done for her—but she couldn't make herself do it. She was too angry. And even though Charlotte had asked why she wasn't interested, she couldn't really say. She'd been getting along with her mother before Sabrina died—as well as she ever had when Sabrina was with a man. But something about her mother losing her temper and jumping on that Vespa filled her with such rage; she was afraid it would come ripping out of her like the chest-burster in *Alien* if she didn't clamp it all down and look away.

Fortunately, she'd learned how to bury her feelings deep. Sometimes her jaw ached from how hard she tried to keep them inside. But it was the only way she could cope from day to day. She was afraid she'd fly apart if she didn't—or rant and rave and scream profanity at everyone around her like her mother used to do.

And just look where that had gotten Sabrina. Besides Lilly, no one had ever really loved her. Steve tried, but even he couldn't do it in the end. No one had wanted to be around her for very long. No one had even been able to muster a small amount of sympathy for her situation. They all thought she deserved what she got—including her own family.

And they could be right. She'd created so many of her own problems. Even Lilly had been able to see how easy it would've been to avoid most of them. If only her mother could've stopped going from man to man. Could've settled down and worked a steady job so she could pay her bills. Could've focused on building healthy relationships and reconnecting with her family instead of just rolling along from town to town, hunting for something she could never find.

Lilly had tried to tell her as much, but Sabrina would never listen. She made the wrong choice over and over again. Maybe that was what made Lilly so mad. Even though she'd always been there, willing to give her mother the love she craved, it wasn't enough. Sabrina had always wanted more.

"What are you up to?"

Sloane had entered the kitchen where Lilly was staring at a recipe. She'd opened the cookbook thirty minutes earlier, while Sloane was handling some work-related things for her design business back home, but she hadn't been able to focus.

She forced a smile as she said, "Just looking for things we could make."

The scent of bacon lingered and dust motes danced in the sunlight coming through the windows as Sloane responded. "You really like to cook, don't you?"

"I do." Planning the meal, shopping for the ingredients and creating such beautiful and delicious pastas, polentas and chicken and seafood dishes for the group made Lilly feel as if she was contributing something special—something they all looked forward to and enjoyed. It was a way to show how grateful she was for her sister and Julian without having to say it. Words were too hard, especially since she was afraid to crack open the safe inside her that contained all the feelings she'd been storing up.

There was so much stuffed in there, she couldn't even guess what would come out.

"What sounds good for tonight?" Sloane asked.

"I haven't decided. But I thought it might be fun to make croissants today. We could do chocolate and lemon. See how they compare to the pastry shops around here."

"Now you're really looking for a challenge," she said with an impressed and slightly overwhelmed chuckle.

"You think it would be too hard?"

Sloane turned the book so she could look at the recipe. "I'm willing to try it," she said at length. "I bet there aren't many people who can say they've made croissants. We're really doing this Italy thing right."

"They offer cooking classes here in town."

"I've had my eye on those, too. I'm just waiting until Charlotte can take one with us."

"That'll be fun." She was coming to enjoy Charlotte and Sloane so much she was growing more and more afraid of when their stay in Italy would end.

"Where is Charlotte, anyway?" Sloane asked. "She's not at the dining table, pecking away at her computer."

"No. She already turned in her sample chapters. Now she's just waiting to hear how her editor likes them."

"I bet she's nervous."

"Has to be. So am I," Lilly confessed. There was a lot hanging on those pages.

"She's an excellent writer. I have no doubt her publisher will love them." Sloane peered out onto the deck but apparently didn't see Charlotte. "Did she go somewhere with Julian?"

The knot in the pit of Lilly's stomach grew even bigger. "No, she's going through Sabrina's things." It felt odd to call her mother by her first name, but Sabrina was technically Charlotte's mother, too, so "our mother's things" felt just as strange. "You just can't see her from there."

"She's doing that today? And you're not out there with her?"

The guilt reared up again. Dropping her eyes, Lilly shook her head.

"Are you sure you don't want to help?" Sloane said. "I'm not trying to put any pressure on you. I'm just afraid you might regret your decision later. Charlotte won't know what's most meaningful to you."

Lilly understood that. The thought of Charlotte or anyone else examining that stuff and throwing away this or that made it difficult to breathe. She wished they could just leave everything where it was until she was ready to deal with the challenge. But that could take years, and they were getting toward the end of their stay in Italy. They had to do *something* with Sabrina's stuff. It didn't make sense to drag all those boxes, most of which were filled with makeup and toiletries, back to the States.

Closing the cookbook, Lilly got to her feet. "I guess I'll go help." The words tasted like gravel in her mouth, but she squared her shoulders.

A compassionate expression claimed Sloane's face. "*I* think it would be for the best. But you're the only one who can determine that. I just . . . I wanted to give you another chance. That's all."

"I know," she murmured and started across the kitchen. As difficult as it was to acknowledge, Sloane was right—Lilly probably would regret it if she didn't take this final opportunity.

She told herself she'd get through it somehow. Life was about making choices—the right choices. If she'd learned anything, she'd learned that. But when she got outside, she found Charlotte so absorbed in what she was looking at that she didn't even hear Lilly's approach.

When Lilly said her name, she twisted around, obviously startled. Then Lilly's heart sank because she could see what Charlotte had been reading.

Charlotte watched the blood drain from Lilly's face. She knew what had upset her. Charlotte was holding printed screenshots and email printouts—ink a little smeared, corners paper-clipped—and other correspondence between Sabrina and a previous boyfriend, something that had probably been turned into hard copy because of the admissions it contained.

This had to be what Steve was referring to when they'd talked on the phone. Walter, the guy Sabrina had been with in Colorado, had put a hidden camera in the bathroom Lilly used. What he'd done was so disgusting Charlotte could hardly believe it, but it was almost worse that Sabrina hadn't gone to the police. Instead, she'd threatened to turn him in whenever she needed money, and he'd paid up to avoid that—until the last time she'd gone to him, after she'd left Steve. Then he'd refused. Charlotte had read an exchange where Sabrina claimed she was finally going to the authorities, and he told her she'd get into as much trouble as he would for blackmailing him.

It didn't look like she'd gotten another payment. She'd told Walter that at least they'd received some compensation to help them on their way. Making him register as a sex offender or putting him in jail certainly wouldn't improve things for Lilly. But Sabrina seemed to have realized that she'd milked the situation as much as she could, or she'd just been distracted by her new relationship with Luca and going to Italy, because she'd seemingly moved on.

How deeply had this incident impacted Lilly? Lilly had to know about the camera or Steve wouldn't have said he'd let her tell Charlotte the story when she was ready.

Lilly immediately pivoted and started toward the house.

Charlotte got up from where she'd been sitting on the deck—where she had more room to spread things out—and ran after her, catching her just before she could go in. "Lilly, I'm so sorry for what happened. Is there any way we could talk about it?"

Tears gathered in Lilly's eyes, but she shook her head adamantly.

"Did he ever . . . touch you?" Charlotte hated to ask, but she doubted she'd have another chance and felt she needed to know so she could get the appropriate help for her sister.

Lilly's scowl darkened. "No!"

"It was just . . . just the camera?" Charlotte clarified.

Lilly said nothing. *Just* probably hadn't been the right word. What he'd done was bad enough, but Charlotte was trying to determine the scope of the problem. "If you don't want to talk to me, can I get you someone to talk to? A therapist or a counselor?"

"I have nothing to tell them," she mumbled. "He never touched me. I didn't even know about the camera until . . . until my mom found it. Then we left."

Thank God Sabrina had done that much. "That camera was such a betrayal, especially from someone posing as a . . . a father figure."

Tears fell over Lilly's lashes and ran down her cheeks. "I don't like thinking about it." She swiped at her cheeks, obviously angry at the tears.

"I can understand why. He's a terrible person, a pervert. But nothing like that is ever going to happen to you again, so you don't have to worry. You're going to be safe from here on out. And I won't bring up the past again. I just . . . I want you to know that you can talk to me about anything—or ask for help—whenever you're ready, okay?"

"I don't need help." She stared at her feet as tears splashed on top of them. "Just . . . don't tell Sloane or Julian, okay?" Finally, she looked up. "Don't tell anyone!"

She found it humiliating, as any girl would. "I won't," Charlotte agreed. "You have my word. Except . . ."

Fear registered in Lilly's eyes—and doubt. She was probably thinking that yet another adult was going to let her down. But that was the very reason Charlotte felt the need to be completely honest and transparent.

"I feel like . . . Well, what happens next depends on you," she continued.

"How?" Lilly asked.

"Sloane and Ben have invited you to live with them after we get back from Italy."

Her mouth fell open, and she dropped back. "Until when?"

"Until you're grown, Lilly. They'd like to raise you."

Her eyes widened.

"If you choose to do that, they might need to know about Walter. It would help them support you in the best way. But only if you agree. You control that story."

She blinked several times. "You want me to go live with Sloane and Ben?"

"That isn't what *I* want, no. It's what *they* want. They asked me, but I think you should be the one to decide." Charlotte caught her breath as she waited. When she'd first arrived in Italy, she'd never dreamed that Lilly would come to mean so much to her, not in such a short period of time.

"I need to decide between the farm and Ben and Sloane?" she asked.

Charlotte inhaled deeply. "Between the farm, Ben and Sloane and . . . me."

"You?" she said hopefully and sniffed as she wiped her face. "Where would we live?"

"That's just it. I can't offer you everything they can. Not yet. First, I have to get back on my feet. And I know you've lived with too much uncertainty as it is. Part of me believes you'd be better off with Sloane—"

"And not Steve?" she broke in.

"Steve seems very nice. And the farm sounds great, too. But I don't really know him. That worries me, especially when *I* love you and would do my best to take care of you."

She seemed even more taken aback. "But if I stay with you . . . What about Cliff? He'd never want me to live with you."

"No."

"So you're choosing me over him?" She seemed stunned, as if she couldn't quite comprehend that.

"I am, and it's the better choice for both of us. I know that. I promise he won't figure into our futures—except I'm staring down the barrel of a divorce, which won't be easy."

"What will your parents say if . . . if you bring me home?"

"I think you know they'd be supportive, which is good, because we'd probably have to live with them for a while until I could finish my book, find us our own place and . . . and see if I'm offered another publishing contract. If not, I won't even be employed."

She knew having Lilly could make a big difference in Sloane's marriage and wanted to be supportive for that reason, but Lilly was *her* sister—her only blood relative, at least that she knew of. She couldn't give her up too easily.

Charlotte took hold of her hand. "Do you feel you can make such a big decision? Because there's no wrong answer. We—all of us—only want what's best for you. If you go to the farm to be with Steve and Old Blue, I'll visit as often as I can, or you can come see me. The same goes for Seattle." She gripped Lilly's shoulders. "So you're in a good place. It's not that you have nowhere to go. It's that you have *too* many people who want you."

A hint of a smile curved Lilly's lips. "That feels good," she admitted. "But I don't know what to do—who's just being nice and who really means it."

"We *all* mean it, or we wouldn't have offered," Charlotte insisted. "But like I said, we won't be hurt by what you decide, so don't be afraid of choosing what would make you happiest."

"How long do I have before…before I have to say?"

They were getting toward the end of their stay. It would be good to know soon, so they could make plans. But Charlotte wasn't going to press her. This was too important a decision. "You can have a few days. Then we'll talk about it again and go from there."

"Thank you," she said and gave Charlotte an impromptu hug.

Charlotte sighed as Lilly went inside. She'd wanted to get to know her birth mother better mostly because she'd craved something to admire.

But certainly nothing she'd found so far was any help.

Lilly almost couldn't believe it. She'd gone from having nowhere to go to having *three* places, and she liked them all. There would be no group home or foster care. The hard part now would be deciding where she'd be happiest.

She'd rather be with her sister than anyone. That was a no-brainer. Her sister was family, and as someone who had so little of it, family meant everything to her. But Charlotte was young. Although she claimed she didn't mind how keeping Lilly might affect her future, there was always the chance she'd change her mind. What if she found someone else, someone like Cliff, who wasn't willing to let her have another person in her life, especially someone who needed time, attention and a home?

Steve was probably the surest bet. She'd lived with him before and knew what to expect. He was all about routine—something her mother loathed, which was partly why they hadn't been able to get along. "Can't you ever cut loose?" her mother would yell at him. And he'd yell back that he wasn't about to let his animals or his property go without the care they needed even if the work he did wasn't exciting enough for her.

And Old Blue was there. She missed that dog so much her teeth ached.

But she also felt a little melancholy when she remembered attending school in Iowa and was afraid it'd get lonely out on the ranch. Steve had been the most decent guy her mother had dated, but what if he wasn't as decent as she thought? What if he was like Walter and would get weird after a while? She had no idea what he might be like as she grew older. Could she really trust him—she, who couldn't seem to trust anyone?

Then there were Sloane and Ben. They both seemed nice. But wouldn't she feel a bit like a guest in their home? She'd never been to Seattle. She was tired of moving around, tired of trying to become familiar with place after place.

Which brought her back to Steve, who was, at least, familiar.

What should she do? And what if she made the wrong decision? Her mother was no longer around to make her go one way or another.

This decision was entirely hers, and she didn't want to screw it up.

"Sloane asked to take Lilly?"

Charlotte could hear the surprise in Julian's voice. They'd just made love and were lying in bed, the house quiet around them. Outside, a single cicada rasped; inside, the air smelled faintly of linen and sandalwood from the soap they'd shared in the shower. "She hasn't said anything to you about it?"

"No, nothing," he said. "But I've been keeping my distance.

I'm afraid she'll know something's going on between us if she ever really focuses on me."

Charlotte chuckled. "I'm surprised we haven't been found out already."

"Everyone's pretty caught up in their own thoughts and decisions. Taking on a child is a big step for Sloane."

"It would be good for her and Ben. In all honesty, I think it would be good for Lilly, too. But . . ."

He'd been running his fingers down her bare arm. When her words fell off, he stopped. "But?"

"I've decided I want her to stay with me."

He shifted so that he could see her face in the moonlight streaming through the veranda doors, which were open to the cool ocean breeze. "When did you decide this?"

"I think I've known I'd do it from the beginning—that I could never really let her go. I was just overwhelmed by what I was going through myself—and knowing Cliff wouldn't be happy if I brought her home while I was married to him—which made me hesitate to offer too soon."

"Are you really committed to raising a teenager?"

"Now you sound like Sloane used to," she said, rolling her eyes.

"Maybe so, but becoming her guardian is a lot of responsibility. It'd be different if the situation hadn't changed, but it has. Now there are other options. Good options."

"I don't care. I want her with me. As soon as I told her today, I felt infinitely lighter. Even if . . . even if I lose my publishing career and the divorce turns into a nightmare, I know I've chosen the right thing. Lilly—and you."

He stiffened. She was generally careful not to say things like that. It upset Julian, made him moody. From her perspective, that was like a cloud crossing in front of the sun. It got suddenly chilly; she hated it. They could talk with their bodies—communicate all they wanted while making love—but he didn't like it when she put her feelings into words. That always spooked him.

"Relax," she said. "I know you care about me."

This was Jules. He wouldn't be making love to her if he didn't feel what she was feeling, wouldn't risk ruining their relationship. They were friends first and foremost, which gave them a strong foundation of trust on which to build.

"Charlotte, we agreed we'd wait to talk about anything serious until after Italy. This is an escape, a time to be selfish, remember? I believe those were your words."

"Because I wanted you to lower your guard." She got up on her elbows, letting her hair fall onto his chest as she gazed into his handsome face. "So what if I want more?"

"Now's not the time to make that decision." Resolute, he slid out from beneath her and got up to go into the bathroom.

She knew she should allow him to withdraw. He did that occasionally, whenever she got too close. Giving him space and time during those periods usually brought him around again.

Besides, she needed to seek her own bed before it grew even later. Morning would come far too soon, and she'd had a particularly emotional day. There hadn't been anything good in those boxes—no memorabilia attached to her birth father or extended relatives—so she'd been disappointed. And she'd been upset by Sabrina's communication with Walter.

Other than that, she'd discovered nothing but clothes, knick-knacks, jewelry and makeup. Charlotte had packed one small box of the best items she planned to ship back to the States—just in case Lilly wanted any of it when she got older—thrown some of it out and planned to give the rest to a local charity.

"You're turning into a curmudgeon, you know that?" she called after him.

"I'm not old enough to be a curmudgeon," he responded, his voice muted so they wouldn't wake up the others.

"Exactly. So lighten up and enjoy life, okay?"

The toilet flushed, the water came on and he appeared in the doorway of the bathroom. "We have another week. I'm going to enjoy that."

"It doesn't have to end in Italy."

He seemed frustrated that she was so confident. But she knew him, knew what was important to him. *She* was important to him. She could feel it in his touch. It was different than Cliff's had ever been. She didn't think Cliff knew what real love was, but Jules did. She was willing to bet her life he felt exactly as she did. "You know you want me."

He scratched his head, making his hair stand up even more. "Of course I want you! But . . . God, have I made a mess! You're never going to speak to me again, and I'm never going to forgive myself."

She gave him a saucy grin. "I'll always speak to you, and you won't be able to avoid speaking to me, since you're going to marry me."

He stopped dead in his tracks. "Charlotte, don't make any decisions yet."

With a laugh, she fell back on the pillows. "I'm not worried. Whatever you're going through, we'll work it out. I'm finally with the right person, and I know it."

He came over to the bed and glowered at her. "Maybe we need to have a talk now."

"Nope! I promised you Italy, and you shall have Italy, but I'm also not going to let you make me think this won't last," she said.

He didn't seem to know how to react. She'd never approached him in quite this way. But she was truly happy when she was with him, too happy to imagine being with anyone else. Whatever he was dealing with, it couldn't be that bad.

At least, that was what she thought until she coaxed him

back into bed, and he eventually relaxed enough to fall asleep in her arms. Then his phone went off, and when she reached over to dim the screen so it wouldn't wake him, she saw the text that had just come in:

> Parkinson's affects everyone differently.
> Chances are good you can still lead a full life.
> Please call and schedule an appointment so
> we can get you started on a treatment plan
> as soon as you return to the States.

chapter 28

Parkinson's. Jules had Parkinson's. Charlotte sat on the deck watching a thin pink seam open over the water as the sun came up. She'd been outside with a blanket ever since she'd slipped from Jules's bed, leaving him sleeping.

Too upset to sleep herself, she'd gone straight to her computer and read everything she could find about Parkinson's, what it would do and how to deal with it. But what she'd learned hadn't been all that encouraging. There was some hope that the disease would not progress quickly. It seemed to differ, depending on the individual, and Jules was young and strong, so he had that going for him. But this was nothing like what she'd expected him to be facing. It'd been too easy to discount a serious health problem when he seemed so physically fit.

At least it wasn't cancer. She kept telling herself that. But the comfort felt paper-thin. Trying to imagine him as he'd be in ten, twenty or thirty years broke her heart. Jules was the strongest man she knew—physically, emotionally and mentally. It just didn't seem possible that anything could steal his coordination and vitality.

But what he'd said and how he'd been acting finally made

sense. At last she understood why he kept trying to push her away.

Hearing the door open behind her, she quickly wiped her tears with the edge of the blanket.

"What are you doing up so early?" Sloane stepped out in a hoodie and yoga pants, her hair in a knot, but with bare feet.

Charlotte hesitated. She didn't feel it was her place to tell Sloane. But Sloane wasn't just Jules's sister; she was Charlotte's best friend. And there was no way to hide her swollen, red eyes. Should she say what he wouldn't—get it out in the open where they could deal with it? She'd promised to give him all the time he needed in Italy, but Italy was supposed to be a chance to heal, not just escape. Keeping his secret felt like watching him tread water while the tide came in. He couldn't heal in any meaningful way if he was still hiding from the truth—and they couldn't help him if he continued hiding it from them.

"It's Jules," she said, fresh tears blurring her vision.

Sloane had come out far enough to see evidence of her emotions and was watching her warily. "What do you mean 'it's Jules'?"

"I know what's wrong with him."

Sloane knelt beside her. "What is it? Tell me!"

She squeezed her eyes closed. "You should hear it from him."

"I'm asking you—right here, right now."

"I can't tell you."

"It's not health related, is it?"

When she didn't answer, Sloane grabbed hold of the chair Charlotte was sitting in as if she'd topple over without its support. "What's wrong with him? Is he dying, Char? Tell me! I'm freaking out!"

Charlotte threw up her hands. It was too late to try to hold back—at this point, it was just cruel. "He's been diagnosed with Parkinson's, Sloane."

"Parkinson's," she repeated numbly. "How serious is that? I mean . . . I've heard of it, but no one I know has ever had it. What will it do to him?"

"It's a progressive disorder that causes the nerves in the brain to weaken and die. It affects so many things—mostly his motor function. There may come a time when he struggles to walk or even talk."

She covered her face. "No . . ."

"I wish it wasn't true."

After several seconds of silence, she said, her voice a shocked whisper, "How'd you find out?"

It wasn't hard to tell that Sloane was hurt to think he'd confide in Charlotte when he hadn't told her. So Charlotte decided it was time for the whole truth—time they dealt with all the secrets between them and figured out how to proceed. Sloane's problems—and hers—paled in comparison to Jules's diagnosis. At least they had their health. And yet he'd been doing his best to support them.

"I saw a text come in from his doctor last night."

Sloane looked confused. "At dinner? Because I was right here with you, and you didn't even react."

"Not at dinner. Later—when I was with him."

"With him where?"

Steeling herself for Sloane's reaction, Charlotte drew in a bolstering breath. "In his bed."

Letting go of the chair, she sank down onto the deck. "You've got to be kidding me!"

Charlotte frowned as she shook her head.

"You and Jules have been hooking up? For how long?"

"As soon as I realized I wasn't going back to Cliff."

Sloane gave her head a small shake. "So . . . what does that mean?"

"It means I'm in love with him, Sloane. It means that we

need to forget about whatever's going on in our own lives and be there for him."

"Of course!" she said. "I'd do anything for him!"

Another tear slid down Charlotte's cheek. "He's not going to like that we know."

"Maybe we shouldn't tell him. Maybe we should pretend we don't know and let him break the news when he's ready."

"And when will that be? Knowing Julian, he'll just keep putting it off, thinking he can deal with it on his own. I say we have that conversation now, while we're all here together and still have some concentrated time with him."

"But that could turn into something big and . . . and disruptive. What about your book?"

She'd believed Megan would get back to her immediately. The fact that she hadn't didn't bode well. It meant she was unsure enough about what she'd read to ask her boss to take a look. "Forget about my book. Whatever happens with it happens. I want to be available to Julian when he needs me most."

Sloane rested her head on Charlotte's knees. "This sucks."

"We'll get through it," Charlotte said. "We'll get through it together."

After a moment or two, Sloane lifted her head. "Are you really in love with my brother?"

"Does it surprise you that much?"

She thought about it for a moment. Then she said, "No. He's twice the man Cliff is."

Charlotte was about to agree—not to be mean; it was simply the truth—when she heard someone call her name. She could've sworn it was Cliff, but the timing of Sloane's mention seemed like too much of a coincidence for that to be true.

He shouted her name twice more before the buzzer rasped. It really *was* Cliff.

"Holy shit." Her stomach dropped; the sunrise suddenly

looked stupidly cheerful. The playoffs had ended in defeat, which meant there was no longer anything keeping him in the States, and although he'd once threatened to come to Italy, she'd never believed he'd really do it!

Julian couldn't stop glaring at Cliff from where he sat directly across from him, partly because Cliff was glaring back. Cliff had traveled for so long and had such a rough flight—delays and bad food—that Charlotte had let him in to meet Lilly and have breakfast. But he must've upset Charlotte when he first got here because her eyes were red and swollen from crying, and Sloane was acting odd, too. Julian was so defensive it was almost impossible to tolerate the other man's presence. He felt none of the hero worship such a big NBA star was probably used to commanding; Julian wanted to throw the bastard out of the villa.

Lilly seemed skeptical of Cliff, too. She kept watching him from under her eyelashes as if he couldn't be trusted. Maybe she'd heard the exchange that'd made Charlotte cry. Julian had been sleeping so deeply he'd missed it. He'd had no idea they even had a visitor until he'd gotten up, showered and made his way downstairs. He'd been worried about the things Charlotte had said to him last night, the confidence with which she'd claimed they were going to get married—until this new threat stole his attention.

"Nice place. It's good to see you're spending my money wisely." Cliff was obviously joking, but what he'd said wasn't funny. Instead of a laugh, his comment earned him a narrowed glance from Sloane, who'd never liked him to begin with. Even Lilly grimaced.

"Well, since you kicked me out so unceremoniously, I felt it was the least you could do." Charlotte spoke with a smile, as if she was only joking, too, but she'd put him in his place firmly enough that Julian didn't feel *he* had to do it. That kept the delicate balance they had going at the moment.

"Jules and I are paying our way," Sloane piped up, drilling Cliff with a laser-like gaze. "We're not taking anything from you."

"I'd pay, too, if I could," Lilly said, her voice small but steady.

"No one expects you to pay for anything, Lilly," Charlotte said. "You're a child. Please don't feel bad about that."

Lilly's attention returned to Cliff, who was looking back at her over the rim of his cup.

"Sorry about your mom," he said as he put down his coffee. "But from what I hear, maybe you're better off."

"Cliff!" Charlotte exclaimed.

"I'm just saying!" He spread out his hands. "Doesn't sound like she was much of a mother."

Sloane jumped to her feet. "You're an asshole. You've always been an asshole, and I, for one, won't sit here any longer and pretend you're not," she said and walked out.

"Touchy," Cliff muttered. "Lilly's a smart girl. I'm not telling *her* anything she doesn't know. Right, Lilly?"

If he expected to win Lilly over with that compliment, it didn't work. The way her eyebrows slammed together reminded Julian of the girl she'd been the day they first met. "I think you're an ass, too," she said, and Julian nearly spewed coffee all over the table when he burst out laughing.

"Sounds like she's turning out more like her mother than you led me to believe," Cliff said to Charlotte as Lilly stomped up the stairs.

Charlotte rubbed her temples. "Please stop. You asked for it."

"I didn't ask for it! I was just pointing out the obvious."

Julian spoke up for the first time. "None of this is helpful. It's time for you to go."

Slamming his hands down on the table, Cliff came to his feet. "*You* don't get to tell me that."

Julian got up, too. Cliff was a significantly taller man, but Julian wasn't afraid of him. He'd been so angry and on edge since his diagnosis, he was eager to have a target—one with whom he felt justified in totally letting loose. "Not only do I get to tell you that, I'm the one who's going to show you out."

"Julian, I've got this," Charlotte said, growing concerned, but Cliff spoke at the same time.

"Like hell! It's because you couldn't keep your filthy hands off my wife that I had to fly halfway across the world to save my marriage!"

Julian kept his voice down. He didn't want to upset Lilly. "A wasted trip, Cliff," he bit out. "Your marriage is over."

"Who the hell do you think you are?" Cliff started to come around the table, and Julian was ready for him, but Charlotte jumped up to intervene.

"Stop it—both of you! I was going to let you eat breakfast first," she said to Cliff. "But if we have to do this now, I guess we have to do it now."

"We have to do it now," Cliff echoed. "Tell him you love me. Tell him we're going to put our marriage back together. Tell him to get lost."

"I'm not going to do that," she said. "Because Jules is right. I'm not coming back to you."

"Why?" he shouted. "I told you Lilly could come live with us. Lord knows we have a big enough house, right? We have the money, too. Think of everything you'll be able to provide for her."

"I'll take care of Lilly just fine on my own," she said. "I'm finished, Cliff. I don't love you anymore. I want to be with Julian."

Stunned, Cliff gaped at her. That declaration, and the resolution in her voice, had shocked him. Julian looked shocked, too. He'd been fooling himself, he realized, trying to believe

Charlotte wasn't counting on too much from him. And now, in this moment, he couldn't avoid the truth. He'd fallen in love with her just like he'd been afraid he would. And she'd fallen in love with him.

But if he *really* loved her, he couldn't foist what was in his future onto her. That would make him even worse than Cliff!

Cliff looked between them. "Fine," he said. "I'll leave. But I'll bet you a million bucks you call me back tomorrow," he said and snatched his bag before shouldering past Julian.

Seeing him go worked like a cup of cold water in Julian's face. What had he just done? "Whoa, wait." He started to follow as the gate clanged shut, but Cliff didn't turn around.

Julian looked blankly at Charlotte. "I think . . . I think he and I *both* need to leave."

Charlotte blinked at him. "What are you talking about?"

"I'm sorry," he said. "I'm *so* sorry. I hope one day you'll be able to forgive me."

"Stop it!" Charlotte said. "I know, okay? I know about the Parkinson's!"

He wanted to ask her how, and why she would still be getting involved with him if she knew, but he couldn't bear the answers. "Then you don't know what you're doing," he said simply and quickly packed his things before pushing past all three women when he left.

Ten minutes later, Sloane sat on the deck with Charlotte—Lilly was on Charlotte's other side—trying to console her. "Give him some time, Char. He'll come around." She was talking about her brother, but she wasn't entirely convinced what she said was true. Julian was the most stubborn individual she'd ever known, especially when he believed he was in the right. The fact that they knew about his diagnosis when he hadn't thought they did only seemed to galvanize him.

Charlotte had been staring out to sea almost since he left. When Sloane spoke, she wiped the tears from her face but said nothing in reply. She'd tried to convince Jules to stay—they all had—but he kept saying there was no way he'd ever allow her to throw her life away on him. And since he'd already called an Uber, they couldn't stop him from leaving.

After shaking them both off, he'd waved goodbye to Lilly, who'd been standing in the background crying by that time, too, and drove away.

Now it was quiet.

"You're going to be okay," Sloane murmured.

Charlotte sniffed as she gazed down at her phone, which was lying in her lap. "Julian's not answering my calls or texts."

"It's too soon." Somewhere on the street below, a scooter coughed to life. "He just found out that we know about his diagnosis," she said.

"He shouldn't have tried to keep it from us," she grumbled.

Sloane had to agree, and yet she could understand why he would. "It makes him feel like he's been robbed, that he's no longer the man he once was. No one wants to feel like they're damaged goods—bound to be a burden on all who love them."

"So he keeps shoving us away?"

"I'll talk to him. I'm his sister. He can't shove me away, and he knows it."

"He can't shove me away, either," Charlotte said defiantly. But then she added a much weaker "I hope."

Lilly threaded her fingers through Charlotte's. "Don't cry. No matter what happens, you've got me." She sent Sloane an apologetic glance before adding, "I love Sloane, and I love Steve and Old Blue. But you're my sister, and families should stick together."

It was such a sweet sentiment that Sloane couldn't even be sad about her choice. She'd known it would probably go that way—that if she'd changed her mind and wanted a child, she should have one. Now that Lilly had shown her that she might like to be a mother, she wasn't nearly as frightened of the responsibility and the changes it would require. "I agree," she told Lilly. "You two *should* stick together. But I hope you know that you're always welcome to visit me."

A smile appeared on Lilly's face as she nodded. "I'd like that."

"Steve might be disappointed when he learns that he's going to miss out, too," Sloane teased.

"I've already told him," Lilly responded.

This pulled Charlotte out of her misery. "You have?"

"I texted him late last night when I made my decision," she explained.

"What'd he say?"

"He said that you're a wonderful person, and he thinks I'm making the right choice. And he invited me to come visit."

Finally, Charlotte seemed to recover some of her composure. Her hand curled more tightly around Lilly's, and her voice went husky as she said, "I'm glad you chose me."

Seeing the pleasure of Charlotte's response register on Lilly's face made the future even easier for Sloane to accept.

"Don't worry," Lilly said to Charlotte. "We'll get Jules back—once he realizes he's meant to be part of our family."

Charlotte brought Lilly's hand up and kissed her knuckles. "Love wins," she said, sniffing through a laugh. "We'll wear him down."

chapter 29

Ben had met Lilly via FaceTime. He thought she was a sweet, beautiful young girl. Smart, too. He would've loved to have had her as a baby, because it would've enabled him to savor every stage of her life. But getting in halfway through was better than nothing. He was so eager to have a young person around, someone he could help and guide, someone who needed him. He knew there were people who didn't agree. The same thing wasn't right for everyone. But he felt his life would be missing something without the opportunity to devote himself to a little human being. And after being *so* hopeful that he'd soon have a child in his home, the news Sloane had just delivered landed hard.

"She's not coming?" he said. "But it was going to be perfect."

"I'm sad, too," Sloane said. "But you can't really blame her. She has so little family. It's understandable she'd cling to what she's got. And Charlotte is wonderful."

"I can't argue with that. But Charlotte's currently living with her parents, going through a divorce and trying to save her career. Is she really the best person to raise Lilly? Because this seems to be hitting her at a really bad time." Which was why they'd been about to step in. They were stable and ready.

He was ready, anyway, and he finally had Sloane on board. He didn't see another opportunity like that—one they were both happy with—coming up again in the future.

"Charlotte's capable of doing a great job, regardless of the headwinds she's facing. You know her. She won't allow Lilly to want for anything."

"At what sacrifice?" Hadn't that been Sloane's argument from the beginning? Why was she so calm and accepting of this news? Because she didn't truly care if Lilly came to live with them?

Maybe her offer to take Lilly had only been an attempt to placate him, something that was easy to offer since she'd known it would never happen.

"Less of a sacrifice than giving her up," she replied.

He said nothing—couldn't speak. He didn't want to say something he'd regret later. Of course Sloane had been sincere. It was terrible of him to suspect otherwise. That was his hurt talking. What was happening right now was *his* fault. He'd let his hopes get up way too high even though he'd warned himself that this could happen.

While cleaning out the spare bedroom, he'd imagined taking Lilly school shopping, reading out loud—she was a little old for that, but he'd hoped she'd still allow it—and helping with her homework. There were so many books he wanted to share with her—Tolkien, Sachar and a dozen others. He wanted to attend Back to School nights and cheer her on as she learned and developed. And *she* probably wouldn't be too excited about this, but he was also looking forward to having her help him with the yardwork because he remembered bonding with his father as they clipped and mowed and weeded.

In retrospect, working together had been more rewarding

than playing together. Those were the times his dad quietly taught him so many lessons, and it was those lessons that'd molded him into the man he was today.

Now the dream of being a father like his own was shattered. Already. He felt sick.

"Ben?" Sloane said.

"I'm here," he replied.

"You seem to be taking the news pretty hard, babe."

"Yeah, well, I'm disappointed. I wanted her to come. I *really* wanted her to come." What he didn't add was that, as much as he loved Sloane and could never let her go, his life was starting to feel empty without children. If that hadn't been the case, he would've quit asking for them long ago. He didn't know why he seemed to need them, and why she didn't. He couldn't explain that, but he knew it wasn't going to be easy for him to go through life without kids.

That was exactly what he'd have to do, however, because he couldn't give up the woman he loved, either. *Fuck.*

Apparently, it was fate that he'd get what he most wanted on the one hand—a wonderful partner to share his life with—and not on the other.

"I've got some things to do here," he said, eager to get off the phone. He was the one who'd made the decision to remain in their marriage and accept what it meant. He needed to abide by his choice gracefully. "I'll have to call you later."

There was a long pause. Then she said, "Before you go, I want to tell you that . . . that meeting Lilly and getting to know her has . . . has changed something inside me."

He didn't say anything. He could barely listen. He just wanted to get off the phone.

"Did you hear me?" she asked.

His coffee had gone cold in his hand; he hadn't noticed.

"Yeah. I heard you. But is there any way we could talk about this later?"

"Sure, I just . . . It's the weekend."

"I know."

"And...since you don't have to work, I thought you might like to spend some of the day turning the bedroom you just cleaned out for Lilly into a nursery."

He wasn't sure what he'd been expecting her to say, but it certainly wasn't that. He blinked. "Excuse me?"

"I told you—Lilly changed something in me, Ben. I've decided I want to have a baby. *Your* baby."

Sucking air in between his teeth, he held himself perfectly still. He was afraid to react for fear she'd retract that statement.

"Hello?" she said. "Are you still there?"

"Do you mean it?" he finally asked in response, barely able to squeeze the words out of his tight throat.

"I know how much a baby would mean to you. I wouldn't have said it if I wasn't completely committed."

"But you're not doing it just for me, are you? I don't want you to resent it later. Pregnancies are hard. So is raising children—"

"I know the risks, honey. I've continuously listed them off to myself for the past few years. But I've decided that, yes, having a child is hard—but it's also worth it. I'm finally ready. Just in the nick of time," she added with a laugh. "I'm not getting any younger."

The lump in Ben's throat made it almost impossible for him to speak. "I miss you so much," he said. "I would've stuck by you. I hope you know that."

"I *do* know that. And now I'll let you get off the phone. I have to go myself. I promised Lilly we'd go to the beach, so she's waiting for me."

"Okay," he said, and she nearly hung up before he overcame his surprise and elation enough to add, "I love you."

"I know," she said teasingly. Then she disconnected.

Ben sat still for several minutes. His whole world had shifted, and he was stunned by the whiplash it caused. *A baby*. Sloane wanted a baby. She'd really said that. He'd be a father, after all.

He laughed out loud, even though there was no one around to hear him. Then he yelled, "Yes!" and pumped his fist as he leaped to his feet.

He needed to find his laptop. If they were going to create a nursery, they'd need some ideas, and he wanted to see what other parents had done. He couldn't make any decisions without Sloane's input—she was the decorator, and a professional at that—but he could certainly send her some ideas.

Charlotte had received an email from her editor. Megan was cautiously optimistic about her new manuscript. She said she personally liked this story better than the first one, but was worried about the difference in tone. She'd had the publisher read her sample chapters to get his opinion—as Charlotte had guessed she was doing—and he was equally concerned that her readership wouldn't follow her into more "emotionally hefty" territory. But they both liked the book well enough to give it a chance.

That meant she was going to get to finish the manuscript and send it out into the world. She was excited, but the uncertainty they felt tempered her reaction. She wasn't any more convinced than they were that her audience would embrace such a big change.

But what she was writing now reflected how much she'd grown as a person. She had to go with what inspired her, what moved her—couldn't conjure up anything else at the moment—so she was going to take her chances.

"What is it?" Lilly asked. "Have you heard from Megan?"

Lilly was sitting at the other end of the table putting a thousand-piece puzzle together and must've noticed the change in her expression because Charlotte hadn't made a sound.

"I have."

Worry entered Lilly's eyes. "What'd she say?"

Sloane was in the kitchen putting together a vegetable tray but was close enough to overhear them and immediately came to the dining room. "Did she like it?"

"She did," Charlotte said somewhat tentatively. "More than my first book. But they're concerned about how it might be received."

"What does that mean?" Lilly asked.

"They're afraid it won't sell," Charlotte clarified. "And if it doesn't sell . . ."

"Well, there are no guarantees any book will sell, are there?" Sloane said.

Yes and no, Charlotte thought. If she'd gone back to Cliff, she would've had as much of a guarantee as anyone could get. Her book would've sold simply because of her connection to him, like the first one did. She had to go with this one on her own, which was terrifying, but it didn't make her regret her decision. She hadn't married Cliff for his fame, and she wasn't willing to go back to him because of it, either.

"True," Charlotte agreed.

"It's going to be a great book, which means it'll do fine," Sloane predicted, obviously trying to buoy her confidence.

"I hope so." Charlotte checked her phone. Julian had only left a few hours ago, but she was already dying to hear from him.

Sadly, there'd been no word, but she kept checking.

"So are you going to try to get a few pages written today?" Sloane asked.

Charlotte nodded. "I can't fall any further behind."

"At least you know what you're creating is good," Sloane said. "Let that encourage you."

"I will." Although Charlotte was worried about the risk, she knew the situation with her career could be worse. Had Megan and the publisher hated what she was writing, she would've been in a world of hurt.

Picking up her phone again, she texted Julian:

> Don't you want to know what my publisher said about my book?

She'd thought that might be just the carrot to get him to respond. But she waited several minutes—and got nothing.

> You're making Charlotte really sad.

Julian sat in a hotel room in Rome, exhausted from the train ride north and feeling sick to his stomach as he read the texts he'd been getting. That one was from Lilly. It was hardest not to respond to her.

He scrolled through Sloane's texts. She was getting pissed off. He'd never ignored her before. He'd have to respond to her eventually; she was his sister. He just couldn't do it now when he was already feeling so terrible. She'd called their parents and enlisted their help in trying to reach him. Although they'd already known about his diagnosis, they now also knew his relationship with Charlotte had changed and were hounding him to go back to the villa and work things out with her, which ticked him off. Sloane shouldn't have said anything to them.

He knew he was lucky to have so many people in his life who cared about him and were willing to stick by him during difficult times. But they didn't understand—he didn't want them to have to do that. He'd always prided himself on what he could *give*. If he was incapacitated, someone who could only take, how could he be of any value to them?

He sighed. He hadn't eaten all day, but he didn't care. He was too tired to worry about that. He hadn't had much sleep since arriving in Italy. At first, he'd been too wound up about his diagnosis and how and when he was going to break the news. Then he'd spent every night he could with Charlotte, trying to collect as many memories as possible—as if that would be enough to carry him through his particular future. He was going to bed. But before he set his phone down, he received another text from Charlotte.

Please don't hurt me.

He winced. That one took a chunk out of him. He didn't want to hurt her. He was trying to *save* her, but he could only do that by staying away from her.

She'd be so much better off in the long run. He wanted to reiterate that, but he knew if he started a dialogue with her he'd crumble. He wanted what she wanted probably even more than she did.

Leaving his phone on the nightstand, he pulled the covers up and rolled over. He was doing the right thing. He had no choice.

He kept saying that to himself, but the minutes ticked away and sleep wouldn't come.

Finally, after nearly an hour, he sat up and grabbed his phone again.

I'm doing this for Charlotte's good. One day you'll understand, he wrote to Lilly.

I can't believe you looped Mom and Dad in about Charlotte, he wrote to Sloane.

And to Charlotte: Please don't feel hurt. I will always love you.

He told himself to leave it at that—hoped that now he'd be able to sleep—but he couldn't help waiting for their responses.

Lilly: If you love her, you'll come back.

Sloane: They agree with me. Charlotte is perfect for you. That's why they keep calling— to say the same thing. Parkinson's doesn't mean your life is over. Fight to live every moment to its fullest, the way you always have. That's who my brother is.

Charlotte: I'm the one who should get to decide what's best for me and my future.

Lilly was too young to understand, he told himself. And Sloane was right, but he didn't feel much like fighting today.

He hoped he'd be stronger tomorrow.

Problem was, Charlotte was right, too. She was a grown woman. She should get to decide what was best for her. In any other circumstance that would apply.

He just couldn't let her make this one mistake.

"You'll be glad one day," he muttered and pulled the blankets back up.

The flight home was long and uncomfortable, made worse by the fact that Charlotte couldn't sleep. She'd enjoyed Italy. She'd loved their villa, too, and definitely wanted to come back.

Next summer when Lilly was out of school, she hoped they could spend another month on the Amalfi Coast. After all, it was the place where she'd met Lilly and fell in love with her, so to speak. Praiano, especially, would always be close to her heart.

But thinking about her time on the Amalfi Coast was bittersweet. Although it wasn't where she'd met Julian, it was where she'd fallen in love with him, too, and yet he hadn't responded to her since he left, except to tell her he would always love her, and he was going to live his life without her for *her* sake, not his. He wanted her to find someone who wouldn't be so much of a burden, wanted her to have the kind of happy and fulfilled life she "deserved."

She'd tried to tell him that she preferred quality over quantity—whatever years she could have with him over whatever years she could have with someone else. But he'd never replied to that text. Last she'd heard from Sloane, he'd started treatment with his doctor and then left for Iceland, where he was taking pictures of the volcano that was erupting there.

She pictured him under a pewter sky, lava lighting his face from below, and felt a lump rise in her throat.

"Are you excited to be home?" Lilly asked. The cheapest flight for Sloane had been through Dallas, so she wasn't with them. Only Lilly was sitting next to her. She'd read almost since they took off—when she wasn't sleeping.

Charlotte had been gazing out the window, watching the ground rush up to meet them as they prepared for landing. "I am," she said and smiled. But she was feeling more tentative than she wanted to admit. She knew Cliff would have divorce papers waiting for her; he'd told her as much. He was now claiming that he was going to try to break the prenup himself and leave her with nothing, and she'd been so engrossed in trying to make progress on her latest book that she hadn't even had the chance to contact an attorney.

She'd figured she'd handle all that once she was back in LA, so that was what she had to look forward to now.

"What about you?" she asked Lilly, to take the focus off herself.

"I'm excited, too." Her sister looked more nervous than

excited, and Charlotte could understand why. Her life was entirely different than it'd been just a month ago. She had yet to meet Charlotte's parents in person, had no idea what living with them would be like. She'd also be in yet another new area.

Charlotte gave her a nudge. "Don't worry. Everything's going to be okay."

"I know." She was probably exuding more confidence than she felt. But they were both pretending. Every time Lilly asked about Julian, Charlotte acted as if whatever happened was going to be fine. That she was resilient and happy. She knew Lilly had been subjected to the ups and downs of her mother's many romantic relationships and didn't want to put her through the same angst and uncertainty. She was determined to remain solid as a rock no matter what she went through personally so that Lilly could finally feel confident and secure. That was the promise Charlotte had made when she'd decided to finish raising Lilly. Although she still wanted to find a mate and have children herself, she wasn't going to burden Lilly with her own heartbreaks.

Rubber thundered under them and the wings hummed as the plane touched down and bounced slightly before settling securely on the tarmac. Lilly's eyes flew open wide.

"The landing can be a bit disconcerting," Charlotte explained.

Lilly relaxed as they taxied more comfortably down the runway. "Do you think Jules will be waiting for us?" she asked as the flight attendant opened the door and everyone started to get into the overhead bins.

For a moment, Charlotte was tempted to believe it was possible. Surely he'd change his mind. Why would he relegate himself to a life of loneliness when she was right there, ready to love him? She'd texted him the date and time they'd arrive in LA and asked him to pick them up from the airport. If he was going to respond to anything, it'd be a request for a favor. Jules was like that; he loved to step up for people.

He hadn't responded, so she had no commitment. Still, she hoped he'd surprise them. "You never know," she said hopefully.

But after they got off and gathered their baggage, it was only her parents who were waiting.

Lilly was going back to a whole new life. She wouldn't recognize a thing.

She knew she should probably be terrified, but she wasn't. As different as this new world would be, she felt safer than ever before. She hoped her mother was happier in heaven than she'd been on earth—that she finally had the love she needed—because Lilly knew *she* was going to be fine. Charlotte wouldn't let her down. As long as she had someone to love her, someone she could love in return, Lilly felt she could handle almost anything. It was trying to take care of her mother when she couldn't seem to make much of a difference that'd been so hard.

She wasn't even scared to meet Charlotte's parents. She'd sort of met them already via FaceTime, so she knew what they looked like, how they acted and how they treated her.

When she saw them standing at baggage claim with a bouquet of welcome balloons and a huge stuffed bear, she was slightly embarrassed—they were drawing a lot of attention from other travelers—but knowing they were excited to have her come home with Charlotte felt wonderful.

"Thank you," she'd mumbled when they handed her the balloons. She didn't tell them that she was getting too old for stuffed animals. What did that matter? She felt so light inside she thought the balloons might carry her away.

Once they got their luggage, she sat in the back seat of their giant black Mercedes with her new bear and the helium-filled balloons taking up all the space between her and Charlotte, listening to Penny describe the bedroom she'd decorated for Lilly as they started home. Although Charlotte had made it clear that they probably wouldn't be living in the house for all that long, Penny said she'd wanted to have a special place for Lilly, because even after they moved out, she wanted Lilly to come and stay on weekends or over summer break.

Lilly got the feeling that Don and Penny viewed her as sort of a grandchild, and since she'd never really had grandparents, she didn't mind.

The bear's fur tickled her cheek as she told Penny she couldn't wait to see her new room. Then Don looked at her in the rearview mirror and winked as if to say he knew she was too mature for the way Penny was treating her, but appreciated her playing along.

That made Lilly smile even wider.

Charlotte reached over and held her hand as if she thought her mother might be a bit much, and Lilly squeezed to let her know Penny was just fine. "This feels sort of like Christmas," she whispered to Charlotte while Penny was telling Don that he was going to take them all out for a special welcome dinner once they'd had a day or so to recover from the jet lag.

"Do you know if Sloane made it home safely?" Penny asked.

"She hasn't landed quite yet," Charlotte told her.

"Have you heard from Jules?" Penny kept her tone light. Lilly could tell she was trying not to upset Charlotte and felt bad for her sister that Julian wasn't being her friend anymore.

"No." Charlotte turned to the window, probably so no one could see how sad that made her. "But it's fine."

She always added that at the end because she didn't want Lilly to worry that she might break down or spin out. Lilly appreciated how hard she was trying, but she knew Charlotte was hurt, and she couldn't understand why things had to be this way. Okay, so Julian had a disease. Anyone could get sick. You didn't stop loving someone because of that. *Jeez*. She'd thought he'd figure that out. He was so smart.

But it would be hard to feel you're no longer lovable because of something outside your control . . . She'd experienced a bit of that, thanks to her mother.

After peppering Lilly with questions about Italy and what she might like to see or do in the next few weeks—and promising to take her to Disneyland for the first time—Penny struck up a conversation with Charlotte, asking about her book and how much she'd written. Charlotte told her that once she'd gotten her publisher's approval, she'd made good progress but still had a lot of pages to write. And Penny said she knew she'd be able to finish them. Then they started talking about Cliff.

Lilly had heard all she wanted about Charlotte's ex. He was being so mean about the divorce that Lilly couldn't think of him without getting mad.

Her phone buzzed. She glanced down to see that she'd received a text from Sloane.

You home, girl? How was the flight?

> Good. Just read and slept. Penny and Don picked us up in a huge black Mercedes.

😂 I bet they were excited to meet you.

> They brought me balloons and a huge stuffed bear.

Nice.

> How's Ben?

Haven't seen him yet. Just landed. We're still waiting to deplane.

> I bet he missed you.

I hope so. And I hope you and Charlotte will come visit us after she finishes her book.

> I'll see if we can.

Lilly was about to put her phone back in her lap and start listening to what was being said again. But because she was also hurt that Julian didn't come get them from the airport, she took a moment to text him instead.

> I can't believe you didn't come get us.

Three dots appeared. She thought he was going to finally say something back, but then they disappeared and she didn't get anything.

chapter 30

Sloane was nervous as she made her way down to baggage claim. She felt like a different person from the woman who'd left Seattle a month ago. Back then, she'd been so single-minded, so caught up in her work and trying to make her business a success that she'd gotten tunnel vision. The design studio was all she could think about, all she wanted to think about. It was a wonder Ben had put up with the neglect.

A month away had given her a better perspective. She still loved her business and wanted to succeed, but Italy had reminded her how much the people in her life meant to her—how much *Ben* meant to her.

He was waiting for her with a dozen roses in one hand, smiling as he caught sight of her rushing toward him.

"Feels like it's been years since I've seen you," she said as she threw her arms around him, nearly crushing the flowers.

He laughed as he stumbled back. She'd obviously hit him with more force than he'd expected. But then his arms went around her, too, as well as they could with the flowers, and she felt the safety and security of being pressed against her life partner.

"I missed you so much," he murmured.

She pulled back to look into his face. "I missed you, too. It's so good to be home."

He handed her the flowers, and she dipped her head to smell one of the fragile buds. "These are beautiful."

"Impractical. But I thought this occasion called for impractical—something that would simply say, *I love you*."

She let the warm glow inside her reflect on her face. "I love you, too."

Other travelers were walking past. Some looked as rumpled and tired as she was, and yet they grinned when they saw the flowers. An old guy even gave them a thumbs-up. They were becoming a bit of a spectacle, probably making people wonder if they'd just gotten engaged, which was no doubt why Ben lowered his voice to a whisper when he said, "Did I dream what you told me about having a baby?"

"That I want one? No, it wasn't a dream. I meant it. I still do."

"What about your business? I know it'll be hard—"

"Lots of moms have businesses. If they can do it, so can I. I no longer see it as mutually exclusive."

"I'll help. I'll do all I can to give you the time you need," he promised.

"I know you will. But I'm not going to have a baby just to pass him or her off to you. I don't want to be an absentee mom. I want to be part of the experience. I'll just have to learn how to become a better juggler."

His eyes sparkled as he said, "I can't tell you how excited I am."

"I'm excited, too," she said and was astonished by the fact that she meant it. She'd loved mentoring Lilly. She was going to enjoy being a mother, too. She'd just needed a little test run to get her started.

"Come on, then. I plan to knock you up right away," he said, and they both chuckled as they approached the conveyor belt that was beginning to spit out the luggage.

Should she call him?

Charlotte had hoped the DNA results would lead to information about her grandmother or possibly her aunt—give her a way to contact them. Although she'd been curious about her father, it didn't reflect well on him that he'd cheated on his wife and gotten the neighbor girl, who was barely eighteen, pregnant. She hadn't considered him anyone she'd ever want to know. But the only thing that'd come through on the relatives' section of her DNA report was a picture and an email address for one Robert Sharp, who shared half her DNA.

He was older—gray and a bit weathered, but in a smooth, citified way. He looked like a retired banker or a salesman of expensive suits. He also looked like a close relative. Even *she* could see how similar his eyes and nose were to hers—his smile, too—which was why she kept opening her DNA report and examining his picture. There had to be a reason he'd had his DNA tested, didn't there?

Maybe not. Maybe he simply wanted to know his ethnicity, or it was a gift from one of his other kids, all of whom would be closer to Sabrina's age than hers and might not know anything about his indiscretion.

She nibbled on her bottom lip as she tried to enlarge his photograph. He'd probably been quite handsome. He was *still* handsome. Maybe that was what had attracted Sabrina to him . . .

What'd happened back then? How did their relationship develop and how did he react when he found out Sabrina was expecting? Charlotte had assumed these were questions she'd be able to ask her grandmother, if she could track her down. But it didn't seem as though any of the relatives on her mother's side had submitted their DNA, at least not to this particular service.

She could submit to all the others and wait several more weeks. Something might turn up . . .

Or maybe they didn't want to be contacted. That was just as possible.

How would Robert react if she reached out to *him*?

Charlotte really didn't want to invite anything painful into her life. Dealing with Cliff had been difficult enough. He wasn't used to losing, and once he realized she really wasn't coming back, he'd grown so vindictive. He'd taken the clothes and other personal belongings she'd left at the Malibu house and thrown them all out in the driveway. She, her father and Lilly had to go collect everything. He'd also been seen partying all over town with numerous women, which had set the internet ablaze again.

None of that was pleasant, but six weeks had passed since she'd returned from Italy. Six weeks that, in the quiet moments of her day—usually when she was supposed to be working on her book—she'd been opening and reopening this email to stare at Robert's picture.

Six weeks had also passed since Julian had walked out of her life. That was far worse than what Cliff was doing; she was at peace with her decision to go ahead and end her marriage. It was Julian's abandonment that cut deeper than anything because she knew a relationship with someone who had his character would bring the fulfillment she'd been missing.

And she was worried about him. She knew he'd started treatment, but was it helping? Did the medication have side effects? How was he processing everything?

At least Lilly seemed to be happy. That was what mattered, Charlotte told herself. Penny had been teaching her to knit.

They'd also started a garden. And she'd been going swimming at night with Don. So she had plenty of love and attention. Don had even mentioned getting her a puppy after Charlotte turned in her book and could help train it—and given how much Lilly still mourned the loss of Old Blue, Charlotte thought that was a fine idea.

Charlotte was grateful to her parents for making Lilly's life so full because it gave her a chance to work. They provided a great distraction even for moments like these, when she couldn't quit thinking about Julian and missing him.

Or she couldn't quit thinking about the results from Ancestry.com.

Was the fact that her birth father had submitted his DNA an invitation? That was hard to believe, but she supposed it was possible . . .

It was late on a Saturday afternoon when she was supposed to be finishing her book, and Don and Penny had taken Lilly to the movies, that she finally decided if she was ever going to move on, she had to at least send Robert an email. He could ignore her if he wanted to. Then she'd have her answer as to whether he wanted to be in touch.

After she wrote him, she went back to her manuscript for a while. But it was only an hour or so later that she switched over to find he'd responded with his number and a question:

Do you mind if we talk over the phone?

Her heart began to pound. She told herself not to call. She wasn't sure she could tolerate it. She also didn't want him to have her number, just in case he was weird and wouldn't leave her alone afterward.

But she could always block her number before she called, which, in the end, was what she did.

"Hello?"

His voice sent a chill down her spine. She knew almost nothing about him, and yet she had him on the phone. Her birth father. "It's me," she said, "Charlotte." She realized he probably wouldn't know her name and added, "I think I might be your daughter." She rolled her eyes at her own comment. He was definitely "closely" related. What else could he be? "Actually, my DNA results suggest it."

"I wondered if there was someone out there," he said. "I'd almost given up. If I hadn't given the DNA company permission for push notifications, I might've missed it. As it was, it popped right up, and I was so surprised I just about crashed my car."

Her chest tightened. "You've been looking for me?"

"I didn't have much to go on, so I couldn't really *look*. I took that DNA test hoping if I did have a child with Sabrina, he or she might contact me."

"Why would you care?"

"Guilt, I guess. Wanting to make things right—or as right as I can at this late date. I know you have no reason to believe this, but I honestly wasn't the type to cheat. I never cheated before that day or after. I also never dreamed I'd have sex with a girl who was barely eighteen and certainly didn't set out to make that happen."

Charlotte glanced out the window, hoping her parents and Lilly wouldn't return quite yet. "You're saying it was all Sabrina?"

"It takes two. I'm not blaming her. But when she came over to my house in a bikini one day and asked me to come kill a spider in her bedroom because her parents weren't home to do it, things got out of hand. I'd noticed her before, of course. And I knew she'd noticed me. She'd always walk over when I was watering the lawn to talk to me or wave every time we passed.

Anyway, that day she let me know she was interested, and I . . . I didn't walk away like I should have."

He sounded totally sincere. And Charlotte *had* learned a lot about Sabrina—knew she'd loved the excitement of the taboo and would've enjoyed feeling so attractive that even the handsome neighbor, who was married, would want her.

"I felt horrible after it happened," he continued. "And what made it all worse was that she kept coming over, trying to interest me again. I was afraid she'd destroy me!"

"Did you tell your wife about what happened?"

"I'm ashamed to say I didn't. I looked at it as a mistake. It wasn't an ongoing affair. I didn't want to crush my wife because of fifteen hormone-fueled minutes. I knew how it would look. It *still* looks that way! Instead, I convinced Cindy to move, and we put our house up for sale. She thought we were moving because I was tired of the neighborhood. But I was doing it just to escape Sabrina. I didn't want to let my desire for an eighteen-year-old girl rip my family apart."

"So you moved away." Charlotte gripped her phone tighter. "Was that before or after you found out she was pregnant?"

"I never learned about the pregnancy. Before my house sold, Sabrina graduated from high school and was simply . . . gone. I didn't know where she went. I never dreamed she was pregnant, and I certainly wasn't sure, if she was pregnant, that the child would be mine. I'd only slept with her once, and she claimed to be on the Pill.

"Besides, I knew from how she'd behaved with me that she was very sexually active. But I heard whisperings around the neighborhood—things her mother, Kathy, was saying to various people. I even ran into Kathy at the grocery store one day, and the scathing look she gave me let me know what *she* thought. I knew Sabrina would never have told her, feared the gossip was true. So I went over to her house to speak with her. If Sabrina was pregnant, I knew I had to come clean, risk the loss of everything I had over one stupid encounter. But Kathy insisted there was no baby and slammed the door in my face."

"She didn't want your financial support?"

"I think she was embarrassed by her daughter. They never got along. Kathy was a very religious woman, felt there was a right way and a wrong way and Sabrina never seemed to choose the right way.

"Kathy also knew my wife. I think she acted to protect her and my children. I can't be sure. But something about the way everything happened left me uneasy. For years I tried to believe that what I did that day would never come back to haunt me. I ran with that because my kids were still young, and I couldn't bear what the truth might do to them. But as the years passed, I couldn't help wondering if I had another child out there, and if that child might need me. So I finally told Cindy about what happened, and she supported me in submitting my DNA, just in case."

Charlotte had thought such terrible things about this man. But now that she'd heard his story—now that he just seemed fallible, human—she didn't feel quite so hard toward him. There was no need for him to make up anything. He was the one who'd put his DNA on that site so she could find him. She doubted he'd do that just to lie to her. The type of person she'd thought he was would've tried to skip out cleanly.

"That was very nice of your wife."

"She's a far better person than I am."

The fact that they were still married and had made the DNA decision together suggested he wasn't as terrible a person as his actions that one day might suggest. "I can't blame it all on Sabrina," Charlotte said. "She was so young."

"I'm not asking you to," he was quick to say. "I guess what I'm hoping for is that you'll forgive us both. I don't know what kind of life you've lived, so I don't know if that's even possible, but I also wanted to let you know that I'm willing to help with anything you need me to make up for . . . for the fact that I'm partly responsible for bringing you into this world and then did nothing to support you."

At last, Charlotte fully believed him. People didn't step up, apologize, and offer to make restitution if they weren't sincere. He could easily have gone on living his life without telling Cindy, without testing his DNA, without inviting her to contact him. Why would he make himself vulnerable to such an ugly truth coming out if he wasn't completely repentant?

And that was what made it possible for her to forgive him, as he'd asked. "Fortunately, I had fabulous adoptive parents who didn't let me want for anything. I've always been well-adjusted, happy."

"Adoptive parents . . . So Sabrina didn't keep you."

"No. I was lucky she didn't," she said and went on to tell him everything she knew—about Sabrina's death and the other child she'd left behind.

"I'd love to meet you one day," he said at the end of the conversation.

Charlotte knew he wasn't too far away. They'd sold their house and left the area where he'd known Sabrina many years ago, and were now in San Diego. She could drive down there one day—or have him drive to Orange County.

"I'd like that, too," she said and meant it.

Julian loved geothermal activity, and Haukadalur Valley had a lot of it. While he was in Iceland, Fagradalsfjall erupted, a volcano on the Reykjanes Peninsula only about twenty-five miles out of Reykjavík. He got incredible photographs, some of the best of his career, likely because he was feeling so fatalistic he was willing to get closer than the other photographers. He'd been offered a lot of money for them, so that was a win. But he wasn't as excited as he should be.

Because of Charlotte. He'd stopped hearing from her several weeks ago, and it absolutely crushed him. He had to keep telling himself he was doing the right thing—that this was what was best for her—to keep from breaking down and calling her. And that wasn't easy. The memories of their time together in Italy plagued him constantly. She was on his mind *all* the time.

It didn't help that he was alone in Iceland. That gave him far too much time to think.

But he didn't feel like staying in close contact with anyone right now, especially his family. They just badgered him to get in touch with Charlotte. Lately, Sloane had even refused to tell him what was happening in Charlotte's life. She said he couldn't use her to keep track and needed to contact her himself.

He hadn't spoken to his sister since then, but when he saw a call from Sloane coming in, he decided to take it. He knew she was visiting their parents and that his mother or father would just call him if he didn't.

"What's up?" he asked as he got back into his rental SUV after trekking out to the volcano to see if there was anything interesting left to capture of the still-smoldering lava flows.

"Charlotte's been in touch with her father," Sloane said. "She just went to meet him last weekend."

He'd been about to start the engine. At this, he dropped his hand and sat back. "You're kidding. How'd she find him?"

"I'm not going to tell you," she said. "You need to ask her. So what if you have Parkinson's? Don't let that stop you! Tomorrow or years down the line, she could get cancer or another disease! Would you quit loving her if that happened? Kick her out of your life?"

"Of course not. But she found out about me in time to avoid being bound to that kind of thing."

"You don't know what the future holds," Sloane argued. "You don't know exactly what this disease will do to you. It varies, depending on the person. They could even find a cure! Life is both precious and uncertain, Jules. You need to grab hold of happiness when it's offered to you. Do you hear me? Anything can happen to anyone at any time. She loves *you*! She wants *you*! Now get your ass home and marry her, or I'm never going to speak to you again!"

She must've handed the phone to their mother at that point because he heard Karen's voice next. "Jules?"

He let his head fall back against the seat. "What?" he said dully.

"Your father and I second what Sloane said."

"You're going to hang up on me now, too?"

"I don't want to. I'm worried about you. Won't you just let the people who love you . . . love you? Why do you have to make it so hard?"

For the first time, he allowed his mind to consider that what he wanted most might actually be good for everyone. He'd stand by Charlotte if she was going through something like this, wouldn't he? So why couldn't he believe that she'd do the same for him? Not out of pity, but out of love and commitment and the happiness they had when they were together.

Suddenly, hope blasted inside him like a giant gas flare on one of the oil rigs he'd photographed in Texas. He'd been trying so hard not to be selfish, not to limit Charlotte to the future he saw ahead of him. But what if the years they could spend together would be worth whatever it cost them?

"You're trying to control too much," he heard his father chime in even though Jerry wasn't actually on the line.

"Do you really think it could work out somehow?" he asked, but he was talking to himself more than to anyone else.

"I think you two are destined to be together," his mother

said. "Don't let her go, Jules. I admire what you're trying to do, but it's just as courageous to accept the truth and fight for what you want in spite of it."

"Fight for what you want in spite of it," he muttered. Those words somehow broke his resistance. He knew it immediately.

Starting the vehicle, he smiled as he put the transmission in Drive and tore down the dirt road leading to the highway. "I'll book the first flight I can get," he said.

"Can I tell her you're coming?" Sloane called out, revealing that she'd been listening in all along.

"No. Leave everything to me," he said. "I mean that."

"Fine!" she yelled. "Just don't fuck it up."

He laughed because he heard his father immediately scold her for her language and because he felt lighter than he had in months.

He could only hope that his family was guiding him in the right direction—and that it wasn't too late.

She'd finished her book, and she was only three weeks late. Charlotte could hardly believe she'd managed to write an entire manuscript—a story she was very happy with—despite everything that'd happened since Cliff first kicked her out, including meeting the man who'd supplied half her genetic information. She'd gone to San Diego last weekend and enjoyed having dinner with him and his wife. He seemed like a decent person, despite what she'd thought of him in the beginning. She liked his wife, Cindy, too. She was intelligent, kind and beautiful. They fit together well; Charlotte was glad their marriage had managed to survive what'd happened with Sabrina.

She was relieved about Cliff, too. Last she'd heard, he wasn't going to try to break the prenup and leave her with nothing, as he'd threatened—probably because his attorney had told him it'd be a waste of time and money. He was going to pay her the eight hundred thousand dollars he owed her in a few months, when their divorce was final. Then she'd be able to move out of her parents' house and get a place of her own—although she wasn't in too much of a hurry to do that. Lilly was thriving right where she was. Don and Penny doted on her, so she had the love and support of three adults.

After submitting her finished manuscript, she wanted to go to bed and sleep off the effects of the last several months—this week particularly, during which she'd worked almost nonstop to reach "the end." But her parents and Lilly were looking forward to taking her out to dinner to celebrate, so, telling herself she had to hang in there for one more night, she closed her laptop and headed to the bathroom to get ready.

"What're you wearing?" her mother asked as she stopped by the bathroom where Charlotte was putting on makeup.

Charlotte found that an odd question. Her mother typically didn't ask her what she was going to wear when they went out, not since she was a lot younger, anyway. "What do you want me to wear?"

"Something nice. A dress? We're going to Fleming's."

Now she had to dress up, too? Charlotte wasn't in the mood. But her parents had been so good about helping out since she and Lilly got back from Italy that she bit back her initial response. "Sure, I can wear a dress."

"That would be wonderful," Penny responded before moving on down the hall.

Her mother seemed more excited about this dinner than she did, but at least Penny had been feeling better. She claimed that having Lilly around helped keep her mind off her aches and pains.

Don and Penny had already taken Lilly to Disneyland twice,

once while Charlotte was visiting her birth father in San Diego. They'd purchased a season pass, so Charlotte knew she'd be going quite often, too, now that her book was done.

"Charlotte?" Lilly knocked on the bathroom door, which already stood partway open.

"Come on in," Charlotte told her.

Lilly came in and sat on the closed lid of the toilet. "Do you think you could put a little makeup on me?"

Charlotte considered her younger sister's beautiful, earnest face. "I remember asking at your age, too. I guess I don't see anything wrong with letting you wear a little blush and lip gloss, like you sometimes did in Italy. How about that? You can wear eye shadow and the rest once you turn thirteen."

"Okay," Lilly said, and Charlotte tilted her face up while using a makeup brush on her soft cheeks.

"Are you looking forward to dinner?" Lilly asked when Charlotte went back to her own face.

Like Penny, Lilly seemed to be *very* excited about tonight, which was a bit strange. Fleming's was a nice place. But Charlotte wasn't sure any dinner warranted as much anticipation as the rest of her family seemed to be feeling.

"I am," she replied absently since she was trying to put on mascara.

"I think you're going to like it," Lilly said.

Charlotte lowered the mascara applicator. "Why?"

Looking a little startled, Lilly shifted her gaze to the tile floor. "The food's good, isn't it?"

"It is, but this isn't like Disneyland, Lil. It's just . . . food."

"I know. I'm happy you finished your book—that's all."

"So am I," Charlotte said and felt a smile creep over her face. She was relieved, but the full sense of accomplishment hadn't hit her quite yet. She supposed that would come later, after she'd had a chance to recover and had heard from Megan.

"We're leaving in fifteen minutes!" Don called from downstairs. "Can't be late or we'll miss our reservation!"

Lilly jumped to her feet. "I'd better go put on my dress."

"You're wearing a dress, too?" Charlotte asked.

"Yeah. I want to look nice," she replied as she hurried out.

Apparently, her parents had Lilly believing that tonight was going to be something special. Charlotte couldn't imagine why—until they arrived at the restaurant.

Julian paced back and forth in the private room he'd requested at the restaurant. He was wearing slacks, loafers and a golf shirt—nothing too heavy—and yet sweat dampened his collar.

That was nerves, he realized. He was terrified to put his heart on the line. And yet . . . that was exactly what Charlotte deserved. He wanted her; he just didn't want her to accept him back into her life out of pity or obligation.

Would he know the difference?

He hoped so.

He heard voices—one he recognized as Lilly's—and stiffened, his heart in his throat. His future happiness hung in the balance . . .

The others let Charlotte enter the room first. The moment she saw him, she stopped abruptly before gathering herself enough to say, "Jules."

He came toward her, but stopped a few feet away. He didn't want to crowd her. "I'm sorry," he said. "I . . .I don't know what else to tell you, except I love you. That's why I was trying to live without you. But . . ." He wanted to say his life was empty without her. Except he couldn't. He was afraid that kind of statement would only guilt her into responding the way he hoped, and he desperately needed her to accept him for no other reason than that she loved him, too.

"But . . .?" she prompted.

The others came into the room and stood behind her, quietly waiting.

"Living without you isn't easy," he admitted. "But I'd rather do that than be a burden."

"Jules!" She said his name as an emphatic whisper right before launching herself into his arms. "You could never be a burden! You're what I think about every moment, what I dream about at night, the man I want to spend the rest of my life with. Why can't you understand that?"

"Because you'll be settling for so much less than you deserve!"

Pulling back, she took his face in both hands. "I'm *not* settling. If you'd let all that go, I'd be the luckiest girl in the world. We'll just make the best of whatever we're given!"

The hope he'd been feeling since he left Iceland rose inside him again. "Do you mean it, Char?"

"At least trust me enough to know what I really want," she said.

He grinned at her. "Even if it doesn't make any practical sense?"

"Since when has love ever been practical?" she said with a laugh, and then he kissed her.

Epilogue

One year later . . .

Lilly had only seen a wedding like Charlotte's in the movies, so she figured it was fitting that it would be in LA. Charlotte had insisted she didn't want anything too elaborate—that she'd already had a big wedding and preferred something subdued and private for her second marriage. But Penny and Don, and Jules's parents, had gotten involved in the planning, and while they claimed it *was* subdued, it certainly looked fancy to Lilly. Her dress alone had cost quite a bit; she'd been shocked by the price. But Penny had said she looked so beautiful she simply had to have it, and so here she was, standing in a sleeveless white gown with a fitted top and a full skirt that hit her just above the ankles—a dress Sabrina would've loved because it looked like something out of a high-fashion magazine. And with her hair styled partway up and partway down, and adorned with fresh flowers, Lilly had never felt so pretty.

Still, she wasn't half as pretty as Charlotte. No one could be as pretty as Charlotte. Charlotte's dress also had a fitted top, but it fell off her shoulders and trailed out behind her on the ground, along with a lace veil. She hadn't wanted a lot of beading or sequins, so her dress and veil were also subdued—if Lilly understood that word correctly—and yet it was the most gorgeous gown Lilly had ever seen.

Charlotte's face was what made it perfect, though. She was happier than Lilly could ever imagine her being.

"So . . . what do you think?"

At the sound of a man's voice, Lilly turned to see Robert, Charlotte's birth father, standing behind her with his wife, Cindy. "About . . .?"

He used a champagne flute to gesture around him at the lanterns that swung above the lawn and the Olympic size pool filled with a tasteful number of floating candles. "The festivities?"

"I've never seen anything like it," she admitted.

He chuckled. "I have a feeling Penny and Don won't let your wedding be anything less than legendary, either."

"Maybe." So far, she hadn't really been into boys. But that was changing. Charlotte said it was because she was getting older; she thought that was only part of it. She was also feeling normal, safe. Happy.

Megan, Charlotte's editor, approached them. "I'm going to take off, but I wanted to tell you how nice it was to meet you."

She was looking at Lilly, so Lilly responded. "It was nice to meet you, too."

Megan smiled at Robert. "I'm glad I came for this. I bet you are, too."

"I am," he acknowledged.

"I know it meant a lot to Charlotte that you came all the way from New York," Cindy told Megan.

"I wouldn't miss it," Megan told her.

Robert took a sip of his drink. "How's the book doing?"

"Excellent," Megan replied. "Sales are growing instead of declining. That's always a good sign."

Charlotte's latest novel had come out two months ago and stayed on *The New York Times* bestseller list for several weeks. Once it fell off, they thought that would be it. This title hadn't done as well as her first, but they'd expected as much. She was no longer in the public eye, not to the extent she'd been when she was with Cliff.

But the book had returned to the list three weeks ago and was still there. Megan said that was a sign that readers were talking about it and sharing it with friends and family. Lilly remembered Charlotte being more excited about its return to the list than hitting it in the first place, because she felt that was because of her writing, not her old connection to Cliff.

Megan said good night and left just as Sloane and Ben came up. Sloane had taken off her high heels over an hour ago. Her feet were swelling because of the pregnancy, so Ben was carrying her shoes. She was due in just a couple of months, which was why Jules and Charlotte had chosen to have the wedding in August, even though it was the hottest month of the year. They hadn't wanted to schedule it later because Sloane would be too far along to be able to fly.

"Lilly said you only have a couple of months before your baby arrives," Robert said. "Congratulations."

Sloane put a hand over her swollen stomach. "Thank you. We can't wait."

"We have the nursery all ready," Ben added.

"Do you know the sex?" Cindy asked.

Sloane gave Lilly a look that indicated she could be the one to reveal it, and she piped up with, "It's a girl." Sloane had called her and Charlotte as soon as she and Ben had left the ultrasound appointment to let them know.

"Do you have a name picked out yet?" Robert asked.

Ben switched Sloane's shoes to his other hand. "We're planning to call her Mila."

"Pretty," Cindy said.

Sloane slid her arm around Lilly's shoulders. "We hope she turns out just like this girl here."

Heat climbed Lilly's cheeks, but she smiled as her phone signaled a call. Everyone she knew or interacted with was at the wedding, so she was surprised—until she remembered telling Steve that she'd FaceTime him so he could be part of the celebration.

"Sorry, I have to answer this," she said before connecting the call.

"Hey, did you forget about me?" Steve asked.

"Not really. I just lost track of time, so I'm glad you called," Lilly said, feeling a bit sheepish. "How's Old Blue?"

"He's good. He's right here." He turned the phone so she could see the dog sleeping on the porch at his feet. "He can't wait for you to come visit."

She was going to be staying with Steve and Old Blue while Charlotte and Julian went back to Italy on their honeymoon. "I'll be there soon."

"Thanks for making it possible for me to attend the wedding—at least virtually."

"Of course. Let me introduce you to everyone," she said and showed him her dress before turning the phone around so he could meet all the other people she knew and loved.

Beyond the screen, laughter scattered like confetti across the lit garden, and for the first time in her life, Lilly felt her whole world fit in one frame.

Turn the page for a sneak peek of *New York Times* bestselling author Brenda Novak's new novel, coming next winter!

Chapter 1

Podcast Episode #1: Define Success on Your Own Terms

Success isn't just shiny titles and braggy bios. If your soul's doing the Macarena in a cubicle, it might be time for a rethink. 🙃

*Craft a life that **feels** like a smoothie on the beach, not just a LinkedIn flex. Because let's be real—a corner office ain't it if your heart's dreaming of sandy toes, coconut drinks, and exactly **zero** Zoom links.* 🏝️🍹🚫💻

Forget society's scorecard—build a life that gives your insides a standing ovation. 🎉✨

Molly Sanpolo stood waiting on the crowded corner of Bleecker and Mercer, near New York University, watching her cousin, who was also her closest friend, read a summary of the first episode of the podcast she planned to start. "So? What do you think?" she asked.

Guinevere—whom she'd called Gwin since they were two because Guinevere was such a mouthful and at that point she couldn't pronounce it—looked up from her phone, a baffled expression on her face. "'If your soul's doing the Macarena . . . '? This doesn't sound like you."

Molly pushed her sunglasses higher on her nose. "What do you mean?"

They started walking north toward Houston Street, as they'd done on many other occasions since Gwin started working at the university. "I mean . . . did you write this? Because it doesn't sound like *you*," she repeated more emphatically.

Students wearing earbuds and toting backpacks jostled around them. So did people walking a dog or pushing a stroller toward Washington Square. "Why does that matter?" Molly asked. "I'm an Instagrammer and self-help guru who writes books that guide people toward living a more fulfilled life. That's what needs to be authentic. This is just . . . marketing material."

"One book," Gwin clarified.

Molly glanced over at her. "What'd you say?"

"You've got one book out."

Gwin had been nagging her to write another. Publishing again was her stated goal. Problem was she'd been struggling to get started. "True, but *Hashtag Happy: How to Live Your Best Life in a Filtered World* has sold over a million copies. An encore after *that* kind of success isn't easy."

"Quit overthinking it. You can do it."

"I know. And I will," she said, but she wasn't nearly as confident as she sounded. She was afraid she had nothing new to say—had been completely blocked. "I've just . . . been busy."

Again, Gwin gave her the side-eye. "With . . . ?"

"Posting content. Instagram's a lot of work!"

"Then slow down a little, let some of that go, if you have to."

"I can't! I have to keep my followers happy, or they'll scroll past me. And I'm going to need plenty of support when I finally do get my new book out."

Gwin's glossy black hair fell in waves, framing her smooth olive complexion. She anchored several locks behind one ear. "Everything's about social media these days."

"Younger generations prefer bite-size content." Molly was starting to think she might be better at delivering it, too. Her following was getting large enough to monetize without ever writing another book. So there was that.

Although . . . who knew how long it would last in a world with bright, shiny objects (i.e. the newest thing) and fleeting interest?

Besides, social media content felt trivial. And the comment section could be brutal. She could get a hundred kind, encouraging messages, but it was the single mean one that lodged in her chest, triggering her imposter syndrome, which was probably the cause of her professional paralysis. No matter what she put up, someone would criticize it—pointing out that she didn't have a psych degree, questioning her right to give advice or trying to poach her followers.

All of which, she supposed, was to be expected. This was social media, after all. You didn't step into the ring and then complain about getting punched. But *expected* didn't make it any easier.

"I'm well aware," Gwin groused. "Thanks to the endless scroll, people are training themselves to have the attention span of gnats."

"At least I can reach readers directly. But I have to be clever, or they'll drift away."

"So that's why you went with the Macarena thing?"

Molly dodged a dog walker untangling leashes. "Oscar suggested I use humor, and I think it's a good approach."

"Oscar isn't the one who got you where you are today."

Although Molly knew Gwin would deny it, she suspected her cousin didn't like the man she was dating, and her slightly disparaging tone confirmed it. But what was there not to like? Oscar was everything a woman could want—he was handsome, charming, wealthy, witty and fun loving.

Maybe he could be slightly materialistic, and he had crazy expensive taste, but he'd been orphaned as a toddler and grown up in a children's home. Molly believed he was trying to compensate for those difficult years now that he was an adult and finally had control over his life. "That's true, but I trust his opinion," she said. "He's incredibly successful."

"So he's told us," she muttered, her words barely audible.

Catching her arm, Molly pulled her to a stop. "What was that?"

"If he's so successful, why haven't we seen his big Fifth Avenue penthouse, Mol?"

Molly blinked. "I've seen it." The art alone in his place was worth millions—not to mention the view. "You know we're only living in my loft while he renovates. Then we'll get married, sell my place and move uptown."

"It's already been . . . a year?"

It'd been longer than that, but Molly didn't clarify. "That kind of project takes time. He's run into one hassle after another. Delayed shipments from overseas, botched work that had to be ripped out. It hasn't gone smoothly. And we don't mind staying right where we are. We love my loft."

"You should. It's not like you're living in a hovel. That place cost two and a half million dollars!"

"NoHo's expensive."

"Ain't that the truth. Why do you think I'm still living in a third-story walk-up with my stepbrother? There's no way I could afford a mortgage the size of yours, not on a starting professor's salary."

"I like the apartment. It has character. Sometimes, I sort of miss it."

"Want to trade places?" Gwin asked wryly.

"I'll trade my mortgage for your rent!" Molly offered.

Gwin gripped her wrist. "Please tell me Oscar's still paying his half."

"Of course! If he wasn't, I couldn't afford to live there, either. I've spent a fortune on promotion the past couple of years. What with the ads, and the down payment on the loft, I have very little savings left. That's why I have to write another book—and soon. Although, the podcast should help, if I can get the right sponsors."

Gwin started walking again, silent.

"Look, I know you've had a bad day." Molly fell in step beside her. "But Oscar's the man of my dreams. Can't you be happy for me? He treats me like a queen."

Gwin opened her mouth to say something, then seemed to think better of it.

"What?" Molly prompted.

"Nothing. Back to the podcast . . . I don't think you should veer away from what is distinctly you."

The walk sign turned green as soon as they reached it, so they started across the street along with the traffic flowing toward NoHo. "But I'm not funny!"

"I think you're funny."

"We're related. You're contractually obligated to think I'm funny." She yanked Gwin out of the path of a delivery cyclist who cut in front of them, trailing the scent of yeast and pepperoni. "Anyway, all the content will be mine. As for the other stuff, I'm a busy person—AI saves time."

Gwin shot her a disgruntled look. "As an English professor who sees her students abuse such tools all the time, I hate to hear that."

"You're acting like it's cheating!"

"It *is* cheating!"

"I'm not turning it in for a grade! I'm using it to make me more productive. AI is going to advance with or without me. I intend to get what value out of it I can."

"And I intend to remain deeply rooted in what's real," she

said. "I'm afraid it won't be long before the whole human race won't be able to tell the difference."

Molly hitched her computer bag higher on her shoulder as they passed a busker playing saxophone. "That should be the least of your worries. Computers will kill us all before that. Haven't you seen *Terminator*?"

Gwin frowned at her sarcasm and spoke louder, to be heard over the music. "Could happen."

They passed beneath one of many trees lining the street, into the relief of shade, only to come almost immediately back into bright sun. It was the second of August. Summer was in full swing, and they were experiencing some of the hottest temperatures on record. "Just tell me what you think of the content of the summary. Does it do its job?"

Pausing under the next tree, Gwin took out her phone and reread what Molly had sent. "Depends on what you're going for."

"You know what I'm going for. I want to entice people to tune in."

"It's catchy," Gwin admitted, pocketing her phone. "But except for the 'Macarena' part, which is sort of dated, it sounds young for someone who just turned forty."

Molly paused to retie the bow over one shoulder that helped hold up her cotton sundress. "My followers are young. I don't have to reveal my age."

"It's not just that. It's . . . trying too hard," she finally decided.

"Ouch!" Molly couldn't help feeling wounded. While sitting at her favorite coffee shop on campus today, working while waiting for Gwin to finish teaching Freshman English so they could walk home together, she'd spent hours going through her past Instagram posts, deciding which subjects to tackle, coming up with bullet points and appropriate headings, editing and reworking what ChatGPT spit back at her for the summaries.

"I'm sorry." A spot of dampness was beginning to soak

through the back of Gwin's pale blue jumpsuit. "I just . . ." She sighed. "It's been a long day spent with kids we call adults who don't want to think for themselves. This afternoon I actually had a student ask me why she had to write a research paper when Google has all the answers."

Molly wiped the sweat beading on her upper lip. "That's disturbing. I get it. But if you weren't in the middle of an existential crisis, would you like it?"

"It'll grab attention," she said at last.

"It will?" Now Molly wasn't sure whether to believe her. "Because I was never going for 'literary masterpiece.' As long as it catches the interest of the right people, I'm golden."

A mixed shepherd, tongue lolling, jerked on his leash, trying to sniff them before being redirected by his owner. "I think it'll serve that purpose," Gwin said, the dog's toenails clicking on the concrete as owner and pet hurried on.

There was still a measure of hesitancy in her voice. Molly watched her suspiciously as they started walking again. "But . . ."

"Can you really tell people to ditch their nine-to-five, along with their health care benefits and 401K company match and chase their dreams?"

"I never said people don't have to work. I'm just releasing them from society's expectations, telling them to live according to their own values. 'Forget society's scorecard—build a life that gives your insides a standing ovation,' right? I'm telling them to trust their instincts and reach for the stars."

"Really? Because sometimes it sounds like you're giving them a license to do whatever they want."

"What are you talking about?"

"Nowadays young people think they have to have everything in order to be fulfilled, and I believe that's setting them up for disappointment. Life doesn't owe anybody anything, even a rewarding career."

Molly tried to peer into her cousin's face as they continued to walk. "Is this still about me? Because it's starting to sound like it's more about you. Don't you like your job anymore?"

"I love my job! On most days," she hedged. "Maybe not *this* day. But chasing 'experiences' over stability could leave people with nothing beyond a TikTok highlight reel in thirty years."

"At least memories are nontaxable assets—unlike my loft," Molly quipped, trying to lighten things up.

Gwin rolled her eyes. "But if you don't pay into Social Security, you won't get much out."

"Who knows if that'll even be around by the time we get there?" Molly asked. "Anyway, why don't you be my first podcast guest? Opposing viewpoints will only make it more interesting. You can tell everyone how our mothers walked to school uphill and in the snow both directions and are stronger for it. And I'll tell them how they lived with so much fear they tried to force us into 'safe' paths, whether it made us happy or not."

"They thought they were doing the right thing," she said, somewhat defensively.

"That doesn't mean we should let them dictate our lives."

"Whether our lives will turn out better or worse for not listening to them remains to be seen," she pointed out. "Anyway, I'm a professor. My mother isn't disappointed with my career."

Molly's was. When Molly tried to explain what an influencer was, her mother had scowled and said, "You get paid for telling people to go to Bali?"

Until Molly had published a book, and it became a huge success, her mother was always harping on how Molly should "apply" herself.

But Molly didn't want to think about her mother. She'd spent years chasing the gold star of Eloise's approval but could never conform enough to earn it. "Your mother wanted you to become a doctor," she pointed out.

Gwin arched her eyebrows. "Because I'm such a caring individual."

"You faint at the sight of blood. And my mother wanted *me* to become an attorney, like her, even though I can't think of anything more soul sucking than spending all day drawing up wills and trusts and talking to people about *dying*."

"Your mother has done well for herself. Gave you everything you needed, even helped *my* mom after my dad walked out."

Gwin's dad had walked out when Gwin was only eight, so neither one of them had grown up with a father. Molly's had already been married when he and her mother were dating—not that her mother knew it. Fortunately, she found out before she learned about the pregnancy, broke off the relationship and never told him she was expecting a baby. She said he didn't deserve to know, that she didn't want someone like him in their lives—and in true Eloise style, once she made up her mind, she never wavered. "Money isn't everything," Molly grumbled.

"It is if you don't have enough," Gwin pointed out.

"Careful—you're starting to sound like my mother."

"I guess I am."

They turned onto the cobblestones of Great Jones Street. "If it makes you feel any better, I have a whole podcast focused on financial literacy," Molly said. "I just haven't sent you that summary yet."

"I think your heart's in the right place. You want people to be happy, and chasing their dreams is more likely to make them happy than working in a cubicle. But what about those who launch out on faith alone and belly flop into reality? What if a woman takes your advice and sets out to become an actress but she's not the next Meryl Streep? Or she can't get the breaks she needs? What if she doesn't marry or start a family because she's so busy chasing this pipe dream? Or she passes up a good job, where she would've made enough to carry her through life? I wouldn't want to see someone like that posting #YOLO regrets from her mother's basement in thirty years."

"Everyone's got to figure out their own way. I'm just trying to share a different perspective—one that might help them breathe a little easier. How bad can that be? Trusting my inner voice worked for me. But there is no one answer for everyone. I can give people some good starting points, but the real magic happens when they figure out what works best for them personally."

"Okay," she said with a note of finality, but Molly could tell she hadn't exactly won the argument. That one-word response had sounded more like "whatever." Gwin remained at least partially unconvinced.

"That's it?" she said. "You're leaving it right there?"

They'd reached Molly's cast iron building. Gwin scrunched her nose as she peered up and down the street, where there were chic boutiques, the Engine Co. #33 Firehouse and famous artist Jean-Michel Basquiat's former loft—now a graffiti shrine. But Molly knew her cousin wasn't really seeing any of those things. She was deep in the well of her own thoughts. "I guess clinging to safety isn't always best, but taking too many risks can be a problem, too. There is no one-size-fits-all answer, as you say."

Molly checked her watch. "We still going for drinks later?"

Gwin dug out her phone. "Silas hasn't confirmed. What about Oscar? Have you heard from him?"

Molly glanced at her texts. "Not yet."

"I'll let you know."

Molly waved, but still felt slightly out of sync as she went up to her loft. Was her advice misleading? Could it cause more harm than good?

She'd often heard that authors and artists saw life in shades of gray, not black and white. That was where the best stories and paintings came from—the messy spaces where people's contradictions collided, and nothing was simple or perfectly true. But when it came to telling others how to live . . .

She didn't want to be responsible for hurting anyone.

With a sigh, she put her computer bag on the marble-topped island. Her place wasn't large, only twelve hundred square feet, but it was überfunctional. With one large open space for the living room, dining room and kitchen, it had a single bedroom and bathroom sectioned off with a partition, high ceilings, plank flooring and exposed brick.

She loved it all, but it was the office on the mezzanine that really set it apart—along with the oversize windows. In the 1850s to 1880s, it was popular to build with cast iron in New York. These buildings had the same columns, arches and scrollwork many stone buildings did but were much stronger, which was why the windows could be so big.

For years, she'd longed to live in Greenwich Village or NoHo, but it was only nine months ago that she'd been able to buy her own place.

An Instagram DM came in. Expecting it to be someone she'd reached out to, offering a collaboration, Molly froze when she read the message.

> I'm sorry to bother you, but I have some information you should know, and I'm guessing it'll be very hard to hear.

Molly was staring at it, too shocked to do anything, when another message came from the same number.

> The man you're dating isn't who he says he is.

Don't miss Brenda Novak's new book, available soon!

Copyright © 2026 by Brenda Novak, Inc.